There was a little girl,
Who had a little curl,
Right in the middle of her forehead.

~ author unknown

a Mackenzie Wilder/Classic Boat Mystery

Where the Bodies Lie Buried

a Mackenzie Wilder/Classic Boat mystery

by

R. J. Minnick

Wingspan Books
1513 Briarwood Lane
Fayetteville, NC 28303

Printed in the United States of America
First edition
ISBN- 13: 978- 0692716656 (WINGSPAN BOOKS)
ISBN- 10: 0692716653

Cover photography: © 2016 Dave Minnick

about this book

Where the Bodies Lie Buried is a work of fiction. Any resemblance to real people or incidents, other than historical, is purely coincidental. Kings Hill is a geographic and topographic counterpart to an actual town, but not identical to the original. Any perceived similarities or dissimilarities is the result of the author's active imagination.

References to real places have been made with an attempt at respect due the places and their real-life inhabitants. Characters throughout the book, even those with historical reference, are fictional.

My gratitude to all those connected with antique boats and antique boat societies who have had a hand in introducing me to these fabulous boats.

Where the Bodies Lie Buried

R. J. Minnick

PROLOGUE

1988

Tammy Wynette wailed in the background - Pop's old record of D- I- V- O- R- C- E punctuating today's event. I shifted my feet impatiently. The selection was no accident.

Mom's face was stony. It amazed me how blank she could make it. If she felt like I did, there was a raging turmoil beneath those smooth facial planes.

Lamberson shoved a pen into Pop's hand. He circled his hand over the paper; unsure of where to land it; unsure, really, of how to sign at all. He set the pen down and switched his hand to a shot glass. Lamberson filled it.

I turned my head away to stare out the window. My neck felt rigid. I wondered where Jake was. The last two dogs lay quiet on the porch, lost without their garrulous human friend. That brought tears to my eyes. When Mom and I left, I hadn't been able to take their mother with me. I didn't know where they'd go now.

CHAPTER 1

My legs cramp marching down the steepest hill in town, flute in hand. We never play on hills; uphill is too strenuous, and downhill just too steep. Memorial Day parades are cool under the shade of maple trees lining the streets. And right now, quiet. Maintaining near-silence in our formation, we exchange whispered pleasantries with our band director and friendly waves with the few parade watchers who choose to line the hillside.

Main Street lies at the bottom of the hill, the river just beyond. Maybe we'll see a grain vessel or a barge making its way upriver to the port. That's the extent of the river's effect upon us here. Unless you own a boat, it's merely a backdrop, paralleling the railroad tracks, requiring a bridge to get into downtown Albany. It's simply there, unimportant, no matter how many times they tell us Henry Hudson sailed it.

I let the car roll down the twisting hillside street, past the cemetery engulfed in various shades of perpetual green. It reminded me of coasting on a bike - steep, slippery, out of control. *I hate being out of control.*

"And the thunder rolls…" Garth's voice filled my car with plaintive, ominous notes.

I don't remember WTRY playing country when I lived here.

As I pushed the 'off' button I caught a glimpse of the sky overhead. Pale sponges of clouds were wringing down their excess moisture. Thunder was rolling.

I'd finished my tour in Scotland three days ago and come directly to Kings Hill. Right now it was beginning to look like the 'bonnie village' I'd left behind: misty, clinging to the valley walls with a tenacity that echoed the stubbornness of its residents.

At the bottom of the hill, the blinking red light had been replaced by a regular traffic light. *What traffic?*

I glanced about. My stomach felt as wobbly as someone going to their first job interview. Which was silly; I already had the job. So to speak. Maybe it was the anticipation. *Anticipation - another old song, really old.*

The Hudson River flowed parallel to Main Street, leaving between the two a flat strip of land wide enough to accommodate businesses, their parking lots, and the railroad tracks. Across the tracks, the sloping lot of Kings Hill Boat Club dropped off into launching ramps for the members' boats. A long pier extended out from the end of the building into the river, two shorter ones perpendicular to it providing tie-ups for the boats. More piers lay beyond the Club house.

I was going to need a place to store my boats and get them in the water. Even more, I needed to get to know the local boaters. Especially any who were into classic boats. Although, if I remembered right, that might be a problem. They called this a boat club, but most of these boats fell into the cruiser or yacht category. I could see a 50-foot Hatteras riding alongside the far dock from here. *Guess I'll just have to ask.*

Another establishment shared the Boat Club's parking lot: Pete's Kings Hill Bar and Grill, the neon sign blinking friendly offers through the rain. Some things never change.

The light did. I turned left onto Main Street then hit the brakes and clutched the wheel. A lone figure in creased navy slacks and matching windbreaker scuttled across the waterlogged street to Smitty's Gas Station. I couldn't tell if I knew him or not.

I cruised along in my blue Subaru wagon, watching for familiar places, since the rain made it impossible to see familiar faces.

Great. I'm rhyming. A sure sign of nerves. Maybe this wasn't such a brilliant idea after all.

A few houses marched along the street, before the village's business section began in earnest. D'Amore's Italian family restaurant; Larson's Bar and Grille.

I unrolled the window a crack, letting the stale atmosphere of a long- traveled car filter out. Over there was Ashley's Grocery, no doubt struggling against the Megamarket I'd seen on the way into town. Next door was "Di's" - another bar.

More than one too many in this town.

The Latest Word, a newsstand and old-fashioned soda shoppe sat next to T. Bear Hardware: "Anything for Any Job You'll Ever Need". One or two small specialty shops had insinuated themselves into this commercial strip like so many weeds fighting for space in the sidewalk cracks.

In five minutes (it only took that long because of the rain), I was at the south end of Main Street. Set back from the corner of Main and Vernon was the Village Hall, two stone columns flanking its walkway. It housed the Mayor's Office, the Town Clerk, and the Kings Hill Library, a two- room affair that probably hadn't updated its set of Encyclopaedia Britannica since I grew up; no telling if it had computers yet.

Down another block, around a small bend. On the right, at the village line, was a low building circa 1950's. Redwood clapboards covered the left façade; a curving bay window of glass brick dominated the right. Between was a door, and set high in the redwood were three short casement windows. This was what I'd been looking for.

I pulled in the C-shaped driveway. No nameplate on the office door, but the grass had been mowed, and petunias were straggling from wood chip mulch contained by old railroad ties around the building. The gutters had been cleaned, judging by the water gushing out the downspouts.

Someone is expecting you.

Across the street was Vernon Avenue and the big house on the corner where one of my friends from junior high had lived. I could still make out the windowed entrance to the Village Hall, too. *Maybe I'd better explain my presence before someone reports a trespasser.*

Butterflies continued attacking my insides as I stepped out of my car, pulled my raincoat close, and headed over to Village Hall. A gust of wind splayed leaves against my coat. My hair curled against my cheeks in dripping tendrils. I crossed the threshold, leaving spatters on the linoleum and more on the wall trying to shake off.

My old classmate Saundra Denniston frowned at me as I approached her desk.

"There is a coat rack in the foyer. Between the doors," she directed with all the severity her position as Village Clerk could command. She hadn't changed much, but the lids of her eyes had grown even more hooded.

"That's all right," I said. "I just stopped in to explain. I parked my car at the doctor's office - "

"Kings Hill doesn't have a doctor anymore. Sydney Kesselman retired. You'll have to move - "

"I know about Dr. Kesselman. I'm parking my car there while I look around. I didn't want anyone to wonder about it."

"Well, you know you can't do that." She fixed her eyes on me. "It's private property."

"I'm sure it will be all right. I'm supposed to meet Brooklynne Jamison."

She was curious, but she still hadn't recognized me.

"Saundra, it's me, Mackenzie Russell. Mackenzie Wilder now."

"What? Where on earth did you come from? You're meeting Brooke?" She slapped her hands on the desk and rounded it in one bound. "You're buying a house from her, aren't you? Where is it? When are you moving in?"

I laughed. "Actually I'm buying *two* properties through Brooke. Kesselman's is one of them. I'm Kings Hill's new doctor."

Her mouth snapped shut, but she spoke again almost immediately. "You're a doctor? You? Wait, what about - "

"Mackenzie? Is that you? Isn't this weather awful? I'm glad you made it okay." The beige London Fog wrapping Brooklynne emphasized an athletic shape with generous curves. Her presence put an end to my dilemma.

"Saundra, isn't it great? Mackenzie's taking over Kesselman's practice." She started to move back to the door. "Listen, I've got all the papers and keys in my car - "

"Wait! Wait, Mackenzie!" Saundra called out. "You said you bought two properties. What's the second one?"

Brooklynne whisked me back out into the downpour to her car. Her silver Camry nosed out onto Main Street. Left and left again, then up the driveway to Sidney Kesselman's old house. She pulled beneath the portico and stopped the engine. She fished something from a dashboard cubby and dangled it over my lap.

"Here's your keys, Mackie. It's good to have you back."

I hesitated. Last-minute jitters. Then I grinned and grabbed the keys from her hand. "Let's go."

Rain was letting up, but we wouldn't see the sun today. The house appeared surrounded by greenery. A narrow strip of lawn disappeared to the left. A short front yard to my right ended its downhill run abruptly in a wild hedge that divided the property from the road. I paused.

The property sheet described it as an 1850 clapboard with three bedrooms, country kitchen and dining room; thirty-foot living room along the front. The yellow on the clapboards would have matched the best creamery butter, the trim a gleaming white in contrast. What had once been a front porch was now enclosed by a series of many-paned windows that reached to the eaves from the old railing. Arches replaced the supporting wall inside, making this gallery an extension of the living room. Its roof served as the floor of the balcony off the master suite, a sort of widow's walk.

The interior of the portico was sedate and spotless except for some dirt spattered up from the pavement at the corners. A single spider web captured the occasional raindrop from its protected nook under the eave.

I knew the garage was around back. Once a carriage house, it may even have served as the kitchen in the early life of the house. From a cabinet in the back of the garage a stairway spiraled down to a tunnel leading to a wide cave whose riverside entrance was overhung with brush. Rumor said it was furnished with the remains of an iron bed and a couple of tattered blankets. The Kings Hill station on the Underground Railway. Every school kid in the village knew about it.

I loved the architectural details on this building: the portico offering protection to the doctor's patients in the days before his office was built across the road; a massive carriage lantern suspended from the center of the domed roof; the custom lock on the oak front door that also boasted an etched glass window.

Once inside the foyer you faced a round marble-topped table with traditional   ball-and-claw   feet.   Gold-framed   mirrors   graced oppositesidewalls. The foyer opened into a corridor that gave the impression of going everywhere. To the left lay the kitchen, to the right the living room. Two sets of louvered doors straight ahead discreetly hid the bath and hall closet.

"Be sure to remember which is which when you have company," Brooklynne teased.

I gestured around me. "Kitchen, living room, all of it, even the bathroom - it's fantastic! Thank you, Brooke!"

"Hey, I'm getting a great commission on this. Not to mention a reunion with my best friend."

I hugged her. "If it hadn't been for you, I probably wouldn't have come back."

"I know. But - " Brooke ran a finger along the table's edge. "You belong here, Mackie. Kings Hill needs you."

"I'm not sure Saundra would agree with you, but I've faced that attitude before. People will come around. And won't they be surprised when they find out I'm not only back, but I'm back at the farm, too?"

The expression on Brooklynne's face flickered.

"So," I continued, watching her. "When do I get to see the old place?"

"Come on in the living room, Mackie. We'll finish the papers in here. The basement door is off the kitchen, by the way." She led me into a room with a wide-board floor, braided rug, and large soft-edged furniture. Past the arches, windowpanes opened onto a shadowland of overcast afternoon.

"Hey, do you have any contacts at the boat club?" I asked.

"The Boat Club? Maybe. Gary Henrey, remember him? He's a J.P. now. I think he's treasurer over there. Why?"

"Didn't I tell you? I've got a couple classic boats. I need a place to keep them. Actually I need a place to work on them, too. Maybe I could put up a small boathouse behind the office, where that inlet is."

She set her briefcase down by a chair and clicked on a lamp, setting loose a pool of light around the furniture. I took the edge of the couch, facing Brooke and the window gallery.

"I like this couch."

"I hadn't realized you were into boats. Look, here. Kesselman signed everything. It's all notarized. He wasn't well enough to come out. He's excited it's you buying the practice and everything."

"Classic boats, yes. He always was a nice man. Especially when Pop was - sick."

Brooke's eyebrows went up, and she paused for a fraction of a second. Then she snatched up a pen and passed it and the papers to me.

"Here. These are for Kesselman's practice, the office building, and this house. And these are the papers on the Russell place." She glanced at me, reddening. "People call it that," she mumbled.

"Hmph," I grunted. "That'll change." I bent over the forms, scribbling my name, feeling a sense of completion. I was coming home. When I saw the farm, it would only be better.

"Brooklynne, have you warned Mackenzie what she's walking into?" That light baritone almost made me miss the significance of the words.

I raised my head and smiled upwards. In twenty years I'd forgotten how tall Bryan Jamison was. His baseball-player body was still long and lean. Where Brooke was curvaceous, he'd kept his trim cowboy lines. He was taller, thinner, fairer of coloring than his twin, but his and Brooke's smiles were identical, from the curves of their generous mouths to the corners of their bright blue eyes. There were a few more lines in all those places now, but the same was true of me.

Bryan pulled me to my feet and hugged me. Then, unexpectedly, he brushed a quick kiss on my cheek.

He'd never kissed me before. I suddenly wondered what his ex-wife was like. And why she was 'ex'.

Bryan repeated, "Have you told her, Brooke?"

She began shoving papers into her briefcase.

"Waiting for me, weren't you?" Bryan sounded less amused this time.

He sighed in the general direction of his sister and looked at me. The direct gaze of those pale blue eyes on top of the kiss did something strange to me. I couldn't recall his ex-wife's name.

"Mackenzie - it's great to see you. Sorry about the rain." He flashed the smile again.

"Not your fault," I assured him. "It's good to see you, too. But - uh - what is this 'thing' I'm walking into?"

"Well, let's sit down. Brooke was supposed to tell you about what's been happening out at the Russell place."

"That's the second time someone's called it that."

The smile was gone now. "Remember those bones that were found on your property?"

"Yeah," I answered slowly. "The ones Brooke told me that the Hicks found."

"Apparently it was the final straw that made them sell. They'd been making a last ditch effort to make things work. When they ran into those skeletons digging up by the barn, they decided it was just too much."

"Right. I told you skeletons don't bother me. I couldn't have finished medical training if they did. So, what about them?"

"The State Police decided -   Well. They've completed the forensics on them."

"Did they identify them?"

"Not exactly, but - they dated them. They're - that is they were - buried about twenty years ago."

"Twenty years - ?"

Brooklynne walked around the furniture and came to sit on the other side of me. "I wasn't sure how to tell you. Sorry."

"*Some*one should have told me!"

"I couldn't reach you, Mackie. The report only came out two days ago. You were on your way back from Scotland. I left messages all over, but I guess you never got them."

"You probably have some other messages, too," said Bryan.

"What? Bryan, how did this happen? And you still didn't explain why you're calling it the Russell place. It hasn't been the Russell place since my father sold out to Vince Lamberson!"

"About five years ago, Vince Lamberson unloaded the place and moved to Florida." Bryan's voice took on an impersonal sort of directness that reminded me of his profession. "This young couple from Tennessee - the Hicks - bought the place; they wanted to raise horses. Lamberson had sold off some acreage to developers, so there wasn't as much land as before, but there was enough. This spring they were clearing some land to build a riding arena behind the barn. That's when they came across the first body. Just bones, really, like Brooklynne told you. About a week later, when the State Police let the workers finish dismantling the silo, the second set of bones turned up."

I nodded. "Brooke told me all this when she told me the place was for sale."

"And you told her to go ahead with the purchase since skeletons don't faze you." Bryan looked just a tad skeptical.

"Right, they don't."

"Okay, well," he reached out and ran his hand through his hair self-consciously. "At that point things were pretty basic, as far as you're concerned."

"When did that change? I assume from what you're telling me, things did change."

"Like Brooke said, the medical examiner's report came out two days ago. The bodies are twenty years old."

"So you said," I said, jamming my hands beneath the elbows of my crossed arms.

"As for calling the farm the Russell place, well, it happens. Your family were the owners when the crime took place."

"Crime? Oh. Burying dead bodies on private property would be a crime, wouldn't it?"

Bryan and Brooke exchanged looks.

"People are going to start talking. In fact, they have. The timing, your father owning the place when it happened. They're going to start speculating that he was involved. So now everyone's calling it the Russell place again. They're going to wonder about you buying it back right now. The State Police already are. They've been trying to reach you."

"They have? I didn't hear - wait, there was something from my medical school. They said someone in New York was trying to reach me, but I just thought it was you, Brooke, and that I'd being seeing you in a few days. What do you mean they're wondering about my buying the farm? Didn't you explain to them, Brooke? It's a pretty big jump, even if they think my father was involved. Which I can't really blame them for, but they're wrong." I turned to Bryan. "Who could those bones belong to?"

"State Police haven't any leads. Everyone from your family was accounted for. No one else around here was missing, and the bodies didn't match up with any known local crimes."

"Well, then, maybe they were from out of town. Maybe someone snuck in and put them there. Where were they exactly?"

"The first skeleton was next to the foundation of the barn, under the ramp. The second one was a little ways away."

I pictured the barn, always big and scary to me. One summer when I'd thought I'd get a horse, I'd spent weeks trying to fix up a stall in the lower level. I cleaned out piles of wood, petrified chicken droppings, rusty tools, old toys. I tried to fix the rotting wood in the ramp that led from the door to the lower field. It had been a summer of hard work that didn't pay off. Divorce ended any horsy ambitions I'd had, and leaving set off the craving I'd felt for years to return to my land.

Three hundred years before my father purchased those hundred acres, ancestors of ours owned several thousand acres in the Hudson Valley - including the parcel I came to be raised on. My father and I both felt enormously strong ties to the land. I'd never understood how he'd been able to break them, and I'd never forgiven him for breaking mine as well. Buying the farm had brought me full circle, back to the land I loved. And, it seemed, back to trouble in the form of skeletons under the very ramp whose rotting boards I'd tried to fix.

"So, the State Police think my father's involved?"

"They suspect it."

"What do *you* think?"

"Until the bodies are identified, there's not much use thinking anything. Not that they're interested in my opinion. It's not my jurisdiction."

I grunted. "How much of a crime is it to bury bodies anyway?"

Bryan studied me long enough for my face to warm.

"What?" I asked, confused.

"They really want to talk with you, Mackenzie."

"Why? So I bought the land back. Brooke, you told them that *you* told *me* about the land being up for sale, right? It's a coincidence. Why would it have anything to do with bodies buried twenty years ago?"

"Well, maybe they see a murder suspect's daughter buying back his property just as the skeletons are found as too coincidental. Cops don't like coincidences, you know."

"Murder? No one said - " I stopped, horrified. *What else could it be?*

Bodies buried on our property. You didn't just bury random bodies on property you were passing by. It couldn't be anything but murder. Twenty-some years ago two people were murdered -   and buried - unbeknownst to anyone, on the farm that my father, my mother, and I owned. That I had just bought back again.

Welcome home!

CHAPTER 2

The little school bus only holds twelve, like its call number, Bus 12. Shaped like an elevated station wagon, it has two bench seats, one along either side. We sit facing each other - great for afternoon conversations about gym or study hall or the funny-looking girl with the frizzy hair. Not so fun for the little girl with the frizzy hair and a father everyone whispers about.

Another aspect of small-town life. Not so bad if you've chosen that town to live in. Lousy if you're born into it.

D   o you want to go out there today?" Brooklynne's tone was
      quiet.

"Yes, I do. Right now." I led the way to the door.

The ride out to the farm was revealing. Nothing to match the skeletons, of course, but I got a good look at things. Kings Hill had grown up in twenty years. Once we'd climbed the hill past the St. Rose Catholic Church and turned by the elementary school to run out Kings Road, it was obvious. Developments barely off their foundations when I left were now established neighborhoods. The interstate passed through just before the state highway, cutting off what had been the Plank Road where our little school bus kicked up a cloud of dust every fall. The new lumberyard now looked like an old lumberyard. My one-time best friend's house was completely gone.

I wondered how many times I'd ridden this road. And why now all I could remember was an evening long ago when, pick-up time forgotten by my inebriated father, I'd walked home along that same road, drenched by rain, eyes fixed on the road to avoid any oncoming cars.

Think of something else.

We turned right onto the state highway, then immediately left in a zigzag that turned us up Wexford Road. Houses lined both sides, small ranches built into the hills, passing by like stairsteps. One large house, many times remodeled, stood at the foot of the hill. Everything seemed at once so much the same and so different. At the crest of the hill was a log home set back in the trees on the piece of land I'd claimed as my own - until Vince Lamberson bought the place.

I shook myself. Forget him. The farm was mine, now. Complete with bodies. I shivered.

Then, it didn't seem possible. The approach around the curve, the straight stretch in front of the house, the dip in the road, the lilacs. It was all there. In the years since I'd lost the farm, I'd thought of it often. In my memories, I could never look directly at the big white house I'd adored in childhood. The pain of loss had become a barrier. Tonight there was no such barrier, and there was no fear or regret or guilt or worry, either. Just simple delight. My ancestor's land was back in the family. It was the Russell place once more, as people were insisting on calling it. Someday it would be known as the Wilder place, maybe Doc Wilder's place.

Brooklynne slowed the car, passing up the first driveway entrance for the second. Trees had grown, been cut down, removed, but much of the landscape remained the same. Well, except for the trees where the open fields had been. Now I owned a big house in the woods.

We turned in down by the barn. A State Police car was parked there, its occupant sitting with head bent over a clipboard. He looked up as we pulled in, and before we'd come to a stop had unfolded his long self from the car. Bryan opened the door for me and waved to the trooper simultaneously.

I was busy staring at soggy mounds of earth outside the rear foundation of the barn, laid bare back to its pilings. It looked as skeletal as the remains it had hidden. I turned my head away from it and felt my chest tighten as I looked into the face of that most intimidating of peace officers, the New York State Trooper.

"Jamison. Ladies. Can I help you? There isn't anything more I can tell you about this case, Jamison. We really don't need sight-seers."

I felt Bryan's arm clench where I'd grabbed it to steady myself climbing out of the car. I hastened to speak. "Officer, I know this is an investigation site, but it seems to me I have some right to come and inspect my new property. I'm Dr. Mackenzie Wilder. I own this land now." I held out my hand.

He was slow to offer his. No expression crossed his face, though I knew I'd been scrutinized carefully. I had the impression he wasn't sure how to categorize me.

"You've purchased this land at an awkward time, Dr. Wilder."

"So I've learned. I've also learned that you are probably looking for me. Am I right?"

Trooper Matheson (the nameplate read) looked me over once again, then cast a sharp glance at Bryan. "I suppose that information came from you, Jamison?"

"Yes, it did. When she heard it, Dr. Wilder came right out here," Bryan added.

"Exactly," I said. "Could we go up to the house, please?" My mother's phrase slipped off my tongue as easily as if I'd heard her use it yesterday, not twenty years before. I led the way, wondering if the trooper was at all puzzled over how familiar I was with my new property. Did he fully know who I was? Once on the porch, I turned to Brooklynne for help with the key. I glanced at Trooper Matheson. With a deep breath, I unlocked the door.

I'm not sure what I expected. I knew Lamberson had gutted the interior of the house to remodel it. I'd never seen the finished work. Maybe the Hicks had done more.

The back door led into a roomy square kitchen, much like the one I'd known. Kitchen carpeting - a thing I'd always despised - covered the floor in one of the less nauseating patterns. A nice enough round oak table and four chairs stood to my left. Basic appliances lined the opposite walls. The pantry and bathroom walls had been torn down. The room now took up the entire back half of the house, and windows looked out on three sides. Except for the hideous floor covering, it was wonderful.

A tremor of excitement crowded aside any apprehension. I couldn't help myself. My dreams of restoring this house were suddenly within reach. I could rip out that floor covering. Or I could leave it for a bit, 'til I knew just what I wanted. I could do anything I pleased.

Trooper Matheson looked at me expectantly.

I dragged my thoughts away from my surroundings. "I told you outside that I've just bought this property."

"And that you thought I was probably looking for you." A statement that he somehow made into a question.

I took a deep breath and seated myself opposite him at the oak table. "The reason I bought this place, Officer, is that several years ago, my family owned it. For a long time I dreamed of buying it back. When it went on the market recently, I found myself in a position to do so."

I was playing with my hands. This was like a dance. He knew. I knew he knew. He probably knew I knew he knew. Things had yet to hit the fan. "The case you're investigating involves presumed murders from about twenty years ago."

"Did you get that from Jamison? It's not supposed to be common knowledge yet." He managed to look as though Bryan had breached FBI security. "Yeah, someplace around twenty years ago."

"Trooper Matheson, let's talk plainly here. The facts: around twenty years ago this property belonged to my family. My parents were Jessica and Wylvern Russell. I'm Mackenzie *Russell* Wilder." I waited for a minute. "How may I be of help to you in your investigation?"

In the stony silence that followed I could almost hear Bryan whistle approval. Inwardly I smiled. If ever he should see the new Mackenzie, the Mackenzie I'd grown into, it was now.

Matheson pulled up a chair and took out a small notebook and pen. With deliberation he started making notes, rubbing his eyes occasionally as is he were tired of the complications life brought him. He spoke slowly.

"You want us to talk plain. All right. *The facts*: your name is Mackenzie Russell Wilder. Your parents were Jessica and Wylvern Russell. They owned this place twenty years ago. When, apparently, two murders took place. You've just bought the place back after, if I understand my information correctly, after two totally decomposed bodies were resurrected." He paused and rubbed his face again. "Do you see why we might want to talk with you?"

Uh-oh.

"Can you explain why you were so interested in buying this property after the bodies were discovered?"

"Actually, the existence of the bodies had nothing to do with my decision to purchase this farm. When Brooklynne told me it was up for sale, I wanted it. This land goes back beyond my childhood, Officer Matheson. Three hundred years ago it was part of a land grant owned by an ancestor of mine. This land is my history. And it's my childhood home. After talking with Brooke, I wanted it back. Skeletons or no skeletons, I wanted my land back. Frankly, I figure the skeletons have nothing to do with me anyway."

He gazed at me. "Right. It didn't, say, bother you to have bodies turning up on the old homestead?"

"I'm a doctor. I 'm around bodies all the time, and dead bodies have a way of becoming skeletons eventually. These *skeletons*," I emphasized, "are very, very dead. I'm not about to let other people's ideas of squeamishness keep me from a long-time goal."

"Which is?"

"To have back what's mine, what was taken away twenty years ago."

"You sure that that doesn't include those skeletons?"

"Matheson!" Bryan leaned over the table.

Brooklynne jumped in. "Officer, Mackenzie didn't have any idea what was going on. She bought the land before anyone found out how old the bodies were!"

Matheson transferred his gaze to Brooke.

"I'm the realtor who sold the land to Mackenzie. Once I'd sold her on the idea of moving to Kings Hill, she wanted her old place back. She wanted it before I ever told her about the bones."

Matheson sighed. "Your name?"

"Brooklynne Jamison. Umm -   Kerns. That is, I use Jamison professionally. My husband is Lloyd Kerns. The attorney."

Why did I get the impression that didn't make Matheson any happier?

"Relation to you?" he asked Bryan.

"She's my twin sister."

Matheson looked from one to the other. "Oh, yeah. So, Jamison, have you advised your sister and Dr. Wilder here about getting an attorney? Maybe your brother-in-law would be interested."

Bryan shook his head. "Brooke and I discussed the matter this morning. I didn't have a chance to talk with Dr. Wilder about it. Should I be calling Lloyd now?"

"It might not be a bad idea - "

"Wait a minute. That's not going to be necessary. I'm perfectly willing to tell Trooper Matheson anything he needs to know."

Matheson shook his head. "This doesn't look very good, Dr. Wilder. I've only the word of your friends and yourself that you didn't care about the bodies when you decided to buy this place. How do I know that you didn't buy up the property in an effort to exercise damage control? How do I know that you didn't know about these bodies long before anyone else?"

"I think I'd better call Lloyd," muttered Bryan.

I waved him off, nodding to the State Trooper, who, I told myself, was only doing his job. "Actually, you don't know anything of the sort, and I realize that. But I'm here, talking with you, not anywhere else. I expect you will realize -   after you have checked me out thoroughly - that all I am interested in doing is getting this cleared up. I don't like the situation any more than you do."

"That could mean a lot of things. We know something about you, Dr. Wilder. That is, about you twenty years ago. Care to update us?"

With that we began a rather long series of questions and answers that entailed my essential personal history and justification for living. It took half an hour, during which he insisted Bryan and Brooklynne go out on the porch. It was still the same as always, a big old- fashioned porch running half the length of the house and jutting out for about four feet over the basement entrance. Through the two windows that opened out onto it, I could see how irritated Bryan and Brooke were. Bryan paced impatiently. Brooklynne muttered to herself and fussed over her purse. Water still dripped from the eaves and made an occasional gurgle along the gutters. Night crowded in, camouflaging the cloudy sky.

I kept being distracted from Matheson's questions by the house. When the investigation - inconvenience that it was - was over, I was going to have so much fun re-doing it. I could feel the house settling around me, sense the barn outside, the one-time fields - now filled in with overgrown Christmas trees - surrounding me, ringed further out by older forest laced with rushing creeks. I remembered the description my mother had given me of standing in front of the house their first night here, feeling the land stretch out around her, knowing it was all theirs. I remembered the fierce love for this piece of land my father and I had shared. Our domain.

Matheson wrote down the last of my answers.

"I don't think I've ever run across this situation before, Dr. Wilder. I'll file a report in the morning." He paused. "You know, this being an investigation site, you can't really move in here."

"I wasn't planning to. Except - well, I have a boat that will need to go in the barn as soon as possible. But I'll be living in Dr. Kesselman's old house in the village. This place - I've been planning on fixing it up the way it should be. Then, maybe..." I shrugged. I'd had big plans for the farm. Now it was mine, I found I wasn't exactly sure what I wanted to do with it. Except hold on to it. Which meant getting this mystery solved, finding out who those bodies were, and who was responsible for putting them on my land.

"Officer, when you make your report, would you do something for me? Tell them I'd like to read the pathology reports. After all, I'm a doctor; I'll understand them. Maybe I can be of help."

Matheson shrugged. "I'll ask, but I doubt they'll okay it. It's not a usual request."

"This isn't a usual situation."

"I'll see. Jamison! You and your sister can take your friend home. We're finished."

"I was about to ask if you had charges to file," Bryan groused. "You okay, Mackie?"

"Fine. Just tired. Can we go back now? I'd like to discuss this with both of you, but not tonight. I just want to get home. Good-night."

"Good-night, Dr. Wilder. I'll drop by tomorrow with your answer."

"Try my office. I'll be there setting up. Thanks."

Bryan glanced in the mirror at me as we drove down Wexford Road. "What was that last bit with Matheson? What answer?"

"Oh, I just asked if I could see the pathology reports on the bodies. I want to get this cleared up as soon as possible. I thought it might help to read the reports."

"You asked a State Trooper for a path report!?"

"Yes. Actually, what I really want to do is look at the bodies myself. Do you think they could arrange that, Bryan?"

In the passenger seat, Brooke was laughing. Bryan shook his head. His voice came softly back to me. "You sure have changed, Mackie."

CHAPTER 3

Winter. Snow piled higher than I've ever seen. So high they cancelled school yesterday.

Will it cancel the Christmas performance in two days? I hope not. I want so much to sing at church this year. I have a solo, my very first, and even Pop said he'd come. I don't know if that's such a great idea, but at least he wants to come.

This year we're singing with the Reformed Church. That means Bryan is singing with us. I can't help it. The thought of singing in the same choir with him is exciting! So what if he's going out with Carol Anne? I still like being around him.

He's fun. He's sweet. He's - nice.

He's my friend.

B ryan had no idea. I chuckled to myself as I scrounged for pans to scramble eggs the next morning. No one in Kings Hill is prepared for how I've changed. Oh, they'll see the same person. I'm still five feet two. My hair is still brown and frizzy - darker now, and I wear it shorter, to my shoulders. My eyes turn a deeper blue under intense emotion. At the slightest exertion, my cheeks still flush an unbecoming red. For some people, that's all they'll see; I look the same as ever.

But twenty years changes people. Some of us throw off our adolescence and become nothing like what we were in youth. Some of us come full circle and embrace the same principles and causes we did in childhood. Me? I'm still serious, but no longer shy. I wept at the silver-seared hand of Johnny Tremain; now I treat injuries so my patients don't have to suffer. In high school I debated hotly for civil rights; now I campaign with my colleagues for support of equal opportunity policies. I used to float paper boats in the shallow creeks that flowed through the farm; now I refinish old boats to show and run in meets around the country. When I was young, I painted my dollhouse walls with tempera paint leftover from school; now I restore old houses for relaxation. I learned to target-shoot from my father, and now I go gunning for my own solutions to problems I encounter. I don't wait on others to solve the riddles of my life.

So I wasn't about to accept the New York State Troopers' explanation of what had happened at the 'Russell place'. There had to be an explanation that did not involve my family.

My family. With my father, you'd wonder at my coming back to Kings Hill at all. Certainly some of the villagers would. I paused as I was pouring myself another glass of tea. Maybe that explained Saundra's reaction. I thought she'd been fussing over the idea of a 'lady doctor'. Maybe it was at my daring to return to Kings Hill - especially in light of the current investigation.

Too many thoughts, too many ideas. What I needed was to get busy. What I really needed was to head over to my new office!

I dressed in old Lee jeans and an even more ancient sweatshirt. Yesterday's rain was gone. Sunlight coated the tops of the trees. On the other side of the house I found metal steps that led to the River Road. Ivy and honeysuckle twined along the ground and up the handrail. A gurgling sound turned out to be a charming brook bedded with large rocks moving away from the stairs at an angle. I paused on the top step, listening to the gurgling, the faint buzz of insects, and the steady hum-whoosh of passing cars. Saturday morning business. I skipped down the stairs and crossed quickly behind a bright purple pick-up truck, fumbling the keys in my hand, jeans brushing through weeds that crowded the sides of the road.

The building was long and low and empty. I walked along the driveway around back to survey the lot. At the near end was a small dike, maybe decorative, maybe not. I strolled back to it, trying to gauge whether or not there was room in the 30- by 60-foot lot to work on a boat. Water lapped at the dike. I saw a couple branches blackened by too long in the river water caught amongst the weeds and grass, sinking in disintegration. Somewhere to my left, barely above water, was the opening to the cave that was the underground railway station.

I turned away from the dike and walked back, inspecting three brown garbage cans near the building, one labeled 'hazardous medical waste'.

The cans stood near the back entrance. My keys were clearly marked, the door double-locked. After a false try, I opened the door into a sleek efficient kitchen incongruously furnished with an old metal Formica-topped table and vinyl upholstered tubular chairs. Everything was enameled porcelain or stainless steel and totally immaculate. Cabinets, sink and a small stove lined the inside wall. The tables and chairs stood against the outside wall below a window. Two small refrigerators stood side by side at the far end of the room. A carefully lettered label on one read "FOOD" - the other said merely "MEDICAL". Of course, anyone *medical* would know the unsavory variety of things that might have to be kept there. The only other piece of furniture in the room was an old set of barrister's bookcases, three high, their glass fronts gleaming when I switched on the light. They occupied the end corner of the outside wall, close alongside the table.

To my left were two skinny closets of rooms: a small bath and a room with a cot and a bookshelf and an old phone. A doctor who would sleep at his office. Now *that* was dedication. The front of the building was given over to office and waiting room, with two examining rooms beyond the office. These were minimally equipped, but again immaculate. Tucked in between them was a walk-in closet. Dustless boxes of tidily filed medical records stood at attention on heavy-duty metal shelves attached to the wall.

"How did he keep it so clean?" I murmured in amazement. I started making a mental list. A cleaning service for the office, a nurse or nurse/receptionist, someone for the house - I didn't know what I wanted that person to do exactly, but I knew I needed someone - and a handyman/gardener type. It all sounded terribly feudal, but when I considered I had money and a great deal of property to manage, I knew it was the only way. Besides, what was money for?

I hadn't let on, even to Brooke, but when my husband, also named Brian, died in 2001, my life changed completely. There was the obvious change: I lost my mate, the man who'd helped me learn to come out of myself, who let me be strong, and I lost him on very nearly the day we decided to start a family. I'd taken the summer to grieve and think over my life. Then came September 11, and everyone's life changed.

I'd put in four years as a hospital psychiatric social worker helping people. Suddenly that was not enough. The work I'd seen the doctors do with Brian and the world-shattering tragedy pushed me in a new direction - I used some of Brian's life insurance to put myself through medical school.

The final change was even more unexpected. I didn't put all my money into my education. I invested some of it - and very well. As a result, I was a woman with property, a profession, and an almost embarrassingly awful lot of money. Finances would never worry me unless I was exceedingly foolish, something even I acknowledged as highly unlikely. So it wasn't the cost of a staff that daunted me, or even the concept. What I didn't look forward to was hunting one down.

I moved on to check out the waiting room. Serviceable, but too dark. Something to change. I turned back to the office.

Someone had cleared the shelves and files. Some personal items - paperweight, a book on homeopathic medicine, diplomas, a framed Bill Mauldin cartoon, a careworn Old Testament - lay in a box on the desk. Propped against the phone was a white envelope with my name on it. I picked it up and held it, still gazing about the paneled room. I could remember so many times that I'd come in here. Kesselman had given me my shots, taken me through measles and chicken pox (no mumps), a broken wrist, a bruised ligament (from when my ex-best friend kicked my instep during soccer practice), and a dozen mysterious aches and pains he called 'growing pains'. He never pampered his patients, but he never put them off either. He made time for adolescent flights of fancy and elderly fears and middle-aged miseries. He was a good, kind man - a caring, capable doctor.

I slit the envelope and slowly unfolded the white writing paper. His writing was spidery, nearly illegible, but with a colleague's intuitive ability I read it.

Dear Mackenzie,

Excuse me. Doctor Wilder! Your letter took me by complete surprise. You never gave anyone the slightest hint you might take up medicine. I remember you as a very bright child, one who would be successful wherever she applied herself. How delighted I am that you chose not only the medical profession, but my own humble specialty. Family Practice! I think I like that appellation better than 'General Practice'. After all, we are not so much practicing medicine generally, but practicing medicine as it affects the family. Or at least, you are. Not me, any longer. Not that I am complaining. The hours and energy a family practice demands can eat one up. It is for the young and able. It has been tiring for me for many years now.

Your letter was most providential. I often regretted that I had no younger partner to leave my practice to. I'd wondered of late just who Kings Hill would find. It isn't easy to attract young doctors to rural communities like our own, particularly with larger cities so close by, but I don't need to sell you on all this. You've already bought my practice.

I could hear him chuckling.

I wish you the best. Be patient with these people. Some will not trust you - 'you are a woman', 'you are new', 'you are young', 'you used to live here', 'you are wealthy', you were poor' -   any reason to see you as different, objectionable. However, it is these same qualities that will lure them to you for a first visit, a 'look-see'. It's up to you to bring them back. Some you will, some you won't. Not every drug is a cure-all; not every doctor is everybody's doctor.

One other thing. Be patient with pain. I remember how stoic you were as a child, with a high pain threshold. Most people do not share that. Don't expect everyone to be a hero. Strapping young men faint at blood or a broken bone. Some women require no anesthesia in childbirth, while others collapse one week a month. Pain tolerance decreases with age, so you must be tolerant. Believe your patients, at least until you know better.

I've studied your record and recommendations. They are the finest I've seen in a long time. Be patient getting started, and you should do well in Kings Hill.

I'm delighted you took the house as well. I think I'll spend part of each day imagining you in it. Perhaps you will eventually bring some children into it. Good luck, Mackenzie, and mazel tov!

P.S. Keep the book on homeopathy with my compliments. I recall reading your own well-documented paper on the subject in JAMA.

I smiled. *Thank you, Dr. Kesselman.*

"Who are you?" The hard voice belonged to a large-boned woman standing in the doorway to the waiting room. She was a head taller than I, her hair a steel gray helmet, her fists upon her hips as she demanded a reply. "Well?"

"I'm Mackenzie Wilder. Dr. Wilder. I've taken over Dr. Kesselman's practice." I stood up and offered my hand.

She stared at it for a minute. "You? You're Dr. Wilder?" She snorted, then decided to shake my hand anyway. "I'm Jean Hesford. I cleaned for Doc Kesselman. I've been keeping the place up. What took you so long?"

"I got here yesterday, Ms. Hesford. The drive took longer than I'd expected. Most of my things haven't arrived yet."

She'd flicked a cloth out of her back pocket and begun dusting the spotless telephone.

"Call me Jean. Moving companies! Terrible! Pack up every bit of cracked china, every broken crayon they can find in boxes with that bubble wrap stuff, load it up and disappear into the blue for a week, then they show up - *maybe* - three days late. Charge you the earth to do it, and then act as if they've done you a favor just showing up! Move that lamp, will you?"

I obliged. After she'd thoroughly and totally unnecessarily cleaned the desk, she faced me, hands on hips again.

"I used to come in daily for Doctor K across the street. 'Course, I cooked for him, too. You probably won't want that. I can still come in to clean if you want. I can do here as well." She paused. "Actually Doctor K, he had Missy Schoonbeck in to clean here. She has a whole round of doctor's offices she does. There's no reason I can't work it in too, mind you. 'Course, Missy sort of specializes in ultra-sanitary cleaning. She'll probably be in to see you about pickin' up her contract." She looked doubtful, pride in her own work warring with her integrity.

"Ms. Hesford - Jean - it might be better if you were to stick to your own area of expertise. Besides, you may be the solution to a more pressing problem for me."

"Oh?"

"How would you feel about supervising two households? I bought my old homestead as well as Dr. Kesselman's house. I plan on fixing up the farmhouse as soon as possible, and I'll need someone who can run out there now and then to keep an eye on the workmen and such. There'll be plenty of clean-up, too. I want to do a lot myself, but I'll be hiring a lot of it out, too. I'll need someone to supervise. This would be in addition to keeping house at the place here. Do you think you could handle that?"

"Two houses! What does one person need with two houses?"

I continued evenly, "The Russell place is where I grew up. It's a wonderful piece of land. I want to help it reach its potential, and that means major renovations."

"They gonna let you do that stuff with those dead bodies out there?"

I kept myself from staring at her. "Oh, you know about that. I'll have to wait until that's all cleared up, I suppose. On the other hand, they may let me start work on the house, since all the action seems to be down by the barn."

"Hmph. How much do you know about all this anyway? If it was your old place - "

"I don't know anything about it yet, Jean. From what I've been told so far, my father was still living at the farm when those - bodies were left there. But he didn't know anything about it." She gave me a skeptical look. "I'm sure of it. My father adored that old place. If he'd caught anyone dumping bodies on it, he'd have been after them with a shotgun."

She looked away, dropping one hand to flick away some more imaginary dust. "You know, Doc, my husband and I only moved here 'bout twelve years ago - from Worcester, Mass. But I work around, and there's already been talk that Wylvern Russell was the sort of man who might have planted a couple bodies there himself. Just thought you should know what was being said," she added, darting a look at my face.

"Pop wouldn't have done that. He wouldn't have. He did many things, and a lot were illegal, but he would never have done that." My knees gave way, and I plunked into the desk chair.

I felt the beginnings of a cloying trap of small-town gossip and censure. How did news move that fast? Suspicions like that could spell death to my fledgling practice.

"Dr. Wilder?"

I raised my head.

"What time should I come by?"

"What?"

"I don't see any reason why I can't handle that job, way you described it. Never been a workman yet could put one over on me. I know that house across the street as well as my own. So, what time do you want me?"

"What was your usual time? I don't want to interfere with your home schedule." I felt almost too overwhelmed to discuss it.

"Don't worry, if I don't like your hours, I'll set my own. It doesn't take more'n two hours to do that place as a rule. How about if I start at ten?"

"That sounds fine. There'll probably be more work as things go on. Sure you'll have the time?"

"Said I could do it, didn't I?"

She was glaring at me again. I smiled.

"Yes, you did. I'm sure you'll work out fine. Jean, I'll figure on seeing you tomorrow. Let me know what Dr. Kesselman was paying you. I'll go fifty percent more. I'm going over to get some lunch, and then I have to come back. I better call those movers again."

"You don't have to pay me that much you know. Not that I couldn't use it. But - fifty percent?" She squinted at me.

"It's what having someone like you is worth to me," I said as I walked her to the door. She collected her purse and looked about to say something more when a flash of blue and orange caught our eyes.

"What are they doing here?" she muttered.

"Looks like Trooper Matheson. I told him I'd be here."

Jean shot me a puzzled look.

"I've asked to see the autopsy reports on those bodies. Maybe I can help clear things up if I do."

She looked at me hard with gray eyes capable of penetrating the most complicated deception. "The quicker the better for you, Doc. These shenanigans are bad for your kind of business. Probably not too good for you personally, either, " she added more softly.

"Thanks, Jean. See you tomorrow."

I held the door for her as she walked out -   and for Trooper Matheson as he walked in.

CHAPTER 4

It's summer, and I'm seven. The ground is dry. It powders up in little explosions where the spade edge strikes the ground. Gravelly pieces pour in the sides of the hole. It seems to take twice as long to dig a hole as when it's damp out.

I hold the bucket of seedlings at my side, pulling them out one by one as Pop demands. Mom follows with a pail of water.

Splash! to tempt the roots into the soil.

Splash! to hold down the dirt.

Splash! to nurture the seedling. Grow, live, be happy.

Sparkling drops of water clinging to dusty bare toes. Scattered drops of precious love to encourage a daughter's wearying spirit. Grow, live, be happy.

M atheson stepped into the room and paced out a small square, his rapid scan of the room a reflex action. He turned a speculative eye on me.

"Do you consider yourself lucky, Dr. Wilder?"

"I never actually thought about it. Why?"

"It seems our county medical examiner knows about you. Friends with one of your professors or something. At any rate, the office gave the okay for you to read the path reports, provided you do it at the examiner's office - in case you have questions. The results aren't secret, technically they're open to the public, but we try to keep a certain amount of control."

"You seem a little surprised."

"It's not every day that the family of a suspect gets to see such information." He spoke evenly, watching my reaction.

"What do you mean, 'suspect'?"

"Dr. Wilder, your father's reputation was known to more than just his customers. New York State Troopers have records of your father's activities going way back."

I stiffened, my chin coming up. "My father was in a good deal of trouble. But none of it *ever* involved dead bodies."

"Maybe, but guns and alcohol and drugs can lead to dead bodies. Don't you agree?"

"In principle, yes."

"Dr. Wilder, those bodies were planted on property belonging to your father when he lived there. Do you mean to tell me you think someone could actually have put them there without his knowledge? It was well- known he shot trespassers on sight."

I turned toward the office door. I didn't like the way this man was probing, poking at scars I didn't want poked.

"Trooper Matheson, let me fill you in on a couple of items. My mother and I left my father before I knew about his illegal activities. I found out about most of them from boys in school. My father helped them find some of the wild times they were looking for. I'll grant you he did them harm. Pop didn't see things the way other people did. But one thing he would never have done is to kill someone. Shoot a trespasser, maybe - but in the leg or the arm, or over the shoulder - "

"Your father had a temper," Matheson pointed out.

"Absolutely. He'd start a fight as soon as end it. But he wouldn't kill anyone. That would be too easy on them."

"He get over his anger easily?"

"Not at all, but he didn't usually do anything about it after the first blow-up."

"Why couldn't he have shot at a trespasser and missed his mark? Maybe got scared and buried the guy?"

"You never knew my father, did you?"

At the shake of his head, I smiled. "Talk to someone who did. Pop couldn't miss a shot if he tried. Dead drunk, sober, in-between, my father was a better sharp-shooter than any TV Western cowboy. No way would he kill someone by accident. Especially not twice."

"You can only kill someone once," he said, with a trace of a smile.

"You know what I mean!"

"Well, that means we're back to killing someone on purpose." He nodded in some kind of satisfaction.

I sighed. "I realize there's no adequate proof for you, Trooper Matheson, but I knew my father. He never killed anyone."

He shrugged, admitting at least that he couldn't convince me, not with proof he didn't have. He gripped the handle of the door. "Call the examiner's office when you want to come in. It can't do any harm."

"Thank you."

He touched the brim of his hat and left.

Rotating my head and shoulders in one simultaneous stretch, I breathed deeply. This wasn't quite what I'd expected when I came back to Kings Hill.

I locked up and headed for the house. I entered by way of the portico again, savoring my ownership. Inside was cool, a result of the gallery and surrounding shade trees. The kitchen hummed warmth and homey-ness. There was something about the old brick and honey-toned cabinetry, the wrought iron baker's rack and overhead pot rack, the French glazed ceramic tile behind the gas stove and the inlaid tile countertop. It was reflected in the Tiffany-style lamp with its glass stained in umber, ochre, and maize. I made a small lunch, padding about the room, observing that I'd have to do some shopping. I wondered if Jean would consider that one of her duties. I'd have to make a list of what I needed soon.

I spent the afternoon unpacking personal stuff, going through the rooms of the house to see what furnishings I liked best, what needed replacing, where things would go. A small room on the first floor would serve as a home office; it already had an undersized rolltop desk. The bathroom downstairs could use new faucets, and wallpaper. I'd need new curtains for the bedrooms upstairs, and definitely a new hall light. It would be nice to find a carriage-style lamp for the hallway to echo the one in the portico. Maybe at a flea market. My inventory continued, and I felt myself settling in.

Collecting houses, buying them, changing them, had been something my husband and I loved. We'd bought four houses during the nine years we were married. Each was different; each was painstakingly redone. We loved working with the wood and stone and paint, but especially the wood. Then, one year, we found another passion.

Not that we gave up on houses. Nothing could change that. But in 1998 Brian and I attended our first classic boat show.

Chris Craft. Garwood. Lyman. Hackercraft.

Runabouts. Cruisers. Skiffs. Even dugout canoes.

Boats made of wood painted white or stained mahogany then coated, no, bathed in layers of varnish. So much varnish, in fact that Brian nicknamed his favorite the 'Butterscotch Boat'.

We were in love. We talked with owners and builders and historical experts. In typical fashion, one owner invited us aboard his 1938 cruiser and gave us a tour of the lake where the show was held. We subscribed ourselves to *Wooden Boat Magazine* and picked up cards from every vendor - from reproduction hardware makers to restoration marinas to varnish manufacturers.

Within six months we had our first runabout, a 1941 Chris Craft Barrel Back with a Chrysler M engine that we spent ten intense months sanding, tinkering, bolting, planing, staining, varnishing and varnishing and varnishing until we were able to deck it out in the jewelry of classic boatdom, the brass and chrome hardware. We showed it at the next meet and promptly arranged to buy our second boat. We were hooked.

Things slowed down as life intervened, and for that reason alone, I still had only the two boats. But, I reflected happily, that would change, once I got settled in Kings Hill.

Mid- afternoon my inspection was interrupted by the phone.

"Hello, is there a doctor in the house?"

I groaned. "Hi, Brooke. Yes, and she's loving every minute of it. Even meeting the housekeeper."

"You mean Jean?"

"Yes, I do. What was she, a Marine Sergeant or something?"

"No, but somebody told me she raised her nine brothers and sisters single-handed."

"I guess that explains it. By the way, that trooper came over today. I can see the path reports provided I go to the medical examiner's for them."

"That was fast!"

"Matheson said the M.E. knew one of my profs or something. He gave me the idea I was getting special treatment."

"Oh, really?"

"Well, actually, I got the impression he figured I couldn't mess things up too much just by looking at the reports."

" 'Mess things up?' Why on earth - ?"

"Pop's high on their list of suspects. You know. Matheson thinks I might be trying to affect their investigation."

"That's crazy! So what if your father gave his gin and homegrown pot to a few kids in town? Those kids could've gotten worse on the street! He was always giving kids a place to crash, or even money. He'd never kill anybody!"

"I tried to tell the trooper that, but you can guess how much he listened." I watched some dust motes drift down a sunbeam to the wooden floor. "Wait a minute, how come you know so much about Pop?"

Silence. "You forget what I was like in high school? I went with some of those guys, remember? And remember what else happened?" she finished softly.

"Yeah. I'd forgotten. That was a bad time for you."

"And Bryan. He's the one who pulled me out of all that. I think that's why he became a cop." Her voice grew brisk. "Anyway. I called to see if you wanted to celebrate with me. I just closed on another sale, and that puts me into the million-dollar club! You've got to come to dinner with me and Lloyd and Bryan next Saturday. My treat. We can go to the Black Carriage. What do you think?"

"It sounds great. Did you say Bryan would be there?"

"Yeah. Okay with you?"

"Sure, fine." *Very much okay with me.* "Who did you make the other sale to, Brooke? If you can tell."

"Man called Jason Fields. He bought that huge tract of river property, near where your uncle had his farm. He's going to build some think tank or computer complex or something."

"Jason Fields? *The* Jason Fields?"

"Well, a Jason Fields. I don't know if he is *the* Jason Fields or not. Why?"

"Brooke, Jason Fields is a very famous, extremely wealthy, enormously talented man, a Leonardo da Vinci and Benjamin Franklin rolled into one, a real Renaissance man. He invented a gizmo that's used on all American-made cars, he's got doctorates in Engineering, Philosophy, and Criminology, writes music and mysteries, and paints. I think he's even written a couple commercial jingles and a country song or two."

"How do you know all this stuff?"

"Fields lived in Baltimore at the same time Brian and I did. Every night on the news you'd hear about something he'd done, was doing, or was about to do. He'll get himself involved in any creative project that strikes his fancy -   which may mean Kings Hill is in for a most unusual time. But look, didn't this guy tell you anything about himself? Didn't you need to check references or something?"

"The sale was handled by an accounting firm, and it was a cash sale, no mortgage. I couldn't believe it. The bank check was good, and the seller gave me a bonus for handling things so fast. What did I care who he was? He sounds awfully intriguing, though. Maybe you two should meet," she said, more than a trace of matchmaker in her voice.

"I wish," I responded appropriately. I would like to meet Jason Fields sometime, but my inner thoughts remained stuck on Brooke's handsome twin - appropriately or not.

"I'd like to celebrate with you, Brooke. Saturday, right? Will you guys pick me up?" I asked, congratulating myself on my innocent tone.

"Sure. See you then, Mackie."

I hung up and made a series of calls myself. A couple dealt with the problems of a gardener and a nurse/receptionist. One dealt with the missing moving company and another with the Long Island marina where my second boat's engine was being rebuilt. And one more set up a time for me to go to the County Examiner's office next Friday.

CHAPTER 5

There's never enough time. Never.

I shovel a forkful of scrambled eggs into my mouth. Papers slide off the table as I grab a book that's toppling from the stack in front of me.

Study. Study, study, study. The latest litany in my life.

Medicine seemed like such a good idea at the time.

It was.

There it is. That little voice again. The little voice that started following me around after Brian's funeral. I can't decide if it's Brian himself, or just me because I'm feeling lonely. It's a friendly little voice, whatever its source.

I have to finish this course. I have to. And the next one, and the next. I will not allow myself to be talked into giving up.

Who's talking about giving up?

Well...

Not me. And not you, either. You're going to finish this.

It's so hard -

You expected otherwise?

No, but -

No buts. You made a committment. You can do this.

I look at the books again. Can I?

You can. You can, you can, you can.... a new litany to harmonize with the previous one.

F riday I was knee-deep in patients, paperwork, and unpacking. My office equipment had arrived safely, along with the Chris Craft. Jean was tracking down the rest of my things. She'd enlisted the help of her friend, Arthur. Arthur was a trucker.

"Speaks the language," Jean said. She set him to work on the phone with the moving company.

Most of what he said was either loud, incomprehensible or unrepeatable, but as he walked past me on his way out, he muttered to me, "Be here in three days." He also offered to help me transfer the boat to the barn until I could either get it in the water or set up my boatworks.

Monday I hired Andrea as my assistant. Andrea was a round person - round figure, big round brown eyes, and a round mouth that she wasn't shy about using. I had a feeling I was going to enjoy her company.

On Tuesday we began office hours. Patients trickled in for a couple days, but Friday the floodgates opened. An epidemic of measles coinciding with a series of accidents on the high school baseball team combined to bring me my first deluge of patients. All I could hope was that whither the children went, so would the parents.

Andrea ushered in the last ballplayer.

"Okay, what happened to you?" I asked.

He grinned back at me. "I'm the relief pitcher. When Dave hurt his arm, Coach sent me in. I musta thrown the best pitch I ever have. Tyler swung so hard to get it he lost his hold on the bat. It flew all the way out to the mound. Stung me right on the fingers. See?" His fingers were cramped in an odd position.

"I can't move them. They don't hurt or nothin', but I can't move 'em." Fear crept into his voice, pushing it higher. "How'm I going to be able to pitch? I need to play ball on Tuesday!"

I examined his hand. Swollen tissue was minimal. None of it seemed to hurt, except when I maneuvered the fingers too hard. "I don't think it's broken, there's not enough traumatic response for that. I want you to go to Outpatients Analysis in Fieldcrest for an x-ray before you go home. They'll call me with the results."

He nodded a little too brightly.

"Meantime, I suspect the bones are pressing on a nerve, paralyzing your hand. It's only temporary," I assured him as he snatched back his hand. "Can you take Advil?"

"Yeah."

"Okay. I want you to take some at home, one when you get there, one at bedtime and one in the morning. It'll help your muscles relax. Apply heat to your hand - "

"Coach always says to ice everything - "

"Coach is usually right, but this is to relax your hand, not keep it from swelling. I think you've jammed the nerves a little. Call me if it hasn't loosened up by morning. If Outpatients Analysis finds anything different on the x-ray, I'll call you. If there's any pain, call me tonight," I added sternly.

"Okay."

His mother appeared at the door, her face frowned in the sort of concern I'd feel if I saw my son's hand like that.

"Well, Dr. Wilder? How is he? Can he play on Tuesday?"

"I think he -   what? Oh, yes, I think so. Provided his hand has loosened up. I think he jammed the nerves a little. I told him to take Advil and apply some heat this evening. You do need to go to Fieldcrest - Outpatients Analysis - for an x-ray. Just to be sure."

She nodded. "No problem. We've been there before. We'll start the heat and Advil as soon as we get home. Kyle, you go wait in the car. I'll be right out."

She advanced into my office. "Thank you for taking such good care of the team. I was a little worried when I saw how many were going to have to come in. Nobody knew much about you -   and no one likes to trust their children to a strange doctor. You seem to have done okay."

I murmured thanks. *I guess it's a compliment!*

"I'm Carmen Anthony. My brother coaches the team, and I'm the team mom. I gave the authorizations to your receptionist. All the parents have signed papers giving me the power to authorize treatment for their kids."

"That's a good idea."

"It was Dr. Kesselman's idea. We lost an athlete several years ago because his mother couldn't be reached to sign for surgery."

"You mean Kevin Buehler?"

She stared at me. "Yes, how do you know?"

"Kevin was a couple years ahead of me in school. I grew up here in Kings Hill, Mrs. Anthony. It was a big loss to everyone when Kevin died."

Her eyes narrowed and her shoulders stiffened beneath her white cotton shirt. "I'd heard it, but I didn't believe it." She paused. "Are you really Mackenzie Russell?"

I hesitated, trying to recall if I'd ever known someone named Carmen. She didn't look familiar.

"My cousin knows you. From what I've heard, I'm surprised you have the nerve to move back here." She turned and went out the door. She didn't enlighten me as to who her cousin was.

I turned toward my desk, but before I'd a chance to start brooding, Andrea popped back in.

"Don't forget you have that appointment at the M.E.'s. You can make it if you step on it. You have to stop in at St. Peter's staffing to make sure they've got you listed. They'll want you for a picture ID, so fix your hair first. Don't worry about the office. I'll close up." She bustled out again, patting her shiny brown bun.

I'd found a gem. Twenty-four years old, Andrea was a good nurse and a great organizer -   something to be valued in an employee who had to be as many things as she was, from receptionist to medical clerk to physician's assistant. Not to mention the value of her not knowing me from Eve. There's something to be said for a lack of history.

"Hey, Andrea, I didn't get a chance to tell you. My stuff arrived, and I've got some prints I want to put up in the waiting room."

She poked her head back in. "What prints?"

"Boats. Posters from some of the antique boat shows I've been to."

She wrinkled her nose at me. "Boats, huh? Okay. Whatever you want. Don't forget your appointments."

I went up to Troy to the County Medical Examiner's office. As I passed the Boat Club I saw a young couple strolling off the dock in the direction of Pete's Kings Hill Bar and Grill. I thought I recognized Jean's friend Arthur right behind them. I had yet to call Gary about joining the Boat Club. I was tempted to turn in right then and talk to someone, but duty called. Not to mention the path reports.

Once past the Boat Club, the road widened and curved outward to the river's edge. This wasn't the two-lane concrete twister I remembered. They'd dedicated some of the county's precious funds to straightening the worst of the curves. There were side roads I didn't recognize that intersected with this new and improved River Road. More changes surfaced as I got nearer to the city. I reflected that it wasn't necessarily a plus to be driving over once-familiar roads. Wherever they changed proved so confusing I wound up wishing it were wholly new territory just so I wouldn't go along thinking I knew what I was doing.

Not a bad description of my entire situation.

I parked my Legacy in a visitor's slot and strode up the walk past budding crabapples. Begonias were being installed in brick flower boxes that lined the cement walk up to the plate- glass doors. Blue sky reflected off a solid phalanx of glass.

Directories bounced me to the right location, and I entered a set of rooms belonging to B. McBride, MD, ASCP, Forensic Specialist. I caught the door before it closed and looked at the name again. It couldn't be.

"Mackenzie!"

A slap on the back and a smothering hug, all in one sweep of motion. Yes, it was.

"Betty McBride! What on earth?! When did you get this job? Why didn't anyone tell me? I didn't miss it in the Alumni News, did I?"

She shook her head at me, a mass of unkempt curly hair enveloping a pudgy face with a wide mouth, a squashed nose, and two of the brightest, most intelligent brown eyes I'd ever seen. This atop a square body that could never be called 'hot' yet supposedly had entertained more than its share of the male student body at our branch of the university system.

"It may have been in there, but not because I sent it in. What about you? When did you decide to enter medicine? What's Brian up to these days? Does he like you being a doctor?" She preceded me into her office, chattering away in a raspy contralto, so she didn't catch my confused expression when she said "Brian".

"Betty - uh, Brian died seven years ago. In fact, that was when - and why - I decided to go into medicine. I've just taken up my first practice down in Kings Hill."

"Where you were born, right? You know I remember the history of every roommate I ever had. I'm sorry about Brian. That was one piece of news I didn't get from Matheson."

"He spoke to you directly?"

"He's in charge of the investigation. Though he does like to downplay things. Claims people open up more if they think he's 'just a cop'."

I must have snorted as I sat down.

"Works, does it?"

"It's effective. I appreciate you letting me see these reports."

She pulled a file from a deep drawer in the regulation putty-colored desk and pushed it across to me.

"I take it you know these bodies turned up on my parents' old property? Which now belongs to me?" I laid my hand on the topmost folder. It seemed to pulsate beneath my fingertips.

"Matheson said you were in an awkward position. It sounds peculiar, even to a State Trooper who's heard all kinds of weird coincidences. You know the police don't - "

"Yeah, I know, they don't like coincidences. Well, that's all it is, a coincidence. One I'd like to clear up."

She gestured at the report. "You have to realize, 'bodies' is a misnomer. The papers prefer it because it has more substance. No pun intended. What these really are, are skeletons. Skeletal remains with only a few things to tell us. With nowhere to start, even what they tell us makes no sense. You know, I think 'skeletal remains' has a much more dramatic impact than 'bodies'." Musing over this she fell silent and left me to the reports.

They were typical McBride: brisk, one page, professional, but with idiosyncratic comments thrown in. They created an intriguing picture of two men, one young, one middle-aged, most likely both white, both spending much of their life on their feet, the older one leading a life of extensive manual labor, neither of them terribly remarkable, but both probably murdered.

About one, Betty was definite.

"The older one was shot?"

"No doubt of it. Found a .357 bullet located in the rib cage. Medium range at best. Not that we'll ever know who he was," she added gloomily.

I glanced up at her. She tapped the report.

"No dental work, ergo no dental records. Body's been laying there twenty years. They're already done a quick check. No missing persons reported around then -   none that fit the description anyway. Without some idea of who this could be, someone to compare DNA with, we have next to no chance of finding out who this is."

"What about this, the bullet crease in the skull?"

She shrugged. "Old news. Man that age, could've been anything from a hunting accident to a random shot in a hold-up. Could've happened anywhere."

I nodded, but something bothered me. We ought to be able to find out who this was!

"What about the younger man?"

Betty snorted and reached for a mug of stale coffee that sat on her desk. It was the only personal item there. "I've got my own ideas about him! See this here? Fracture lines on upper tibia - both of them. That's the kind of thing you see when something cracks you across the legs - like a baseball bat! My guess is this guy got in trouble with some of the local bad guys."

"Maybe a tree fell on him?"

"Maybe, but my gut feeling is this guy was in trouble once, and maybe again. The mob doesn't always use finesse when it wants to unload a troublemaker. He died from a conk on the head."

I re-read the Opinion. "But you're not sure it was a homicide. It could have been an accident."

"That's what I had to say, but my instinct tells me it wasn't." She plunked the empty mug down for emphasis.

"What's this piece of rock you mention?"

"Darned if I know. May have had something to do with cause of death, or it may have fallen in after. Have a look." She reached back into that deep drawer and tossed a bag at me.

She answered my surprised look with a shrug. "You wanted to see the reports, I figured you'd want to see this too, so I got it out of the evidence room."

Amazing. I turned the bag over in my hand, smoothing it to see through the plastic shine to the 'unidentified rock' Betty had found in the younger man's skull. It was triangular in shape and thicker on the short end, growing thinner as it approached the opposite point. One side was smoother than the other, more worn, and it was dark gray, almost black in color.

I held the bag as if to open it. "May I?"

Betty thought about it for a moment. "I think it's okay. It's been printed, and you can't hurt it. I should tell you I'll have to make a note that you handled it."

I stared at her, then opened the bag thoughtfully, remembering who and where I was.

I wanted to feel the stone, and get a look at its grain and striation. Rarely had I ever felt stone of this particular polished texture. It was the smoothness born of wear and tear, like stepstones in an ancient footpath. I returned it to the bag. Keeping my voice even, I said, "I don't think this kind of stone is native to this area."

"No? That's interesting. Makes it seem more likely to be cause of death then, but who carries around a rock, ready to bash someone on the head? Have to get another opinion." She made a note and tucked it into the file folder. "Thanks for the tip."

"Sure. Look, I'd better go. I have to pass my credentials over at St. Peter's. Any chance I could have copies of those, Betty?"

"Nope, sorry. Even I can't bend the rules that far. If you have to get yourself a lawyer, then he can have 'em. You can look at these whenever you want. Just stop in and see me."

She stood up and walked me to the door. "Call me anyway. We need to get together and talk. Mackenzie, don't worry over this stuff. It'll blow over. An investigation into something this old is basically a formality. They always drop them when the evidence peters out. We don't know who these men were, let alone who might have had a reason to kill them."

"So, what happens then?"

She shrugged. "It remains an open file. Eventually it goes on microfilm or computer and gets buried in a file someplace."

"But nothing gets resolved."

"Huh?"

We'd stopped at the door. I turned to her.

"Nothing gets resolved with an open case. If a person is under suspicion, he not only doesn't get proven guilty, he doesn't get proven innocent."

"I suppose. But, who's under suspicion? Your parents? They're both dead. And no one else is in the picture."

"Exactly, Betty. My parents are dead, so maybe it shouldn't matter. Still, I've moved back to Kings Hill. I'm not really keen on having people think my parents had something to do with this. I have enough from my father to live down without adding that. Look, what about this business of reconstructing a likeness from the skeleton? Could that be done?"

She shook her head at me. "Sorry. There's only one expert in the area, and he's in England for the next six weeks. By then this'll be file fodder."

"A cold case." I nodded slowly. "Thanks, Betty, for letting me see this anyway. I'll call you soon."

She gave me another brutish hug. "Don't stew over it, Mackenzie. Good to see you."

I left the building in a fog and dealt with St. Peter's staffing department so distractedly that I'm sure the clerk was questioning whether I was fit to be on their staff. I drove home on automatic, nebulous thoughts flitting through my mind.

Jean opened the door for me, ready to discuss her latest phone adventures with the moving company, but I passed her by. I climbed the stairs to my room, crossing to an old trunk I had put in a corner. I sat staring at it, wondering if I was remembering correctly. I reached toward it slowly, running my hand over its dried-out finish.

It was a handmade wooden trunk, one of my father's rare finished projects. In it were World War II ration books, a small stamp and coin collection, old photos. Stuffed in the corner was an object wrapped in a scrap of decrepit blanket. I pulled it out and unwrapped it. I hefted it by the handle, marveling at the balance. Once upon a time some ancient hunter had labored with animal bone and hide and stone to create himself a tool, a sort of hammer cum ax cum chisel. It was a crude weapon, the basis of my father's collection of man's armory, and one of the few things I'd kept from my dubious inheritance. I fondled it, rubbing the head over and over, trying to massage away doubt about the scarred surface where a wide chip had broken off the end of the stone mallet, a chip that would have been triangular in shape, and thicker on the short end, growing thinner as it approached the opposite point.

CHAPTER 6

Easter Sunday. Pop's not home for dinner. He's late. Mommy's mad.

I play with my ham and mashed potatoes, glancing out the porch window every now and again. The sky is getting grayer. Maybe it will snow. Easter came early this year.

Almost done with my chocolate rabbit dessert, I hear Pop's old green pickup roar into the driveway. Quickly I finish my rabbit and take my plate to the counter. I skip to the porch door, ready to hold it open for Pop to make a grand entrance. But he is nowhere in sight.

The pickup door hangs open like a shutter ready to fall off its frame.

"Mommy! Pop's not here!" I cry.

Mom comes running, drying her hands on a dish towel. She scurries out the door with me right behind her.

"No, Mackenzie, stay inside."

"No, I want to help - "

"Mackenzie!"

I stay behind the door, listening to her call.

"Wylvern! Wylvern! Wyl - vern!"

She disappears too, over the hill beside where Pop stopped his truck. I wait, obedient to her command, but picturing what awful fate my father has met. Robbers. Wild animals. Heart attack - whatever that is.

Movement. Grasses and shrubbery moving, and my parents make their way up the slope, Mom supporting Pop.

They reach the porch, and I open the door, ever-helpful.

Pop leans down unsteadily, scratches from the weeds and burrs dotting his face. His eyes are glazed over. He leans into my face, peering as if to figure out who I am. He smells.

Mom grimaces behind him and maneuvers him past me into the house.

I pull the porch door closed behind them. My shoulders sag now, just like Mommy's. I want to get mad, too.

I was in no mood for a festive dinner with Brooklynne and company Saturday night. I hadn't slept well. Maybe it was the farm, maybe it was remembering Pop, but I'd been bothered by a dream I hadn't had in years. An analyst would identify it as the result of the stress I was under in my teenage years. Freudians might interpret parts of it as deriving from adolescent sexual turmoil. Like many such dreams, it was made up mostly of anger - and fear.

Pop is angry with me. Wordlessly he approaches. His steel-gray work clothes match his eyes. Eyes showing white at the edges and round, glazed, blind centers. He points his finger at me in fury and comes toward me. I rush downstairs to the kitchen and race, not to the door, but down the cellar steps. Worn wooden steps bending round, descending between musty walls of plaster and lathe dotted with mouse turds and draped with stringy cobweb garlands. Kitchen cleaners and garden tools crouching on shadowy shelves. Footsteps behind me. Panic edging in. Should I lock myself in or get myself out?

I seek a hiding place in the cellar. A waste of time. I pull the outside door open. Noises of keys jingling. He's locking me in! Or is that the car? I dash out into the dusk. I dive down the steep hill below the house, sliding on shiny weeds and grass, shoving burdock and blackberry canes aside.

I reach the bottom of the hill and press my way to the shelter of the dying apple trees. I sense he is still behind me, but I don't know where. I've got to make it to the road! I push on. It's dark, and I'm feeling my way through chest-high growth. Infant Christmas trees are tucked here and there. I stumble over one.

Here's the embankment that leads to the road. If I gain the road I can get away. I reach the gravel shoulder and clamber out. I start to pound away with my feet, running as hard as I can. Headlights approach. I flag the vehicle down.

Disbelief and horror commingle to become some intolerable emotion: it's Pop's pickup truck!

I wake up.

Four a.m. I couldn't go back to sleep, and I couldn't face getting up, either. Instead, I lay there letting thoughts swirl through my head.

Pop hadn't been *that* horrible. Perhaps that was why the dream had never finished. I was always afraid of him doing something absolutely unspeakable, but he never had.

Had he?

I spent most of the day working furiously. At least, that's what I tried to convince myself I was doing. I unpacked boxes, put things away in closets. I tried to do it in an orderly fashion, but I'd find myself absent-mindedly shoving things on shelves, hanging my quilted winter coat in my bedroom closet instead of in the store closet, putting magazines on a kitchen shelf. I scolded myself, then wandered to the stove where I explored how the oven worked. I decided to have lunch, couldn't find anything I liked in the fridge, finally fixed a sandwich and left the cheese on the counter. I must have wandered into my bedroom a dozen times. One of those trips the doorbell rang, but I didn't try to answer it.

Trying to clear my head, I drove out Shallot's Road to where my mother and I had lived after we left Pop. The tiny little house was overrun with foliage and lilac and wisteria. It needed paint, but it looked happy.

I cruised toward home. Rounding a curve, I was transported back twenty years. A big house, two stories of cedar shingles, dormers, sashes, and porch. A broad lawn bounded by pines on the sides and dual sentinel maples at the front. A long gravel driveway that disappeared around the side of the house. On the lawn, the porch, the driveway, even leaning out the upstairs window: kids. From an infant in a stroller and a toddler in a walker, up through what looked like a fifteen-year-old wiping the mouth of his younger sister, there were kids all over the place. Weirder still, they looked *exactly* like the kids who used to do the same things twenty years ago. Shaking my head, I checked the mailbox. "The Coopers."

I backed up my car and pulled onto the shoulder. The fifteen-year-old boy approached, waving the others back. Two other teenage girls gathered up the younger ones and kept them from coming any closer than ten feet.

"Can I help you?" the boy asked.

His voice was even like Bob's! "Does all this still belong to Frank and Mary Cooper?"

"Yeah, they're our grandparents."

"My name is Mackenzie Wilder. I'm the new doctor. I used to live here, and I went to school with Bob and Sandy Cooper."

"Oh! Okay, then you know my Dad and Aunt Sandy."

"That sounds right. Are they here?"

"Well, no. They went out for Granddad's birthday. We're supposed to be getting the cake and ice cream ready." He turned to call out, "Josie! It's okay! Get everybody working on the decorations. They'll be home soon!"

"You're all kids of - " I hesitated. The thought was mind-boggling. There must have been seventeen children there. The Coopers had run towards lots of kids, but....

"We're all Coopers, one way or another. We're cousins, mostly. Well, some brothers and sisters. Look, what was your name? I can tell Dad you came by... unless you'd rather wait for him?"

"No, that's okay. I don't want to intrude on a family party. Tell your Dad that Mackenzie Russell was by, and to check by Dr. Kesselman's old office. Tell him I said 'hi'."

"Sure. See ya." He waved a hand as he turned back to the house.

Seeing the younger generation of the Cooper clan was a great distraction. All the way home I speculated over what kids might belong with which adult. It seemed to me there had been eight Cooper kids when I was in school. Stairsteps, with Bob and Sandy only ten and a half months apart. Could each Cooper have had two children? Naah, I thought. They were some future genealogist's dream - or nightmare.

All the good feeling drained out of me as I entered the house. I glanced at the clock. Still only two-thirty. I marched upstairs to my room and paused in the open doorway. It was still there, I thought stupidly. I opened the lid and began to unpack the trunk, item by item, examining everything in the hope I'd find something to make me think something other than what I did.

I found the ration books, each inscribed in old-fashioned handwriting with the name of the person it was assigned to. They'd belonged to my parents and their friends. I went through the stamp and coin collection piece by piece. Pop had started them for me. A Liberty-head dime for my tenth birthday; a Colombian Expedition stamp for sixth grade graduation; three 1884 silver dollars.

A gun-cleaning kit with its instruction book. Inside the kit was a card with a list of guns on it. His gun list! He always kept an inventory of his various collections. Not terribly formal, it was just a running list of everything he owned. Even inside the stamp and coin box were sheets of paper listing all the items. The gun list had a few lines crossed out, notably a .22 rifle and a BB gun. Those would have been the two I took with me when Mom and I left. I scanned the list idly, until I saw his .357 magnum pistol and suddenly remembered the wood-handled gun he'd let me fire once. I stared at it, wanting to toss it away but finding I couldn't move my hand at all. Just as well, because if I had, I wouldn't have noticed the faint markings. A line was drawn very lightly through the .357, and beside it was a question mark.

Now, what did that mean? He'd sold it and couldn't remember who to? Not unusual. It was stolen? Possible. Lost? One thing I was sure it meant, *he didn't have it anymore, or he wouldn't have marked it out.* I breathed a little easier.

I lifted out the handtool and set it aside. I'd already seen enough of that! Next I found a box of jewelry that had belonged to my grandmother. Some jelly jar glasses, wrapped in an oily pillowcase. A manila envelope filled with pictures of people I didn't know, taken before I was born. A couple of old plates lay hidden under a copy of a 1947 *Saturday Evening Post*. A box camera, its black exterior rubbed shiny, its levers rusted shut. A cotton shirt crumpled into a ball.

I was beginning to feel guilty that I'd never unpacked this stuff before. I'd used the trunk as a table to hold plants or books or knick-knacks. One year I put my Christmas tree on it. Somehow I had never wanted to open it and examine what was inside.

Finally I reached the bottom, dusty and oil-stained. A couple of notebooks lay in the back corner. Pop's lists! I leafed through them. Copies of the lists of stamps and coins. A list of the fields of Christmas trees we'd planted, with their planting dates. I guess you could call that a collection. A list of vintage comic books. I'd entirely forgotten he'd had those! A list of dates and locations on the farm and people's names, followed by dollar amounts. Oh, this was embarrassing. This looked like his moonshine list. These were kids to whom he sold stuff, and the locations probably represented stills or pot gardens. They weren't the right places for anything else. I scanned the list. It made sense, except for one or two names. He sold stuff to Judge Robinson's daughter? Good grief!

The second notebook was devoted to a single list: his weapons collection. It was written in bold letters, straight and uncompromising. At the top of the list was the handtool, purchased for $12.00 at an auction in Ravena in 1953. A note had been added in smaller letters in ballpoint pen. It read: "End of blade chipped 1988". The lines of the numbers were wavy, as if his hand was shaking as he wrote.

CHAPTER 7

We lie on the bed, panting.

"Come on. Let's try again."

The bed is torn apart, sheets tousled. A musty smell pervades the air, part dirty clothes, part sweat, part heat-triggered fabric softener.

My jeans cling tight along my legs, flaring out in enormous hand-embroidered bells, as retro as I could find. They pull across my abdomen, dryer fresh, gapping desperately as I try to zip them up.

Brooklynne has some luck with hers - jumping up and down, yanking on the zipper tab with each upwards jump. Then she flops down beside me on the bed again. Both of us yank and tug and struggle with the badge of teenhood fashion: faded grungy jeans tight in all the right places.

Once we cajole and slide and force those tiny metal tabs to the top of their toothy columns, we lay there 'til we catch our breath, staring at the crack that splays across her ceiling, trying to figure out how we're going to stand up.

M y hands shook as I applied my make-up. I'd wanted nothing more than to discover who was responsible for planting those two bodies on my farm. I'd wanted to clear Pop's name of the suspicions that were blowing about town. Now I wanted the investigation dismissed, buried in those boxes of files Betty McBride had told me about. Most of all, I wanted to forget everything I'd read in those damn reports.

"I wish I hadn't told Brooke I'd go tonight!" My frizzy flyaway tresses rivaled Frankenstein's bride's. Blotchy make-up didn't help. My dress was all wrong - too new, too green, too stiff. I didn't feel like seeing anyone tonight, and I certainly didn't want Bryan to see me like this! But bad hair wasn't enough of an excuse. I sighed. Maybe I'll ask Brooke to put it all back on the market. Maybe I'll join Doctors Without Borders, go to Bangladesh.

Bryan had been elected to pick me up. He looked spectacular in a sharp black suit, bow tie, and off-white shirt. The lock of hair that kept dropping down his forehead only emphasized the boyishness his face had, even at thirty-eight. His eyes widened in appreciation as he looked me over. This might be okay after all.

If you can forget about what you found and that Bryan is a cop.

We had a moment of awkwardness as he tried to hold my jacket for me. No one had done that in years - except for male chauvinists who seemed to think I couldn't find my way into my own clothes and whose ulterior motive was to help me find my way out of them. Bryan was just being helpful, I told myself as I allowed him to slip the jacket on my arms.

His car was a dark green four-door with comfortable seats and a complex-looking dashboard. Besides the usual speedometer, tach, and fluid gauges, there was an assortment of dials and bandslides I didn't understand. A sleek microphone dangled discreetly from a coil under the dash. As we pulled away I sensed greater-than-normal horsepower. Bryan grinned at me.

"I use it for work."

I didn't want to talk about his work or anyone in his line of work. There were other difficult topics to be tackled.

"Then I guess it didn't come up for negotiation in your divorce."

He flashed me a look. "Yeah. But Deb always had a car of her own anyway."

"That was her name? Deb?"

"Yeah. Deb Voag is what she goes as professionally. She still uses my name privately, I don't know why."

"Your ex-wife is Deb Voag, the fashion model?"

"Yeah, and that has a lot to do with why she's my ex."

"Voag. Did she make that up?"

Bryan sighed. "Yeah. 'Voag' equals 'Vogue', you know? Awful, but it worked. Her public loves it. Mackie, why are we discussing her? She's not exactly my favorite topic. Especially when I'm out with another, far more congenial woman."

I blushed. "I know it's not really any of my business. Brooklynne didn't tell me very much about your situation, though, and - well, I'd rather understand it properly so that I don't make a worse gaffe sometime. I'm sorry to seem nosy."

"That's okay."

"I always thought that Deb Voag lived in New York City. I thought she was single. Everyone thinks she's single."

"Mackie!" Bryan said sharply. The speedometer crept upwards. His knuckles showed red lines against white. Then he sighed. "Yeah, Deb always tried to project that image, even when we were married. Her agent thought it made better copy. Now she's got an apartment in New York and a condo up around Loudonville. That's where Rachel is tonight. Our daughter."

"Rachel? How old is she?" I watched out the window as black emptiness drifted into the outskirts of Albany. Streetlights danced as we went through the city.

"Nine - and smart. She's a good kid, too. She's nuts about animals. You'll like her. I'll bring her by to meet you."

"I'd like that." The cheer had come back into his voice at the mention of her name. A nine-year-old daughter, huh? Surely I had known when this child was born; why hadn't I thought of her before? Had the thrill of seeing Bryan again wiped memory of his daughter from my mind? Since when was I so excited about Bryan Jamison anyway?

We drew up in front of the restaurant, a building covered in gleaming white clapboard. Black and brass carriage lanterns hung beside shiny black double doors. Black shutters framed windows alight with candles, and a black canvas awning stretched over the twenty-foot walkway from door to curb. Two valets in black flamenco jackets sprang forward to open our doors. He motioned to the second valet and handed him some cash and the keys.

"Only guy in the city I let park my car. He's a cadet at the Police Academy. He knows what I'll do if anything bad happens to it." He laughed as the valet sketched a salute and took off.

A man in spotless black livery and top hat swung open the door and bowed low. The interior was lit with electric candles, except for a grand old carriage spotlighted among ferns and begonia and ficus along a brick walkway lined by gaslights. "The Black Carriage" was lettered in gold flourish on its door.

Brick arches stood to either side. A corridor just behind the left one led to the back to rest rooms and the catering office; a small foyer behind the right archway housed the cashier. Two flights of stairs flanked the entrance and mounted to a gallery where intimate tables were laid out. The floor was paved in flagstone, and as I stood, transfixed, we were approached by a hostess wearing a snowy white blouse with black vest and black ballerina skirt. I grinned at Bryan as we were escorted back to the private room Brooklynne had reserved.

"Mackie! Meet my husband, Lloyd Kerns. Lloyd, this is Mackenzie Russell Wilder. She's your new doctor, Lloyd, so be careful what you order."

Lloyd, a redheaded, sturdy man with an impish grin, waved. Brooklynne stood up and rounded the table to hug me. She wore a creamy white satin suit with a sparkling diamond pendant and matching earrings. I laughed. We'd done it again. Whenever we'd gone anywhere as teenagers we had managed to coordinate our outfits without discussing it at all. My satin suit was forest green trimmed in cream, and I wore a necklace and earring set of old pearls.

The men shook hands, and I lapsed into an old habit of comparing the twins. Brooke was only five foot seven; Bryan topped out at six one. Their skins had the same delicate tones, and their eyes and smile were identical. Their faces differed significantly. Where Brooke's always appeared ready to smile, Bryan's could be a mask, closing down when things got serious.

We ordered, making sure to include champagne for toasting Brooke's success.

"I finally met Jason Fields today. He is intriguing. Very personable and easy-going. Not at all self-important. I invited him to stop by. I told him about you, Mackenzie. He seemed terribly interested."

Bryan raised his eyebrows at me, his mouth twitching.

"Great," I groaned. "Brooke, we aren't teenagers anymore. You don't need to play matchmaker."

"I'd never dream of it. Besides, Bryan here would put a stop to it if he thought I was trying that again."

"Oh?" I turned to Bryan.

He reddened. "From what I understand, you did well enough on your own to find your husband. You don't need my sister stepping in and running your life. Besides, her matchmaking doesn't always work out the way she expects. I should know," he added beneath his breath.

I didn't let on I heard him.

We sat down to appetizers of shrimp and oysters. The champagne arrived, and we toasted Brooke.

Putting down her glass, Brooke grinned at us. "I can't believe it. First you, then Jason Fields. Now - are you ready - the Lt. Governor! His office contacted me. He wants me to find a family retreat for him up in the Adirondacks! I am sooo excited!"

"That calls for another toast!"

There was a general clinking and congratulations, and then servers bustled as salads of radicchio and Romaine with a house specialty of cheese dressing arrived. Music drifted in from the main dining room.

Still bubbling, Brooklynne gestured in that direction. "We'll have to dance after we're done. The band here is terrific. They do requests, too."

"Brooke, you are *not* asking them to play 'Louie, Louie' tonight. I forbid it," ordered Lloyd. He whispered to me, sotto voce, "Once she gets going, you can't stop her." Then he raised his voice and asked, "Dr. Wilder, what made you choose Kings Hill, anyway?"

"He never pays attention to my work. Lloyd, you know Mackie was my best friend in high school. I talked her into coming to Kings Hill. Didn't I, Mackenzie?"

"I'd never have known Kings Hill needed a doctor if it hadn't been for you. There were some other reasons, too. My family's land. Once Brooke told me it was for sale, I had to have it. That was a big factor. Also, there's a trauma specialist at Albany Medical Center that I want to work with. He specializes in the kind of injury that ended up killing Brian. I figure I know the grief those injuries cause, I need to know the best possible treatments for them. Who knows, maybe I can help Dr. Tolbrecht devise some new ones. Anyway, I have a couple of letters of introduction to him."

"Sounds like a lot of good reasons to me. Welcome to Kings Hill, Mackenzie!"

"Thank you." I liked Lloyd.

"Lloyd! It's welcome *back*. Mackenzie grew up here. Do you not listen?"

Lloyd chuckled at his wife's exasperation.

Brooklynne huffed. "Mackenzie, have you had a chance to check out the underground passage yet? Can you still get down to the river?"

I shook my head. "There hasn't been time. Besides, it's not something I want to do alone. If anything collapses on me, I want help handy. I did check out the lot. I think I can fit a boatworks back there. If I can work out a ramp to get the boats in the water."

Lloyd looked confused.

"I'm into classic boats," I explained. "Brian and I refinished a Chris Craft stem to stern, and I've got a Hackercraft getting its engine rebuilt on Long Island. I don't want to waste that riverfront."

"How many boats do you need?" Bryan teased.

"As many as I can refinish," I said. "Want to help? You'd love being out on the water in these. The wood looks fantastic, and the power in these old engines is unbelievable."

"Not me. There's a reason I'm a cop and not a sailor. I hate the water."

"Really? You hate it?"

"If man were meant to be on the water, we'd all have paddles for feet - or something like that."

"Oh. Well, okay. But I'll bet I can change your mind eventually." I backed off, but it wasn't easy. *He doesn't like the water?*

The server arrived with prime rib, asparagus, crab, and rice. We dove in with the enthusiasm of old friends reunited, and the momentary tension dissipated.

We weren't halfway through when I noticed Brooklynne watching the door. She touched Lloyd's arm, and he paused his fork mid-lift. I looked at Bryan who looked at Brooklynne, then laid his napkin on the table and turned his head in time for our ears to be assaulted by a shrill voice.

"I've been trying to reach you! Where have you been?"

A tall, lean beauty coated with a sublime if unnatural tan stalked our way. Her eyes were an alluring combination of hazel and emerald, almond-shaped, almost narrow, and her hair was a cascade of chestnut curls artfully laid out to look casual. The gold and black dress she wore screamed its designer's name. As we looked on, she draped herself over Bryan's shoulders and squeezed. From a distance it might have looked playful. From right beside him it looked deadly. Bryan winced in annoyance if not actual pain. The small, impeccably dressed man who'd followed this siren into our dining room murmured to her.

She hissed at him over Bryan's head. "It's all right, Monty! No one will think anything of it. After all, Bryan is the handsomest man in the room. Why shouldn't Deb Voag be seen with him? Now go find us a table. I want to talk with my ex."

Bryan's face was expressionless. Brooke, Lloyd, and I watched in silence.

"Deb. What do you want? Who's with Rachel?"

"Bryan, don't fuss. She's with a sitter, that Brandi she likes so well. Rachel is what I wanted to discuss with you." She cast an appraising look around the table. "Dance with me. We can talk out there."

"Deb, I'm eating. We can talk right - "

She stood up, and smoothed the taut silk over her thighs. "Come on, Bryan. Being seen with Deb Voag will be good for your reputation." Her perfume floated over the table like a poisonous cloud.

I watched dumbfounded as Bryan stood and let her lead him out to the dance floor. The little man she'd arrived with passed them coming back into the room.

"Can't you do something about her?" Brooke hissed at him.

"What would you like me to do? Muzzle her?"

"It would be a start!"

"Brooke, honey, as much of a brat as she is, she has more charisma and savvy than any other model I've ever seen, even those ten years younger. She may have the sensitivity of a boulder, but she knows what serves her interests. There's no stopping her."

"Yeah, like a downhill train," Brooke muttered.

"Well, Deb is ... Deb. Listen, I've got to get out there. Another client of mine is supposed to be Deb's escort. I have to smooth ruffled feathers until this dance is over. Be good now, Brooke."

I raised my eyebrows at Brooke.

"Monty is Deb's agent. He's okay; he just doesn't want to blow his own deal. Deb Voag," she mimicked the model's self-important tone, "is lucrative property right now."

"Not the most polite person, is she? No wonder they're divorced!"

"You're telling me! She's always been like that. I feel responsible, since I introduced them the year Bryan got out of college. She's always been selfish. Always 'me, me, me'. You should have seen her when she found out she was pregnant. She wanted an abortion; claimed being pregnant would ruin her chances for a career. Bryan put his foot down. Threatened her with legal action, divorce, everything. She was still starting out, and she was terrified of being on her own. So she had Rachel - under duress - but she's all but ignored her ever since."

"That's terrible!"

Lloyd spoke up. "Brooke, you have to be fair. When Rachel had appendicitis? Deb sat up with her the whole night. Stayed with her in the hospital and played games for five days straight. You know that's not her style. She loves Rachel. She just doesn't have any idea of what it means to put someone else first. Her mother was like that, too."

I was surprised. "You know her family?"

He grimaced. "When Bryan and Deb were married, I walked her down the aisle. Her mother is my cousin. But Deb would prefer to forget that, so.... Notice how she never asked your name? She can't stand other beautiful women stealing the limelight she thinks is hers -   especially around someone important to her."

I blushed. "But - they're divorced."

Lloyd shrugged. "Doesn't matter. Way she sees it, you're competition. I'd watch out if I were you."

Somehow I couldn't see myself in competition with the sensuous and veneered Deb Voag. Still, it wasn't like the Bryan I remembered to stand for such humiliating treatment. And what about Rachel?

The music ended, and Bryan returned, alone.

"Deb's date took over. Sorry."

"I hope your food is still warm."

He pushed his plate aside. "I got all I wanted. All I deserved, I guess. Damn that woman!" He glared across the table at his twin. "Do you know what she wants now? She wants me to let her take Rachel to North Africa for a photo shoot! Take her out of school early, at test time, to go and hang around with models and photographers and strangers! Says it will be educational. I won't let her take Rachel to live in New York City, and she thinks I'm going to let her go to Africa! Rachel gets heat sick, for God's sake!"

"Oh, Bryan, no!" Brooklynne exclaimed.

Lloyd was shaking his head. "She can't do it, Bryan. You're custodial parent, you're in charge of Rachel's welfare."

"Yeah, I know. But she makes me so mad, Lloyd. You know she'll try her best to make my life miserable over this. Not to mention the ideas she's filling Rachel's head with!"

I didn't know what to say. Actually, to me a trip to North Africa did sound educational. Although I didn't know what kind of care Rachel would get in her mother's custody.

The busboy began discreetly clearing the table. The server consulted with Brooklynne as coffee and tea was poured. Lloyd began a funny story about what happened the week before when one of his clients, an animal lover, called him to her home to make out her will. It seemed she was concerned she might die suddenly because of one of the many snakes she rescued from construction sites. Occasionally one of them would bite her, and she wanted things taken care of in case the ungrateful recipient of her kindheartedness should turn out to be poisonous. Lloyd was a great storyteller. We chuckled at all the right places, but I noticed that Brooke had reached over to take her twin's hand. I had to control an urge to do the same.

"All right if I join you?"

A tall man with a mop of curly hair and big eyes stood in the door. Six foot three; large-boned; wide, grinning mouth filled with horse teeth below a Roman nose. Everything about him seemed big, even his hair. He wore a black tuxedo, with a bow tie in iridescent colors, a musical staff filled with notes flying across the wings of the tie.

"Jason Fields! Sit down, please!" Brooke invited him.

He shook each of the men's hands heartily upon introduction and held mine in his as Brooke explained who I was. His eyes were the palest green I'd ever seen, afire with intelligence and creativity. I could swear I felt ideas radiating from him.

Brooke requested an extra place setting. When the Ice Cream Romanoff was served, Jason dug in with a gusto that seemed to characterize everything he did.

"So, you, Bryan, you're a cop. Homicide? Must be fascinating. Tough, no doubt. But somehow I bet you enjoy it. Brooklynne, you're his twin sister, and you're in realty. Lloyd, you're an attorney. Good to know. I always like to set up with a local barrister when I move into a new area. Mackenzie Wilder, you're the new physician in Kings Hill. How's the country doctoring business?"

"It's coming along, but Jason, I'm impressed. You seem to recall quite a lot about us for just having met us."

He tapped his head. "Necessary. I remember everything that might be important until I know it's not. Especially when I'm starting a new project."

"I'd have thought a man like you would have a large retinue of secretaries and assistants to handle details," commented Lloyd.

"Yeah. People like you don't usually travel on their own, do they?" put in Bryan. "The department's always getting calls from some bigwig's secretary that Mr. Hotshot is in town and needs special services."

I dropped my head down and looked at Brooke from under raised eyebrows. What was with Bryan? Was he taking his annoyance at Deb out on Jason?

Jason leaned in conspiratorially with another toothy grin. "Not my style. I'm a loner. All my secretaries, assistants, managers, and underlings are kept corralled at my offices. I only let them out when I need them."

Even Bryan laughed.

As we continued eating, I asked, "Bryan, was baseball a dangerous sport when you played in high school?"

"No, but then, we didn't play that hard. Why?"

"The baseball team was in my office yesterday with no less than seven injuries. That seems kind of excessive."

"Well, Tim Franklyn teaches those kids a lot more than we ever got. I wonder sometimes if he pushes a little too hard, but they don't seem to mind. His sister's a big help. She mothers the kids, in a tough kind of way."

"Carmen *Franklyn*! That's who that was? Dianne Franklyn's cousin?"

Brooke and Bryan nodded.

"No wonder she looked at me like I'd crawled out of the morgue with entrails dripping from me!"

"Mackenzie! Please!"

"Sorry, Brooke, occupational simile." I caught the question on Jason's face. "I grew up in Kings Hill, Jason. My family - well, my father - was kind of notorious. Dianne Franklyn was my best friend until about junior high. Then she made my life miserable all through high school. She had a very low opinion of my father and considered it her duty to tell me and anyone else within earshot so. There's no telling what kind of stories she's told her cousin."

"That was all in the past, right? Why should it matter now?"

"Some things take forever to go away. I don't want old stories hurting my medical practice. Besides, something's brought it all up again."

"You mean those bodies they found on your place?" He met my eyes and grinned. "I always check out potential property very thoroughly."

"Well, apparently, everyone is talking about whether or not my father was the one who killed these guys. I'm sure he didn't, but it's not likely anything can be proven after this many years." I spoke as if I hadn't looked in the trunk that morning. "They don't even know who the men were."

"Are they sure they're men?" asked Brooklynne.

Bryan nodded. "One's in his mid-thirties, the other guy's about sixty. One was bashed on the head, one was shot."

"I thought you said the State Police never told you anything!"

"I have my sources. Decided to use them to keep tabs on this for you. In case you need help. And Lloyd here said he'd go on retainer for a buck."

Lloyd nodded, his mouth full of ice cream and raspberry sauce. Brooklynne beamed at them.

"Thanks guys, but I don't think I'll need any help of that kind."

"Chances are they'll drop the case in a week anyway," Bryan said.

"If they drop it, people will still think Pop did it. They may not want me as their doctor. Some of them - like Carmen Anthony - won't want me anyway. I sure didn't bargain on having to fight this kind of a battle."

"Mackie, I'm sorry. I feel responsible," Brooklynne looked miserable.

"Why? Did you kill those guys?" I teased. "Look, I'll survive. If the worst happens, I'll let you re-sell it all and you'll get another fat commission."

She brightened. "Hey, that's right, I would, wouldn't I?"

"I could use a private physician for my new organization," Jason offered. "Interested?"

"I'd like to hear about it."

Before he could reply, Bryan tapped my arm. "The band is starting up again. If we don't dance, Brooklynne will be at us forever. Excuse us, won't you, Fields?"

"Oh, certainly. We'll talk about the project another time, Mackenzie." He waved as we left the table for the dance floor.

Brooklynne wore a bemused expression.

I hadn't danced with Bryan Jamison since fourth grade. He hadn't been so much taller than me then. He'd been gawky and clunky when we'd danced the Virginia Reel in gym class. I remembered he swung me so hard my arms pulled out of their sockets and my feet left the floor. Tonight he moved with confident grace and held me closer than I expected. I made no effort to pull away. I could feel him turning his head occasionally. Watching out for Deb, I expected. I turned my face into his shoulder. Oh well.

CHAPTER 8

We've never been a river town, not in my lifetime anyway. Where once Kings Hill needed the river, flourished on it, drew from it and contributed to its economy, now it merely squats, nothing more than blocks of wood and concrete barely watching the river pass by every day.

It makes for a lack of identity, felt by every one of my generation. We're cynical teens, too cool to show sentimentality, deeply serious about public social issues, but too disillusioned and suspicious of the power of the status quo to try anything really effective or noteworthy. We spend far too much time disenfranchising ourselves - and the lack of a real river town identity is a contributing factor.

We've pulled away so far that we can't put down roots to connect us with our past, weave ourselves into history. We can't acknowledge the part of our lives that is the River, because the River flows on forever and would carry us away with it. We have to deny it, and in so doing, we have defined ourselves.

I called my ballplayers first thing Monday morning. They seemed like a nice bunch of kids. Carl and Donnie were going to be a little sore from their collision in the outfield, but otherwise they were fine. Their parents seemed a little short with me, absent- or maybe other-minded. When it came to Kyle, Carmen Anthony was downright cool.

"Kyle's fine. Hand loosened up Saturday afternoon. He'll be playing again Tuesday. Dr. Jenkins over in Fieldcrest will check it on Wednesday."

"Fieldcrest? Oh! Actually, I was thinking I could come by practice or the game tomorrow and go over all the players. That would save everyone a trip, and - "

"That won't be necessary, Doctor. Our boys are fine now. They don't need you."

The rest of my calls brought similar responses. It was thought the team would be playing with a full roster tomorrow - but no thanks to me.

" 'Morning, Doc. More patients coming in. Here's a list of supplies I thought we'd better have on hand. Okay if I bring in sandwich makings and store them in back? It's easier than making a lunch to carry in every day. Fresher, too."

"Fine, Andrea. I'll keep a supply of fruit. Maybe I can con Jean into baking us something once in a while."

She whispered to me. "Do you know she makes the best chocolate cake with buttercream frosting in three counties?"

"Really!"

Andrea nodded solemnly, the soft curls of her new flowing hairstyle jiggling. "We'd better not have it too often, though. It's almost *addictive*."

"How about you bring in our patient?"

The morning passed quickly. Only a few patients stopped by, but they were all pleasant. One young man owned up to the fact he was more curious than ill. We talked, and I gave him a cereal sample for his baby girl. He assured me he'd be back. I was feeling reasonably self-satisfied when Andrea popped in with a frown on her round friendly face.

"I don't understand it, Doctor. There's a detective outside to see you. He's not from the State Police - you know, like you told me to look out for - and he's got his *daughter* with him! What do you suppose he wants? You're not in more trouble, are you, Doc?"

"I'm not in trouble at all, Andrea. I think I know who this is." I eased by into our still-dull waiting room. "Bryan? What are you doing here?"

He stretched out his arm to a leggy young girl with strawberry blond hair. Her face was pale except for flushed cheeks and a dusting of freckles across her nose. She glanced at me uncertainly, but the look she gave Bryan was full of adoration.

"This is Rachel. This is Dr. Wilder, honey. She's taking over for Dr. Kesselman. We were in school together."

"Hi," she said softly.

"Hi, Rachel."

She was beautiful, a feminine version of the fourth-grade Bryan, but with golden-red hair where his had always been flaxen. I didn't try to hug her as my Southern friends would have. Some young people are very private about their personal space.

"Rachel, you can call me Mackie if you like. Your dad and Aunt Brooke call me that."

"Are you and my dad really friends?" she asked.

"I think so. Your Aunt Brooklynne has been my best friend for years."

"Okay. I'll call you Mackie." The smile she gave me revealed the resemblance to her mother, but it wasn't tainted by the Deb Voag attitude.

I looked up to ask Bryan, "She isn't sick or anything, is she?"

Rachel piped up. "Nope. Daddy said he wanted me to meet you. We're going to the museum in Albany. It's his day off, and," she whispered dramatically, "he's keeping me out of school. He calls it a 'family field trip'. We do this sometimes. We *always* go someplace *educational*. Then we go eat and do something fun." She hung on his arm and grinned.

He flushed and tossed his head awkwardly. "Yeah, well, with a job like mine, I'm not always around when Rachel is, so I take a few liberties. Her teachers don't mind. Rachel's a good student. I think she gets something out of our trips. I know I do." His grin matched hers glow for glow.

"What are you going to see at the museum?"

"There's this guy who does these tricks with bubbles? He makes all these neat shapes, and puts smoke inside them and everything. He's great, really cool. And then Daddy said we'd see some of the regular stuff, too."

"Sounds pretty good to me."

"Want to come with us, Mackie?" Rachel invited generously.

I caught Bryan's eye. There was an echo of her invitation lurking there.

"I'm afraid I can't. I have office hours today. Besides, I think this is a pretty special day for you and your Dad. You two have fun. You can tell me all about it."

"Daddy says you bought the farm where you used to live, where the Hicks were going to build a riding arena. I was going to take lessons, wasn't I, Daddy?"

"We talked about it."

"Now I won't be able to. Unless, are you going to have horses? Could you show me how to ride?"

"Rachel - "

"It's okay, Bryan. Rachel, if I get horses, you can certainly come ride. Okay?"

"Sure!" There was that incandescent smile again.

"I hate to break this up, but we really should get going. Thanks, Mackenzie. Come on, Rachel."

"Bye, Mackie!"

We closed the office for lunch. I sprinted across the street to meet with Jean. I found her in the kitchen slapping sandwich slices together and muttering to herself. A half-empty pitcher of iced tea sat on the counter. She reached out a brown arm for a glass and drained it, setting it back down with a firm chink to pour herself a refill.

"Jean?" I asked hesitantly.

"Hi, Doc," she said. "Sandwich? Tea? I'd better make more. Just a minute."

She moved to put my beat-up kettle on - we agreed on the superior virtues of fresh-brewed tea - while I carried lunch plates to the long oak table. She poured the tea, pulled up the knees of her workday khakis, and settled herself in the chair across from me.

"How was - " I began.

She held up her hand, lettuce protruding from a corner of her mouth. "Not yet. How was your morning?"

Puzzled, I reviewed the morning for her. It took only ten minutes for us to polish off the thick whole grain sandwiches and proceed to fresh cut-up fruit. Jean made a habit of eating hers with a small pickle fork. She speared a slice of apple, held it up for examination.

"I don't know how you're going to be able to do anything with that place out there, Doc. It's a mess!"

"It didn't seem too bad when I looked at it. The kitchen has possibilities."

"Hah! That's the word! Rip up that ugly carpeting, put in a decent floor and cupboards - didn't you notice there weren't any cupboards?"

"I - well, yeah," I admitted.

"No cupboards, and no downstairs bath - you need at least a half-bath downstairs. That floor feels weak, and some of the window frames have wood rot. Front door needs replacing, the lock and doorknob don't work - "

"Never did." I crunched into my own apple.

She glared at me. "And upstairs is a rat's nest! There's papers and dust and discarded stuff left all over. I don't think those Hicks cleaned up when they moved out."

"I understand they moved in a hurry. There probably wasn't time."

Jean snorted. "Didn't need to be in that much of a hurry. You need to redo the floor up there, too. That shiplap stuff looks stupid. And someone put in a fireplace in that upstairs front room and didn't make sure it was supported right. Floor sags. I didn't get to the basement. No telling what's down there," she commented darkly.

I couldn't tell if she were worried about finding awful conditions or another dead body.

"You seem to know a lot about house structure. I thought you were just going to check out the cleaning."

Jean rose to bring large slices of chocolate cake with a buttery-looking frosting to the table. This must be the confection Andrea had described in such hushed tones. I could feel the calories staking claims on different parts of my body. Applying my fork to my slice was sinking into condoned sin. Jean smiled in satisfaction at my sigh of delight.

"My husband was in construction with my brother. I learned a lot from them, especially about older houses."

"My husband and I used to buy houses and fix them up for a hobby way before it was popular. I hadn't realized how valuable you were going to be, Jean. That was before we got into boats," I added.

"That's another thing! Those boats! I don't know where you plan to put them! It's going to take a lot of work out there, no matter how you decide you want it. I suppose we can do it. Provided those State Troopers get out of our way." The dark note was back in her voice.

"Did they give you a hard time?"

"They tried. I showed them the key *and* the letter you gave me, but it wasn't until that Matheson showed up that I could get in. Not the barn, though. By the way, he asked if you could meet him out there around four this afternoon."

"Four? Did he say why?"

"He did not! I reminded him you were a doctor with a schedule of your own and that I didn't know if you would be free. Right?"

I'd like to have seen Matheson's face. "I'd better show up. I wonder what he wants." I smooshed the remains of my cake.

"Probably wants to dig under the house. We won't be able to get started out there for weeks!"

"I need to get the boat under cover out there, soon, too. Unless I can get it in the water. But that'll take a ramp. Maybe the work crew can come down here and put one in for me. Think Arthur might have some ideas, Jean?"

She stared at me. "I know one thing. He's going to love you being here. At least you two talk the same language. Antique boats. Doc, you've got a practice to build!"

I pushed back my plate. "I know. These leisurely lunches won't last, I'm sure. We're going to need to keep some stuff at the office for those times I can't get away."

"Just like Dr. Kesselman. Once that man got going I never could make him eat a decent meal! Better let me stock that kitchen."

I began clearing our plates. "Can I take some of this cake over? Andrea told me it was the best in three counties, and she wasn't exaggerating." We stacked dishes in the sink.

Jean beamed at me as she ran the water. "Take some of my apple kuchen, too."

"I'll get those from you in a minute. I've got to bring Andrea the prints for the waiting room. I can't stand empty walls. These'll look great."

Jean saw the prints and threw up her hands. "Boats!" was all she said.

When I returned to the office, Andrea's eyes got bigger than ever (if possible) at the piece of cake. She wasn't impressed by the prints, though. I settled myself on the leather couch in my office and sifted through the packet of mail she'd handed me. I read about computer programs that would make my patient tracking easier, computer tie-ins to hospital networks, a new drug a local pharmaceutical firm was touting, a new professional journal that was proclaimed a 'must-have' (by its editors), and a diagnostic computer program that, if I read the literature correctly, was so good it would make me obsolete. Computers!

Andrea came in, chocolate crumbs at the corners of her lips, another envelope in her hand. "There's one more you need to see, but you're not going to like it."

My hands went numb as I read. I glanced up into Andrea's concerned face. "No kidding I don't like this. Where did it come from?"

I'd never seen anything like this. Though poorly worded, its essence was clear. It read:

> Doctor Wilder,
> It has come to the attention of many dwellers at this community that you are the new Physician in Residence. This determines to be a situation unpleasing to the majority of us.
> Kings Hill was better off twenty years ago when the likes of you departed this community and will be as well again when you are gone.
> It would behoove us (and you too) to leave our town as soon as possible. Or else.

Actually 'Or else' was crossed out, but carefully, with only one line, as if the writer wanted me to see it. I held the letter by one corner and started to crumple it, slowly at first, then faster and faster. There was a great deal of satisfaction in the crunch and crumple of that wad imprisoned in my fist.

"You sure you want to do that?"

I opened my hand and dropped the distasteful epistle into the wastebasket. "The only way to deal with dirt is to toss it out. If Kings Hill doesn't want me, we'll know soon enough. A lack of patients will show that." The memory of the morning's phone calls to the ballplayers' parents stole some of my bluster.

Andrea pursed her lips and moved toward the door. "I think whoever sent that letter should be arrested! You're a good doctor, a really good one, and a good person, too. That person is crazy. Just plain crazy!" She exhaled and stomped off to her desk.

I made myself put the letter out of my mind. I had too much to do to build up my practice. Worrying about phantom mail like that wasn't going to help me. I started going over some of Dr. Kesselman's old records. I was going through them a box at a time, trying to familiarize myself with patient histories. I was on my fourth record when Andrea buzzed the intercom. She'd never bothered with it before. Who was she trying to impress?

"Dr. Wilder, your next patient is here. A Ms. Deb Voag."

Oh. My finger slipped off the intercom button. *Rats!* "Send her in, Andrea. Wait, has she filled out the new patient forms?"

"I shouldn't have to. Don't you have my records there? I pay cash." She pointed to the file box on my desk.

I shifted the box to the floor as she sauntered in. She wore a leopard print dress that should have looked totally out of place but succeeded in looking damn near perfect. Staring me straight in the eye, she sat in the chair in front of my desk. She was taller than me. It was more noticeable sitting down, as funny as that sounds. She must have been five-six to my five-three, and I'm short-waisted.

"I'll have to ask you to fill out the forms on your way out, Ms. Voag. Dr. Kesselman didn't leave me all his records. And - were you one of his patients?" Okay, I lied. But she got on my nerves.

"I came to see him once," she asked vaguely. "Today I wanted to see you. Where did you study medicine, Dr. Wilder?"

"Johns Hopkins. I did a stint at Columbia Hospital for Women in Washington, D.C."

"Your husband didn't object to your having a career?"

"My husband died some time before I decided to enter medicine." I waited to see where this was going.

She rose to meander about the office, squinting unbecomingly at picture frames and lampshades. Jean wouldn't have left her any dust to find.

"Your old man had to die before you could do what you wanted, huh?"

I cringed. I'd never liked that term, even when it was popular. "No. I don't know why you need to know, but to make it clear, Brian," - she looked up, startled - "my husband was Brian Wilder - would never have stood in my way if he'd known I wanted to become a doctor. I never stood in the way of his dreams, either. I was a psychiatric social worker for four years before Brian died."

"He never pressured you to have kids?"

I rubbed my forehead. "Ms. Voag, not that it's any of your business, but Brian and I both wanted children. We were planning for that when he died. Now, *why are you here*?"

She returned to my desk, and leaned heavily forward over it. "Well, Dr. Wilder, I'm here to get a good look at my husband's old girlfriend. And I see that your doctor-patient relationship with him is closer than I like. Back off!"

I stared. "Ms. Voag. First off, I was never Bryan's girlfriend. You can ask your former sister-in-law about that. Brooke and Bryan have been helping me move back to Kings Hill. We're friends. But I don't understand something." I stood up and took a couple steps in her direction. "You're divorced. You and Bryan aren't even friends. So what interest is it of yours *what* my relationship with Bryan is?"

She slid her eyes around at me, her lips curving to heighten the leonine resemblance her hair and jungle print dress gave her. "It interests me, Dr. Wilder, because it interests me. Bryan was my husband. What was mine is mine. You say you weren't his girlfriend, maybe, but he knows an awful lot about you. I repeat, back off. I don't like trespassers!"

"I don't let other people dictate my relationships, professional or otherwise, Ms. Voag. If you have a complaint about my friendship with your *ex*-husband, I suggest you take it to him. Now, if you have no medical problems, I have patients who do." I walked to the door and pulled it open.

For a second I thought she was going to refuse to leave. She tossed her head and started to brush by me. She paused and looked me over, head to toe.

"I can see why you weren't Bryan's girlfriend." Her nostrils flared. Beads of perspiration dotted her upper lip. Ms. Voag's poise was slipping. She all but spat her final words at me. "But how come he admires you more than any other woman he knows? Including his twin sister. Including his own *mother*!"

She stalked past three stunned waiting room patients, flicked a tissue from the hand of an alarmed Andrea, and swept out the exterior door.

CHAPTER 9

"There are five tribes in the Iroquois Nation: the Seneca, the Cayuga, the Onondaga, the Oneida, and .... "

I stare out the classroom window. New York State history. Indians, Dutch, French, English - none of it's real.

Last year was the first time I even began to get a handle on our Dutch heritage. My cousin Perry took us walking in the cemetery where we found gravestones from one of our forefathers. The inscription read: "Loving Father, Honored Mother -   Peter and Jane Van DerVeerden." The colonial equivalent, Perry said, of Vandevender.

There's a Vandevender in the class ahead of mine. Probably a distant relative.

That night I checked out the phone book. I never noticed before just how many surnames there are that begin with 'Van.' Van Allstyne, Van der Vahl, Van Eyck.

I sat with the book spread over my knees, counting. Fifty-six families with 'Van' in their names. And places! Stuyvesant. Muitzeskill. Catskill. All Dutch names.

We have a past. A past right here in Kings Hill.

I sigh. I doubt that any of my classmates care.

A large hand grabbed the closing door, and its owner turned to ogle the model's departing figure. He wore a dusty T-shirt with jeans whose fading had nothing to do with a custom acid-wash, and his face was permanently tanned under his gimme cap. He started hollering before he was even in the waiting room.

"Doc, help me out here, would you? I got a real problem here... hell! Mackenzie Russell! It *is* you! How 'bout that!"

I peered under the cap. "Doug? Doug Pulaskey?"

"You bet! Pulaskey Dairy. But, hey, look, I got me this problem. Can we go in there?"

"Sure, come on in. Andrea, get some forms ready for Mr. Pulaskey. The ones our last patient didn't need."

"Ms. Fashion Model flying out the door there? What's her problem?"

"She's just mad about something."

Doug nodded. "Usually is, unless she's getting her own way. Doc, take a look at this arm, will you?"

He held out his left arm. Three fat puncture wounds were laid out diagonally along his forearm, piercing flesh and muscle, narrowly missing the bones, blood gleaming where it hadn't already caked. I could see bits of rust and metal flakes at the entry points.

"What happened? Come in here."

"Idiot dropped a hayfork out of the mow. Didn't even holler that he'd dropped it, and there I was talkin' to a guy right below. Jesus, this hurts!"

"Why on earth didn't you go to the ER? Or did you think you had to play Superman? Let's get this cleaned up. When was your last tetanus shot?"

"Too long ago, Doc. I'll need another one. Superman, huh?" He leered. "How've you been, Mackie?"

I ran water on the wound. "Pretty good. Trying to get my practice going. I take it the grapevine told you I was here."

"Yeah - sssttt! Ouch! Easy, will ya? - Saundra over at Town Clerk's told me last week. Didn't believe it 'til I came in here, though. Man what *is* that stuff?"

"Disinfectant, for starters. You've got the dairy now. Are you married?"

"Yeah, married Kathy Trindle. Remember her? Got three kids. Why, Mackie, still pinin' away for me? All those years in band finally get to you?"

"Hah! Fat chance!"

"You know, I wouldn't mind showing you around the new places - not here in Kings Hill maybe, up towards Albany. What do you say? We could work something out."

I stared hard at him for a moment. "I don't think so, Doug. That's not my style."

"Sure? Your loss."

I finished bandaging his arm in silence. Some people never changed. Doug considered himself a stud in school - even with girls older than him like myself.

"Okay, let's see about your shot. Turn around and loosen your pants."

"Now you're talkin'!"

"Doug!"

"Well, s'pose I don't feel like turnin' around?" He unzipped his pants as he spoke, an impudent expression on his face.

"I don't know if you want to do that, Doug. What if you don't compare favorably? Or I might miss." I held up the needle.

He blanched and turned around and let me give him his shot without any more smart remarks. When he straightened up, though, he was grinning again.

"Damned if I know why your old man felt he had to protect you. You know how to handle yourself."

"What do you mean?" I stopped writing in his chart.

"You never found out? I figured for sure you'd know by now."

"Know what?"

"It sounds a little stupid, but.... Back when we were in high school, ever notice how nobody asked you out or anything?"

"Believe me, I noticed."

"It wasn't so much that no one wanted to ask you out. You were kinda cute, even if you were serious all the time." He paused for minute. "You're real attractive now."

"Gee, thanks. What about high school?"

"A lot of us hung out with your Pop, you knew that. And he always made a point to warn us off you."

"Huh?"

"He threatened to shoot us if we ever laid a hand on you."

"*What*?" His chart slipped out of my hand and clattered on the countertop.

"Aw, Mackie, you know how he was. We didn't know for sure he'd do it, but none of us meant to find out. I mean, you were cute, but not worth getting shot over."

"Doug, are you making this up?"

"Nope. Swear it. Ask Brooklynne Jamison about it, or her brother. He got warned off, too. We all did. I'm surprised you didn't know."

"There's a lot of things I didn't know, Doug. Keep that arm bandaged and protected. I don't suppose there's a way you can take off for a couple days - "

"Cows get real pained if they have to wait, Mackie. But I'll be careful. I got my help, such as it is. Thanks." He started for the door.

"Andrea'll have some papers for you. Say hello to your wife for me," I added maliciously.

"Right." The door shut.

I washed my hands a second time, scrubbing hard as I thought. Well, that certainly explained a lot. My father!

It took forever to get through the rest of the afternoon. I was still going over this news when I turned onto Wexford Road, narrowly missing the purple pick-up truck pulling onto the highway. How many purple pick-up trucks are there in Kings Hill?

Matheson was sitting on the front porch looking comfortable. It was a real effort for him to stand up. He looked like Marshal Dillon.

I paused at the grove of white lilacs that grew in front of the house. They needed trimming back. After twenty years, the centermost trunk was gnarled and gray and over fifteen feet high. Smaller trees about ten feet high attended the central one like ladies-in-waiting attending a queen, circling her skirts and shielding ever-smaller trees. Beneath their leaves was a dappled fairyland of three-inch seedlings. Florets sprayed forth from every branch, ready to burst. Some had opened, and their fragrance drifted downward.

Matheson joined me, craning his neck to inspect the upper branches. "You know this is one thing I've liked about this job. Watching stuff come into bloom."

"Mmhmm, lilacs are my favorite," I agreed, inhaling. Over by the house I spied the back of the Chris Craft's trailer.

"By the way," I said to Matheson. "When am I going to be able to put that in the barn? I sent it out here because I thought we'd have access soon."

Matheson stared over my head and sidestepped my question.

"I wonder if you'd take a closer look at where we found the remains?"

I followed him to the barn. I felt a little guilty as we followed the path past a rusted fuel pump and the cement block milkhouse where Pop had stored bits of wood. I probably should have come out here yesterday, but I hadn't felt ready. I ducked under the bottom branches of the mulberry tree, bumpy with aging bark. I sniffed a little.

Downhill from this was where the excavation had begun. The old silo - never safe - was torn down to make way for construction of the riding arena, which of course led to these grisly discoveries. To the left rose the foundation of the barn, rock on rock, well over a hundred years old. Here and there above the rear foundation boards had been removed, exposing the skeleton of the structure: pilings and timbers and joists. Rusted stanchions and drinking faucets created archways amongst the pilings. Bird and bat guano mingled with the packed dirt to create a brown-gray mat. Except near the entrance where freshly dug dirt scattered across the floor.

"This is where they found the second body."

Right under the ramp my horse should have walked up. I shivered. Revulsion at the present? Or anger at the past?

"Here's where they found the first one." This spot was further away from the silo, probably once sheltered by the cedar tree that lay uprooted to one side. I caught sight of what appeared to be daylilies tangled in its lower branches.

"May I?"

The trooper nodded. I crossed over the upturned earth and stood midway between the two sites. Twenty feet apart. One under a bug-infested wooden ramp, one beneath an inviting tree. I stared at the cluster of mulberry trees that stood beyond the construction. The breeze fluttered the baby green leaves like supple petals. There was a pleasant view of the field and creek from this little rise.

"Which body did they discover under the ramp?"

"The second one - sorry, the one with the skull wound. See, they called us when they found the first one under the tree. When we arrived, the workmen were already dismantling the silo and that wooden thing that was there. We held them up for about a week, but we had to let them finish so the thing wouldn't collapse. That's when they found the other one."

I nodded. If what I dreaded was true, finding the bashed-skull body under the ramp didn't surprise me. But why was the other body under the trees? And who were these guys?

"Dr. Wilder, I know you've read the reports. Does this jog your memory at all? Give you any ideas?"

I turned toward him. "No. I don't know anything about this, and I don't believe my father did either." I had a sudden urge to feel my nose to see if it had grown.

"Just hoping. We'll be filing all this in a week or two. It's got a pretty low priority as far as the department is concerned. It's just...."

"Just what?"

He rubbed the back of his neck and squinted into the distance. "Ever have something that bugged you? Something you wanted the answer to?"

I nodded.

"I'm like that about these old cases. Most of the time there's either an obvious answer or none at all. Sometimes I'm the only one who wants to know what happened. It doesn't seem fair for a person to be murdered and forgotten both. The truth may be the only justice these souls will see." He gave an embarrassed laugh.

"I know you suspect my father had something to do with this, but you're wrong." I still thought he was wrong, fears to the contrary. "I don't want people thinking Pop did something he didn't, something as horrible as that. I don't want people thinking my father was a murderer. He left me enough to live down without that."

Matheson started walking up the slope. "Yeah, I read the file on your father, Dr. Wilder. Were you aware he was suspected of supplying these kids with hard core drugs?"

"Wh - oh, come on, Matheson, surely not!" I froze in my tracks behind him. "He wouldn't have!"

He turned around to gaze down at me, the tall figure of the law made taller by the topography. "Come on, Dr. Wilder. You can't tell me what a bad reputation your father had and then defend him at every turn. There were hard drugs traveling a clear route from New York through the port of Albany into the Capital District. There were a lot of stations along that route, and a lot of distributors. It can be a short step from pot to speed and cocaine. Your father made it even shorter."

"Are you sure?" I asked.

"He was never caught, but I talked with a trooper who worked out here. He said he could see it clear as day, your father stashing stuff and driving it down this road in one of his pick-ups to move it to the next stop. Or, sometimes, having the kid make the stop out here himself. They knew all right. They just never caught him." He gestured towards the barn, and his face was grim. "Looks like maybe at least one of his customers might have been better off if they had."

With that he went on to the house. I waited, looking around at the trees, the mulberries, the grapevines, raspberry canes showing new growth. Irises and daylily shoots stood tall, crowding out surrounding weeds along the embankment behind me. A huge elm towered overhead, marking the spot where in my dream I charged down the hill to escape my father.

I love this land! I thought desperately. *But Pop's presence is poisoning it for me.*

He was with me here in daylight as surely as he was in the dead of my nightmares. Had this been a complete mistake? A pigeon flew over my head and disappeared into the black square hole at the peak of the barn's gable. How many pigeons had grown up between this one and some great-grandfather from my teenage years? Did this pigeon have some unspeakable family history to live down? Some ignoble aunt or uncle who hadn't been able to find their way home? Did he care what his predecessors had or had not done? Or did he just work on his nest and worry about where today's grain was coming from? I scurried to catch up with Matheson.

"When can we start work on the house?" I asked, panting as I tagged him at the porch steps. "And when can I put my boat in the barn?"

"You can work on the house anytime. Don't touch the barn until you hear from me. I'm talking with Vince Lamberson tomorrow. I might even bring him out here."

"That - ?" I heard the echo of my father's voice; 'son-of-a-bitchin' bastard' he would have said. "Why? What for?"

"He took ownership around the time the murders were committed. Time-wise he's as much of a possibility as your father."

"I hate the man. He hasn't a clue about ethical business practices. He's scum! But murder? He thinks too much of his own hide to risk it. Besides, he's too smart to stash bodies on property of his own. He'd cart them away in one of his sand trucks and stash 'em in cement someplace."

Matheson's face contorted with amusement. "Don't think much of him, do you?"

"No. If it were his body you'd found, you'd have a right to suspect my whole family and probably lots of others as well! He's an easy man to hate, and I hope you make him exceedingly uncomfortable tomorrow."

"Dr. Wilder, you'd better calm down. I don't know if I can let you drive in this condition." He actually smiled.

"Thanks for turning the house loose. According to my housekeeper I have to get workmen going on it before it falls down. I'm sure it will keep us busy until we're allowed in the barn. You sure I can't move my boat in there? It just needs to be under cover. I could put it on the main floor, on the opposite side."

He sighed. "Okay! Okay! I'll give you a hand."

I hustled behind him. With me pushing and Matheson pulling, we managed to get the trailer maneuvered into position for me to hook up to my car. I pulled up the circular drive, swinging into place to back it in.

I slammed the door and went in to make sure there was room. Matheson had walked up while I parked.

"This place is packed," he observed.

"Yeah. Looks like no one's thrown anything out since we left. I think there's room, though. Guide me, will you?"

I backed the trailer up the old ramp slowly. Matheson waved me to the right a couple times, but she went in as smoothly as if she'd just been waiting for the opportunity. I unhitched her, then checked to see how close I was to anything that might mar the finish Brian and I'd worked so hard on.

"I've never seen one like that. Pretty."

"Yeah. You should see it in the water. There's nothing like it." I glanced around. "You know, I could put the boats up here and still stable a couple horses below. What do you think?"

Matheson looked nonplussed.

I grinned and waved as I got back in the Subaru and drove away. Keeping him a little confused was not a bad thing.

CHAPTER 10

Yuck. I glare in the mirror as I pass by.

Scuttle. I *scuttle* through the halls, I think in disgust, and stick my tongue out at my own image.

Frizzy hair. Dark frizzy hair that could be an Afro with a little work, but stops just short and looks horrible on a white girl anyway. Not that my friends would know.

Sue Overstreet called me "Turtle" again today. Then she led her friends to the opposite end of the cafeteria table where they whispered behind their sandwiches, glancing at me with every sip of their milk.

What is wrong with me anyway?

I look at myself thoroughly.

What's wrong with *them*?

I'm a decent human being. I'm not mean to anybody. And I'm reasonably smart without being *too* smart. I like Janet Jackson, Phil Collins, and Blondie. Okay. I like Willie Nelson, too, but does that have to mean I'm weird?

What is wrong with them anyway?

I was beginning to hate having to think so much. Practicing medicine was no strain. I loved it. However, establishing my practice against the onus of my previous life in Kings Hill took a level of social skill that demanded concentration. Add to that the fact I was learning more and more about a man I'd never wanted to think about again.

For as long as I could remember, my father was the bad guy in my life. His drinking made our lives miserable. Endless arguments, repeated car wrecks (twice he'd been nearly killed, once he'd permanently disfigured another driver), broken appointments, ruined family get-togethers, wasted money, not to mention being related to a persistent outlaw. Although, to be fair, a lot of the lawbreaking came after my mother and I left him. He'd been the cause of all my mother's pain and much of the embarrassment I'd felt in my teenage years. Way before Doug's crazy revelation, my father was the reason I'd found it so hard to establish relationships. He was why I worked so hard to be perfect.

I could have admired his outlaw point of view, in a skewed sort of way, if he hadn't messed up our lives so badly. When he lost control of his life and took it out on my mother and me - that was more than I could take. Mom stood by him for years, and she made me stand by him, too. Even after the breaking point came, it took all of my youth coping with being Wylvern Russell's daughter. It took my first two years of college to figure out how to forgive him, and by that time he was dead. What I had never truly been successful at was forgetting.

Most of the time I managed to stuff memories of him into a box in the corner of my mind I reserved for the unpleasant things of life. Periodically they spilled out in some unforeseen way - a wiry old man walking down the street holding onto a cigarette in Pop's blue-collar way, a novel about bootleggers, the smell of bean soup simmering. A memory would trail out across my mind and have to be tucked back in before it caused too much pain. Most of the time I could cope.

Sometimes the old dreams would crop up. Hazy dreams of him lurking around corners, locking me downstairs in the cellar; nightmares of him pursuing me across the fields, of my never being able to get away. Things that never were. In nightmares he was worse, but life had been bad enough. My conscious mind had directed a lot of effort toward keeping thoughts of Wylvern Russell far, far away.

Now he was plunged into my life once more. Part of it couldn't be helped. I'd returned to Kings Hill knowing I'd have to combat old impressions. I thought I could handle it. I had even anticipated the dreams coming back. What I hadn't expected was a whole new controversy, let alone murder.

All these thoughts gave me a headache. Worse, what I could not, dare not admit to anyone else, I had to admit to myself. I was morally certain that my father had committed one of the murders. Whether or not he had a hand in the other - who knew?

I knew my father had never let anyone but family handle his weapons collection. Since Mom and I left, there was no one but himself - with one possible exception - left to handle his ax. From the evidence, I was certain this ax had been used to bash in the skull of the second victim. If I accepted the premise that only my father would have handled that ax, then no matter how sure I'd been that murder was not in his make-up, I also had to accept the conclusion that Pop had killed a man.

Why? I wanted to think he had justification, provocation. I wanted to think he'd been somehow threatened, but the victim had been hit from behind. Even I was familiar with the concept that a blow in self-defense is seldom delivered to the back of the head.

The righteous voice living in a corner of my psyche said I ought to tell the police. They already suspected Pop, I argued back. So far he was their only suspect. I wouldn't be contributing anything. *Except confirmation that he owned the murder weapon*. Minor detail. It explained nothing about who the dead man was, or why he was killed.

Or why he was buried under a horse ramp. That, too, was Pop's style. I'd worked on the barn. I knew how easy it would have been to plant something under that rotten ramp. I also knew that my father had a healthy, peasant-like respect for the dead. He would never bury anyone he respected in a place like that. Unlike the grave of the other body. Purposely or fortuitously, that person had received a decent burial. By Pop? Who else, I thought, though I couldn't see what sense it made.

I wanted to talk this all out with Bryan. I hadn't heard from him since Monday when he brought Rachel by the office, and today was Wednesday, my self-appointed day off. I could call him. I could find out if Deb Voag had said anything about our little tête á tête in the office.

It would be tempting fate. I was attracted to Bryan - who wouldn't be? I'd like to see what might grow from the seed of our childhood friendship. And events of 2001 - personal and otherwise - had taught me not to waste friendships. Still, the idea was a bit scary. As far as confiding in him, he was still a cop, bound by their loyalties and ethical constraints. My own ethics were making my life difficult enough.

"Aaauugh!" I screamed, and stood up from the little desk in my downstairs office. I needed action. Maybe I could tackle that box of boat hardware that needed sorting. I stopped by the kitchen and found Jean frowning at the paper. She was leaning on the counter, the paper spread out beneath her arms. As I approached, she straightened up and folded the paper back and down, over, and over once more, creasing each fold sharply. She rapped it against the counter and handed it to me, her finger pointing to an ad.

"Brace yourself, Doc," she said.

Physician Sought: With the aim of meeting
our as yet unfulfilled need for quality medical care
in our community, Kings Hill is seeking an MD

with expertise in Family Practice and family values, fully licensed and certified to take up practice in its rural community south of Albany. Candidate must have references and submit to background check. Submit curriculum vitae to Box K, c/o this paper.

"What is this?"

"Just what it looks like, I'm afraid," Jean answered.

"An ad - for - here? For my practice! What on earth! Who would do this! They can't do this! Can they?"

Jean sniffed. "Some people will do anything they damn well please. Especially that bunch," she added, walking away from me.

"Wait! You know who did this?" I followed her to the table, which she was polishing vigorously with beeswax and linseed oil.

"I have a fair idea. Andrea told me about the letter you got. I've heard a few things around the village, too." She rubbed vigorously.

"Well, who - ?" I followed her around the end of the table.

"Not telling yet. I've got to check around a little."

"I'm not waiting. I'll call the paper and find out."

"They won't tell you."

"Then I'll go see them. This is such a chicken, backstabbing way of doing things," I ranted, grabbing my car keys and storming to the front door.

"Wait!" yelled Jean.

"I'm not standing around waiting while someone tries to steal my livelihood! With everything else that's going on, it's too much!"

She came up behind me and reached past me to the door.

"If you think that's too much, take a look at this." She flung open the door and stood aside.

"Oh my God!"

Strewn about the portico was a heap of garbage, trash and refuse three feet high. Chicken bones and slimy tomatoes, soggy newspapers, produce peelings, crumpled notebook paper, squashed milk cartons, food cans, soda and beer cans, greasy fast food wrappers, and other things unidentifiable thrown all over the place!

I walked out, skirting things, watching a stray breeze pick at the pile, snatch some of the fast food wrappers away and sail them across the yard. Jean traipsed after me.

"Had to climb over this stuff when I got here this morning."

"Why didn't you tell me?"

"Didn't see any point in bothering you. After all, that was the point of dumping it here - bothering you. The only way I could spike their guns was by not letting them get to you."

" 'Them'? You mean you know who did this, too?"

Jean took me by the shoulders and turned me around and marched me into the house. "Like I said before, I have my ideas. Now you let me handle this. I'll get it cleaned up - "

"That's an awfully big mess, Jean." I turned back to her. I could still see the mound of trash over her shoulder. How on earth would she manage it? I felt awful for being the magnet that drew her all this extra work.

"I know it is, but I've a good idea where Arthur and I can find some young people itching to help." I wondered where that could be. "You let us handle it and go have a nice day off."

"A nice day - good grief!" I threw my keys on the table in passing. Moved by impulse, I changed direction and headed for the kitchen phone. I dialed Information and was rewarded with a number for Jason Fields.

There was something refreshingly cozy about dialing straight through to a VIP. He answered with a vague, abstracted air.

"Jason? It's Mackenzie Wilder. We met at the Black Carriage last weekend."

"Mackenzie! Yes, I remember! We were about to discuss my project when you were waltzed away by the tall blonde policeman. I hope he didn't find it necessary to detain you," he added in mock seriousness.

"Hardly." I laughed. "However I was thinking, if you have the time, I'd like to hear about that project after all. If you still need a physician, I might be interested." *No kidding. The way things are going, I need to follow up all the opportunities I can!*

"Splendid. Why don't you come out here now and see things and - I know, I'll have lunch sent in. How soon can you get here?"

"Well, Jason, that depends on where you are." I smiled into the phone.

"Actually I'm in an empty room in the building Brooklynne Jamison works out of. She was kind enough to rent it to me until we get a portable set up on- site. Should take about a month, considering I haven't made up my mind which site I'm using. Do you need directions?"

"No, it's okay. I can be there inside of fifteen minutes." Brooklynne's. *Wouldn't you know*, I thought.

"Terrific! I'll see you soon."

Lunch was waiting when I entered his office, and I began to realize where the Jason Fields reputation for never doing anything halfway came from. I'd expected brown bags decorated with crowns or arches and the usual cloying aroma of fried food, possibly green stuff on the side, brought in by a crew member or secretary on a half hour dash to the nearest stop. Not even close.

A shiny delivery van was parked in a shaded slot outside the building entrance. Inside I found a door hung with a temporary sign reading 'Fields Enterprises, Inc.' Behind that was a spacious room furnished to meet the needs of an eccentric, privacy-hungry executive. A standard receptionist's desk with computer and telephone stood empty in one corner, a mute testimony to Jason Fields's preference to fly solo. Behind it, to the left of a sleek cherrywood desk, stood a folding table laid with gay restaurant linens. The wall behind it was slapped with colorful dragon posters. Potted orchids on slender stems bobbed in the center of the table. Massive green stoneware plates heaped high with an Asian salad of greens and garlic and chicken and peanut slivers reposed amongst spot-free utensils. A serious young woman in a short white coat poured sparkling cider into stemmed glasses (chilled, no doubt). A basket of rolls stood on one side, and on the other were two covered dishes that eventually revealed grilled shrimp with a gingery sauce spiked with sherry, and our dessert, fruit flan.

Jason slid from the stool of his drafting table and met me mid-floor. He grasped my hand and led me immediately to a chair on the near side of the table.

"I'm so glad you called. I hate to lunch alone, and this will give us an opportunity to plan." He drew out the chair for me and seated himself opposite. As soon as we were seated he told the server she could go. "Brooklynne told me you used to live in Baltimore."

"About twelve years ago. My husband and I were in the middle of remodeling the second floor of our house the year you received the Casement and Club Award."

"The Casement and Club Award! Yes! *Shoot Me When It's Over*! I had fun writing that. I never expected them to give me that award, though. Great dinner that night. Ever eat at the Annapolis Club?"

"No, but I heard of it. Brian and I had some friends who recommended it to us." I settled my napkin and studied the salad for a good starting point. "We went to our first boat show with them."

"Bryan?" He looked startled.

"My husband Brian, with an 'i'. Same name, different person."

He smiled at me, looking through to something he thought he could see. Then his smile grew to a grin, and he dove into his own salad.

"Baltimore was lucky for me. I hope Kings Hill will be. I'm having a devil of a time getting things started. Location, you see. That's why I wanted that bit of real estate on the river. For the view. I want my team to enjoy their surroundings." He paused to swallow a large mouthful of chicken. "Which site do you think I should use?"

I stopped my salad fork an inch from my mouth. "Jason, I haven't seen the sites. And it might help if you tell me a little about the project."

He stared at me, then smacked his forehead. I'd never seen anyone actually do that. "Of course! I'm jumping ahead, as usual. This salad is terrific! Brooklynne told me about this catering service."

I agreed it was wonderful - it was - then prodded him again about his project. He leaned forward conspiratorially.

"Not that it's government secrets or anything, but I'm not ready for anything to get about, so excuse me if I'm a little secretive about this. How familiar are you with computers?"

"I use them, of course. Personal and business. Our billing is all computerized. At the hospital, there's diagnostics and patient records. A friend of mine is head of Infomatics at Prince Georges County in Maryland."

"How do you feel about computers in education?"

"I never really thought about it." *You don't think about these things when you don't have children.*

"Suppose I were to tell you that the use of computers - in schools - as ubiquitous as it seems, is only in its infancy?"

I frowned. "Okay. But I thought they were in all the classrooms already? I thought every kid used a computer for homework."

"True - or near enough, anyway. And every kid in America knows how to get on the Internet for research and social networking. I believe there's more to come.

"The Internet has replaced television as the average kid's time waster of choice. And like TV, it can be - not always, but can be - destructive."

"Depending on what they do with that time."

"Exactly. Kids love being online. They love it for itself. Therefore, if they're encouraged to do positive things online, time spent turns into something positive."

"Okay. I see that point, but how do you compete with all those distracting sites out there?"

"As you'd expect, we're developing new software and sites to lure the kids in. But there's more. I have in mind a project that I call FRIDAYS. It stands for Friendly Reinforcement of Introduced and Discovered Abilities of Your Students. The title serves to assuage teachers who might still resist the 'intrusion' of computers into their teaching. It emphasizes that these are the teacher's students and that this computer work is only to reinforce material the student has already been taught, or alternatively, to help the student develop talents the teacher has discovered. It also is geared to be an activity for the end of the week when many students can use added stimulus."

I helped myself to the shrimp. Tender, juicy, smoky shrimp, grilled to a lively crisp pink and black. "What do the kids do?"

"You have to understand: what I'm building on the river is a sort of hardware/software R&D center. It will have several goals - software and web development are two. I want to connect with the education community big-time. I'm talking with schools in four counties about giving their kids a chance to beta test our products. In exchange the students will get the benefits of the programs they test, and the schools will get computer time for vocational students, computer science students, and special projects. We'll provide unlimited Internet access, including their own web servers if they want. We'll outfit the school computer labs with state-of-the-art hardware, and we'll network with them. Classes can visit the facility, too. If any students have a particular interest in development, we'll arrange for an internship or mentoring. That's some of the reasons I'm being so careful with the physical plant. I want to create an ideal atmosphere for my team, but I also want to seed the idea with these kids that work can be exciting, even fun. I want to affect the minds that are going to set the work environments of the future."

Whether it was his enthusiasm, his sincerity or his commitment to what he was proposing, something shone out of his eyes and compelled you to listen. You wanted to leap in and ask, 'What can I do to help?'

"What can I do to help?"

"You're interested! Good!"

"Definitely. But what can I do?"

"Our industry has hazards just like any other. Carpal tunnel syndrome, VDT eyestrain, EMF's, radiation. And of course, there's stress. Creative types are driven, particularly when they get hung up on a project and there's a deadline to meet. I need someone who can come in regularly to conduct physical exams, advise on stress management, and generally watch over the health of the employees. I don't want someone to shoot x-rays once a year and grill an employee over whether or not he's really sick when his temperature is a hundred-and-one. I want someone who understands the conditions my people are vulnerable to and who cares about helping us maintain an environment that is as healthy as possible."

I cocked my head to one side. "You know, concern like that is highly unusual. Admirable, but unusual."

"A long time ago I promised myself never to ask a person to do something I wasn't willing to do myself. That includes working in an inhospitable environment. Dessert?"

I reached for the plate he offered me. The slice of flan was generous and light and tasted heavenly. After a couple luscious bitefuls I told him, "I'm beginning to understand why you've always been given such good press. Your employees are lucky. I'd be glad to contract as your company doctor or house physician or whatever."

"We'll work out the title. There will be some sort of retainer, of course. You know what I'd like to do? Are you free this afternoon?"

"Pretty much. I think," I added cautiously. "Why?"

"Come to one of the malls with me. There's a store called Computer Outfits. They offer every make of hardware and help you build yourself a customized system. They also have all the simulators and emulators ever invented to allow one machine to run programs written for another. Knowledgeable salespeople, too. I'd like to show you a couple set-ups of the type I'm considering for the FRIDAYS program."

"All right. Maybe you can recommend a laptop for me. I'm finally breaking down to get one. My desktop is loaded with work stuff."

"Great! We'll go as soon as we're done here." He grinned his great toothy grin that was so much like a kid's, and I thought of all the times I'd heard him described as eligible.

We set to scraping up the last few crumbs of flan. His office fronted on the parking lot. A silver car had pulled up, and Brooklynne and Bryan got out and headed towards the outside door. Brooklynne poked her head into Jason's office.

"Hi, Mackie! Jason, everything okay? I see you took my advice on the catering service."

"Yes, and it's wonderful, isn't it, Mackenzie? We've had a charming lunch."

"Glad to hear it. Hey, Mackie, has Dorsey Wegman been out to see you yet?"

"Who?"

"Dorsey Wegman. She's the Welcome Wagon Lady. She was supposed to have seen you by now. She's usually pretty good about visiting people as soon as they move in."

"You mean you actually have such people? I haven't seen her yet."

"Don't laugh. It's good for business. I'll have to give her a call."

"Mackenzie has consented to work with me, Brooke. She's going to help me pick out the plant site, too. Say! We could go there after we've been to the mall. What do you think, Mackenzie?"

That much time spent with Jason all at once might be misleading, not to mention exhausting. "Not tonight. I have things I need to do at home."

"Okay, we'll do it another time."

Bryan leaned in past Brooklynne. "Hey, Fields. Mackenzie, could I see you for a minute?" He surveyed our table. "I don't want to interrupt."

I glanced at Jason as I laid aside my fork. "No problem." I followed Bryan into the foyer. "What is it?"

"I understand Deb stopped by your office the other day."

"Yes, she did."

"Yeah, well, she had no business doing that. She told me what she said. I hope you didn't let it bother you."

"Bryan, I've long since passed the stage where what people like Deb Voag have to say bothers me. She's not about to run my life." I hadn't meant to put it quite like that. "She talked to you?"

"Yeah. I want to talk with you about it. Can we have dinner tonight?" His eyes searched my face for a yes.

"I - not tonight, Bryan. I have things I have to do." I was beginning to feel repetitious.

"When?"

"Soon. Call me tomorrow?"

"Okay. There's more I want to discuss with you. I want to catch up on this thing with your father. You know Matheson plans to interview Vince Lamberson?" His eyes bored into mine, the intense blue not leaving me any personal space.

"I know, Bryan. You don't really have to keep watch over me. Matheson and I had a long talk on Monday. He's agreed to keep me posted. I'm taking care of things myself."

"Well, if you don't want to discuss it with me...." Bryan's voice trailed off.

"It's not that. It's just - you don't have to take care of me, Bryan. I can do that for myself."

"Sure. I still want to talk to you about some other things. If that's all right. When you have time." His jaw was set.

"Of course. Call me tomorrow." I walked back into Jason's office. He'd finished his lunch. I let him know I was done, too, and we headed out to Computer Outfits. Brooke's eyes twinkled as she watched us leave, but I don't think it was my imagination that scowl lines made furrows in Bryan's brow.

CHAPTER 11

There was a little girl,
Who had a little curl,
Right in the middle of her forehead.

And when she was good,
She was very, very good,
But when she was bad, she was horrid.

She dumped out all the trashes
And played in all the ashes
'Til they covered her with soot and cinder.

Then she stood upon her head
In her little trundle bed
And banged her little heels against the winder.

Her mother heard the noise
And thought it was the boys
Playing in the empty attic.

She rushed upstairs
And caught them unawares
And spanked them most emphatic.

~ author unknown

Mama never ever spanks me. Except for the time I asked her to - to see what it felt like. Mama always says that all she has to do is look at me cross-eyed and I burst into tears, so discipline's easy.

But sometimes I think - sometimes I'm just sure - that I really am the little girl who has the little curl right in the middle of her forehead.

A ndrea, I'm going to drop these papers by the farm to Jean. She's out getting estimates. Probably harassing Matheson, too."

"All right. Do you have your cell with you?" She reached out with one hand to jot down a number while with the other she flipped through an office supplies catalog, never looking up.

"Cell phone, cell phone," I muttered, rummaging through my purse.

"You should get a clip-on. Want me to order you one?"

"No, then I'd just have to decide which one to wear. I've got my cell phone and the beeper that I bought. Then St. Peter's and Albany each insisted I take one of their pagers to be on their networks. Albany Med even insisted I take on a special cell phone from their system since I don't have my own office there. Then I let Jason talk me into that new laptop. And a notebook to synch with it, if I ever figure out how!" I dug deeper.

"Find it yet?"

"What? No. - Wait here it is." I pressed the power button, but there was no familiar buzz. "Oh, no. The battery's dead."

"Got the other one?"

"Here it is. Wait - oh no, that's dead, too! How on earth?" I stared at Andrea. "That fancy charger I bought yesterday. I had all my electronics hooked up to it. It must not have worked."

I dug even deeper into my purse, pulling out everything and frantically stabbing power buttons.

"Nope, nope. That stupid machine must have drained them all."

"That's not good," Andrea said.

"I'll say. Now what do I do? I have to get these papers to Jean. And it would be stupid to just hang around here waiting for this stuff to charge. There's no one here and no one scheduled to come in."

Andrea thumbed her catalog rapidly. "Just check in with me as soon as you're done. I'm ordering you extra battery packs *and* a new charger. *This* outfit's reliable," she called out as I headed to the door.

"That laptop I bought better work," I said, "or I'll have Jason's curly head on a platter!"

Like I'd commented, the afternoon had slowed to a halt. I wanted to get busy, do something. Somehow yesterday Jean had charmed members of Kings Hill High's baseball team into cleaning up the portico. When I'd gotten back, three of them were bagging the last of it. One of them was Kyle Anthony.

"Nice job! I'll tell Jean to pay you extra."

They glanced blankly at each other.

"Dr. Wilder." It was Kyle. "You - uh - don't need to do that."

"Shut up, man!" one of the others said.

I smiled uncertainly at the two young men holding a rake and a broom.

"Mrs. Hesford already took care of us," Kyle stammered.

"Well, you did a great job. Here's a tip." I held out six ones. Slowly the other boys pocketed theirs. Kyle shook his head.

"No, Doc. Keep it. Please." He glared at the other boys who shrugged and started to walk off.

"Comin', Kyle?"

"Yeah." He looked back at me, then lunged off.

When I told Jean, she wagged a finger at me. "You'll spoil those boys, giving them tips. I'd already given them plenty." She smiled once more, leaving me wondering what kind of spellweaver I'd hired.

This morning I'd sent her out to try her magic on the professionals. I wanted to see how she'd done. The afternoon sun was bright, the breeze was cool, and the cows were turning contented heads as I drove out to the farmhouse. I breathed deeply and felt like I was drawing peace right from the land.

I rounded the curve in front of the high school and saw a purple pick-up truck parked at the side door. About a quarter-mile later that same pick-up truck swung into view in my rear mirror. It had to be the same one - how many purple pick-ups can there be in a place as small as Kings Hill? It followed me across the highway, on up Wexford Road, passing by when I pulled into the driveway. Its driver must live up here.

There were no vehicles besides Jean's in the yard. I wondered if Jean had scattered the workers on various errands or if she'd simply scared them off. As I put my foot on the first step up to the back porch, the pick-up came trundling back the other way, a flash of orange at the driver's window. I asked Jean about it when she opened the door.

"That? That's Dorsey Wegman. She's pro'bly looking for you."

"Me? Why?"

"Welcome Wagon Lady," she answered.

"Hmm, well, she's missing me," I said as the truck slipped on by. "Here, I've got papers for you. How's it going out here?"

"Come in and I'll give you the ten cent tour." Jean stepped aside.

She wore her baggy jeans today, sure sign she was working more than supervising. She led me through to the front hallway and confirmed my suspicions.

"I've sent Bret and the crew out tracking down materials. Keeps 'em out from underfoot. They'll be here tomorrow. I already went over with Bret what I expected to see done out here the next time I come. I've got them hunting down trim for the stairs here. See where it's all chipped?"

"That decorative stuff wasn't there when I was little. But I like it. Good plan. What else?"

"Okay. They're pulling up the carpet, but I'm going to clean it first. Much as I hate it, we can give it to Re-use. Somebody will get some use out of it. I got most of the trash out of upstairs - you would not believe how much trash was left!"

"Okay, okay, Jean. Not everyone has your standards, you know."

"Hmph. What's wrong with old-fashioned clean I'd like to know? You'd never catch me leaving behind a mess like that! Here. These are notes from Bret about the floor and the basement. He left one about that boat of yours, too. He wrote down the address of some electrician he knows who works on old cars and might be able to do your boats, too." She handed me the slips of paper, her mouth working.

I thought for a minute she was going to say something more, but she just frowned, as if the papers were dirty. I glanced at the address and phone number.

"You know, if we've covered everything, I think I'll get the boat out and take it down to the village. I want to see if I can get it into the water from behind the office."

Jean stared at me. She'd been doing that a lot lately. "You know you are crazy. Crazy. All boat people are crazy." She stomped off.

I shrugged and went out to run my car up to the barn. This would be fun. I hitched up the trailer and pulled the Subaru forward. Just as I'd pulled the boat clear of the ramp, the Subaru's nose aimed toward the road, a car horn sounded.

Actually, a truck horn. It was the pick-up again, whirling into the driveway in all its purple glory. A tall woman climbed out, rather soft and heavy-set and with hair the color of bright carrots. The huge willow basket of goodies she carried swung forward with each of her long strides. Jean came out onto the back porch, and the woman pointed to me. I jogged up to her.

"This her, Jean?" Her voice was loud, jovial, and warm.

"Well, of course it is, Dorsey. Who else would it be?"

Dorsey Wegman strode toward me, the basket dangling from one hand as she stretched out the other.

"Dr. Wilder, I've been havin' the absolutely worst time in the world trackin' you down. I've knocked on your door, rung your bell, driven to the doctor's house, driven here. You're a tough person to run to earth! But - hey! Welcome to Kings Hill!" She presented me with the basket and pumped my hand. Then she pulled me toward the house and whisked me past Jean into the kitchen.

"Actually," she continued, "I know it's more like welcome *back* to Kings Hill, but it didn't sound right to say it that way. Of course, it's been so long since you were here, I'll bet most of my sponsors are businesses you've never heard of. Except for Brooklynne Jamison and Lloyd Kerns, of course. They're two of my top sponsors. Brooklynne insisted I get these to you. She wanted you to get the full treatment." She beamed at me.

Jean looked dourly at me from behind Dorsey and went back to her work in the front room. I liked Dorsey immediately. Her plaid shirt and jeans spelled farm, but I sensed more, and I was right. That purple pick-up was a clue to all that was Dorsey Wegman.

While she ran through the free samples and coupons that comprise every Welcome Wagon Lady's goody basket, Dorsey gave me a fair-sized portion of her life history as well. She was a farmer's wife. They had a dairy farm south of Kings Hill along the river. Her husband's hobby was stock car racing. She was his official timer. They had three children, all of whom attended Kings Hill's schools - one at each building. To augment their income and prepare for college bills, Dorsey earned money at her 'Welcome Wagoning', selling Avon products, delivering phone books, and boxing and hauling gift packages to UPS at holiday time. She manned their vegetable and Christmas tree stands in season, too.

"Anything I can do from my truck," she said proudly. "With all the carting I have to do for my kids, I figured I might just as well stay in the truck all day. It's my second home. It's a beauty, too. C'mon, Doc. I'll show you. Got to get your other basket out anyway."

"A second basket?" I asked as I followed her out to her truck.

"Sure! Bought two houses, didn't you?"

I laughed. "That's okay, Dorsey. One's enough."

"Nope. You take two," she insisted, pulling a second basket from the truck bed. "You never know when you can use that extra coupon. Besides

- I'm glad you're here. Hey, can I put you in for a coupon, Doc? Or a refrigerator magnet with your address and office hours on it? It's good business, you know."

"I hadn't thought about it, but okay."

She opened the driver's door. "Look in here, Doc. King cab, tinted glass, custom paint job. She's got a 4-wheel drive, 5- speed, tachometer, a phone, A/C, CB, CD, am /fm stereo - "

We were interrupted by the 'bleep' of her carphone.

She leaned into the cab to pick it up. "Yeah," she said. "Sure. You were right. No problem." Then she handed me the phone. "For you."

Me? Who...? I took the phone from her. "Yes. Dr. Wilder here."

"Hey, boss. It's Andrea. Bob Cooper just called. His father's not feeling too well. Might be indigestion, but there's been heart trouble in his family, so Bob was wondering if you could stop out there. I told him you'd get there as soon as you could. Boss, you need to get one of these things for when the cell phone doesn't work. It gets better reception, too. I'm going to order you one from the catalog."

"Okay, Andrea. But how did you know you could reach me by calling Dorsey?"

"Oh, she called this morning to find out where you were going to be. I figured she might still be with you. It was worth a shot."

I grunted. "Listen, I'll go by the Cooper's right now. Pull any records we have and leave them on my desk. If I admit him, I'll call you. Check with you later." I handed back the phone. "Dorsey, thanks for everything. I've got to run. I'll think about those magnets. Jean, I'll see you later!"

I ran back to my car, hoping Mr. Cooper was only suffering an upset stomach. Why hadn't they called 911? I tossed the basket of goodies in the back alongside my bag. I pulled out carefully with boat attached and headed down Wexford as fast as I dared over the bumpy macadam. It would have been prudent to unhitch the boat, but that would have delayed me as much as driving safely. I wished I had Bryan's little blue bubble light to pop on my roof.

It took me twelve minutes to get to Shallot's Road, five more to reach their house. The straight driveway made pulling in with the boat easy.

"Good girl," I whispered to it as I got out. Both floors looked quiet. The blinds were drawn on all but the front room. Cars were pulled up tightly to the garage. Were they all inside? I hoped they weren't crowding him. People tend to crowd 'round way too much in emergencies. I remembered Frank Cooper as a big man with a smoking habit. The front door opened as I walked up. Sandy hurried out, glancing over her shoulder. I thought I saw Bob through a window.

"Mackenzie! Thank goodness! It's so great to see you!"

I pulled out my bag. "Sandy. How is he? Has he complained of any more pain? Did you call 911 yet?"

She shook her head. "I think he's doing better. He lay down for a bit - and frankly, belched a lot. He wouldn't let us call Emergency, so Bob hit on the idea of calling you. Come in here, please."

Bob held the front door open for us. The floral wallpaper looked the same, or at least similar. Large couches, big-screen TV with some kind of games system hooked up to it, crocheting lying in a chair, piano in the long open living room. We hurried past the curving staircase into the dining room. It was crowded with people. Sandy tapped shoulders and drew me through. I prepared to tell everyone to back off. At the head of the table sat Frank Cooper, big as ever, and eating - of all things - an extra large burrito! He scowled, no doubt at the scolding he saw coming. He stood up and leaned over to catch my hand in his.

"It's good to see you, Mackenzie. Welcome home." He looked over his shoulder and roared, "I said, 'Welcome Home!' Come on, woman!"

"Frank Cooper, don't you call me that! I am your wife, not your 'woman'. Give me a hand there, Bobby." Mary Cooper backed into the room, Bob holding the door for her. Still puzzled I stood there watching as she turned, her red round face shining with pleasure as she set down a huge homemade sheet cake with "Welcome Home!" dancing across it in my favorite sky blue.

I stared at the cake. I stared at her. I stared at Frank. A couple of snickers came from the back of the room. Frank glared at the source, and Bob and Sandy smiled at me.

"One - two - three - " said Frank, raising his arms.

"Surprise!" came a disjointed but heartfelt cry.

"You're not sick?" I asked Frank.

"As smart as you always were, you sure are thick sometimes, Mackenzie," Bob said. "We're giving you a welcome home party!"

"You need to cut your cake, dear," urged Mary gently.

I set down my bag and took the knife from her. "You know, it isn't nice to play tricks on your doctor. What will Andrea say?"

"She knew," Bob told me, stuffing his mouth with cake.

"Figures!"

"The kids told us you were by the other day. We decided we had to do something." He signaled for seconds (already!).

"Have you gotten settled in yet?" Mary asked as she deftly passed pieces of cake. "What is the doctor's house like?"

"I heard he had a whole collection of different-sized skulls in a hidden cupboard." That comment from another Cooper brother.

"Mike, that story was old when we were kids!" Sandy punched him on the arm. "Come on, Mackie, what is it like?"

"Actually, it's gorgeous. I bought some of the furnishings, too, so I wouldn't have to move into an empty house," I kept cutting and passing slices of cake. It's amazing how many slices of cake large families need.

"How's the practice coming along?" asked CeeJay.

"Slow. Not everybody is as warm as I'd like, but I think I'll make it."

"Tough luck about your old man," Linda commented, immediately shushed by her sisters. "What? What did I say? Okay, okay, tough luck about your old place. Is that better?"

"Linda, it's okay. I know what you're getting at."

"Well, I do mean, tough luck. Nobody should have to go through what you are. I'm really sorry."

"Thanks, but it'll be okay. I'm glad to be back. What about you? Everyone. I mean, that was some group of kids I saw here the other day. Just like old times. Who do they all belong to?" Everyone answered, everyone had a story for me, and soon I was catching up on what all the Coopers were doing, whose offspring was whose, and where they all fit into the scheme of things in Kings Hill.

Finally we got around to my former classmates, Sandy and Bob. Bob was not quite eleven months older than Sandy, and they'd both been in my class. Now he was a computer programmer and writer of software manuals. He also taught programming at one of the community colleges. His eyes gleamed when I told him about Jason's project. "I'll introduce you to him," I reassured him.

Sandy was a full- time mother to eight (two sets of twins!) as well as being an artist. Her husband was an accountant and full-time father. Somehow between them that meant four jobs, but I had the definite impression they excelled at all four. Certainly the behavior of their children was sterling, as demonstrated by the young girl who wandered in and waited patiently for a break in the conversation. She had a long wait.

"Excuse me," she said at last. "What kind of boat is that out there?"

"Boat? What boat?"

"Behind the blue Subaru," the girl answered.

A couple Coopers looked at me, but more grabbed their drinks and headed outside. Frank took me by the arm and escorted me to the yard, Mary close behind.

"Don't mind, Mackenzie, we're always like this. I swear it's worse now they're all grown up." Mary smiled at me.

"It's fine. Gives me a chance to show it off."

Sandy was talking to her daughter, fourteen-year-old Whitney. Bob and Mike and Sandy's husband Terry were poking into the cockpit, while

Linda and her husband ran their hands along the finish on the engine compartment.

"What is this, Mackenzie?" Linda asked. "I've never seen anything like it!"

"It's an antique boat. Specifically a 1941 Chris Craft. What they call a barrel back."

"For the shape?" asked Mike.

"Yup."

"Where'd you get the thing? 1941? Man!"

"My husband and I found it at a small marina in North Carolina a few months after we went to our first boat show. It wasn't in bad shape. The owners didn't realize what they had, so we got it pretty cheap. Took us ten months to bring it up to par."

"Have you ever shown it?"

"We took it to one show. They're a lot of fun. I've got another one getting a new engine down on Long Island."

Whitney spoke up. "Dr. Wilder, could I ride in it sometime?"

"Whitney - " warned Sandy.

"It's okay," I told her. "I'll take everybody out for a ride once it's in the water." I turned to Bob as others waved and drifted inside. "That's what I'm doing now. I'm taking it down to the village to see if I can get it in the water behind my office."

"Good luck with that."

Frank and Mary leaned in. "Mackenzie, you drop by whenever you want. Someone's usually here," Mary said.

Frank added, "Be careful out there on the water. It's not all that warm yet, y'know."

"Thanks, Frank. You take care of yourself, you hear me? I don't want to come out here on a real emergency!"

"I'll take care of him, Mackenzie." Mary assured me, hustling Frank ahead of her.

Sandy stopped beside me for a quick hug. "It's good to have you back, Mackenzie. We'll have to get together soon. Maybe we can get Bryan and Brooklynne and Lloyd in on it, too. Have a regular reunion."

"Sounds good to me. Just let me know when and where."

Bob was the only one left with me now.

"Thanks for the party. It's the nicest surprise I've had in a long time. Today was good timing."

He shook his head at me. "I don't get this business of trashing your place."

"Somebody isn't happy about my being back. Anyway, some things about this place haven't changed much. The people who were broad-minded still are, and the people who are small-minded always will be. I'm just not sure who's in the majority."

"Hey, the Cooper clan constitutes a majority all by itself." His eyes twinkled at me.

"Oh, you." I laughed, leaning against my car to look at him.

"Sandy said Andrea told her you were going to put a boatworks back of the office?" Raised eyebrows telegraphed his skepticism.

"Maybe," I said, a bit defensively. "That's part of what I'm checking out now." I gestured toward the boat. "I want to be able to get the Chris Craft in the water. Maybe I actually need a boathouse. Unless the Boat Club could rent me dock space. I need to stop in there and see about joining."

"Why not let me introduce you? We're not members, but Gary has us out as his guests a lot. He'd help you out."

"Bob, thanks. That would be terrific. And I'll have to take you out on the river sometime. Ever been in a wooden boat? "

"Don't know if I've even seen one until today."

"It's unbelievable how different the experience is. Not like in a fiberglass - "

"Say, Mackenzie?" he interrupted.

"What?"

"Watch out for Deb Voag. She can cause you real trouble."

"Trouble?"

"Word got around she stopped by your office the other day mad about something - "

I sighed and pulled my car door open. "This town doesn't miss a trick, does it?"

"Small town, Mackie. Maybe you better remember that. Teachers - and doctors - have to be circumspect."

"Little too late for me, don't you think? Nothing circumspect about dead bodies on your property." My tone reflected what was in my mind. This topic was not going to go away.

He gave me a quick hug. "Just be careful, okay?"

I climbed into my car. "I'll do that. And make sure your dad behaves himself."

Okay," he laughed. "Take care, Mackenzie. I'll give Gary a call."

CHAPTER 12

Sometimes I wonder if I'm schizophrenic. I mean, how can you tell?

I wonder if anyone knows how I really feel? Sometimes, at school, when I do really well in a class, I feel really smart. Other times, even if I do well, I feel like I'm really dumb, and the teacher just doesn't know it.

And those days when I'm at home, and I can't even get my best friend on the phone, and I know all the boys think I'm weird? Sometimes even then I think I'm lucky, and special, and will have all kinds of adventures soon.

I think about what it feels like to run down a long hill, arms stretched out, feet flailing the air, moving faster than the eye can follow, until it feels like the ground is rushing up at you and you're going to crash. I think that's what adventure feels like. That's what power feels like.

I hummed as I eased my way back to the village. That had been a really sweet thing for them to do, I thought. I pulled around back of the office. I considered going on home, but I spotted Brooke's car in my parking lot.

"What's up?" I asked, walking in on her and Andrea in deep discussion.

"My hair should be, don't you think?" Andrea held it piled on her head in soft curls. "How was your party?"

"It was fun, but I'm not going to trust you again," I said. I told Brooke, "Coopers gave me a little surprise 'Welcome Home' party. This one was in on it."

"That's nice," Brooke said, but she looked as if her mind was elsewhere.

"Brooke? Come on with me. I want to show you something. Andrea, you come, too."

They followed me through the kitchen and out the back door. My boat filled up the entire back lot. I'd maneuvered her around and parked her end in, the gold-painted name bannered across the stern just above the exhaust ports.

" *PsyKe*?" Brooke's eyebrows rose.

"That's her. This is the Chris Craft Brian and I got started on. We almost called her *Obsession*, but I didn't think that fit." I chose to ignore the look I caught passing between Brooklynne and Andrea. "See how sleek her finish is? Thirteen coats of varnish, then four more for luck. I had to talk him down from thirty-two."

I leaped off the back steps. "Brooke, do you know how far back this property goes?" I pushed past *PsyKe*, dodging the blade of the rudder peeking out from its underside. On her far side was tall grass and weeds, overgrown dandelion and chicory. Farther off I could see cattails, but I couldn't tell how far away they were, or how deep.

"To the river."

"I *know* that. Do you know how much *space* I've actually got?"

"This part should go back about thirty feet."

"Doesn't look like it. Damn!" I'd been slashed by an old blackberry cane. I started watching my footing more carefully. I didn't want to get slashed again, and it wouldn't do if I suddenly started sinking into river water.

I paused and looked back. The low wall at river's edge near the far end of the office marked the point where the river water occasionally swelled to. There should be a relatively straight - or at least even - line from that point to somewhere near here. Where was the river edge?

Andrea wasn't quite as careful as her boss. One minute she was to my right, barging ahead of me, and the next her pony-tailed head had dropped from view, accompanied by a loud shriek. Then silence.

"Dr. Wilder?" came a cracked cry.

"Andrea! You okay?" Brooke and I rushed through the weeds to get to her.

There she sat, head barely higher than her knees, rump deep in water. She shook water and mud off her hands, and her shoulders shook, too, but I couldn't tell if she was laughing or crying.

"I found you a ramp," she said, disgust in her voice.

I held my hand out to help her up, examining where she'd landed. It was a ramp, a rough concrete ramp that must have been here for years. Water lapped up between the stems of grasses and cattails, which I realized were leaning, stretching over here from either side of the ramp. There really was a clear - so to speak - entry to the river here.

"Come on, ladies. We've got a boat to launch!" I kept hold of Andrea's hand and headed towards the boat.

"What? Doc, you've got to be kidding!"

With careful guidance by my two reluctant cohorts, I maneuvered the boat to the ramp, backing through the weed-strewn shore to where the flattened grasses signaled the top of the ramp we'd discovered. After checking the placement one more time, I handed one of the lines from the boat to Andrea.

"Here, hold on to this no matter what. And stay up here where your footing is secure!"

"Secure? You call this secure? Remember what happened a few minutes ago?" Her voice squeaked higher and higher.

"You'll be fine. Brooke, come here a moment, okay?"

"You know, I'm not that much crazier about the water than Bryan is!" Brooke told me.

I climbed out of the car. "Look, you'll have to back her in."

"What?!"

"It's easy. Just back her straight down until I yell. When I yell again, pull the car forward, and park it. Andrea? Once the boat's in the water and I give the okay, untie the second line that's tied to the trailer. You can drop both lines in the water then. Go back to the office after. Brooke, after you park the car, get yourself down to the pier by Pete's. I'll pick you up there."

"This seems like an awful lot of work - "

"Come on! It'll be fun!"

"The things we do for the people we love!" Brooke said, but she was grinning at me.

Andrea still looked dubious, but she followed my instructions.

While Brooke took over the car, I climbed into the boat. As Brooke backed into the water, the river gently lifted the boat from the trailer.

"Hold it!" I yelled.

Andrea took care of the lines. I had a couple misfires trying to start the engine, but then it caught. *PsyKe* hit the Hudson just fine. I waved at Andrea and Brooke to get going, and then I carefully nosed my way out of the backwater into the river.

It was a straight run to Pete's. I took my time, checking for debris or signs the water was more shallow than I expected from the charts I'd studied a couple nights ago in preparation for this moment. Main Street looked vastly different from the river side. Buildings were flatbacked, devoid of window trim, barren.

The water was smooth, good for a first run. The engine seemed to be in fine shape, no misses now that she was warmed up. Yachts or no, the pier itself was deserted as I pulled up to where Brooke was waiting. I was just as glad. I didn't know if the Boat Club officials would be annoyed at me for this.

Brooke stepped aboard and gave me a funny look as I reversed the engine and backed away from the dock far enough to swing the boat toward open water again. I concentrated on avoiding the precious yachts, then put some additional distance between us after I cleared them before opening up the throttle.

I stood at the wheel, my head above the windscreen and my hair blowing wildly about me. Brooke had seated herself next to me in the cockpit. I caught her grinning at the pleasure of being here, but she laughed out loud when she looked directly at me.

"What? You're having fun, right?" I yelled above the rush of wind and water.

"Yes, I'm having fun. But it's so funny to see you steering this thing. I would never in a million years expect to see you doing something like this! It's great!" Then she squealed as spray blew into her hair as well.

I laughed, pointing ahead to where I was planning to take us. Before us lay Kings Island, opposite Jason's construction site. I wanted to run up there and scout out the shoreline for future reference, then head back home. This was only a quick run after all, though it would take about forty-five minutes. But even a short run felt great.

I slowed down a little, to make talking easier as well as to savor the trip.

"Okay, Mackenzie, I'm starting to feel the attraction these boats have for you. But I don't get why this is so different than riding in any other boat."

"I think that's the mystique. There is no explanation of why, it just is. It's said the designers and builders of these boats put way more into them than was strictly practical. Lord knows they didn't make fortunes with them. Some of them even lost fortunes. The Dodge family - you know the cars? - supported Horace Elgin Dodge's design habit for years with money from the auto industry. He was a fabulous boat builder, but it didn't make money. They lost nearly two thirds of their fortune. That's the thing, even when wooden boats were the norm, these boats got under your skin. It's no different now."

"So it's just one more obsession?"

"Maybe. I love 'em, that's all."

Seagulls were tracking us now, checking to see if we had bait or other food aboard. A couple branches drifted by, followed by a large turtle that looked too far from shore.

"Brooke, what does Bryan have against the water? He took me by surprise with that the other night."

"That's something he'll have to explain to you, Mackie. It's not my place."

I turned quickly, but caught only a profile, no facial clue as to what was behind that response. "I guess he's entitled. I hate flying."

"You do? How'd you ever make it across the Atlantic then?"

"Pills. Nothing like self-medicating." I grinned at her shocked face. When she didn't say anything, I asked her, "You know, you're not saying much. You were kind of pensive when I got to the office, too. What gives?"

She didn't look at me. "Mackenzie, I know you're new at the hospital, but have you heard anything about a Dr. Reid?"

"No, I don't think so." I glanced at her sharply but had to pull my attention right back to the river. There were more logs floating around out there than I would have figured. "Why?"

She sighed. "I just wondered. I started going to him about a month ago, and I - I guess I'm feeling a little skeptical."

"You said you were going to make me your doctor."

"I am."

"So, this Reid. Is he some kind of specialist?"

"Yeah. He's - he's a fertility specialist. Lloyd and I are trying to have kids." She glanced my way furtively, afraid to meet my gaze.

"Well, that's good news. I mean, that you're seeing someone. What has he said so far?"

"He's not terrifically hopeful. He found a lot of adhesions when he examined me. They're from - Damn, why is this so hard to talk about with you?"

"It's okay, Brooke. This is me. I was there, remember?"

"I know," she said in a small voice.

"Except I never understood why you didn't come to me before you had the abortion." I eased back on the throttle until we were moving only fast enough to beat the current.

"I was afraid you'd talk me out of it. I couldn't take it. Not Bryan knowing, not Mom or Dad. I knew you'd make me ask them for help. You'd make me go back."

"They found out anyway. You did go back."

"Yeah, eventually. After I realized how stupid the drugs were. Like I've said before, that whole experience was one of the reasons Bryan became a cop. Thank God your father was around. He's the one who helped me get off the hard drugs. If it hadn't been for him - well, who knows what I might have tried? I got pretty desperate there for a while."

I grunted. "It's ironic, your saying that. Matheson told me how it was in the trooper reports that Pop had been trafficking in hard drugs. I'm surprised he helped you stop," I added bitterly.

Brooke leaned over and took hold of my wrist. "Mackenzie, let me tell you something *I'm* sure of. Your father had a thing about hard drugs. They were chemicals, and he was always going on about 'natural highs'. Only things I ever saw him offer people were pot and homemade whiskey. And I *mean* 'offer'. He never made anybody do anything they didn't want to do."

I pushed the throttle forward again, picking up speed. "That's what I always thought, Brooke." I waited for a minute, unsure. "Matheson says they have proof."

"What kind of proof? Their reports? Hah!"

"Now, Brooke - "

"You know how things were back then - "

"Just because there were those scandals doesn't mean all the police were incompetent - "

"They were worse than that!"

" - *or* corrupt. I have no real reason to doubt what Matheson said."

"Yes, you do. You have my word that your Pop wasn't pushing drugs!"

I shook my head again and looked up- and down-river. Nothing there. I directed the boat to port, heading for the island we'd been creeping up on. I wanted to scout out the shoreline on this side at least, but I'd have to hurry. This was taking longer than I'd expected. And there was nothing for me to say to Brooke's assertion.

"Look over there." I pointed at the island. Gulls ran over the rocks at the water's edge, with a few floating in the water itself. Other birds could be seen in the trees. There was no other sign of animal life, or human life either. Oh, yes there was.

"Will you look at that! I hate that!"

In a small cove on the northerly side of the island was a boat, or the remains of one, partly sunk in the water, it's tow line snagged on rocks, it's windshield smashed, the upholstery of its seats gashed with foam hanging out. The trim had bled rust onto yellowed fiberglass, and the steering wheel dangled into the water. Wrecked, abandoned, it lay half-submerged in the water, polluting river and island alike with its non-degradable components of plastic and fiberglass and petroleum fuels.

"I hate it when people do that! And it's that much worse just because it's a modern boat. I'll take a classic wood boat over one of those Clorox bottles any day!"

"Clorox bottles?"

"You know, all plastic and fiberglass. You can't destroy them if you try. That stuff never breaks down. Now a wooden boat is biodegradable. But, you know what I'd do?"

Brooke was looking amused. "No, what?"

"If one of my boats wore out and I absolutely couldn't fix it, I'd give it a Viking funeral. That's what I'd do."

"How on earth do you give a boat a Viking funeral?"

"I'd set it up on the water. I'd remove anything from it that wouldn't burn safe - like the leather upholstery, and the engine and so on. Then I'd pull it out into the water, and I'd set it on fire. Let it be its own funeral pyre."

"What if it floated back to shore or something. Couldn't someone get hurt?"

"Okay, anchor it then. Let it burn itself out. Point is, I wouldn't be polluting the river with stuff that won't ever break down. Plus, a wooden boat is more dignified, more classy than those stupid things. It deserves a dignified ending."

"Sure, Mackenzie, sure."

"Are you patronizing me?"

"Who, me?"

I'd seen enough for now. As irritated as I was by that abandoned boat. I was also excited by how *PsyKe* was running on the Hudson. This was going to be great. I swung the boat around to starboard and began the run back to the Boat Club. It was faster going back, with the current pushing us along. I let the speed creep up, still alert for more floating logs and debris. As I scanned the water, I came back to our other conversation.

"Brooke, I know you mean what you say, but we would need hard proof. Even *I* need some convincing Pop didn't push the hard stuff some of the time! The troopers think he killed somebody! They don't have any trouble at all believing he helped move hard drugs."

"Well - oh, I don't know how to prove it. It's not like you can call all the people who hung out with him and ask!"

I steadied the wheel as the current pushed the boat towards the mainland. I wasn't too sure about what lay beneath the surface yet. "You know, I could almost do that. Except it would be too embarrassing for all of us."

"What? How? I mean, I could give you a few names, but like you say...."

"No, actually, I have a sort of... list." I throttled back again. We were coming along behind the buildings on the north end of Main Street.

"What kind of list?"

"Um... a list of people Pop sold stuff to."

"He kept a *list*?"

"Yeah, crazy, huh?"

"You aren't kidding crazy." She drummed her hands on her thighs. "You know what though? We couldn't call them up, but, well, couldn't you check their medical records? See if there was any sign of hard drug use?"

There *were* those records in the back closet.

"I suppose I could check some of them," I said. "It will take some time."

"I could help. I don't mean looking at the records, but I could help you pull them, couldn't I?"

"If you're willing to do that...."

"I want to prove to you that your instincts are right. You get back to the office and I'll be right there." Her voice had a hard edge to it.

As quickly as I'd picked her up, I dropped her off and headed for the office. As I idled in to shore, I saw her backing down the ramp, Andrea trotting down to assist. Together we got the boat loaded onto the trailer and out of the water. We pulled around back and marched inside.

Brooke must have told Andrea what we were up to, because she dove right in and started bringing out file boxes from the closet.

"I'm helping," she said, grinning as she pulled boxes past me. While she and Brooke set up, I ran across the road to my bedroom and Pop's trunk. I pulled out his collections notebook with only a passing glance at the ax. If we could settle the issue about Pop moving hard drugs, maybe that would affect the murder case. I paused. Of course, if Pop *had* been moving drugs and someone found out about it, *there'd* be a motive for killing. But Brooke was so sure. We had to find out.

I settled myself cross-legged on the floor of the office alongside one of the six boxes Andrea and Brooke had brought out. I laid Pop's notebook in my lap, open to the first page of his sales records. Brooke looked over my shoulder.

"I can't believe he kept this! What was he thinking?"

"Knowing Pop, not much. No, actually, he had this thing about making lists of all his collections. He had notebooks on his coins and his stamps, even the Christmas trees we planted." I wasn't about to mention the gun collection.

"Well, okay, look," Brooke ran her finger down the list. "Here's one: Bill Van Dyke. He was staying with your father the same time I was. I think I even remember him getting the same lecture about hard drugs from your Pop as I did. Let's try him."

We pawed through the files, Andrea checking the boxes that remained in the closet, and Brooke double-checking our current file cabinet.

"Bill must have gone to Dr. Morrissey. I don't have anything on him."

"Me neither, " added Andrea.

"Let's try Mary Kulwicki."

"Okay. Any particular reason why?"

"Just try her. Her name's right here on the next page anyway. Hey, I didn't know the Murray boys bought from him!"

"Who do you suppose his first customers were? I think they discovered one of his stills and offered to help him with it. You know how they were."

"True. Found Kulwicki yet?" Brooke prodded.

"All right, all right. J - K - K - A - Kaslowski - K- E - Kelley, Kimbrough, Koger, Koontz - Here it is. Kulwicki. Mary. Okay, let's see." I looked at the others, then held my breath. As if that would change the outcome.

I scanned the record. Kesselman had never put any of this on film or computer, the way the hospitals would have. Still, Mary's file wasn't very thick. I thought at first that meant she'd left town when she graduated. Actually, it was that she'd died without graduating. I glanced at Brooke. Her expression told me she'd known. I read further.

Mary Kulwicki had died in October of her senior year. Cause of death had been.... I stared at Brooke. "She O.D.'d! That doesn't help at all!" I slapped the file closed, its pages sliding around in the folder.

"Look again, Mackie. Think about the dates."

I picked up the folder and read the final report more thoroughly. She'd died October 8, 1989, of an overdose of amphetamines compounded by LSD. I shuddered. Then Kesselman's final notation registered.

It has been rumored that this young person has been involved with drugs for approximately six months. I have seen this patient seven times in the past year. While her health has deteriorated since August, I saw no evidence of drug usage prior to then. From conversations with Mary during her visits, I think she had just begun to experiment with controlled substances. Physical findings at this time are consistent with this theory. It is very sad that such a beautiful young person should have made such a very bad choice. I wish I had said something that would have prevented it.

An unusual note, but in character for Kesselman. And it nailed down a time frame for Mary's drug habits, a time frame that excluded my father. When Mary died, Pop had already been dead for six months. If Kesselman was right, she didn't even try the hard drugs until four months after he died.

I put the file to one side. "Okay, that's one we can be sure of. Let's try another one."

There were more. When we finished, we had a stack of seventeen medical records of teens my father had assisted at one time or another and whom he had supplied with either marijuana or whiskey. While Mary's case was the most dramatic, it was clear from the records that none of these young people, whether they eventually got involved with hard drugs or not, had ever been supplied with them by my father.

I sat back, steadying the pile with my hand and thinking, while around me Brooke and Andrea replaced file boxes and picked up bits of stray litter that we'd strewn around. Andrea brought me an empty box.

"To put these in," she said, arranging the first of the files inside. I deposited the completed box on my desk.

"Thanks, Brooke, for making me do that."

"Well, I couldn't let you go on thinking he'd pushed the hard stuff. I know what he did to your life, but he about saved mine. Somehow I think he knew he'd screwed up with you, but he still loved you. He liked kids in general. I think taking care of us was his way of trying to make up for what he'd done to you. I couldn't stand hearing him get blamed for something I knew he didn't do." Her eyes were bright and steady.

"You're right. Despite what he did to my life, I can't stand him getting blamed for those murders. Because somehow I know he didn't do them, either."

"If New York State Troopers can be wrong about one thing, they can be wrong about another," Brooke said grimly.

"Don't let them hear you say that! But... you're right. They can be wrong, and they are. I just don't know how I'm going to prove it."

CHAPTER 13

I trudge along, yanking the rope whenever the sled catches on a hummock of grass protruding from the crusted snow.

Pop's several feet in front of me, periodically calling over his shoulder for me to catch up. He's not mean about it or anything, but his impatience is one more annoying characteristic of our relationship.

We're supposed to be finding a Christmas tree to cut down and bring back home. We've passed a number of perfectly good 'possibles' - and I'm fussy about Christmas trees! But we've kept on going anyway.

Sunlight glints off sparkles in the crust like diamonds. The sky is that never-ending blue that looks like you could fall right into it. Every tree in the field stands out, every branch fanning out its twigs, every individual needle having a place marked all its own. And everything is silent. Silent as a Little League park at midnight in the middle of a school week, except for our huffings and chuffings.

We've come to a thick grove of trees formed by several pines and three or four birches. The trees are so close together we actually have to push our way through. It's like entering a small stockade. The inside of the grove is completely hidden from view. For good reason - the grove is home to the oldest of Pop's stills.

This is my first sight of one of the working contraptions, though I've seen coils of copper hose lying around the barn often enough.

I watch as Pop checks the settings and pokes at flames that are not quite out. I watch as he pulls off some clear liquid into a cup, sniffs it, sips, then downs the whole thing, wiping his mouth on the back of his other, still- gloved hand. I watch, incredulous, as he pats the machine, sets down his cup, and leads us out of the grove, back down along the path we've come, ready now to decide on a tree, now that he's had his drink.

F riday was quiet. No one was sick, no one needed attention, and I didn't really care. I sat in my office and shuffled files and composed a letter to Dr. Tolbrecht about working with him at Albany Med.

Andrea bustled in and out, fetching files and forms and mail.

"Do you want me to set up permanent files on Kyle Anthony and the other ball players?"

"I don't know. They certainly didn't act like they were coming back, did they?"

"Well, it'll be their loss if they don't. Look, I'll make up files anyway. You never can tell."

"Okay, go ahead." I sighed. "I'm not so sure about whose loss it would be, though."

Andrea glanced at me as she scribbled names on labels. "You're not really worried about them, are you, Doc? We've had plenty of patients in here for our first couple weeks. You've got to remember, Kings Hill is a small town. Sometimes just everybody's healthy."

"I know all about Kings Hill being a small town. But I have to confess, I'm a little worried about this stuff that's been happening. You know - the letter, the newspaper ad, the trash." I stopped. It wasn't any fun to feel you weren't liked.

Andrea carefully placed color-coded stickers along the edge of a folder and added it to a growing stack. "I've been wanting to ask. I didn't want to intrude, but well, why do you suppose this is happening? Is it because of those - those skeletons they found?"

"I'm sure those aren't helping any, but no, I don't think that's the only reason."

She waited for me to continue, but I wasn't sure I wanted to tell her. One of the charms Andrea held for me was that she didn't know much about my past history in Kings Hill.

She came over and stood in front of me. "Look, Doc, I like you." She spoke softly, standing with her hands on her hips. "As far as I can see, there's no reason for me not to like you, but it looks like *someone* has a reason. I think it's only fair I understand what you're up against. Please explain it to me. It's not going to change how I feel about you." She grinned at me. "I'm a very loyal person, really."

It was impossible not to smile back. "Okay. Basically, the whole reason everybody in this town thinks my father had something to do with those skeletons is because it fits his reputation. They think Wylvern Russell was perfectly capable of doing something illegal and outrageous. Heck, he *did* things that were illegal and outrageous. Just not murder. But that didn't mean he might not. Pop's behavior made him very popular with one segment of the town's population, and made me very unpopular with another."

"What do you mean?" Andrea moved back to her stack and resumed her filing.

"It's kind of complicated. I was very quiet and shy, sort of brainy. You know how some kids will mistake that for being stuck-up."

She nodded. "Oh, yeah."

"Well, I wasn't stuck-up. Almost the opposite, in fact. Still a lot of the kids thought I *was*, stuck-up that is, and that I had no right to be, considering what my father was like."

"Which was?"

"Pop was sort of a renegade. A law unto himself. He thought it was all right to grow marijuana in our fields and dry it and smoke it and sell it to local teenagers. He had a couple of stills back in the woods, too."

"I sort of knew that from what you and Ms. Kerns were saying yesterday, but was your father really a moonshiner?" Andrea's eyes went round.

" 'Fraid so. After Mom and I left, he always had kids coming to the house to buy pot or whiskey - what he didn't drink himself that is. Funny thing was, he always had a soft spot for kids in trouble. He helped out a bunch of them, like Ms. Kerns said. Let them stay with him at the farm, if they needed to. Fed them. Gave them money.

"And there was the drinking. He'd been drinking so long, he probably thought he always had, but he couldn't handle it. When he still could hold a job, he thought anyone in authority had it in for him. I can't tell you how many times I had to call in sick for him when I was a kid. He worked nights, you see, and I had to help get him off to work. If he'd spent the day drinking then he wouldn't go, but someone had to call in. Mom would still be at work, so he'd make me do it. Then, if I was lucky, he'd just pass out. If not, he'd turn into one of those troublesome drunks. He'd take off in the truck to go drinking again. Or he'd pull out one of his guns and start waving it around. He'd threaten to 'shoot the next s.o.b. who walked in the door'."

Andrea stared at me. "Doc! You just said - "

I waved away her concern. "Yeah, I know. But that was the drink talking. I mean, Pop could shoot. Heck, he taught me to shoot a rifle. I know there is no predicting what a person who's drunk will do. My point was, though, is that's what he was like. He was the reason I thought I never wanted to come back to Kings Hill. He's the reason a lot of people have no use for me."

"So why did you come back?"

"Every time I thought about the kind of place I wanted to live in, it was always like a clone of a Kings Hill. Eventually I started thinking about coming back and fixing all the things my father had touched." I stood up. "Come out front a minute."

We made our way through the empty waiting room and out the front door to the parking lot. I turned Andrea to face north, up Main Street.

"See that street? There's a house around the bend that my father crashed into with one of his trucks. Drunker'n a skunk, as he'd say. No one badly hurt, but the lady who lived there finally moved out, she was so afraid it would happen again. There're at least three bars on Main Street that Pop was intimately familiar with. Thanks to him and his moonshine, a lot of teens were, too. And then there's those the State Police think he introduced to hard drugs, too," I drew a breath. "Though thanks to you and Brooklynne yesterday, I stand a chance of showing that it didn't happen that way."

Andrea shrugged off my gratitude.

"Anyway, I wanted to come back to make things better, different. When Brooklynne started trying to convince me to come back, I thought about how I could make people look at the Russell name differently. But it doesn't look like people want me here. Maybe Pop's memory is too strong."

"Doctor Wilder, there are plenty of people who want you here!"

"I know, but - whatever. Let's put those files in here." I pulled out a file drawer. "We'll make this drawer for patients who've been in once. If they come in again within six months, or if they look like they'll come back when they need us, we'll move them into the other drawer."

"Doc, I like to set up my own system, you know that. But that's a good idea. I'll do it. I'll put the old files on computer, too. When I have time. Now, where did Jason Fields take you?"

"He wanted to tell me about his work. He's building a sort of computer/think tank complex further up the River Road. We lunched, and then he took me to Computer Outfits. Ever hear of it? He showed me around some, then he let me muddle along on my own. He wants to connect with the schools and provide resources for projects with them."

"Kind of a strange date, Doc."

"It wasn't exactly a date. Speaking of Jason and organizing, Andrea, we'll need to set up files here for his employees. He's asked me to be company doctor. I'll have an office at the complex, but I think I'm going to want some kind of files on it here, too."

"No problem, I'll set you up. See what I mean? Jason Fields wants you here."

"Okay, okay." I laughed. "He's one!"

The phone rang.

"Here's someone else, I'll bet. Doctor's office. Yes, you can speak with Dr. Wilder. May I say who's calling?" Suddenly Andrea's smile twisted into a grimace. She handed me the phone gingerly. "It's Deb Voag, Doctor Wilder."

Really. "Hello, Ms. Voag. What can I do for you?"

"Doctor Wilder, I understand my husband - my ex-husband - brought our daughter Rachel by to see you on Monday. Is that correct?"

Was she going to give me flak about this, too?

"Yes, they came by the office. Your daughter is lovely, Ms. Voag."

"She - what? Oh, thank you. Now, Bryan didn't give me any details. How is Rachel's health? I'm her mother, don't you think I should know?"

"Certainly, you ought to know your daughter's health status, Ms. Voag." I waited, but apparently irony was lost on our fashion queen. "Rachel seemed fine. It was just a social call. Bryan wanted me to meet her."

"There's nothing wrong with her? You wouldn't keep something from me?"

Where was she headed with this? "No, I wouldn't keep any information about Rachel's health from you, Ms. Voag. Now, if you'll excuse me - "

"Dr. Wilder. You're a woman. You understand a child's need to be with her mother. Don't you think a stay in New York with me would benefit Rachel? Maybe we could work in a little side trip to my shoot in Africa."

"Ms. Voag, I really can't - "

"All I need you to do is to write a prescription for Rachel to miss a few weeks of school in order to come see me. You can do that for me."

"No, I can't."

"I'll just stop by and pick up the - What do you mean, 'no, you can't?' "

"No, I can't. What part of that don't you understand?"

"I don't understand why you can't."

"It wouldn't be ethical. There is no medical need, and in view of stringent school attendance policies, I would have to recommend against it. I'm sorry." *No, I wasn't.*

"No, you're not. You're not one bit sorry. Bryan talked to you, didn't he? I should've known he'd get his girlfriend to side with him!"

Girlfriend?! I hadn't spoken to Bryan since I saw him at Jason's office, and that hadn't exactly been friendly. "Ms. Voag, I don't know what you are talking about. I can not recommend Rachel go on this trip with you, and that is that. Good-bye."

"No, that isn't that, b - "

I hung up. Andrea's round eyes were on me once again. "That wasn't one of my fans, Andrea. Come on, let's get back to this."

We worked in silence for a bit. I stared at the computer screen, trying to focus on the darned letter to Dr. Tolbrecht.

Instead I suddenly thought of what Doug Pulaskey had told me the other day. Had Bryan wanted to date me in high school? Had my father's threats really kept him and the others away? It might explain a couple of odd things. Getting stood up. A relationship fizzling out senior year before it had even begun. It could be comforting to think it wasn't me after all. Although it was frustrating to think of all the emotional turmoil and self-doubt an insecure teenager had gone through because of a father's cockeyed sense of protection!

If that was true, did it have anything to do with the vibes I was picking up from Bryan? He said he wanted to see me, but he hadn't called me yet. Wednesday he'd seemed almost jealous around Jason, but he didn't have anything to be jealous over. I liked Bryan. A lot. I was grateful to him for his help and friendship, but I needed to keep some distance. I didn't want to discuss what I'd come to think of as Pop's case with him. Not even the part about pushing or not pushing drugs. I didn't trust the cop ethic that would send him to the state authorities with what I had found. And I didn't much trust myself not to tell all if I saw him.

I sighed.

"Hungry, Doc?"

"Hmm?"

"It's lunchtime. I brought salad. It's in the back."

"Okay. Know what though? I need to run an errand. I'll pick up something while I'm out. Want anything?"

"No. I want to get the filing done as soon as I eat. I've got a hair appointment."

"I like your hair that way," I protested. This pulled-back style at least was sleek and contained, with only a few wisps straying about her face.

She shook her head. "It's too plain. I want something more exciting, more exotic."

"As long as it doesn't get in the way," I warned.

I'd decided I couldn't stand one more time of saying how I needed to contact the Boat Club. I was going down there to talk with Gary Henrey.

I'd found out he kept an office right at the clubhouse, between Pete's and the docks. I averted my eyes as I walked past Pete's. Too many memories.

The inside door to Gary's office stood open behind the screen, catching a breeze off the river. I rapped on the doorjamb and walked in.

"Gary?"

A sandy-haired man in dockers and a navy polo shirt stood up from his desk. He'd gotten a little broader, but no taller, topping me by only five inches.

"Mackenzie! How are you? Bob Cooper called me about you. How's life at the other end of the street?" He shook my hand and led me to a captain's chair, one of a pair standing along the short wall by his desk. A tidy stack of *Yachting* magazines under a narrow shelf was the only messy spot in the room. Potted plants strategically filled corners, and two upright wooden file cabinets stood to the right of the door. It was all - okay, shipshape.

"It's fine, Gary. The practice is setting up all right. It's good to see you. And I hear you're a Justice of the Peace?"

He waved it off. "It's not so much. I take my responsibilities seriously, but Kings Hill isn't that big, and my work is pretty tame. This is what I really love. " He motioned toward the river.

"The boats?" I asked.

"The boats. And their owners. You'd be surprised how complicated things can get. Yachtsmen have strong personalities. Sometimes I don't know who's harder to deal with, teens in my court or boaters in this office. Anyway, Bob told me you were asking about dock space for - what - a couple classic boats?"

I nodded eagerly.

"Define classic for me." He leaned back in the chair. The light in his blue eyes had been replaced with a graver, grayer look.

"Classic, with a capital C. Antique. Vintage. My Chris Craft is a 1941 barrel back with an M engine. I've got another runabout, a Hackercraft from 1936, but it won't be needing space yet - unless you've got a workyard. The Chris Craft is fully restored and needs to get in the water right away. I'm getting the engine rebuilt for the Hackercraft. It's down on Long Island right now. When it's done, I'll just need to put one more coat of Spar on her and find the right cleats to mount - "

Gary was shaking his head at me. "That's what I thought."

"What?"

"How big are these boats?"

"The Chris Craft is nineteen feet, and the Hackercraft about seventeen."

"They're motorboats, right?"

"Runabouts." I didn't like the condescension I was hearing in his voice.

He fiddled with a small airhorn that sat on the shelf over the magazines. Shiny brochures advertising the boat club lay beside it.

"The Boat Club is really for owners of large boats, modern boats. Yachts really. Even though no one supports using the word Yacht in our name, it's really what we're about. I don't think we have anything smaller than thirty feet or older than 1981. George Ferris thinks that's old!" He chuckled.

Gary Henrey chuckled? At me? My boats? As if boats that were newer and bigger were by mere existence better!

I tried to smile. "Well, what about just renting me a slip? It's not like I can't afford one. I can. I could, in fact, afford any one of those yachts out there, but that's not what I happen to have!"

"Take it easy, Mackenzie. I don't have a problem with vintage boats. I just don't share your interest. Some of members, however, are very particular over who uses our facilities."

"Particular?" I raised my eyebrows at him.

"Don't take offense. It's just how it is. You don't want to put your boats at risk, do you?"

"Risk of what?" Visions of the trash under my portico flashed through my head.

"Well, I don't know where you've docked before, but putting antique wooden craft next to a hulking yacht - no matter how well you tie up - in a storm or swell, there's bound to be some banging and bumping around. You wouldn't want your new varnish to get scraped up, or worse."

"Don't you have protected slips?"

He shook his head. "Not for your size boat. And, before you ask, the members won't be interested in adapting any, either. Nothing personal - except for the preference for modern boats. Sorry, Mackenzie."

I exhaled, deflated. "You're sure?"

"I'm sure. I can ask Fred or Dave McDonald if you want. They're on the membership committee. Frankly, though, they're the toughest on guidelines, too."

"Okay, okay." I gave in. I'd find my own solution, but this conversation had made me even crosser than I'd been earlier. "Do you have any suggestions on what to do with my boats?"

He drew breath, and for a second I wasn't sure what he'd say. Then he smiled and looked more like the kid who'd stood in line next to me in fire drills. "Well, if you can afford it, why not build your own dock? Or even - and don't say I told you - set up a Classic Boat Club. Personally I think it would be good for Kings Hill. There's a whole different following for boats like yours, and Kings Hill could use another draw. There's a couple people in town who like old boats. Art Swandeck is one."

"Jean's friend? Jean Hesford, my housekeeper."

"That's him. Maude Davenport is another one."

"I remember her. I'll have to track her down, I guess. Okay, Gary. If you're sure...."

"I'm sure, Mackenzie. Thanks for stopping in, though. Listen, can I buy you lunch? We can go over to Pete's."

"I - well, okay. I need to eat somewhere."

Gary closed up behind us, and we headed over to Pete's.

I walked into Pete's ahead of Gary, closing my eyes momentarily before I crossed the threshold. I was always like this whenever I entered a bar. Not that I never drank. I did, but drinking in my own environment was not the same as entering one of Pop's old haunts. I hadn't visited a place like Pete's since college, and never one where Pop had gone.

"Pete makes a terrific Reuben sandwich," Gary told me, leading us across red and brown flecked carpet to a booth. He waved to a man behind the bar as he sat down. The man grabbed a menu card and hustled over.

"What can I get you? Hey Gary. Want yer usual?"

"Sure, Pete. Mackenzie?"

"I'll just have a Coke® and one of those Reubens - to go. Sorry, I really do have to get back."

"Afternoon patients?"

"Yes - no - " I thought of how slow it had been. "You know? I don't have to go back. Pete? I'll have that Reuben here."

"Still want the Coke®?"

"Yup."

"Can't sell you on a Shirley Temple for old times' sakes?"

"What?"

Behind Pete stood a bear of a man wearing a tight red sweatshirt and baggy faded jeans and grey curly hair circling a bald pate.

"Mackenzie Russell. Come in here every day for two summers in a row with Wylvern Russell, and he allus' ordered a Shirley Temple for his little 'halfpint'. How are you, Mackenzie? How's them bodies they found out there on yer old farm?"

"Tommy, isn't it? Tommy - ?"

"Tommy Maynard. Didn't think you'd remember, you was so little when you used ta come in with yer Pop!"

"I remember all right!" I hesitated. This was one of the men who'd continued to pour Pop drinks, then would throw him out on the street. Two strikes against him. But, he could be a patient someday, too. "How are you, Tommy?"

"Can't complain, much. Just figgered I'd say hello, seein' as how you were here." He peered at Gary. "That Justice Henrey? Got him helpin' ya out with them bodies? Never hurts ta have influential friends." He loomed over us.

Gary cleared his throat, eyeing me across the table.

Maynard edged away. "Don't worry. I ain't sayin ' nothin'."

"There's nothing to say! What makes you think I'd need Gary's help?"

Maynard snorted. "You'll be needin' some kind of help. Yer Pop left you a real problem out there!"

"My Pop didn't have anything to do with the skeletons out there, Mr. Maynard!" I stood up.

"Sure, sure. Whatever ya say." He turned away.

"Maynard!" My tone pulled him around to face me. "Mr. Maynard, just because you know so much about my father's failings - " I stumbled over the next words -   "and you should because you certainly took advantage of them enough - that doesn't mean you know it all!"

"Sounds a little high 'n' mighty for the daughter of Wylvern Russell. Sure you ain't hidin' somethin', girl?"

"You son - "

Gary jumped up and grabbed my forearm as I moved in Maynard's direction.

"Hold on to her, yer Honor. Better check her purse and see if she's got a gun in there!"

"Get out, Maynard. Mackenzie, sit down. Sit! Maynard, get out of here before I call Jensen."

"Hey! It's her you need to be worryin' about. Her and that drunkard dad of hers!"

"Get out of here now, Maynard," Gary warned again.

"Come on, Tommy. Let's go." Pete came up behind him and clapped one hand on his shoulder and swung him around with the other. "I'll buy you a beer before you go."

"Mackenzie."

"I'm okay. Let me sit down."

"You always treat senior citizens like that?"

I flushed. "No. Of course not. I guess I'm a little sensitive on the subject."

"Of your father, you mean? Or the bodies?"

"Both, I suppose. You know, Gary, I like you, but this has been one lousy lunch. No boat club, no lunch, and Maynard all over the place."

"Well here's lunch anyway," he observed as Pete returned with a hefty-looking bag.

"I put a dessert in there. On the house. Sorry 'bout Tommy." He handed me the bag, but he stood there, seemingly reluctant to leave.

"Yes?" I said, wary of what he might be thinking.

He flushed. "Oh, nothing. It's just -   I couldn't help but overhear. And, I wanted to ask - Is it true there was still some flesh on those bodies they found? Even after all these years?"

"Come on, Mackenzie." Gary actually pulled me out of the chair and dragged me out the door before I could stop sputtering and formulate a reply.

CHAPTER 14

I blush as I stumble between the seats to go up onstage. I've won another math award!

The applause isn't exactly deafening. I hold my head high, though. My friends are there. I even hear a couple "Go, Mackenzie!"s

It's okay. I know I'm not the most popular of girls. I relish this particular award.

I've always liked puzzles. That's what math is, one big puzzle. Finding the answer always seems to me like solving a mystery, and the feeling I get makes me feel powerful. I can do this. I can figure things out!

Mom isn't here today. She has to work so she doesn't usually get to see school assemblies. That's okay. I know she's proud of me. Knowing that makes up for her not being here.

Knowing that makes up for a lot of things.

1 :00 p.m.
       I walked into the back room of my office. Andrea had left, just as she'd said. A note on my desk read "Getting hair done. Finished files. Ordering more technology."

More technology? What now?

"Guess I'll find out tomorrow," I said to myself, tossing the sack with the Reuben in it on the table. The whole episode at Pete's had been frustrating. Bad enough the Boat Club had these notions about what constituted a proper boat, but to have to face Tommy publicly about Pop had been more than I could take. Or wanted to.

One more strike against this move to Kings Hill. Still, I hated the idea of being run off.

I sat down and tried to enjoy the sandwich. At least Pete was a good cook. Too much mustard, though.

1:07 p.m.

Matheson was supposed to interview Lamberson this morning. I hoped he would make Lamberson sweat bullets. I hoped he'd put he fear of the Almighty in him. I hope he'd - well, I couldn't think of any more clichés, but I hoped he'd given him a hard time. Lamberson had been the other s.o.b. in my life, and I didn't use a term like that lightly. The man was cruel. And if it turned out he had some connection with the bodies on my farm - well, I couldn't think of anyone I'd rather see in trouble.

It had started, like so many of my father's adventures, in a bar. Lamberson owned a sand and gravel operation, supplying cement companies and other customers with raw materials. He and Pop made a deal, and for a while he'd purchased gravel from my father, developing an unsightly gravel pit in the field across from the house. It was actually a monolith of black and gray gravel and sand encircled by a road he'd dug out across field and creek. At the top you could see where the soil had been ripped away from the roots of trees, right up to the fields of

Christmas trees. Scotch pines threatened to topple over the edge. Apparently Lamberson had been giving the property a real good look whenever he was out there. One day, in Mimi's Tavern, where Pop had a plastic-covered stool permanently imprinted with the shape of his backside, Lamberson made a casual-sounding offer, an offer to buy the house, barn, and all the land. He was careful to make the offer late in the afternoon, when Pop had entered that twilight time of mind when a drinker is the only one convinced he is in full possession of his faculties. To Pop, the offer sounded great. More drinking money. No more hassle over illegal hooch and garden plots of funny-looking weeds.

To my mother and me, it sounded less than terrific. Not that we were against selling. We felt we could get a better deal if we put the farm on the open market. Both of us were suspicious of how Lamberson conducted business. Mom in particular was wary. I was graduating high school, and as a present, Pop had given me ten acres of my choosing. Lamberson's deal was contingent on purchasing all of the land, my ten acres included. I wasn't sure how I felt about it, but college was only a summer away, and money was scarce.

Mom had watched during the last few years as Lamberson hauled truck after truck of gravel out of there. He'd spent an awful lot of time with my father and at the gravel bank itself, more than she'd thought the business warranted. Now we knew - he'd been studying the land. Mom sat in on business conferences. Although divorced, my parents held our farm jointly and shared in all the legal profits. She listened as Lamberson made big talk about his contacts and business opportunities, municipal contracts, grades of gravel, truck capacity, manpower and hauling costs. Her sharpened business sense and her intuition warned her about men who spoke like him. She'd never been able to catch him in anything specific, but she didn't trust him, and she wanted badly to find another buyer.

Vince Lamberson was not pleased. He was a big man with a big beer belly that he swaggered behind and used to intimidate people. He thought he could persuade my mother to his way of thinking. When his brand of hearty charm failed, he demanded to know what right my mother had to stand in the way of his business deals. When bluster and forthright pressure failed, he turned to deviousness and trickery. If it hadn't been for Pop's buddy, Jake Terry, we might never have known what Lamberson was up to.

Jake was a devoted sidekick to my father in all his cockamamie schemes, legal and otherwise. He was also a self-proclaimed admirer of my mother's. When we left Pop, she'd told me, "I'm glad Jake's around. Your father is going to need him."

It was Jake Terry who warned us that Lamberson was trying to submit sale papers with our signatures forged on them. It was Jake who confirmed for us that Vince was getting Pop drunk then putting him up to making late night phone calls to put pressure on us. It was Jake who made a special stop by our house -   not so easy as it sounded, the man had no car or even a bicycle, and his feet pained him from so many years spent working on them -   to warn us that Vince had been boasting he had a fool-proof way to force the sale through.

He told Mom, "Don't worry, missus. I've put the bug in Willie's ear. He's watchin' hisself more careful now that I've told him some of Lamberson's stunts. I'll keep ol' Willie out of trouble."

"Thank you, Jake. I know you're trying the best you can. It's not an easy job. Wylvern's no match for someone like Lamberson, especially when he's been drinking." Mom could always sound so gracious.

"Well, you know how I feel about you and Willie, missus. Anything to help."

"Thanks, Jake."

Somehow, despite Jake's efforts, Lamberson managed to keep anyone else from making offers on the farm. And whether it was through pressure brought to bear or some kind of trickery, he managed to build a time clause into his offer that, since it had my father's consent as majority holder, forced us to sell to him. Closing was a bitter day for my mother and me. One final disappointment on top of all the others in my father's repertoire. My teeth clenched at the memory.

Tammy Wynette wailing in the background - Pop's old record of D - I - V - O - R - C - E punctuating today's event. I shifted my feet impatiently. His selection was no accident.

My father, shirtless, at the end of the table. My mother sat across the table from me, her back rigid. Lamberson paced the room.

Mom's face was stony. It never ceased to amaze me how blank she could make it. If she felt like I did, there was a raging turmoil beneath those smooth facial planes. My hands were cold, and my knees felt weak.

We'd all read the contract at least twice. Finally, Lamberson shoved a pen into Pop's hand. He circled his hand over the paper, unsure of where to land it, unsure, really, of how to sign at all. He set the pen down and switched his hand to a shot glass. Lamberson filled it.

I turned my head away to stare out the window. My neck felt like it turned on two iron rods. A breeze ruffled the leaves on the purple lilac beyond the porch. The yard seemed deserted. I wondered where Jake was. The last two dogs lay quiet on the porch, lost without their garrulous human friend. That brought tears to my eyes. When Mom and I left, I hadn't been able to take their mother with me. I didn't know where they'd go now.

My father signed away my heritage. And I went to college. I don't know what he did with the dogs.

Months later, my father died of acute alcoholism. Drunk himself into a stupor one night and never woke up. The stench when his landlady found him was horrible. She never forgave him. As Pop's sole heir, Lamberson's monthly payments were transferred to me. I'd too much sense to make a gesture of nobility and refuse the money, but each month, as I deposited the check, bile rose in my throat when I considered its source.

When the farm was paid off in ten years, I felt nothing but relief. By that time my mom had died, and Lamberson was paying the whole amount to me. If I hadn't had Brian helping me put that money to good and enjoyable use, I might have been a lot more unhappy.

Thinking about my years with Brian was infinitely more pleasant than thinking about my single past, but my brain didn't seem to have time for him now. Instead, I wondered what had happened to Jake Terry. It seemed to me he had stopped coming round after the sale of the farm went through. Maybe his failure to stop the sale had bothered him. Or maybe even he had become disgusted with my father's behavior, loyal though he was. He'd been such a funny man. No family. No real home as far as I could tell. Pop often let him crash in our barn, and later I knew he'd stayed at the house with Pop.

I always pictured him in hunting clothes, plaid jacket, baggy brown pants, fluorescent vest, and mismatched plaid hunting cap. He smelled faintly, as if his clothes needed washing. His black hair hung in his eyes, covering the spot where, when I was a child, he'd told me surgeons in World War II had put in a metal skull plate. It was, he said, to cover the tremendous head wound he'd received.

I leaned back in the kitchen-style chair, thinking how many times he'd told me that story, putting his hand to his head and making the scalp shift so that it looked like he was slipping a hairpiece back and forth. It was a funny thing to tell a child. It had fascinated me in a macabre sort of way. I kept waiting for a strong wind to blow the hair off so I could get a look at that metal plate. I smiled to myself as I tried to picture where the surgeons would have placed it.

It's astonishing the faith in childhood stories that we carry into adulthood. I was thirty-seven years old. I had never before questioned what Jake Terry told me. Yet now, the absurdity of it was totally clear. There was no metal plate, never had been. It had been a tall tale told to a pal's little kid to keep her in awe-filled admiration. Jake Terry had never had a life-threatening head wound. Probably he had never served in World War II, although I could be wrong about that. He'd just wanted to spellbind me, and I had to laugh at how thoroughly he'd done that - for nearly thirty years. I must have been about eight the first time he told me. I'd believed it ever since. Why, the closest thing he'd probably ever had to a head wound was that time he got in the way of my father's bullet (that was how Pop put it) when they were hunting, and it grazed the right side of his skull. They'd been in the brush by the creek, and Jake had forgotten his cap. Pop heard movement and fired almost immediately. Jake came out holding a big kerchief to his head, moaning about how Pop was losing his touch and if he was going to shoot at his best friend, Jake wasn't goin' huntin' with him anymore. Pop rushed Jake to Dr. Kesselman and got him sewn up, and the two of them spent the rest of the afternoon drinking away the crimp the mishap had put in their day.

I dropped my sandwich and ducked into my office to stare at a skull model I kept there on a shelf. How long does it take to outgrow a case of stupidity? I pulled my desk phone towards me and dialed Betty McBride's number, wondering if she'd be willing to give in to my unprofessional request. I had no chance to find out then, for there was no answer in her office, not even a receptionist or voicemail.

I grunted and redialed, this time Matheson's number. No doubt he'd like my request even less.

"Matheson? This is Mackenzie Wilder. I wanted to check with you on something. Is there a chance - since I've been allowed access to the autopsy reports - is there a chance I could actually see the remains involved in this case?"

"You want to see the bodies? Dr. Wilder, that's unusual. Even for you."

"I'm aware of that, but I thought perhaps...."

"I have no objection, but Dr. McBride will have to approve it, and she'll have to supervise. Not that you'll have any trouble getting your own way. By the way, I should probably tell you, I had Vince Lamberson in today. He's leaving now. He couldn't shed any more light on this than you could."

"I hope you were tough on him."

"Well, he wasn't too anxious to cooperate, so I might have been a bit short with him." I could hear the Trooper's quiet smile in his voice.

"Good. Couldn't happen to a nicer guy."

"Just so you know, we're probably going to shelve this case."

I made some kind of noise into the phone.

"I'm sorry. I realize it leaves a shadow on your father, but in my opinion he's our most likely suspect. I know you don't agree, but it's a moot point, really. We can't prove anything. Does this change your mind about asking Dr. McBride's permission to examine the bodies?"

"Well... no. I don't think my father did it, but even if he did, I'm like you, I like these things cleared up. I think it might help if I see the bodies for myself. Dr. McBride was thorough, but maybe I'll spot something." *Or, more accurately, recognize something.*

"You've got my go-ahead. I'll jot a note to her - wait a minute, hold on. Someone here wants to talk to you."

There was the fuzzy sound of a receiver exchanging hands.

"Yeah, Mackie? It's Bryan."

"Bryan? What are you doing there?"

"Stopped in to see how Matheson made out with Vince Lamberson - "

I could hear a gruff voice asking a question, then Matheson answering. It sounded like 'You can go now'. There was a disgusted mumble in reply.

Bryan's voice came back. "Sorry, that was Lamberson. He's ticked off, especially since I sat in on this interview."

"You did? I thought you and Matheson didn't get along."

"Aah, it's getting better. He's got a brother-in-law who's transferred to my division. He's decided I'm not such a bad guy after all, for a city cop. Listen, go out to dinner with me tonight. I'd like to take you to the Black Carriage again. A little more private this time. You can tell me about this exam you want to do - I overheard - and I'll tell you what Lamberson said. And, well, we need to talk. So, what do you say? - um, wait a minute. Excuse me, Mackenzie." He muffled the phone. Against his chest? The brief image gave me an unsettled feeling.

"Sorry. Lamberson forgot something. Anyway, will you go?"

"I - I - hang on, Bryan. I'm not sure. I might have something on my calendar," I lied.

"We need to talk soon. I need to see you."

What is there about this man's voice that weakens my knees and my resolve?

"All right. Tonight. At the Black Carriage."

"I'll pick you up around five, all right?"

"Okay."

"Good."

I dangled the phone from my hand before I hung up. *Was* this good?

CHAPTER 15

Watching guys play baseball. Bryan plays ball. Throws like a pro; pitches for Babe Ruth League and Kings Hill High.

For one whole summer I sit on the bleachers, staring at that five-foot-eight frame throw ball after ball, strike after strike.

Watch as sun glints off cornsilk hair that strays out from the jammed-on cap. Watch muscle lengthen and strength increase and grace improve and flow along outstretched arm and leg. Watch as baseball turns my gangly friend into a man.

E ventually I hung up. Okay. Bryan asked me to dinner.

That's nice.

He wants to talk about the case.

Great.

I'd like to see him.

Good.

He wants to "talk".

Hmmm.

About the ex-Mrs. Jamison perhaps? About "old times"? What old times? The ones he remembers or the ones I remember?

Maybe he wants to discuss this sort of buzzy feeling you get whenever he's around. Maybe he feels it, too.

You think? But, it doesn't matter. I'm still not ready to talk with him. Especially about Pop's case. Not until I check out those skeletons. Because if I'm right....

That's where my brain broke down. I didn't dare go out with Bryan tonight. Too much of our talk would center on my father and those stupid bones! I didn't want to even think of the consequences if I spoke too soon.

I have to get out of it. How to do that without hurting Bryan's feelings? He seemed awfully prickly about our relationship, whatever it was.

Furious with myself I hacked out a letter to Dr. Tolbrecht and then finished my weekly addenda - a sort of report I make myself keep. Really more of a journal than the kind of documentation found in medical charts. It was a way I'd devised to keep a focus on my patients as people. I hated doctors who recalled only cases and symptoms instead of people. Some of the entries this week were just as depressing as the dilemma I faced right now.

I finished the last entry, shut down my computer, and sat staring into space, an activity that was becoming a habit with me. I still couldn't think of a good way to cancel. Besides, I really wanted to go. Contempt for my own indecision made me reach for the telephone. Surely I was grown up enough to deal with this!

The phone rang beneath my hand. Jason's voice snap-crackle-and-popped at me from the receiver.

"Hello, how's my favorite country doctor?"

"Fine, Jason." *Even I don't think I sound it.*

"I have a proposition for you. How would you like to come over to my place this afternoon? Not my office, the River Road property."

"Jason, your 'place' is a tract of land covered with dirt and construction equipment!"

"Sure, but Mackenzie, you have to come. I'm trying to pick the site for my building. I need your help."

"How am I supposed to help?"

"You're a doctor. Isn't helping what you do? Seriously, please come. I want the company. I value your opinion." He switched to wheedling. "Please say you'll come. You promised me you'd come look someday. This is my someday."

"Well, I - "

"What if I promise you dinner afterward?"

"Jason, I - " Wait. This could be the answer. Not exactly a prior commitment, but at least it was an excuse. "All right, Jason. What time?"

"Twenty minutes. I'll be right over."

"Wait, let me change first - "

"What are you wearing?"

"Linen slacks and short-sleeves. Running shoes."

"Perfect. I'll be right there." He hung up.

I shook my head at his madness. Maybe it was just what I needed. I looked at my watch. If I called right away, I could still catch Bryan at the station.

"... so I really should go. It's a promise I made him. Do you mind too much?" I had rushed through my explanation without pause, hoping to sound apologetic, pressured, and disappointed all at once. Well, I *was!*

"I can't say I don't mind, Mackenzie, but I understand. I guess. Fields again, huh?"

"Bryan, we'll do it another time, I promise. Okay?"

"Soon. I need to see you soon." He hung up.

I closed the outer door to the office just as Jason circled the parking lot in his red Land Rover. In ten minutes (he slowed down through Main Street) we were at the site.

Already dirt and rock were piling up on the river side of the road. Drainage equipment was being set up and a levee built. This was precautionary, Jason said, against the high flow of the river at this juncture. In all likelihood, this side would be a public park, with river access. Some of the space would be used for parking.

Hmm, river access. That's something to note.

Across the road was the easterly wall of the valley. Hills of pine and maple and elm, skirted with brush, dotted with white birch, and broken by a couple of clearings. Muddy ruts climbed upwards, a daunting challenge to all but the Land Rover. Jason needed to choose between these two clearings, and he wanted to do it tonight.

"I've let this drag on too long. I've finished the design and gotten the specs drawn up. All the contractors are set to go. It's just that I can't make up my mind. I'm tempted to use a dartboard to make the decision."

He pulled a frame out of the back of the Land Rover, and for a moment I thought he'd actually brought a dartboard with him. It was a folding table. While he laid his drawings out, I wandered about, checking the view from this site. There was a nice grove of healthy birch to the left of where the entrance would have to be. Sumac crowned the hill, leaning off toward the road and river. They screened the road from view, but didn't block the river. The Hudson looked like a large plate of glass stretching outward to its far banks. Much as the Native Americans might have seen it when no boats but their own birch bark canoes and dugouts toiled through.

"Mackenzie, come here."

I joined Jason at the table. He leaned on the blueprints, long wide-boned arms supporting a torso that seemed to loom over the plans.

"Here," he pointed to the paper then gestured behind us, "is the main entrance, approached by a brick walk from the parking lot. It's recessed to offer protection in bad weather. Glass-paned walls, revolving doors, a central lobby with sign-in security desk and ample seating. If we're inviting students, we need to have a place for them to wait without being in anyone's way. Directly behind the security desk, more glass walls enclosing a sunken room and courtyard. Benches, a garden, fountains. Sort of indoor/outdoor. The courtyard and the interior room will be where we'll begin tours or classes, as well as conduct informal meetings and provide alternative surroundings for brainstorming. Programmers do a lot of that." He flashed me a grin. "I'm thinking of calling it 'The Bit' - you know, something like 'The Pit', but more computer-like."

I groaned. "What's in these two wings?"

"Ahhh. Right Wing and Left Wing. Right Wing for works in progress, focusing on existing hardware and traditional software. The Left Wing will probably take up less space than the Right. It's for my more avant-garde creative people. They're the ones doing most of the brainstorming, coming up with innovative approaches. Their work will generate new projects, which will probably move to the Right as their status changes."

I stared at him. "I don't believe you, Jason!"

"What?"

"Right Wing for conservative approach and Left for radical?" I started to laugh.

He joined in. "I can't help myself. I've always enjoyed puns. It's why I write jingles and country songs. Any country song worth its grits depends on wordplay. And sometimes I just like to be silly."

Famous Jason Fields, so irrepressibly corny he can't keep it out of his work! It struck me as far funnier than it probably was. The sudden opportunity to relax, to not worry about what someone - anyone - was thinking about me went to my head.

Jason's bright eyes ran over my beige pants, my creased running shoes that misled everyone into thinking I was a health nut, my pale blue shirt chosen because it made my eyes look bluer by comparison. He laughed that fantastic laugh of his, like a shout spun out to reverberate against the treetops.

"Here." He handed me a handkerchief for my flooding eyes.

"I've never met anyone like you, Jason. You're unique!"

"Of course I am!" He beamed at me. "So's my project. This - you're still laughing."

"Sorry. I'll stop. Go on." I pressed my eyes and covered my mouth with the handkerchief.

He continued, pointing again at the plans. "This building is the most important. However, I'm building three others, making a sort of quadrangle behind the main building. At either end will be a one-story square building, nothing fancy. One is a dining facility. I prefer one separate from the work areas. People fuss at me because they have to walk so far, but I'm trying to create a separation opportunity for their psyche. Even if they decide to work on their project while they lunch, having the break in time and location, that walk from office to dining hall, allows them to separate themselves from the work environment. Even a short break of five minutes can be a refresher for someone doing intense cerebral work - and a refreshed thinker is a better thinker. The other building will be a fully equipped gym, with an indoor/outdoor pool. Again, I'm trying to provide opportunities for my employees to keep physically fit. It makes sense in terms of health insurance, in terms of productivity, in terms of psychology, and employee longevity, and in terms of...."

"Loyalty? Ethics?"

"The rightness of things."

I touched his arm. "I'm impressed, Jason. You're thorough, and true to your word. What's the other building you've planned?"

"That's my multi-purpose building. It's there to allow for overflow, expansion, and the unknown. My architect calls it my mystery building. He swears at me every time he sees it on the plans because I can't tell him what to put in it. So far it's 'a series of large rectangular cells whose main purpose is to divide up space so that Mr. Fields can play with it.' That's his description."

"Wouldn't it make sense to wait until you know what you need it for?"

"To some people it would, but the quadrangle has a symmetry that pleases me, and I've found if you create space, you'll find a way to fill it. I have big expectations for this project. If it turns out I can't use it, I might lease the space out to compatible businesses - peripheral designers, forms suppliers, even copy houses."

I nodded. "Profit either way."

"Exactly! Now what do you think about this site? Bear in mind, there's a second story with another open lounge over the entrance, fronted with plate glass. That's why the view is so important. There will be entrances on each side of all the buildings to allow for easy access. Despite 9/11 and security issues, I don't want to make it awkward to get in and out. Our internal security is topnotch. There will be tunnels for bad weather. On the quadrangle side of the courtyard in the central main building is where we'll place storage and housekeeping closets. These will be on the interior wall with a corridor running along the courtyard."

"What's in the quadrangle?"

"Two opposing corners are loading areas. Then we'll have landscaping, pathways cutting across it, benches. In good weather someone'll operate an outdoor canteen. Picnic tables, grassy areas so if family comes for lunch in good weather there's a place they can enjoy."

The description brought to mind scenes from my past. "You've set this up like a college campus! Lounge, quad, dining hall, everything right down to the Frisbees!"

"You caught on!"

I leaned over the plans for a better look now that I understood what he was after. Exciting. An academic atmosphere created to foster original thought in the workplace. The workplace tailored for the worker. Not only was Jason's project exciting in itself, his approach had the potential for making an indelible mark in personnel relations.

I looked at the site more critically, considering the lay of the land, what trees would have to be moved, how the slope of the road might rise. I tromped over to the second site where trees were thicker and pine needles coated the hillside. These were old pines, ones who'd weathered many a Hudson Valley winter, tall and proud and unstripped by disease or wind. I turned to face the river, and caught my breath at the unexpected sight of what looked like a sunset over water. An illusion. Such sights are only seen on the West Coast or over the Great Lakes. Thanks to a trick of geography, the sun seemed to be dropping between two purple-hued mountains into the glassy Hudson.

In the foreground lay a small rounded island, a breast-shaped mound thrusting out of the water, an island of Native American ruins and ritual for which the village of Kings Hill was named. Its proximity had been one more reason I'd chosen this place to settle in. Kings Hill Island featured heavily in Native American medicine, a direct influence on the branch of homeopathy that interested me. Below us on the hill grew more birch and sumac, but interspersed with them I spotted maple and a large clump of roadside lilacs someone had allowed to run rampant.

"Jason, come here! This is where you need to build. Look at that view! Place the dining hall at this end of the quad and diners can get all the mind-refreshing tranquillity they need just by looking out the window!"

I tugged at his arm, turning him back and forth so he'd see what I did. "Oh, Jason, you have to use this one!"

"It is magnificent. We can bring the drive around this way and drop off some of the hill in natural terraces. Perfect!"

He scooped me up and swung me around, his height and the hill and the excitement rendering me dizzy. Gently he set me down. "I knew you'd be a help." He leaned down and kissed me.

Kissing Jason was nice, even a little electric. Even more electric was the expression in his eyes when he straightened up away from me. Shivers ascended my spine.

He grabbed my arm and raced us back to the table. He rolled up the plans and shot them back into their tube, handed it to me, folded the table and led us back to the car.

"We need to celebrate! I promised you dinner, didn't I? Shall we?" He held my door, then leaped in and started the engine. "I have the perfect place. In fact," he added mischievously, "I made reservations."

"You did? Where are we going?"

"You'll see. Sit back, relax. And," he frowned, "don't mind if I seem a little off-stride. I didn't expect to kiss you back there." He looked at me then, all honesty and directness, all eccentricities aside. "I didn't expect you to kiss back, either."

Directness warranted same. "Neither did I. But you did, and I did, and it's okay, Jason."

For a moment he said nothing. "It is okay. Come on, put in that CD and close your eyes. When we arrive, it'll be a surprise," he chanted.

So I did. Soothing jazz on a superb stereo, car gliding along on the River Road, me trying to guess where we were. For an off-road conqueror, the Land Rover maintained an on-road serenity that was startling. I kept my eyes closed the whole time, despite Jason's occasional teasing. He offered no hints as to our destination, and the car's flawless performance provided no clues. I waited until he told me to open my eyes.

I opened them at the awning-covered entrance to the Black Carriage.

CHAPTER 16

"Get that filthy stuff out of my kitchen!"

I look up, startled at Mom's tone. I didn't do anything wrong. Did I? I look back down at the unsanded boards, the unevenly nailed one-by-twos (I am so proud of knowing what that term means!), the sawdust collecting below the unfinished cut I've labored over - well, it is a mess.

"Yes, Mom," I say, and scurry to remove the offending material.

Pop's outside, walking down to the barn. I hold the uncompleted project awkwardly and scuffle up behind him.

"Pop! Mom kicked me out of the house!"

He turns around, startled by my words. Then he sees what I'm struggling to keep in my hands.

Cigarette smoke twirls up past his nostrils, and a twinkle lights his gray blue eyes. "Here, let me help. Kicked you out, huh?"

"Yeah. Well, I guess I was making a mess."

Pop's shoulders twitched in silent laughter. "I reckon she'd like to be able to kick me out when I make a mess, but..." he leans in conspiratorially, "I think she doesn't know she could."

I look up at him quizzically. His eyes are far away.

"She doesn't know I'd do anything she told me to."

S urprised?"

"Yes! I'm not really dressed for this place, you know."

"It's no problem. One of the advantages of being a bit of a celebrity is you don't have to dress according to the rules."

Right. The valet took our car and we went in and were seated in the main dining room. Panic set in. *I am not supposed to be here, at the Black Carriage, with Jason.*

Jason, enthralled by the choices on the menu, didn't notice my mood had changed.

Good. Try to ignore it yourself.

"Let's have the Poco Plata Internationale," I suggested. "It sounds like fun. Two of everything so we can taste it all."

He scowled, reading the description of what purported to be a series of appetizers and hors d'oevres-size entrees designed to tantalize and thrill the taste buds. The list included Lobster Medallion au beurre, angel hair pasta with morels in garlic, couscous, Siaopao en Deux, chapati, and Bengali crab.

"What is Siapao en Deux?"

"Not 'syoh- pao'; 'show- pow'! It's a Philippino dish -   a sort of steamed dumpling with a filling, usually of pork, chicken, vegetables and egg. I presume 'en Deux' refers to being for two. Or maybe cut in two - made smaller for the platter."

"Oh. Is it good?"

"Yes, it's good! Come on, let's order it!" I laughed at his glum look.

"Don't make fun of me, young woman. I was frightened at a tender age by a leaf of Chinese cabbage, and I've harbored suspicions of foreign food ever since."

"Ice Cream Romanoff last week, Asian Salad the other day! What do you mean you don't like foreign food?"

"Uh, yes. Well. Interesting you remember." He twinkled those crystalline green eyes at me. "Anything would taste great tonight. Thanks for helping out."

"No problem. I had fun."

"Enough fun to take your mind off your troubles?"

I stopped fiddling with my water glass. "You noticed. Yes, actually. Add that to the list of things I need to thank you for."

"Thank me? You don't have anything to thank me for yet."

I smiled vaguely. "I was thinking about the area across the road from your site, Jason. Are you really going to have river access there?"

"Yes. I saw that the Boat Club has only left one narrow ramp for the public to use, and Kings Hill had to petition them to do that much. There's no reason my little park can't include ramp space sufficient for local boaters."

He paused to place our order, then turned his eyes on me again.

"Why, Mackenzie, have you designs on my access ramps? Maybe for those two antique boats of yours?"

"You remembered that too? I'm tickled!"

"Not hard to remember such a passion as yours for those boats. Tell me more about them."

I told him about the boats, about Brian and my purchasing first one, then the next. About how we'd fallen in love with the natural materials and mechanical engines. I described the sensual thrill of planing and sanding until a wooden hull was as smooth as bone. The smell of stain and Spar.

"Marine varnish," I explained.

"I'm familiar with it," he murmured, chin resting on his hand as he watched me.

"And finding parts! It's like a treasure hunt! Online, old boatyards, reproduction shops, eBay. Someplace there is bound to be a part to replace the one a boat is missing. I've even heard of people finding spare parts under fishing piers."

I paused for breath.

"You do get excited about your subject," he observed as the waiter served our Plata. We began to pick apart the dish as I resumed.

"Know where my second boat is now? On Long Island. There's a marina there that specializes in vintage motors. I'm having a rebuilt engine installed. They actually had an original Chrysler 70HP engine! A little work, they said, and it would run as smooth and strong as new! This boat's already been to Michigan for an expert rebuild on the keel. It needed a repair that I'm not good enough to do yet. When it gets here, I'll still have to re-sand and stain the whole hull. Then layers of Spar, new hardware. Oh, Jason, you should see the chrome and brass hardware I've got - "

"Mackenzie."

" - it's beautiful. And that gleam against the mahogany? You have to see it. I'd like to take you out on the water when it's all done, and - "

"Mackenzie!"

" - well, no, we don't have to wait. We can go out in the one that's here. You can't imagine how much nicer these boats are than - "

"Mackenzie!" Jason bellowed. Other diners turned their head. The waiter passing behind Jason stopped in his tracks.

"What?"

"Do you know when you babble you sound just like Katherine Hepburn?"

"I do? Really?" I beamed. "No one's ever told me anything like that before."

"Yes, you do. Can you pause long enough to answer a question?"

"Of course, what is it?"

"Do you want that?"

"Want what?"

"That." He pointed to the plate where four siapao were all that remained of our Plata.

"I want my share, but you need to try these."

His expression was one of suspicion, but he popped an entire siapao into his mouth - not the way they're meant to be eaten, but considering his reservations about trying new food, I kept quiet, focused on my own siapao. Two remained on the plate. One disappeared into his mouth, which snapped shut as he closed his eyes in gustatory pleasure.

He swallowed and searched for wine to wash it down. Clearly he liked this food he'd been so afraid of trying. Once more he looked at the plate. A gleam lit his eye, and he raised his fork. I grabbed the remaining siapao before his hand touched it.

"Oh, no, this is mine!"

"But it's good!"

"I know. And I want mine! I'll make you a batch sometime." I nibbled daintily at my siapao.

"You can't!"

"Can too! Philippino woman I knew in Washington taught me. They're easy."

"I don't believe you."

"You should. My talents are not limited to doctoring and old boats, you know."

"Okay, but - Waiter! I'd like to see the Chef!"

"Shh. Shh! Jason!"

He ignored me. The waiter returned immediately with the chef while surrounding patrons looked on, whispering.

"Yes, sir? Is there a problem?"

"No, no problem. Everything is fine."

"Then what is it, sir?"

"My companion here. She's a professional woman. Intelligent, talented. Do you think she is capable of re-creating your fine dishes?"

The chef - portly and grizzled, of medium height with fiery red hair - looked me over as closely as he might a piece of fresh meat.

"She seems intelligent enough." He cocked his head at me as if to consider further.

"Enough already, Chef. I made the mistake of offering to make my friend his own batch of siapao. He chooses to believe I can't do it." I glared at Jason who was starting a laughing fit.

"It is true, the basic siapao is not difficult, but then surely you realize I have not prepared the basic siapao. Nothing Chef Almirez prepares is basic!"

"Certainly not, Chef. I detected something extra in there. A mango chutney, wasn't it - just a dollop?"

He beamed. "Finally a set of discriminating taste buds. Miss - "

"Doctor Wilder."

"*Doctor* Wilder. I am honored. A physician who also appreciates fine cuisine, and with such knowledge and discernment. Sir, this woman knows what she is saying. If I were you I would definitely allow her to prepare me siapao. Good- bye, Dr. Wilder. Please honor me by stopping by, and I will give you some of that chutney, eh?" With a wave he marched back to his kitchen.

A smatter of applause gave sound to the grins that surrounded us. I blushed. Jason chuckled quietly. The chuckle was threatening to outgrow itself, so I swatted at his arm.

"That has to be one of the most embarrassing - "

" - funniest - "

" - exhibitions I've ever - "

" - sat through."

" - been put through, thank you!" I glared at him some more, then blotted my eyes with a napkin as my aggravation collapsed into laughter. My laughter eased, winding down like a toy losing its wound-up power. Suddenly, everything inside me seemed to deflate.

I wished - how I wished! - that this sort of embarrassment was the worst thing that could happen to me.

That I wasn't trying to fight my way back into a town I wasn't sure wanted me.

That I wasn't trying to prove my father hadn't been guilty of murder.

That I wasn't falling in love with Bryan Jamison.

Like most unwelcome truths, that one sneaked up on me. Now it had to be faced.

"What's wrong, Mackenzie?"

I met Jason's eyes. I couldn't tell him what I'd been thinking! In my haste to cover up, another awkward truth wormed its way out.

"Jason, what do you think of someone who hides something from the police?"

"Probably not a good thing, but what are we talking here? Stolen goods? A drug habit? What?"

"No. Information -   well, sort of information, but really more confirmation, but still not for certain - "

"Whoa. Back up, slow down. Let me order coffee -   wine? Then we'll talk."

I breathed deeply, unsure what else was going to come loose right now.

"Okay, someone - you? - has information the police want. I take it this has to do with the bodies over at your old homestead?"

I nodded. "I have some evidence, circumstantial, but pretty strong, that could confirm that their suspicions are -   might be -   in part -   correct." I couldn't take it further.

"And their suspicions are...?"

"They're pretty well convinced that my father is responsible for those bodies."

Jason's lips formed a silent whistle. "You say you have evidence?"

I nodded, sipping my wine. "I think so. Actually, I have evidence he could have killed one of the men. The other, I'm almost positive he didn't kill."

"Why?"

I studied him over the rim of my glass.

I spoke slowly. "I have a hunch I know who the other one is. If I'm right, there is no way my father would have killed him."

"Who do you think this man is?" His voice was quiet to match mine, his eyes alert.

"I think - no, not 'til I'm sure. I'm trying to get permission to examine the remains myself. Then I'll know."

"And when you know, you'll do what? Talk to the police? So, you're just waiting to be sure?" He crossed his arms and looked at me. "You're holding back what are actually two important facts. The identity of one victim. And, the identity of the other one's killer. You think this is a good idea?"

I squirmed. "You don't have to put it quite that way, you know. We're not talking about some killer running around loose ready to shoot someone else or bash someone else's head in. Whoever did this is probably as dead as my father. I mean, he might not have done it. Just because he never let anyone - someone else *could* have used the weapon."

"Wait a minute. What do you know about the weapon?" His voice rose.

"Shh. That's what makes me think he *might* have killed the one guy. I think one of the weapons was something that belonged to my father. It's something he never let out of his possession, but I could be wrong about that, couldn't I? I mean, if I told the police, it wouldn't change anything. They think he's guilty anyway."

I continued gloomily. "What gets me is, what happened? I mean, it makes sense that the same person killed both people and buried them there. But Pop would absolutely never have killed his - . Someone else must have killed both of them!" I looked up at Jason. "See why I'm not ready to tell the police anything?"

He reached out and took my hand. "I see that you haven't got it all figured out, and that you've got to see those remains to reach any more conclusions. So no, there's probably no point in talking to the police until then."

"Do - do you have any theories? You're the criminologist. You write mysteries. What do you think could have happened?"

He traced a finger lightly over my knuckles. "Well, no offense, but you *have* been babbling again, so I'm a little unclear. Any number of things could have happened. Maybe your father and these men were all there fighting, and only your father was left. He buried the two bodies and kept the whole thing quiet. Maybe the two deaths are unrelated, improbable but not impossible. Maybe your father only killed one of them. Or maybe he had nothing to do with it at all. He might be completely innocent, just as you've contended all along. You don't need to go to the police yet. Not 'til you're sure."

I sighed in relief. "That makes me feel better."

He looked over my shoulder, considering. "You know, I don't think you need to go to the police, but don't you feel close enough to Brooklynne's brother to relate all this to him?"

"Uh-unh. Bryan has a very strict sense of ethics, and I respect that. I wouldn't want to put him in a difficult position."

"Too bad, because he's sitting right across the room. Behind you. And hullo, who's that lovely with him?"

I twisted in my seat, a warm flush creeping up my neck at the very thought that Bryan saw me here with Jason. Not fifty feet away, at a table identical to ours, sat Bryan - and his ex-wife. Bryan stared at me, his face a mask I could not read. I saw Deb Voag catch sight of me. She scowled, then thrust her face in front of Bryan's as she talked at him. She clutched his lapel, and he lowered his gaze to her face. I turned back to Jason, feeling sick inside.

I flushed. "That's Deb Voag."

"The model?"

"Also Bryan's ex-wife." I stumbled feebly over the 'ex' part. Things do change, I thought.

"Interesting. There must be more to Bryan Jamison than I thought."

"Could we leave?" The room seemed to be closing around me.

His gaze flicked from me to the couple behind me. "We may want to wait a few minutes. Mr. and Mrs. Jamison are leaving."

I turned. Stupid, but I couldn't help it. Bryan was behaving with precise correctness. He offered her his arm, rigidly bent and held away from his side like a Marine's. He held his head erect, not speaking at all. He was watching me.

I stared at my plate, thinking he didn't look particularly happy with me or his ex. Wife.

Jason cleared his throat.

"Finish your wine, and I'll take you home. If that's still all right with you." He inclined his head in Bryan's direction.

How transparent had I become? I didn't know if Jason thought I was upset over Bryan being there because he was the police, or because he was Bryan. *Well, he doesn't have any other alternatives to choose from, does he?*

"It'll be fine, Jason. You've given me a great evening."

"More to come, if you're interested," he said lightly.

I managed a flat little smile. Jason called the waiter over to settle with him.

Some nights it doesn't pay to even try. As we came out, Bryan and Deb were waiting at the curb for the valet to bring them their car.

We walked up behind them, Jason signaling for his vehicle. Bryan nodded coldly to Jason and cast an empty look at me. Deb gave Jason a quick once-over, then began spouting fiery disdainful glares at me, all the while clinging like a dragonlet to Bryan's arm.

Jason's hovering presence was a welcome protection against this hostility.

Bryan didn't like it. He kept pulling his head back in small jerks, and shrugging his dinner jacket higher onto his shoulders.

"Where's that valet?" he demanded

"Looks like they're having trouble sorting things out. Maybe we'd better see what's what," Jason suggested.

"Yeah, sure," Bryan muttered. He shook loose of Deb's clutches and walked over to the desk, Jason sauntering behind. They became engrossed in trying to untangle the confusion of keys the valets were handling.

Deb shot me another glare.

Traffic, which had been light when we came out, began picking up. Headlights flipped by. Tire tread sucked the pavement in whispered rushes. Mostly the cars remained in the left-hand lane in order to allow passengers to get out at the Black Carriage's canopied entrance. Only one car had pulled up while we waited.

Ms. Voag stalked a tight little circle between me and the curb, fidgeting with her bag. She extracted a lighter and cigarette and toyed with them. Her eyes flicked towards me and away, her disgust becoming more apparent with every flick.

I tried looking over her head, around her. Streetlights and store lights, traffic lights and headlights all hung suspended as orbs of glowing color. Neon lights and computerized billboards added animation. She cut into my line of vision. I glanced away to the left. A dark sedan approached the canopied walkway.

Deb turned, lighting up her cigarette and called out, "Bryan, come on back. Let them straighten it out. It's their job!"

The sedan's approach seemed reckless. It slid in toward the curb without slowing.

I reached out to touch her shoulder, to suggest she step back.

"What do *you* want?" She snatched her arm away.

"I just think - "

"Bryan!" she called. "Come on!"

The gunning of an engine overran her voice.

There was a thud. A smack. A blur of print silk and chestnut hair thrown down from view. A streak of light dazzling my eyes and the smell of burnt rubber.

I pulled my hand back from empty air. There was one long moment as tail lights flashed around the corner and other bystanders and I stared at each other.

Reality streamed in.

Why hadn't I grabbed her and pulled her back?

I rushed forward and knelt beside her. Bryan came and dropped down beside me, staring at her face. Jason was studiously turned away, keeping people back, his skin white and drawn.

I began to palpate her neck, searching for a pulse, checking for what other injuries she might have. "Bryan - call it in! I'll take care of her."

He hesitated a fraction of a second, then moved away and pulled out his cell phone.

I undid the front of Deb's costly blouse, noting as I did that there was already blood trickling from her ear and mouth. Her eyes fluttered and rested on me.

"I guess you get your second Bryan after all," she said in her sulky voice, then her head dropped aside, limp.

I made the necessary final checks. I'd be the one having to fill out forms. I placed my purse where it would shield her face. It was a small gesture to afford her some dignity and try to ease Bryan's pain.

Bryan. It had taken that much time for him to get through. He hurried back, pulling off his dinner jacket as he ran up and skidded to a stop.

"You'll need this to keep her warm 'til they get here. Ambulance from Albany Med's on the way." He knelt down to drape the jacket over her. "What else can I do? Did you see what happened, Mackenzie?"

I rested my hand on his shoulder. I wanted to stop him seeing her face. I wanted him not to hurt. His face whitened. His lips formed a straight line, and he swallowed as if he'd eaten a hunk of granite. Ever so slowly, he pulled the jacket all the way up, to the curls of her fabulous auburn hair.

"Mackie?" he whispered.

"Bryan, I'm sorry."

How strong love was to block out recent troubles and cut to the quick of life's relationships. The loss in his eyes! The woman he'd shared life with, made life with, dead in a mindless split-second.

He rose slowly and reached back, blindly gripping my hand. I held out my arms to him. He moved into them, bending his head over mine to stare down at his dead wife.

People circled around us.

"She pushed her! I saw her pulling hands back!"

"Must have been a drunk. Did you see how crazy he was driving?"

"Did you see how those guys left the women standing all alone? I bet it was a set-up!"

I pulled away from Bryan. Jason reached us and passed me a small flask he'd gotten from the bar. Behind him hovered the valets and the Black Carriage's manager. The valets were trying to herd people back away from us, but they lacked experience at this sort of thing. Bryan's cadet Ted wasn't among them. I unscrewed the cap from the flask and sniffed. The very fumes helped.

"Bryan, Bryan -   here, take this. *Take* it. It's brandy. Bryan, I'm sorry."

He gulped some, and blinked. The hand that grasped my arm was a good deal firmer and steadier. His face grew firmer, too. The mask was back in place.

"Thanks. Mackie, I'll have to call Betty McBride. Will you wait 'til she gets here? She'll want some answers from you. So will Homicide."

"Homicide?" asked Jason.

Bryan nodded. "Homicide always covers hit-and-runs. There's always an autopsy, too. I don't think there's going to be any surprises over this one." His voice cracked drily. "In other circumstances, this would be my case." He stared at Deb's body. "Mackenzie, did you get a look at the driver? Man or woman? Did they look drunk?"

"Easy, Jamison. We'll take it. Come on, pal." Out of nowhere uniforms had appeared, and one lone suited figure. Camera flashes strobed. The crowd now efficiently held back, Jason, Bryan, and I made a closed circle with this business-like man who seemed so concerned about Bryan. He turned out to be Bryan's partner, Steve Adderly.

He took us through the steps of what had happened. From the corner of my eye I could see uniformed men asking questions of the valets and others who'd been nearby. Our statements would be thoroughly checked.

Strange enough to be such a close witness to her death, I was also the physician in attendance. Even nights riding ambulance duty in Baltimore had not prepared me for this. Adderly was gentle but resolutely thorough. We covered our stories three times each, separately and together. He also asked me to remain until McBride arrived so I could answer medical questions.

Jason led me to the open door of a squad car, then produced the brandy flask again. "You need this."

I took it without protest.

"You don't have to be a superwoman, you know."

"What?" I asked wearily.

"I think I know what this is costing you. You've had a long day, and the end of it was emotion-charged, even before - this. No one will blame you if you break down."

I met his eyes, still pale, but warm and caressing. "Jason. I don't know what I'd have done without you here tonight."

"Just part of the service, ma'am."

"Mackie? What is this? They said Bryan Jamison's ex is the victim? That right?" Betty McBride bustled over.

Jason gave me his hand and pulled me up. "I'll be waiting over here. I'll take you home."

I rubbed my arms. "They've told you right, Betty. I was right behind her when the car came up. I guess I couldn't believe my eyes, because,

Betty, I didn't do anything! I mean, I tried to tell her to step back, but I didn't pull her back or anything! Betty, I just let it happen!" I was shaking now, confusion and guilt and shock overwhelming me. Even Betty's familiar face seemed more condemning than comforting. She looked from me to where the body lay a short distance away.

"Adderly get your statement?" she asked.

I nodded.

"Okay then. Can you stop by my office tomorrow to fill me in when I do the autopsy?"

I hesitated. "Yes," I whispered, "I can get it together by then."

"Okay. We'll take care of this - and those other matters you wanted to see me about. - Matheson called me," she added.

Vaguely I remembered my request. Nothing had ever seemed so pointless in comparison to what had just happened.

"Sure." My voice cracked. I cleared my throat. "Sure. Ten o'clock okay?"

"Fine. Now let that tall curly-headed hunk take you home and put you to bed. One way or another."

A semblance of a smile passed over my face, and I walked over to Jason.

"I can go. Thanks for waiting for me, Jason. I - hold on. Can you get the car? I'll be right there."

Bryan was sitting in his partner's car, his jacket slung across his lap, his shirt rumpled, his hair falling over one eye. He watched me approach, drawn as irrevocably as a magnet.

I touched his shoulder. "Bryan."

He grasped my wrist. "Mackenzie. How am I going to tell Rachel? Deb is still her mother. What do I say? 'Some jackass got tanked up and jumped in his car and killed your mother'? I can't say that to her! She's only nine years old!"

Worry dug into his face. He held my hand between his, rubbing it. "Mackenzie, help me."

My mouth went dry. Help him? He'd been having dinner with his ex-wife! How could I help him get over the woman I'd finally figured out was my rival?

"Do you want me to call Brooklynne?" My voice broke on the words.

"Adderly did that. She and Lloyd are on their way."

"Bryan, Brooke can help. She'll be here for you. I -   I have to get home."

"This has been rough for you, hasn't it? I expect Jason's taking you home." He dropped my hand and resumed his cold tone of voice.

I nodded, not trusting myself to keep my feelings silent.

"Well, that's okay then. You're taken care of. Thank you, for your help tonight."

"Bryan, I - I - " My resolve was dying.

"Here's Brooklynne. See you." Deliberately he stood up and pushed past me.

Tears swam in my eyes, and in a final enveloping chill as cold as Deb Voag's body, I walked stiffly toward the car where Jason waited to take me home.

CHAPTER 17

How many times does Mom have to tell this story?

"I used to baby-sit for this guy up in Albany who worked for Mayor Corning. Even though he worked in the Mayor's office, he had another job, too.

"Maybe it was the same job, just a different part of it.

"He was a collections guy. He collected money for the numbers racket - policy, we called it. On Saturdays he'd go around and take up money from the storekeepers who took the bets in and deliver it to one of the ward bosses in Albany.

"His run went between there and Hudson. Sometimes, if it was nice out, he'd take me and his two kids along for the ride. We'd wait in the car while he went into places - stores, mostly - and collected the money. He paid off winnings, too, only not so often."

"Wasn't that scary?"

"Well, no. You see, it was what you did. Nobody was afraid of him, so long as they behaved. And people knew how to behave around people like him. I don't think he even carried a gun. Not that I ever saw. It was just part of his job."

Then she'd get a gleam in her eye. "People think that the fifties were so dull. Life wasn't all that squeaky clean. It was a jumble, just like now."

I always want to ask her if that was how she met Pop.

D octors and medical examiners work on Saturdays. Death doesn't take holidays, Betty would say. I wasn't feeling philosophical or even professional as I entered Betty McBride's office that morning. I was weary, sick, and frightened. Friday had been the ugliest day of my life.

"Here. Have some coffee." She thrust a mug into my hand and poured something hot and dirty-looking into it.

"I hate coffee!"

"Drink it anyway." She sat down behind her desk. "Well, you look like hell. Almost as bad as you did last night. Didn't your tall friend take care of you properly?" She leered at me over her cup.

"Jason took me home and kindly fixed me a snack, then waited 'til I went to bed. So stop looking at me like that!"

Actually he'd been sweet, fixing me a potent hot toddy, then sitting at my bedside holding my hand until I drifted asleep. I didn't add that he'd still been in the chair by my bed when I woke with the terrors at 5 a.m., or that he'd fixed me breakfast while I showered, then left discreetly before anyone could see. Betty would never believe things had stopped there. His attentions were all that were getting me through this. Left to my own devices I'd have crawled in a closet and started screaming.

"Mackenzie, what happened at the Black Carriage last night?"

"We were standing at the curb. The valets had some trouble with the car keys, so the guys went over to try and sort it out."

"You were all together?"

"We were leaving at the same time." I hesitated. "Actually, there was a bit of - well, awkwardness. Deb Voag didn't like me very much. She had it in her head somehow that Bryan was interested in me, so she was busy giving me all these dirty looks and stuff."

"She didn't like you. What about you and Bryan?"

"Bryan and me? Nothing. We're old friends." *Right. Nothing. Remember that.*

Whether it was the coffee in my belly or the slow burn I was starting to do over Betty's line of thinking, I was feeling warmer, more alert.

"Anyway," I said firmly, "Deb started calling Bryan back from the valet's desk. She was turned away from the street and didn't see the car."

"Which you did."

I nodded. "It was a dark sedan. It sped up, kind of wobbling from side to side, not quite weaving, you know? I tried to get Deb's attention to get her to step back. She was so busy being nasty I never had a chance to get the words out. She was fuming at Bryan and yelling to him about the keys, and the car hit her. It was that fast. It threw her against the pavement. Killed her almost instantly. The car was gone before she died." *I* started wobbling from side to side at the memory. I gripped my mug tighter.

"Did she say anything?"

I didn't answer right away.

"Mackenzie?"

"Is this Dr. McBride or Betty I'm answering?"

She shrugged, fiddling with a paper clip, unwilling to commit. Well, so was I.

"She said something which I took to be a private remark addressed to me. It wasn't anything about the car hitting her." I paused. "She knew she was dying."

I stared at the ring in the bottom of my coffee mug. I hate coffee.

"How did you treat her?"

"There wasn't time to, Betty, you know that! I'd barely begun to examine her when she died. I told Adderly that!"

"I've got his report. Just needed to make sure we hadn't missed something in the confusion. Where was your bag? I didn't see it last night."

"Still in Jason's car. We didn't have time to get it out. If you've done the exam, you know how fast she went."

"Yeah. It was pretty conclusive. Broken collarbone, broken pelvis, ruptured spleen. Typical hit-and-run."

"God, Betty. Don't."

"Sorry. These accidents of stupidity get me."

Accidents. Thank God. I'd begun to feel like I was responsible. The finger of accusation did not point my way, and the heavy weight of the law's arm was not, after all, lying along my shoulders. It didn't do squat for my severed relationship with Bryan, and it certainly didn't change anything for Deb Voag, but it left me feeling a heck of a lot better. Ready, even, to tackle other things.

"Betty, if you're done with this…?"

She waved an arm at me. "Yeah, sure, I am. I know it's been the pits for you. Why don't you go on home?"

"Actually I want to get this other thing over with. Can I examine the skeletons?"

She nodded, yawning and stretching her way out of the chair. "Come on. I have to be there with you."

"I know."

"This may hit you funny, seeing as it involves your family. Don't be surprised if it's different than doing a routine autopsy. This is personal for you."

Oh yes.

"In here."

We gowned up. I followed her along a bare corridor, through a set of steel operating room- style doors. She had them ready for me: two tables of bones laid out on display. On a nearby table were plastic evidence bags. One held some tattered pieces of cloth.

I took a deep breath as I always did before an autopsy, even though there was no stench to conquer this time. It seemed curiously dry and clean, like a lab mock-up. So unlike dealing with a fresh body as Betty had this morning.

Don't think of that.

The skeletons were laid out in position, puppet limbs come off their strings. Their color conjured up pictures of their burial places. Bone absorbs the soil color when it's buried unprotected. A surreal feeling of model- building time passed over me. I gave myself a shake. This was no game.

I approached the first table, the toe tag (attached in this case directly to the tibia) identifying this as Case # 08-23758-B, the younger of the two men. I examined it, confirming all the findings Betty had described in her report. I ran a gloved hand along the fracture lines on his tibia, wondering if she was right about their cause. The back of the skull was quite simply smashed in, fragments clinging to the edges of the opening. I fingered them carefully. Had my father's ax done this? As I moved away, I glanced at the evidence bags. I'd deal with them later.

I went on to Case # 08-23758-A.

I moved carefully. I didn't want to seem to be looking for anything in particular. This skeleton was supposed to be a stranger to me, not someone I had once looked forward to laughing with. I wasn't supposed to be looking for recognizable fracture lines or old bullet wounds. I looked him over, skull to toe, as evenly as I had examined the first one. Without a doubt, the bullet crease was in the right location, and could be old enough. There wasn't any steel plate. The teeth could conceivably be the same stained and broken teeth Jake had so proudly bared in laughter. In my mind's eye, I fleshed out and clothed the skeleton: baggy pants, oil-stained undershirt, gray-green workpants of polished cotton, old greasy Army-issue shoes pock-marked from dribbles of gasoline. Although it made me shudder, I imagined that black hair, the pug nose, and the Irish ease ever-present in his face. It was possible.

I crossed to the evidence bags. The first contained what had been found with Body B. Large scraps of material, labeled as having been on the legs, probably pantslegs. This was expensive material. It had come through twenty years in surprisingly good shape. Not so the shirt, which had apparently been of some natural fiber.

In a separate bag I found the rock chip Betty had said was found inside the skull. I squinted cautiously as I examined it. It took all I had to set it back down with a steady hand. I was certain. It had come from my father's ax.

Next I looked in the bags that went with the second body. In the first I found the .357 bullet. It looked like any other that had shattered ribs and torn apart a heart. It might have come from any gun, including my father's. If, that is, I considered only the bullet, and not the one whose life it had ended. There was a second bag for this body, too.

I looked at Betty in surprise. "You didn't mention this."

She shrugged.

I went through the items eagerly. More tattered cloth, nondescript, meaningless in my search. A left shoe, size 10, black leather, creased, dusty, and pitted as if some chemical had repeatedly dripped on the upper. I sucked in my breath. At a nod from Betty I pulled the shoe out of the bag. It was crumbly, as old leather would be, buried unprotected for so many years. I searched it over, looking for something somehow conclusive.

A pebble loosened in the toe and rattled around. I tilted the shoe, trying to see. I reached in with my fingers. Little black flakes showered out. I could feel a knobby shape slipping about. It rolled along my fingertips, evading them. I shook the shoe and reached in again. This time I caught hold of the stone and drew it out. It rolled around my palm as I turned my hand up to examine it.

There's a story in my family about my father starting out as a respectable young man with great expectations. For six years he worked for Isaac Hillin learning the jeweler's trade. He had an eye for beauty and picked up a knack for judging gold and gemstones. When old Hillin died, a cousin moved in and took over the business, a man with an eye for profits but not artistry. In no time he had fired my father and hired a less knowledgeable, less ambitious young man.

Whenever Pop referred to the 'good old days', we knew he meant not his youth, but his time with Isaac Hillin. Gifts of jewelry from Pop were always pleasing to the eye and finely crafted. He remembered everything Hillin ever taught him. He cherished the present Hillin gave to him before he died: a ring of solid gold flaring out into a medallion embossed with jeweler's tools. He'd worn it daily for so many years, I'd been surprised when it wasn't on him when he died, nor in the trunk of things I inherited. Now I knew where it had been. Pop had buried it out behind the barn, in the shoe that still protected the dead foot of his best friend, Jake Terry.

There was my proof. Case # 08-23758-A, was Jake Terry. The police would see it as proof that my father had been behind the trigger of the gun that killed poor Jake.

"Did you find anything?"

I froze, then carefully dropped my hand, curling my fingers and nestling the ring within them. I frowned at the shoe I still held in my left hand, and made an elaborate show of shaking my head. Once again I reached into the shoe, but this time I deposited the ring, wedging it firmly into the seam between upper and sole.

"No," I said loudly. "I thought I had, but it's just part of the shoe." I returned the shoe to its labeled bag, sealed it, and returned it to the table.

"Thanks, Betty. I don't know what I expected to find." I started removing the surgical gown.

"You had to try. Here, leave those things over here. I - "

Her overhead page interrupted us. A phone call.

"I'll meet you back in the office. Find your way okay?" She hustled out the door.

A compelling urge came over me to reopen that evidence bag and remove the ring. Leaving it was tempting fate. Burying Jake was the last thing Pop had done for him. We'd undone that. I couldn't bring myself to take away the last gesture Pop had made, the gift he'd left with his faithful friend. I'd have to rely on no one's being interested in the case and my care in wedging it into the shoe. With luck, no one would find it. If they did, I was probably the only one alive who could identify it. Which I wouldn't.

I regretted it's going out of the family. Pop had chosen to give it to the one honorable friend he had. I couldn't take that away from the two of them. Knowledge of the ring bound me to Jake and Pop. For their sake I had to find out what had happened twenty years ago. I could accept arguments that Pop had killed the other guy, assuming the circumstances had been extreme. He couldn't have been responsible for both deaths. Jake and Pop and I knew better. They had the advantage of knowing the whole story. I had to discover what my two ghosts knew and find a way to make it public.

I dropped the scrubs in the bin Betty had designated and went after her. She was hanging up the phone when I walked in.

"You're not going to believe this!" she fumed.

"What?"

"Deb Voag? They think the hit-and-run was deliberate. She was murdered."

"Deliberate? My God, Betty! That's awful! Who would want to - kill her?"

"For real? No one has any idea. One of the valets called in this morning, scared shitless. He didn't want any part of it, but he was scared someone would blame him, and it wasn't his fault - you know the kind of thing. Anyway, seems somebody slipped him some cash to lose those keys. Told him they were playing a joke on Bryan Jamison and his date. A prank, and would he take his time getting their car?"

"Betty, that's awful! Did the valet describe the guy who tipped him?"

"Yeah, but he might as well not. His description fits somewhere between a shoe salesman and a Sumo wrestler, depending on how rattled he is at the time. It's useless, except that it tells us this was deliberate."

"God, Betty! This is unbelievable! Does Bryan know?"

"Yeah, he knows. He's got some tough questions to answer, too."

"What do you mean?"

"It doesn't look good when an ex gets killed. Especially when the former spouse is on the scene. There are some who think Bryan might have arranged it himself."

"He wouldn't do that, Betty. Bryan is - "

"I know. Bryan is totally clean; most ethical person I know. Some people who probably *aren't* clean are taking advantage of the situation."

"No one is taking them seriously, are they?"

She shrugged. "Who knows?"

I stared at the speckled industrial tiles. Wanted to play a joke on Bryan. Some joke! How could even a kid fall for a line like that? Didn't he get suspicious?

Sometimes our body reacts to a thought before we even put it into words. A chill passed over me. My knees buckled. I dropped into the chair by Betty's desk.

"What the hell? Bryan'll be okay, Mackie. No one is going to believe those characters for long."

I shook my head frantically. "That's not it." Now was not the time to hide things from my old roomie. "Betty, I was supposed to be Bryan's date last night!"

It was her turn to stare. Yet she thought to grab a pencil, and I noticed.

"What are you talking about?" she asked sharply, pulling a pad towards her.

I touched her arm. "Wait, no notes until I'm done. Bryan asked me to dinner at the Black Carriage. This thing with Jason came up, so I got out of it. *I* was supposed to go with Bryan until I called him late yesterday.

Then Jason wound up taking me to dinner us right at the Black Carriage. I don't know when or why Bryan decided to take his ex-wife, but I was supposed to be the one with him, his date. That hit was meant for me!"

"How can you be sure?"

"Remember in college when I told you that I didn't like the way that English professor hung over me? Two weeks later he guaranteed me an 'A' if I slept with him."

"Well, sure, but we all knew his reputation."

"Maybe, but I was the first one in our class he hit on, and I knew in advance he would."

"Are you saying you're psychic?"

"Nothing like that. There was that party at Theta Chi, too. Where those two girls tried to slip something in my drink? Remember I wouldn't drink that night, even though it was hot and I was really thirsty. Later you heard them talking about how mad it made them that they hadn't got me, how they'd spiked my drink."

"Yeah, but you knew they hated you."

"Yes, and I think because of that I sensed that they were up to something. I don't think I'm psychic. I'm sensitive to emotions directed at me. And I tell you, there's someone out there - " I wet my lips, my tongue hot against the dry skin "someone who dislikes me a lot more intensely than those Theta Chi girls did!"

CHAPTER 18

It isn't easy, senior year with the Methodist Youth Fellowship, making Christmas wreaths to earn money. We reshape wire hangers into circles, then pull at spools of telephone cable to tie the bundles of evergreens on to the hanger.

Some people are in charge of twisting and tying.

Some are in charge of breaking down the branches and stripping them of extra twigs.

Some - with cars - are in charge of going after more greens, gathered from the trees at the farm. And I have to ride along so that Pop will give them to us free.

I t took a lot more convincing, but Betty finally agreed I had a
point. Then she had to convince me to talk to Bryan, his partner,
and Matheson.

"Matheson! Why Matheson?"

"Mackenzie. There aren't too many reasons people are targeted for a
hit-and-run kill," she explained. "All those reason require enemies. You
don't make enemies. Not unless you've changed a hell of a lot more than
I think you have. From what you said, only Deb Voag herself had reason
to hate you, and she's the one who's dead. So ask yourself, what are you
involved in that might make you enemies without you knowing? What's
going on in your life that is that serious? A murder investigation, right?"
She raised her eyebrows at me. "Unless there's something else you've
done to make people hate you."

I thought briefly of the hate mail and the garbage. "Other than
setting up shop where I'm not wanted, no." I waved away her questioning
look. "But this is a twenty-year-old murder, and hardly an investigation!
No one even cares about it but me!"

"How do you know? You've kept insisting your father didn't kill
those men. That means someone else did, someone who didn't get caught.
Look - " she ticked items off on her fingers - "the bodies have turned up.
The daughter of the guy the police have conveniently blamed is making
waves trying to prove he didn't do it. If he did do it, well, obviously no
one cares. If he didn't do it, well, your activities could be making
someone awfully uncomfortable." She paused. "Talk to Matheson."

Which was why on Sunday (another day off shot to pieces) I found
myself back out at the farm, not to work on the house or my boat, but to
track down Matheson one more time and try and explain why Betty
McBride and I thought I might, just might, need some protection.

Well, I thought, this has to be easier than facing Bryan. That was
next on my list of fun things to do today.

I'd talked to Adderly on Saturday. It took all afternoon. He'd questioned me closely, then agreed I should be the one to talk to Matheson and Bryan. Matheson I couldn't reach until today. For some untold reason he was supposed to be back out at my place. I wasn't ready to intrude on Bryan and Rachel yet. Adderly didn't feel he could order me protection until he conferred with the others. For at least one night, I was on my own.

Much to Jean's surprise, I'd called her and asked her to spend the night with me at the house. I did it on the pretext of making plans for the farmhouse, but the fact was I didn't want to be alone. If someone out there wanted me dead and had the resources to hire a professional, there was no telling what he'd try next. Not that I was clear on the idea of what Jean and I could do to stop him.

The night went slowly, what with Jean passing me funny looks and me keeping us up 'til three a.m. with idiotic ideas and uncontrollable yawns. When we did go to bed, I didn't sleep, just stared at the new dresser I'd bought and thought about being dead.

Like Deb Voag.

I parked by the house, facing the purple lilacs that grew in the hillside by the crumbling stone steps that led to the lower lawn. Pre-summer sun bathed the farm. It looked peacefully deserted, quietly awaiting the verdict of time before pressing on into the future.

I found Matheson sitting at the kitchen table, filling out reports. He stood when I entered.

"I heard about what happened Friday night. Tough on your friend Jamison." Beyond that rough sympathetic statement his voice was noncommittal.

I nodded and slung my purse on the table. I wandered about the kitchen, rubbing my upper arms, mentally ticking off things I wanted to do with the space. Trying to contain myself.

"Did you talk with Betty McBride?" I asked.

"Not since Friday afternoon. Why? Won't she let you see your skeletons?"

Jean was right. Some of the subfloors were going to need replacing. I could feel the give beneath my feet, not the frolicking bounce of a spring floor, but the unhealthy sag of rotting wood.

"I don't have a sense of humor today. That isn't the problem. I was wondering if you'd spoken with her, because she was going to tell you she thinks I need protection."

He had to work to hide the smile. "Why would she think that, Dr. Wilder?"

I took a deep breath, scuffing my toe against the carpet with the nauseating pattern. Wood floors again, absolutely, no matter how many layers down they were.

"Betty and I were discussing what happened to Deb Voag Friday night, and the possibility occurred to us that the hit-and-run might have been meant for me."

"Why would you think it was 'meant' at all?"

I stopped eyeing the woodwork with its worn green paint.

"You haven't heard. It was no accident. The Albany police concluded it was a contract-style hit-and-run. Apparently aimed at Bryan Jamison's *date*."

Matheson raised his eyebrows. "So?"

"I was supposed to be Bryan's date for dinner Friday night."

"Maybe you'd better tell me about it." He pulled a chair out from the table and sat, stretching his legs out before him.

I explained what Betty and I had worked out.

"Okay, I see why you think the word 'date' stands out a little. But hey, the guy's divorced, right? And who knew you were going to dinner with Jamison that night?" He smiled. "Besides me, that is. On the other hand, who would expect him to be taking his ex-wife to dinner?"

"Meaning what?"

"The person referred to by name is Bryan Jamison. I find that more interesting than anything else."

I thought for a moment. He had a point. Was I being self-centered to think this was about me? "But it wasn't Bryan who was killed, it was his ex-wife."

"Yes, and you can see how that might look to some people. Perhaps that's what was intended." He looked at me steadily.

"Would someone go to those lengths, killing a person to discredit someone else?"

"It's happened."

"But why?"

"You'd have to ask Jamison what cases he's been working on. What kind of connections the people he's been investigating might have. My professional curiosity aside, why bring this to me anyway? You should be talking to his partner - or him - and let them take it up with their superior. If it's valid."

"Coming to you was Betty's idea. She said if I've gotten someone mad enough to kill me, it must have to do with the murders out here. I talked with Adderly about it yesterday, but he won't do anything until he compares notes with you."

"Maybe he thinks Jamison is the real target here, same as I do." He clasped his hands behind his head and turned his gaze to the ceiling. "Let's look at what we know. Deb Voag was killed the other night by a hit-and-run, which turned out to be intentional. You, not Deb Voag, were supposed to be Bryan Jamison's date on Friday. I can verify that. He talked to you from my desk, remember? Some unknown person paid the valet to delay Jamison, theoretically so they could play a joke on him and his date. But his *intended* date, you, are sitting here talking to me, while Deb Voag is lying dead in the morgue." He sat forward and drummed his fingers on the papers lying on the table.

"Taking the assumption that the car was meant for you, wouldn't it be simpler for you to un-involve yourself in this investigation? In other words, quit nosing around and let the professionals - me, Adderly, Jamison - handle it. Let us do our jobs." He placed a faint stress on the word 'us' and raised a finger to make a new point. "If that hit was designated for you - you were there. Why did they hit Voag?"

I opened my mouth. "It's not that simple," I wanted to say. Then I shut it again. I'd spent all evening Friday letting Jason convince me my own agenda was appropriate. This was not going to be when I changed my mind.

"I don't know. Maybe it was hired out and the guy didn't know what I look like. It seems pretty clear to me someone wants me out of the way," I said carefully. "I don't see how stopping now would help. This goes right back to what Betty said: the only one who would be upset over an investigation would be the real killer. So I must be right about that. My father is not the one responsible for these murders!"

The look Matheson gave me was impassive and unconvinced.

"He wasn't distributing hard drugs, either. I found proof!"

"Proof?"

"Yes, Brooke and I went through the records of all the young people we could fi - think of that my father had supplied with pot or whiskey. Dr. Kesselman's records included seventeen of those people - and all seventeen of them showed no sign of any hard drug use!"

"That may just mean that it didn't show up. Unless Kesselman was looking for it, or treating them for a drug-related problem, he might never notice. Some doctors try not to notice. Or even leave things out of their records if it was damaging to their patients."

"Kesselman wasn't that kind of man. You could tell that by reading his records!"

"I'm afraid that's just another case of your word against ours, Dr. Wilder. Still, if you're right and if I assume you tried to investigate this fairly, then not only have you knocked off one of the biases against your father, you also may have found a real motive for the murders. As many people are killed over drugs as by drugs themselves."

We stared at each other, our mutual thought unspoken.

"All right. Get back to me after you talk with Jamison. Today."

"Right." I stood up and went out the door.

It was only my reluctance to face Bryan that kept me from peeling out the driveway and tearing off down the road. That and the conviction that Matheson would get a perverse pleasure out of coming after me and giving me a ticket. I drove more reasonably as I neared the bottom of the last hill.

I slowed down even more as I made the turns leading to Bryan's. I kept remembering the crowd that night. The accusations. Those people were only making judgments based on what they'd seen. Their conclusions weren't unreasonable, just wrong. Bryan would be so hurt.

He wouldn't be hurt by the way you deserted him?

I didn't desert him. He needed to be alone to deal with his grief. Besides, there's probably a whole community of long-time friends to help. And he has Brooke. Twins are important to each other in times like these.

Times like what?

Losing - losing a loved one. So there. He had Brooke. He didn't need me cluttering things up.

So that means you couldn't even call him yesterday? You saw the way he held on to you Friday night. Why couldn't you be there for him?

I saw the way he looked when she died. They'd been at the restaurant together. Think how devastated he felt. They were getting back together, and now she's dead. He has to help Rachel and put his own life together.

What, you can't help?

No. Not when I've just realized I love him. It would be - it would be taking advantage.

What makes you think they were getting back together anyway? After all, he'd asked you to dinner first.

She cared for him. Look how jealous she acted. Probably she's who he really wanted to ask all along. I was just a substitute.

Are you sure she wasn't the substitute?

Doesn't matter. It doesn't matter.

No matter how hard one tries, it does not take long to get anywhere in Kings Hill. I pulled in the driveway at Bryan's house and drove around back. Two cars stood there, Brooklynne's silver Toyota and Bryan's nondescript Ford. No one else. No neighbors, no church members, no pastor. Only his sister.

See? You did desert him. How do you suppose he feels about that?

I sat behind the wheel, waiting for my hands to stop their tremors. I closed my eyes. I wouldn't be able to face Bryan if I couldn't get it together. I had to be able to be his friend. When I opened my eyes Brooklynne was standing at my window.

"I'm glad you've come," she said.

She led me into the house, a large comfortable ranch built in the 1950's and remodeled in the 1990's. The layout had been completely opened up, with almost half the house given over to a circle of interconnected spaces divided into kitchen, dining, living, and study rooms. An open stairway led down to the re-fashioned family room; atrium doors replaced the old glass-panel sliding door onto the deck. The other end of the house contained the bedrooms, and these were private, but the overall impression was one of openness and light.

We went through to the deck. Tubs of begonias newly planted sat clustered together around a large clay pot containing a tall conifer. Teak benches flanked the arrangement. A couple of deck chairs were pulled up to a round glass-topped table, and not far off, a faded lounge rested at an angle to house, deck rail, and everything else in sight. Rachel lay on the lounge, hiding behind some pre-adolescent novel. Bryan, in jeans and short-sleeved shirt, stood with one foot on the lower deck rail, his forearms resting on the upper, a glass of beer in his hand. He could have been contemplating the ground below or the two acres beyond it evenly divided between a child's play-space and an extensive garden. Twittering carried in the breeze; swallows had taken up residence nearby. He turned as I walked out onto the deck.

"Mackenzie!"

It was his smile that did it. It broke all the barriers I'd been trying to erect between myself and falling in love with him. I plunged off that cliff without a backward glance or a safety line or toehold.

I held my arms out to him as I had Friday night, but Rachel was there, probably watching from behind her book.

She was. On disentangling ourselves from our hug we found her beside us, her arm going round her father's waist, her chin tucked into her shoulder. Cautiously I put my hand out to stroke her hair. I wanted to help, but could I? I didn't have a nine-year-old daughter. I didn't remember what it was like to be nine. All I could relate to was the loss, the gut-wrenching, hole-in-the-chest, world-collapsing loss you feel when a person on whom your world depends is no longer there.

I spoke softly. "I know we've only met once, Rachel, but I'm very sorry you lost your mother. It's a terrible thing to have happen to you."

She nodded, her eyes wide and red. A swallow that could encompass a golf ball passed down her throat. I moved around in front of her and bent down, pushing her hair back with both my hands.

"If it's okay with you, before I leave, I'd like to talk with you. I'd like you to tell me about your mother. Would that be okay with you?"

She nodded again, but then she pulled her arm from around Bryan's waist and encircled mine. I hugged her tight. From the corner of my eye I saw Brooklynne wiping her face.

"C'mon Rachel," she said. "Let's head off to the kitchen and get some food together."

We watched them go, and I joined Bryan at the deck rail. "Do you want something to drink? We have tea, and soda, and...."

"Don't bother. I'm here to see you, not have you play host."

He leaned forward on the rail again, and we stood silent for a few minutes. "That's the first time she's done anything but stare or read since I broke the news to her."

"I hope I did the right thing. I *will* have that talk with her. She won't know it, but talking about Deb will help the pain." I scrutinized my hands where they lay along the rail. "It will help you, too, Bryan. I'll listen, if you want."

He eased a step closer, covering my hand with his. "You might not hear what you expect to, but thanks. I'll take you up on it."

We settled ourselves in the deck chairs nearest the table. A breeze ruffled his hair and stirred the plants growing nearby. He turned the beer glass round and round with his long fingers. Then he stared over my head, eyes narrowed as if trying to focus on where to start.

I cleared my throat "Where is everybody, Bryan? I figured you'd have a slew of friends here to help out."

"I'm looking at a very good friend right now," he said, smiling.

"You know what I mean."

"Yeah. Well, it's complicated. A bunch of people came by yesterday. Bob Cooper was here. Doug Pulaskey even called. Steve came by in the morning. Told me I was on Administrative Leave until this gets ironed out. Not that I was surprised. We went over to Deb's mother's house, but that really didn't work out too well."

I looked questioningly at him.

"Deb's mother tends to be a little intense. The gloom got to be too much for Rachel. Besides.... Well, Deb's mother... Barbara's made a big deal out of shutting me out of all the arrangements. Because we were divorced. And because she blames me for getting Deb killed. Barbara's got Lloyd handling everything for her. She even blames me that they won't release Deb's body until the case is resolved." He took a long drink of beer.

"Anyway," he continued, "we came back here in the afternoon. Reverend Thibault brought over some ladies from the church with a bunch of food. Brooke handled all that. And today - well, you can see for yourself. I'm glad you came out, Mackenzie."

I swallowed hard. Time to be the understanding friend. *You're on!* said my little inner voice. "Bryan, about Deb. Are you sure your relationship wasn't getting better? I mean, Friday night - you seemed so - you were there together - "

"Mackenzie, let me tell you something about my marriage."

He hesitated, and behind his tousled hair clouds puffed out against the blue, blue sky. With his dark red shirt, it was a throat-catching picture. I glanced away, tears stinging my eyes before he even spoke.

"When we got married, Deb was a good kid. Pretty, clever, talented. I didn't know she was so ambitious. She had a Bachelor's degree in Design, but she really wanted to get into modeling. She took some courses, learned how to walk, how to fix her make-up. She even had a touch of surgery. I backed her, of course. I didn't know I was financing the demise of my own marriage. When she was pregnant with Rachel, it was awful. I never thought I could love and hate a woman at the same time, but I did. I kept telling myself that when Rachel was born, it would be all right. She'd come to her senses. Well, she didn't. When Rachel was three, Deb filed for divorce. Ever since, it's been one long battle over Rachel's welfare. I've tried not to let the kid feel like a war casualty, but Deb's made it hard."

"You've been divorced six years? She made it seem recent, like she still had feelings for you!"

"Deb was complicated in some ways. When we were married, she loved us both as much as she was able. She thought she loved us 'beyond measure' - her words. When it came down to the nitty gritty, she couldn't see why we - why I wouldn't do things her way."

"Why did she dislike me so much?"

He chuckled. "She saw how glad I was to see you, how much I wanted to help you deal with the problems out at the farm. She knew what a fine person I thought you were, and that I thought you'd be a good influence for Rachel. All the kinds of things she'd never been. It infuriated her that there was someone I thought could fill the role at which she'd failed."

I stared at an ant tugging a scrap of leaf along the edge of the tabletop. Had I heard him right? I glanced up. He was smiling, but almost as if he were afraid to.

"Bryan, why was Deb with you last night? I mean, after you had asked me?"

"After you decided to go with Fields, you mean?" The smile faded.

"Um, yeah. Well, I'll explain that."

His voice was very even. "After you cancelled, I decided I wanted to see Deb to tell her to leave you alone. I was going to tell her I planned to start seeing you. I was also going to make it clear that Rachel was going to get to know you, and that she was going to continue living with me. She dragged me to dinner, and as I had the reservation, it seemed a shame to waste it."

We were silent for a moment.

"I'm sorry I missed our dinner."

It was Bryan's turn to clear his throat. "We were both upset to see you and Fields there. How did that happen?"

"Jason surprised me with it. When we were done at the construction site, he invited me to dinner. I had no idea we'd be going to the Black Carriage. Bryan, don't read anything into it. I enjoy Jason's company. He's bright and different and fun to be with. I count on him as a friend, but he's not you."

He lifted his glass. "Thanks," he said before he tilted it back and drained it.

My next words came slowly. "At least that explains what Deb said to me before she died."

"She spoke to you?"

"She knew she was dying." My cheeks grew warm. "She said, 'I guess you get your second Bryan after all.'"

He rubbed his hand over mine, then stood abruptly. "Come on, I want to show you the garden."

We went down the sun-baked steps and across the open grass past the swings and playhouse to the arched trellis that opened the path through the garden. Budding azalea shrubs and low-growing rosebushes green with new leaves lined the path followed by swords of irises. Then came beds for annuals. An herb garden preceded berry canes, the herbs springing up to soften the rocky surroundings of an ornamental pool. Small fruit trees separated the berries from the vegetable garden, and then we came back through to more flowers and another reflecting pool. The swallows pursued us, dive-bombing us whenever we approached their nests. Bryan dropped my hand and pointed to where the path split and curved.

"Down there is a small greenhouse. I've got orchids in there, the only flower Deb ever was interested in. In the other direction is a grove of slow-growing pines I keep trimmed back. We've got a little picnic area in there. Just some grass and a small table and benches, but it's enclosed by these pines, and it makes it seem like you're far away. Come here."

We stepped off the path into a miniature glade. Scattered amongst the grass I spotted clover, and violet leaves cropped up close to the pine trees' shade. A shovel was propped against the table. Bryan took it up and stepped over by the trees.

He glanced over his shoulder to angle himself the way he wanted and shoved the point of the shovel into the ground. He dug two or three spades full, then grunted.

"Rachel and I are going to plant a tree in memory of her mother. A dogwood, I think. Rachel's going to pick it out."

"I think that's a great idea," I told him as he continued digging. "Something like that can be very comforting."

"Yeah, well," he wiped the sweat away. Then he stood staring into the hole. "But it shouldn't be necessary. Dammit, it shouldn't be necessary!" He threw the shovel aside. "For all the trouble she was, I can't stand that she's dead. It shouldn't have happened. Rachel shouldn't have to face this!" The birds stayed silenced by his outburst.

"Bryan, I have an idea why Deb died."

"What? Why?"

"Remember what the valet said about that night? About what the guy said to him about playing a trick on you?"

"Yeah, he said he wanted to pull a trick on Deb and me and would he help set us up? Set us up so he could kill her!"

"Bryan, that's not right."

"What do you mean, of course it's right, that's what he was doing! It's what he did, for God's sake!" He ran his hands through his hair, then bent to pick up the shovel. We started back up the path toward the deck.

"That's not what I mean. I mean, the guy didn't say he wanted to trick you and Deb. He said, he wanted to trick you and your date. Not 'Deb' or your 'wife', your *date*. Kind of an odd thing for him to say if he had Deb as his target." By now my words were coming out flat and harsh.

"So?"

I really didn't want to say this out loud. I didn't want to say "I think it was meant for me. I'm the reason Deb was killed."

Bryan stopped at the trellis and swung around to face me. "You were supposed to be my date Friday night!"

"Watch the shovel," I warned.

Bryan got a better grip on the handle and let me pass. "You think the car was meant for you, but got Deb by mistake because she was with me. Okay, why?" He followed me across the yard.

"Because of the word 'date'."

"I mean, why would someone be wanting to kill you?"

"It's mostly a feeling, I suppose, but I think there's someone out there who is against me. I know that by itself a feeling doesn't mean anything. But look, I've been trying to prove my father didn't kill anybody. If Pop were responsible for those two bodies on the farm, no one would have any reaction. I think whoever is responsible for them is afraid I'm going to figure it out. They want to stop me."

By now we were back on the deck, standing at the head of the steps. His hands beat a tattoo on the rail, and then he pushed away from it, much like he must have wanted to push away from the whole thing.

"No. No, I don't think so. Mackie. Thank God it wasn't you, but maybe the real target was not Deb or you. I'm the one they referred to by name, the one they knew. Maybe I was the one they were trying to hit. Or what if they were trying to warn me, or hurt me by killing someone that mattered to me? Killing Deb hurts me, but it hurts Rachel more, and that hurts me. Killing you - " I could hear him swallow "would have been a different matter entirely."

I sat silent. It was an aspect I hadn't considered once Betty and I hit on the Mackie-as-target scenario. It made a certain amount of sense. Matheson had said something similar. Bryan had far more enemies than I did. Besides, despite my work on Pop's behalf, I knew my father was responsible for at least one of the murders. Whoever might be after me would know that, too. It would be safer to rely on that and the police's predetermination of my father's guilt than to come after me. Maybe this whole thing was a case of overactive imagination. Maybe it was a nervous reaction to having come so close to violent death.

I tilted my head to look at Bryan. "Do you think it could be that way? Someone trying to get at you?"

Those pale blue eyes bored into mine. "I think it's a lot more likely. I hope so, because then we stand a chance of deflecting the fire away from you. I don't want to think that someone might be after you, Mackie. It would be too much."

I couldn't agree more, I thought, stifling an unreasonable pang of jealousy at being wrong. A much more reasonable feeling of relief that I wouldn't have to watch my back so closely followed it.

"What about you, Bryan? Betty and I thought, well, it sounds foolish now, but we thought maybe I'd need protection. I even talked to

Adderly and Matheson about it. They both wanted to hear what you had to say before they did anything. I guess I don't need protection, but what about you? Are you going to be safe?"

His grin was meant to be reassuring, but it didn't do much for my peace of mind.

"I can look out for myself. It's an occupational hazard."

"Yeah, right. Just because you're a guy you figure you can look out for yourself!"

"Mackie, not because I'm a guy, because it's my job. Come on. Look, I'll talk things over with Adderly and Matheson. Your idea isn't totally off the wall, just not too likely. I'll see what they think. Truth is, if I'm the target, you could still be in danger of some kind of fallout. If that car was aimed at my date, and you were almost my date.... Maybe we need to be extra careful around one another."

"Oh great," I muttered.

"Besides," he continued, "despite the circumstances, it probably would look a bit strange if we were to start dating right away. We need to let people get used to the idea."

I looked over to the deck door, which was opening to let Brooke come out bearing a tray of sandwiches and iced tea and beer. "You mean people like Brooke?"

"No, not Brooke. She'd be delighted if we started seeing each other. Wouldn't you, twin?"

"What, you and Mackie, seeing each other? Not my idea!" She grinned at me. "Jason Fields not enough of a match for you, huh?" She spread out the food for us.

"Brooke, you faker. You've been trying to work this out since I got here. Since before, maybe?" I eyed her thoughtfully.

"Guilty. Can't help it. Deb never was the right one for Bryan. You were."

I spoke before Bryan could. "It might look a little odd if Bryan and I were to start dating the week after she died. Plus what would Rachel think? We're going to need to be low profile about this."

"Speaking of odd, isn't that Monty's car, Bryan?" Brooke pointed to a rather large black limousine that maneuvered around the bend approaching the house.

Moments later Deb's agent, Monty Lyons, strode around the corner. He climbed the steps with his hand outstretched, a somber expression on his face.

"Bryan, I'm devastated. It's terrible. We need to talk. The New York papers and the trade magazines are all over me about Deb's death. I need to have some answers. When's the funeral?"

"Thanks, Monty. Sit down, won't you? Have something to eat. You know Brooke. And this is Dr. Wilder. Look, there won't be a funeral. At least not yet."

Monty cast a sharp look my way, as if in recognition. "What do you mean, no funeral?"

I helped myself to a sandwich and a glass of tea and sat down. The others followed suit.

Bryan explained the policy regarding homicide victims. Monty looked appalled, then thoughtful.

"Have you given much thought to how you are going to handle the publicity?"

"Monty, for God's sake, she's dead! Publicity isn't going to do anything for a dead model - or her agent, either!" Bryan rose from the table. "You don't have a client anymore, Monty, but I've got a nine-year-old little girl in there who's lost her mother, and I'm not about to let you or anyone else turn her life into a circus! Have you got that?"

He rapped the table once with his knuckles and turned away, chest heaving.

The dapper little agent sat with his head bowed. Neither Brooke nor I dared speak.

"Bryan, I've known you now - eight years, no? Have I ever steered Deb - or you - wrong? You look at publicity as an invasion, a sacrilege. For me, it's business. It's because of Rachel that I came. I couldn't agree with you more. Publicity now does nothing for me, but publicity of the wrong kind would be harmful for you - for Rachel - for - " he looked hard at me " - whoever. I want to help you control the damage."

I passed him some tea. "Bryan, he has a point."

Bryan turned toward the table, arms folded across his chest. "All right. What did you have in mind?"

"We need to take the initiative. I can issue a press release about her death. Make it very routine - sad, tragic, but not newsworthy, if you catch my drift. If they think they're getting the story, no one'll be on your trail with questions. After all, a hit and-run is news, but it's no nine-day wonder! It's not like it's murder."

My eyes met Brooke's.

"Technically it is, Monty," Bryan said smoothly. "It's investigated by Homicide. Even if it's accidental, there is the matter of fleeing the scene, and so on."

"Yeah, yeah, but we don't put that kind of spin on it, Bryan. Emphasize 'routine' and 'ordinary' and the press will go away. Isn't that what you want for Rachel? Routine? Normalcy?"

"It's what I've wanted for Rachel all along," said Bryan, sitting down.

"Then what you need to do is give me the particulars, and I'll sift through them for the right information to give the press. The sharks'll be fed, and you'll be sailing in smooth waters." Monty beamed at his cleverness and bit into a sandwich.

Bryan stared dubiously at his plate.

"Speaking of Rachel, how is she?" I asked Brooke.

"She's doing better. I sent her in for a nap. She hasn't slept much since yesterday. She asked for you to be sure and see her before you go."

"I will. Bryan, do we need to -   uh, tell Brooke what we talked about?"

"Yeah," he agreed, "later, though." A swift glance at Monty.

With a genial smile Monty pushed back his chair. "No doubt there are some things I'm better off not hearing. Bryan, walk me out and give me those details I need. The quicker I get a release out the better. Ladies." He wrapped a napkin around his sandwich and took it with him.

As Bryan slid the door into the kitchen shut, I leaned toward Brooke. "He seems good- hearted, but...."

"But strange," she finished. "It's his job. Personally I think dealing with images and selective dissemination of information results in permanent skewedness. He'll do right by Bryan and Rachel, though. In fact, he'll probably be more helpful than we realize. Now, what was it you and Bryan talked about?"

I finished explaining our theories to her just as Bryan returned to the table.

"Oh, God!" she groaned. "Just what we've always been afraid of! Should I be looking out, too, Bryan? If someone's after you, they probably know about me. And it's pretty well-known how close twins are."

"Mmm. You've got a point. Isn't there a realty conference you could go to? Leave town a few days? Maybe take Lloyd and Rachel and Mackenzie with you?" His words were muffled by the bites of sandwich he was cramming into his mouth.

"I thought you weren't worried about me."

He swallowed. "Yes and no. If I'm right and someone is after me, they may already know we're close friends. If you're right and they're actually after you, it wouldn't hurt for you to be out of town anyway."

"I'm not leaving town if there's no one after me! My practice is too new to desert. I'd lose what little ground I've gained."

"I'm just trying to cover all the bases."

"I'm not leaving town."

"You are stubborn, you know?"

Like a wake, I thought, as we went on, alternating between banter and sober discussion. About as much of a wake as Deb Voag was likely to get. Only it wasn't just for Deb. It was for all of us and the security - however relative - we'd lost.

CHAPTER 19

Brian....

I can't think. There he lies, and I can not think. He is so handsome, and he lies so still. I want him to move.

He is supposed to move.

He is supposed to sit up and tease me about the paint on my nose and the plaster in my hair and tell me how he plans to put the footings in for the deck just as soon as his leg heals, but there he lies, and I can't think.

His long legs make ridges under the sheets like mountains waiting to be climbed and traversed, a journey for the two of us to make throughout the years, but there he lies, so still, and so still and so still he'll stay, and I can't think except that I am so, so angry that there he lies and I can't - can't - ever - again - think.

I stayed 'til late afternoon. Brooke and I cleaned up from lunch and made sure there was something for dinner. Rachel came out from her room around five. She curled up in a cozy shapeless sort of chair in the study. I followed her in and sat on the end of a burgundy loveseat. She tried to look at me politely, but I could see it was an effort. Sleep still hung in her eyes the way stray hairs hung in her face.

I cleared my throat. "Tell me what it was like to have a glamorous model for a mother."

A grimace told me she knew it was as much of a a lame opening as I did.

"Mommy wasn't like other mothers. I mean, she wasn't the kind who made cookies for special days at school, she didn't join PTA, and she didn't like to read me stories and stuff...."

She picked at her shirt for a minute.

"She liked to take me shopping. We'd get these really neat clothes - like this shirt. All my friends were jealous because their mothers wouldn't let them buy stuff like that." She shrugged. "I'm not that crazy about clothes, but the shopping was fun. It was when she'd really listen to me."

"Brooklynne said she stayed with you when you had your appendix out."

"Yeah." Rachel grinned. "That was terrific. I can't remember when she ever played so many games with me. She even let me win, and she hated to lose. She brought me a new Barbie doll every day. They're up in my room, in their doll house." Pause. "Mom could be okay sometimes."

A sad summing-up.

"I know she and Daddy didn't get along. He didn't approve of some of the things we did when I stayed with her." She giggled. "There are some things he never found out about. But Mom thought I could be a model, just like her. I don't want to, of course. But she thought I could. She thought I was beautiful."

"You are, you know."

She shrugged. "I might have done it, someday. When Daddy thought it was okay."

She chewed on a thin strand of her beautiful hair. "But, Mommy's dead. Does that seem real? It doesn't seem real to me. I keep thinking she's going to come in and tell me my clothes aren't right, or show me pictures of her modeling. I almost wouldn't mind if she did come yell at me. Dr. Mackie, what was it like when she died?"

Umm ... "What do you mean exactly?"

"What was it like when she died? Please tell me."

"It was sudden, Rachel. But not sudden like a switch turning off. More like a wave washing back into the sea, sliding away."

She sat absorbing my words. "I like that, sliding back into the sea, like sliding back to God. I think she's with God, don't you, Mackie? I mean, she wasn't perfect or anything, but God forgives us for what we do wrong. I think He'd forgive my mother. I did."

I found myself blinking furiously. "I think you're probably right, Rachel. Would you mind - Could you use - How about a hug?"

I told Jean about Rachel at lunch on Monday.

Jean shook her head. "Sounds to me like a very deep child. You'll have to watch her, though. These things creep up on a person."

"I know."

"Is that why you had me stay here the other night? Because of what happened to the little girl's mother?"

"Sort of. I think we made some progress planning too, though, don't you?"

"Ye-es, but I wish you'd told me what happened." Jean switched to her dark tone of voice. "I suppose you'll want me to go out to that place today."

"Is there a problem?"

"Not so long as that trooper stays out of my way."

"Okay then," I said, brushing aside her remark. "I made another list of contractors to call. When Walker Brothers get there, have them start on the floor first. You were right about that. Pull up everything to the sub-floor, the joists if necessary. We'll discuss what to put down after they've made the repairs."

"You'll have plenty of time to make up your mind."

"Jean!"

"That house is in a hell of a state!"

"You're a pessimist."

"I know what I see, is all. What else do you want me to do?"

"Find me some masons -   good ones. We need to rip out that fireplace, but I want to put another one in the front of the living room, between the two front windows. There should be two columns with a wooden mantle between, and I want a mirror put over it."

"That'd have to be an awfully small fireplace," Jean warned.

"Not so small. I'm pretty sure there was one there once upon a time. When I was a kid, I always imagined one there. I used to hang my Christmas stocking from the mantle. We need a heating contractor, too. I got the impression the system hasn't been updated since we converted to oil in '79. I want to check out solar heating systems. The house is set high enough to catch the sun. And I want a greenhouse put in beside the cellar, by the boulder wall. What? What is it?"

She was staring at me, her hands holding her teacup as if she'd drop it.

"Do you know what kind of money you're talking here? A fortune! That old place isn't worth it!"

"To most people, no. Look, I know I won't ever get my money back from the house. It's not about investment, Jean. Or about the place being worth it. I've wanted to fix that place up right since I was a kid. My parents were never able to do it. In the good years, they couldn't agree on what to do, even if they could have afforded to do it. I've had ideas about that land since I was old enough to follow my father around with a hand drill and a hammer. Things that should've been done years before we even had the place. And there are things that need to be undone now. I've got more than enough money to spend however I want to, and this is how I want to. This house doesn't need fixing up, just maintenance, thanks to the care you've given it. All I need to do is add furniture. The farm is what needs attention."

"Seems to me people here are giving it plenty of attention right now."

I threw up my hands. "Just do what I said, all right? I'll worry about what is and isn't affordable."

She sniffed. "No need to go off like that. I'll do whatever you say. I'll order a gold-plated bathtub if you want. Do it up right!"

"I'll come out there after work and see how things are. If you have to leave before I get there, don't worry about it. I'll see you tomorrow."

I charged across to the office. The waiting room was deserted when I walked in. Another slow start. That didn't bode well at all. Andrea answered my call from the kitchen in the back. She was lingering over her dessert, a romance novel (the only kind of book she could put down and pick up later without feeling like she had to go back and retrace the thread of plot she had lost) accompanied by a square box of chocolates. She brushed aside her hair - today worn down and straight - to pop a chocolate in her mouth.

"Only way to read this stuff," she said. "I'm almost through."

"Take your time. Nobody's here. Any calls?" I crossed to the end of the room and opened the "MEDICAL" refrigerator.

"Only the hospital about some fundraiser. I told them I'd try and catch you." She smiled impishly.

I grinned back. "Did you get those specimens sent off to the lab?"

"Yep. Picked up about eleven o'clock. Messenger service is raising their rates, Doc. We ought to see if we can't find another one. Missy Schoonbeck says her brother is starting up a delivery service. I think he'd be pretty reliable, if she's any example."

I nodded. "We can give him a try. Anything else?"

"My sister's having a baby. And her boyfriend is actually sticking around for the event!"

"That's something. Do you like him?"

"He's okay. He's always been pretty good to her, actually. Me, I want to find me the marrying kind. Start having kids, and this living together isn't all it's cracked up to be." She squashed the empty chocolate box and brushed off her uniform. An efficient sweep of her hands and her lunch trash was on its way to the basket, her book in her pocket, and her glass on its way to the sink for washing.

"Stick to your guns, Andrea."

"I intend to," she replied and returned to her desk in time to answer the phone on its first ring. "Dr. Wilder's office. Yes, she's here. Yes, sir, right away."

She covered the mouthpiece with one hand and hissed at me, "It's that Trooper - Matheson! The one out at your place."

I nodded and went to my desk to take the call.

"Yes, Officer Matheson. What can I do for you?"

"Dr. Wilder. I'm glad to hear you sounding so much better today. I've just finished talking with Adderly and Jamison."

"And?"

"And we just don't feel there's enough weight to your theory to warrant police protection."

"Aha."

"Jamison told me you and he discussed your theory, and that he proposed another one."

"Yes. He said it was more likely the person wanted to get at him by hurting someone he cared about, and that's why the wording was so non-specific."

"You have to admit, his theory has a greater probability than yours."

Did he have to sound so damned officious? "Yes," I said slowly. Wasn't I satisfied with that? Was I annoyed I wasn't important enough to draw a killer's fire?

"You don't sound convinced, Dr. Wilder."

"Are you? I mean, the way Bryan explained it, it made sense. But so does my theory, if you accept the premise that there is someone else behind these murders."

"A mighty big 'if', Doctor. One my superiors are not inclined to take. They're making us drop the investigation."

"Are you serious?"

" 'Fraid so. The file will say that it is believed Wylvern Russell was responsible for the demise of two unidentified males circa 1988, but that there is not sufficient evidence to prove or disprove. Technically it will remain an open case, but they'll never do anything with it." His voice was kind. "It's probably the best you can do. I know it leaves your father's name under a cloud, but people forget."

It was what I wanted, wasn't it? The pressure off. The matter dropped. So what if they were blaming Pop for both murders? It was only one more than what I was convinced he did. It would go down on the record as speculation, theory, no proof. If the investigation were kept up, I'd be compelled to tell what I'd discovered. They'd know Pop was involved, and they'd lay the blame for both murders on him anyway.

He hadn't killed Jake. He'd buried him with love and honor. It would be wrong to provide the police with evidence that would make them put it all on him. I had to work it out on my own. I had to find the truth of what really happened. Then I'd ask to reopen the case. Let them close it for now. That should satisfy whoever was out there that I was no threat.

That was when I realized I didn't buy into Bryan's theory.

"Dr. Wilder? Are you there?"

"What? Oh, yes. Does this mean you're done with the farm?" I picked at the edge of my desk blotter.

"Yes. I'll get someone out there this afternoon to clear out our equipment and tape. You can do what you want with it." His voice had turned cheerful, probably relieved to unload his burden after all.

"Thanks for your help."

I hung up the phone and sat staring at the bookcases. Andrea tiptoed in.

"Dr. Wilder? I've seen that trooper around - Matheson? Do you know if - is he married?" She rushed on. "He's awfully good-looking, and his voice is absolutely sexy, and, I mean, someone who's a cop, a State Trooper, he's got to have a good character and all, doesn't he?"

I laughed. "I don't think he is married, but I'm not sure."

"Could you find out?"

"Probably not. Well, maybe. The investigation is being dropped. I don't know if I'll have the chance to see Matheson again, much less find out if he's married."

"Shoot, then you probably can't introduce us, either."

"I don't think so, but don't worry. Someone else will come along who's got just as much character."

The day had grown warm by the time I reached the farm. It was deserted. Jean had left. No police cars, no Matheson hanging about. Except for the mounds of earth around the barn and the back foundation laid bare and a few remnants of yellow police tape, there were no signs of the investigation. A breeze had come up, stirring the tips of the cedar trees, bending the overgrown grass in a gentle wave.

I stood by my car and turned in a circle. The ridge the house was on lay between the fields of Christmas trees we'd planted thirty years before. Where the creek circumnavigated the property it was lined with birch and sumac and alder and scrub. Hills rose up beyond the creek, forming the bowl the ridge bisected, like a toddler's sectioned eating bowl. To this horizon I lifted my eyes, the same horizon I'd looked to as a child, fearful of the lightning of summer storms, awed by crystalline winter snows, bedazzled by autumn foliage. It welcomed me home. I felt a deep flutter of pleasure.

Inside the house lay a minefield of disaster. Kitchen furniture stacked in the living room. Sections of kitchen floor pulled up, exposing the floor joists. Islands of sub-floor were left behind to provide platforms on which to cross the rooms and view the progress. Shafts of damp cool air rose from the basement, despite what the laws of physics might say. Cautiously I crossed joists and platforms to the untouched floor of the front hallway. At least the workmen had cleaned up behind themselves, even to vacuuming up the dust. Of course, that was probably Jean's doing.

I crossed to the front door with its flanks of four-by-nine inch windowpanes that ran floor to ceiling. Same old door; new hardware, though. Jean was fast. Or else the workmen were tired of going in the back door. I propped it open to let out some of the dank cellar air and headed upstairs.

Boxes awaited removal in the upstairs hall. They were full of trash and papers and the general detritus left by people moving out in a hurry. Jean must have cleaned up the mess she'd reported to me. Every room was broom-clean, ready to be renovated.

Somehow we expect time to both move forward and stand still. So much had happened in my life; it seemed that everything here would have changed. That was logic. Yet, my memories would only let me see the house in one particular light. Differences jarred, irritated.

Now, however, it was not a difference that startled me, but something that had remained the same.

My old bedroom. The closet still an open plasterboard enclosure unpainted on the inside. Pencil-marks, made during construction, made me catch my breath. Pop made those marks.

On the corner wall, where new wallpaper had been put up, silhouettes of horses were outlined in dark ink. I crossed the room and ran my hand over the paper. Embossed figures threatened to burst through the paper and canter out into the room. Whoever had redone this wall, either by design or laziness, had left up the Contac® paper images I'd traced from horse magazines when I was eight. Someone else, another horse fan, had carefully traced the outlines, bringing the horses back.

I leaned on the windowsill, steadying myself against waves of memory that wanted nothing less than to overwhelm me. Traced with my fingertips the image of a child's profile I'd once carved on the sill. The image of a child a young girl dreamed would be hers one day to love and raise.

Horses, children, dreams. Tears started down my cheeks, dropping onto my shirt. I slid to the floor, putting my hands over my face. An emptiness I didn't recognize twisted me like a rag. Sorrow at everything lost, past and future. Pain at lives taken, or thrown away, or never begun. And infinite regret. I cried and cried and cried.

CHAPTER 20

It's berry-picking time, and I rush to call my friend Dianne. She has the cutest older brother! But that's not really why I call her. She's my best friend. She has been since kindergarten.

She rides her bike up to my house. We take some coffee cans and head down the hill, through tall weedstalks to the hill we call Strawberry Hill. There, my father insists, are the biggest, juiciest strawberries in three counties.

Strawberry plants carpet the hill, and the berries are indeed as big as my father's thumb. For a while we pick enthusiastically, talking about boys, what the other girls are wearing, how hot the sun is.

We talk only a little about the argument Dianne had with her mother and how her mother slapped her before she left for my house.

Dianne and I tell each other everything.

I sneak a look at her, her hair held back with a rubber band, her short T-shirt revealing tanned skin and a flat navel, her short shorts faded but hugging her rounding hips, the dark mark still on her face where the slap had landed. I vow to never, ever hit my children in the face.

I feel bad for Dianne.

I know she and her family don't think much of my father. Like most people who know him, they think he drinks too much.

But, I think fiercely, Pop has never hit me.

I don't think he ever would.

I wiped my eyes. My horses would have to come down. I was touched they'd been here to welcome me home. I sniffled. I needed to come up with some idea of what I wanted on this floor. No idea was forthcoming.

What was coming was a car - engine roaring, wheels tearing up the road. I scrambled to my feet and reached the window in the front bedroom in time to see a black Jeep sweep into the driveway, scattering gravel, barely stopping short of my car's back bumper.

"Who - ?"

'Who' was a stunning woman with short dark hair and tan skin. She wore a white shirt, deep blue Levis, and polished Western boots. Heavy gold jewelry encircled her neck and adorned her ears. She held a broad-brimmed hat decorated with a designer scarf in her hands. Her expression bordered on disgust. I went downstairs wondering why she'd bothered to come.

She'd worn the same look the last time I'd seen her. She finished her hostile survey of my blue Subaru and the yard. Now she turned towards me, open distaste curling her lip.

"Dianne. What can I do for you?"

Her eyes narrowed. "Depends. How soon can you leave town?"

"Not likely to happen."

"We don't need someone like you in Kings Hill!"

Really, this refrain was getting old.

"A doctor. You think that finally makes you too good for the rest of us? You weren't back then, and you aren't now! Your old man was a drunk! Always causing trouble. We don't need a murderer's daughter for our doctor!"

She marched up to me, her tan face sharp, shrew-like. "Why don't you take a hint and leave!"

"What my father did or didn't do has nothing to do with what kind of doctor I am! And I never thought I was better than you!"

"Yeah. Right." She stomped over and kicked at my car's tire. Volatile as ever. "Why did you come back, Mackenzie? No one wants you."

"Some people do," I said evenly.

She snorted, pacing in circles. "Why here? You could have set up shop anyplace in the country. Why did you have to come back here and stir up trouble?"

"Trouble was already stirred up when I got here, Dianne. I didn't have anything to do with it."

"It was your father who killed those men and put them there! I'd say you had plenty to do with it!"

"Dianne! My father was not a murderer. I don't know where those bodies came from!"

"But you aim to find out," she interrupted, sarcasm all over her words and her face.

"Yes, I do."

"So you won't leave."

"No. I came back to Kings Hill for a lot of reasons. I missed it, for one thing. Believe it or not. And yeah, I guess I wanted to show off what I'd made of myself. But you want to know why I really came back? To fix everything. So much was wrong when I was a kid. So much was just wrong! I wanted to make things right. I couldn't do anything about the past, but I could fix the house, and I could show everyone I was *not like my father*." I paused, then went on more slowly. "But nothing's quite like I imagined it would be. Things aren't the same here now. I don't think they were then either."

"Huh?"

"I mean, I'm learning things. Not everything was what it seemed."

"Oh." She stood with her body still, absorbing what I'd said. Her hands busied themselves sliding her hat round and round, twisting its scarf. Her next words struggled to get past her lips.

"Remember that camping trip you took with us in junior high? You kept hanging around me and my boyfriends and carrying on about how great you thought Mike was."

"Yeah, I had a crush on Mike," I said warily. "You - you were the most boy-crazy thirteen-year-old I'd ever seen! Your mother made me keep hanging around you. To keep you out of trouble. Those guys were eighteen and falling all over you!"

"Whatever. Then you went and got so homesick, you made us bring you home!"

"I did not make your folks bring me home. I wanted to ride back with Mike when he left early. They were the ones who decided to cut things short and bring me back!"

"They had to. You were driving everyone crazy - moping around and crying at night."

It was the same old fight; the one that had broken up our friendship. Maybe this time we'd finish it. Maybe she needed to know how much her family had hurt me.

"They could have let Mike take me. But no! Your family was so sure I'd tell some stupid lie that he'd - what was it you told me? Oh - 'taken me across state lines for immoral purposes'! God! I'd've never said anything like that. I thought your family knew I didn't make up lies. What kind of people were your parents anyway?"

I felt a little foolish carrying on, but I couldn't help it. This ancient history was meaningless compared to what was going on now. Yet it was all tied up in it, too.

Dianne was looking at the sky, tapping her foot. "Yeah, well." She turned her head. "Leave town, why don't you?"

"I'm not going anywhere."

She stared over my head. "That wasn't really it, you know. I mean, that's what I thought they meant."

"Huh?"

She sighed. "Look, I misunderstood, okay? My parents took us home early so Mike wouldn't get bent out of shape at their not letting you ride with him. He was too old for you. He was nineteen!"

"I told you it was a crush. I knew it even then. I never expected him to take me seriously. I knew he had a girlfriend waiting back in Kings Hill. I just wanted to go home, and since he was going back, I figured it made sense to have him take me. I was excited at the idea of spending five hours in the car with him, but that was just kid stuff!"

"I know. I knew you wouldn't tell a lie about somebody. I don't think either of us would've known what to say to tell that kind of lie."

"So, what was the deal? Why didn't your parents want me to ride back with Mike?"

"Like I said, I misunderstood. I was so glad to have Mike back. He'd been gone for two years. I'd missed him so much. I didn't want anyone making trouble for him. How was I to know they weren't talking about lies?"

"What?"

Dianne sighed again. "They weren't afraid you'd lie that he'd done something to you. They were afraid he would do something."

"What? Why? Mike wasn't interested in me!"

"That wasn't it, Mackenzie. God, you are still so naive, how do you do it? Mike might have done something on the way home, molested you, raped you - happy I said it? That's what my parents were afraid of."

"Why would they think he'd - ?" I stared at her, my mouth gone dry. "He'd done it before?"

She nodded. "That's what those two years were about. Some girl in Albany."

"Oh, God. You thought your parents were saying I'd tell that kind of story. So you got mad, and told me."

"I didn't know they were afraid it would really happen. Then they made us go home anyway. I thought you spoiled everything."

"When did you find out you were wrong about what your parents meant?" I asked. She acted like it was all still fresh.

She twisted the end of the scarf round her finger. "A few years ago. Mike got caught again. Only this time, it was worse. There - were pictures - several girls - some from almost ten years back. A couple of them had disappeared completely." She looked at me hastily. "They never proved he had anything to do with them disappearing, but they had enough other stuff on him. They put him in jail. Ten years."

"Oh, Dianne." I raised my hand, reaching out to her.

She pulled back. The gulf was too great, too old. "I don't want you here. You remind me of all of it. You can say it doesn't matter what your father did, but it does! Just like it matters what Mike did! Get out of here, Mackenzie! We don't need you here in Kings Hill! We don't want you here!" There were tears in her voice.

"Dianne, my father didn't murder those men! Somebody else - "

"Sure. Sure! Mackenzie Russell couldn't be related to anyone who'd do something horrible! Only other people could! Hah!" She turned and stomped off to her Jeep. Threw me a dirty, angry look and backed her Jeep out, wheels spinning. Took off with one hand on the steering wheel, scrubbing tears away with the other.

Suddenly the air was still. Twilight was coming. Twilight was coming to too many things in this town. Mike - ! And I'd wanted to - I shivered. I looked out across the road. Where deer once picked their way through waist-high goldenrod and Queen Anne's lace to drink at the meandering creek, now there was solid forest of pine. Our Christmas trees grown up.

Why had I come back? What did any of it matter? If Pop had killed someone, was I really so surprised? He'd been a renegade. He'd broken laws. If he got angry enough, wouldn't he have killed someone? What did it matter if it was proven or not? What did it matter if it was one man or two? It didn't affect me today, did it? Mom and I had left him. She worked hard to make it up to me. I'd become enough of a lady to satisfy her. I'd made good use of my education. She'd been proud of me. Wasn't backing Pop letting her down?

I paced the gravel driveway. I could face up to what Pop had been. I'd had it thrust in front of me for so long, I was used to it. This new stuff was still in character. Even burying Jake. Pop was a law unto himself, but loyalty figured heavily in his philosophy. He'd held it against Mom and me that we'd left him. Jake never had, and Pop had honored that faithfulness with his own. With all his flaws, for all the rotten things he'd done, I had to admire the good things about my father. That was where it all lay.

I'd come back because I wanted to. All the stuff about Brooke talking me into it was smoke. I'd wanted to come back, just as I'd told Dianne, to make things right. Long ago, in a childhood pledge that my adult self had never really expected to keep, I'd vowed to come back and fix everything up the way I'd dreamt. How many of us ever get to keep such vows?

I owed it to the land to keep my promise. I owed it to my father to see he carried only the burden of wrongs he'd actually committed. The man had done little enough that deserved recognition. What there was should not be obscured by false assumptions of guilt.

Falsehood, no. Truth, yes. Whatever Pop had done, he must be accountable for. For what he had not done, he should not be judged guilty. So, it mattered. Truth mattered. It mattered to me as it had mattered to my mother. Defending Pop wasn't letting her down. Not defending him would only let us all down.

The mental gyrations were stabilizing. I felt calm despite the bizarre confrontation with Dianne. It was time to go. I made a couple of notes for Jean, loaded some boxes of trash into the wagon and left.

I turned right out of the driveway for a change, taking Wexford Road to its other end. It wound over the hills with dips and turns, barely two lanes wide, re-paved every few years to keep the dust down. I'd gone maybe a mile when I heard an engine behind me.

A quick glance in the mirror showed the grille-work of a black Jeep close on my bumper. Dianne? I sped up a little.

She moved up closer. The interior of the Jeep was dark, but I thought I saw a flash of pink. I had to look quickly because of the twisting road. We were surrounded by forestland belonging to my neighbors. Outcroppings of rock dotted the shoulder, bedrock close below the surface.

I was going as fast as I dared. Forty on this road was stretching things, even with my Subaru's maneuverability. The Jeep swung out for a brief moment, then back in behind me. She wanted to pass? On this road?

"Dianne, are you nuts?"

She pulled out again, then swerved at my rear fender. I pulled to the right, kicking up twigs and leaves and dirt. The wheel jerked out of my hands. I grabbed it again, played it carefully, pulling back on the road. I had to keep going!

The Jeep slowed, dropping back. It took a run at me, bashing against my rear bumper. My head snapped back and then forward. That wasn't Dianne back there. It couldn't be! I pressed hard on the accelerator. There was a straight stretch up ahead.

Crash!

Straight except for the enormous drop that about flattened the Subaru's undercarriage when it landed. Boxes of trash bounced and slid. I grit my teeth and spared a look in the mirror in time to see the Jeep plunge and bounce and keep on coming.

"Who *is* this?"

I thought ahead, trying to recall the layout of the road. The trees closed in up here, I thought. With so many turns, the Jeep's driver couldn't see far enough ahead to formulate a good game plan. He wouldn't have time to get alongside to force me off. He could only make me drive too fast for the road and kill myself. If I let him.

I had to think faster than I was driving. We had to be near the end of the road. There were houses clustered there, some magnificent ones, a ways from the road. There was an open pond. I didn't know how deep, but I didn't want to end up in it anyway. What came before?

Another slam from behind, throwing me against the wheel. The car rocked as it tried to take over. I fought the wheel. My cheekbone seemed to vibrate. Tears were coming with the pain. I'll need a doctor for myself, I thought. Maybe.

I regained control and a memory at the same time. That next curve. It had been the focus of a tale used to train our Driver's Ed class. The story about prom night, and four kids in a convertible, the drinker at the wheel, a large rock and two kids who returned to school two weeks later. Cliché though it seemed, it was something that had really happened on Wexford Road.

If the Jeep knew about this curve, it would be where he made his next move. I didn't think he'd ever sat in on one of Kings Hill's Driver's Ed classes, though.

I concentrated. The trick, my mother had said, was to enter the curve taking your foot off the accelerator. I eased it back. At the deepest point of the curve, step on it. I practically stood on the pedal.

Another crash. Only not me. This sounded far worse than before. I braked swiftly. Behind me the Jeep lay butted against the rock, smoke and steam rising from it, its silver grille and sleek black fenders crumpled like paper. I didn't wait to see more.

I pulled away, getting out of there at a slightly safer speed. I headed for the Trooper Station on the state highway, about a mile from where Wexford Road ended.

A handful of trooper cars were in the lot. I pulled straight up to the door. I guess the look on my face made the desk officer think better of reprimanding me for leaving my car there.

"I - need help. Someone - force me off - the road. I - he crashed."
I leaned on the counter top. My breath came in gasps. Someplace far away
in my head I diagnosed shock.

"Where?"

"W - Wexford Road. By the big rock - you know, the turn - "

She was nodding. She grabbed the radio's mike, then changed her
mind and called over her shoulder.

"Hornung, Davis. Get over to Wexford Road, you know where.
Lady here - "

"Mackenzie Wilder. Dr. Wilder," I interrupted.

"Dr. Wilder here says she was being forced over when the car - ,"

"A black Jeep," I interrupted again.

" - when a black Jeep crashed into the rock on that curve. I'll call
out an ambulance to follow."

The officer named Hornung said, "Better make it the coroner."

I hiccuped. "I'll ride back with you. I'm a doctor."

"You don't have to do that, ma'am. You look like you've been
through enough. Officer Young here needs a statement. You're hurt," he
insisted as he saw me waving his words aside.

"She'll get her statement later. You need a doctor with you. I'll be all
right." I hiccuped again.

"Let's go," said Davis.

The presence of two six-foot New York State Troopers did wonders
for me. I was mostly frightened, shook up, and bruised. Now an unfeeling
curiosity took over. In the short time since the Jeep crashed, part of me
realized that the driver had not been at all familiar with Wexford Road,
or things would never have turned out the way they did. That led me
straight back to someone being hired to hurt - or kill me.

If the person in the Jeep were still alive, we should be able to get a
line on his employer. Those words were creepy. 'If he were still alive.'

Even the trooper saw the need for taking care at this end of Wexford. He dropped his speed to thirty-five as we approached the backside of the curve.

"It's right up here."

"Yes, ma'am. We know." He pulled up and swung across the road, blocking it.

Davis climbed out with a couple flares and a light.

I stared at the accident site from my seat in the back.

Hornung glanced over the seat at me. "Maybe you better wait here, ma'am."

I ignored him and followed him over to where tracks dug into the forest floor at the edge of the road. Leaves and rock were thrown everywhere. Fresh scars were etched into the rock, evidence of one more battle fought. Of the Jeep itself and its driver, there were no sign.

CHAPTER 21

Grandma Bessie is dead.

At least, that's what Pop said when he explained to me why Mom was so upset.

I'm nine. Old enough, you would think, to understand at least that death means Heaven and never coming back. But that isn't for Grandma Bessie.

Grandma Bessie is about baked potatoes topped with broccoli and cheese and sour cream and black olives with iced tea on the side. She is about a to-the-wall game of Pokeno for a-penny-a-pot. She is about lobster at the shore with French fries, cole slaw, and blueberry pie for dessert. Oh, and don't forget the iced tea. She is about crossword puzzles and murder mysteries and "Oh Gawd, did you see the dress she had on at church today?"

Grandma Bessie is one live wire who will never be extinguished, and I stubbornly resist any idea otherwise.

And Mom lets me.

"Let her be, Wylvern," Mom says. "Maybe as long as we let Mackie think that way, maybe Bessie will still be alive."

I hear the catch in her voice and know her eyes are bright with tears.

Pop puts his arms around Mom.

"Yeah, alive and kickin'," he says, and winks at me.

L ucky for me the road and my car told a convincing story. That and having Matheson vouch for me. Still, no one had any idea what happened to my pursuer or who he might have been.

Scratch that last one. Some of us were sure of his occupation if not his identity. A professional hit man. Even Bryan was convinced. He scarcely left my side once I called him from the station office. He came out and sat with me while they questioned me about the incident. He took me home in his car, calling Jean to get Arthur to take mine to the shop next morning. Brooklynne met us at the Kings Hill house.

I threw my purse and medical bag on the kitchen table and zeroed in on my favorite chair in the gallery. Flopping down, I shut out the world with both hands over my eyes.

"Here, Mackenzie." Brooke brought me some tea. "Hey, Bryan, who do we call to doctor our doc?"

"I'll be okay, Brooke," I said, sipping at the tea.

Brooklynne looked at Bryan pointedly as he ambled into the room, trying to seem casual, lightening the expression on his face with a smile. He sat down in the chair across from mine and leaned forward, reaching to cup his hands around mine.

"The paramedics checked her out," he reassured her. Then he gazed intently into my eyes. "How are you doing?"

"I don't know. Lousy, I guess. My neck and arms hurt. My shoulders are tight. You know, having someone try to kill me is not high on my list of fun things to do. It's creepy, and I'm scared. And why do I keep feeling defensive, as if *I'm* the one who's guilty? Does that make any sense?" I drew a long shaky breath and drank more tea.

"It's just a reaction to someone coming after you."

"But why guilty? He's the bad guy! I didn't hurt anybody. All I tried to do was - wait a minute! You agree it's me he's after?"

"I think someone is definitely after you. I'm not sure why. It might be a way to get at me, but that's not really important. Someone is after you, and I have no intention of letting them get any closer than they did today."

I sighed. "Thank you. How can we stop him? Do you think Matheson'll believe me now? Will he help protect me?"

"I don't know. He believes you about what happened today, but I don't know if he'll agree with our interpretation. Especially now that he's closed the case."

"Shouldn't that make whoever this is stop? I mean, if the case is closed, why am I a threat?"

"Whoever is after you may not know it's closed. Or he may not think he can count on it. Maybe it's not related to this case at all."

"Of course it's related to her father's case, Bryan. Can't you convince Matheson to get Mackenzie the protection she needs?" Brooke asked.

"I'll protect Mackie," Bryan said.

She raised her eyebrows at us.

"Bryan, you can't protect me constantly. Especially right now. Rachel needs you. This is no time to desert her."

"Besides, Bryan, Rachel may need protection, too," added Brooke.

I was feeling warmer, and angrier. Wordless indignation, rage that someone was doing this, had done it before. I had to put a stop to it.

"Brooke, would Lloyd come over tonight? I'd like to talk with him about this. Maybe work out a few things."

"What about Rachel? She's with Lloyd right now."

"Bring her along. It may be safer that way anyhow. Maybe Jean could come back, too. She could watch out for Rachel and find out what's going on all at once."

"Jean won't mind?" Bryan asked.

"She'd probably be mad if I left her out." I rubbed my hands over my face.

"Hurt?" Bryan asked. He put his arms around me briefly.

"Yeah, some. I feel really tired. That takes a lot out of a person." *And I'm trying to screw up my courage to tell you something you won't like.*

"They're on their way," Brooke announced, returning from the telephone.

"Good. Let me call Jean, then I need to call Jason."

"What do you need him for?" demanded Bryan.

I wasn't about to admit I wanted Jason there for moral support. I needed to convince Bryan that the person after me was indeed connected to Pop's case. I was about to tell him and Brooke - and Lloyd - exactly why I must still be a threat to my unknown assailant.

"He was there when Deb died," I reminded them. "He helped me - and you, for that matter. Besides, the more people in on this the better, don't you think? Jason is an idea man - one with lots of power to back them up. And he's my friend," I finished firmly.

"Oh, well, if he's your friend, by all means...." Bryan looked disgusted. "Can I call some of my friends, too?" he asked of Brooke, who hit his shoulder.

I hid a smile as I turned around. Amazing what taking action could do for the spirit!

Jean would be right there. Jason, too. His concern over what had happened was kind, too generous to be rewarded with news of my new relationship with Bryan. That part of things was going to be sticky.

I came back smiling brightly at Bryan. "They'll be right over. Will you two help me get some food together?"

"You sure you feel up to it?" Brooke fretted.

"I'll be all right. I'm ready to fight back. Food-wise, what we don't put on the table, I'm sure Jean will. Maybe she's got some of that chocolate cake around here someplace."

A half-hour later, there was a chocolate cake on the table - although it came in with Jean, having been on its way out of the oven when I called. Platters of meat and rolls and cheese were there too, accompanied by coffee, tea and lemonade, potato chips, pickles, leftover macaroni salad, and some fruit we'd scrounged together. Arthur had sent over a humongous salami via Jean.

"If this army was traveling on its stomach, we'd be there by now," observed Lloyd.

"What army, Uncle Lloyd?"

"Just an expression, child. I'll take that as a compliment, Mr. Kerns. Dig in, everyone. Rachel, do you want some salad with that?" Jean had already taken up post as guardian over Rachel's welfare.

We built sandwiches and took seats around the table.

Rachel wiggled into her seat. "This is good, Mrs. Hesford. Daddy, why are we here? Did you find out who killed Mom?"

We all looked at one another. Bryan answered slowly, "No, Rachel. This isn't about that."

I wonder. "Rachel, I asked everybody to come over because we need to do some planning." I had to shift my hand as I picked up my tea. My fingers were stiff.

"Mackie, what's wrong with your hand? Are you okay?"

"Rachel, honey - "

"It's okay, Brooke. Rachel, I was in an accident today. A car accident." I paused at the frightened look on her face. "Yes, another one. Rachel, we think maybe there could be a connection between the two accidents, and we need to talk about it."

She stared at her plate.

"But, you know what? You don't have to listen to us. I'm going to have Jean show you upstairs to look at some books we found here. Some of them will be too young for you, but you might get a kick out of them. They were written for children before I was even born. There's some from when I was growing up, too. Is that all right with you?" I could still feel her anxiety. I didn't want to scare her more, but I couldn't lie about things either.

"Sure," she said weakly. "I don't mind being gotten rid of."

"Thanks. You can take your cake up with you." I caught Jean's disapproving frown. "We can start quicker."

As they got up to leave, Bryan pulled Rachel over to him and gave her a hug. "Sweetie, don't worry. We're all fine, and we're right down here. I'll check on you. Or you can come back down after a bit."

Brooklynne pulled out a long yellow pad and paper. "I used to act as Lloyd's secretary back before I got my realtor's license. I'll take notes as we go. What do you say we start by listing things? Two unknown dead bodies on Mackie's property. No one knows who killed them, but most people believe it was Mackie's father. She's trying to prove that's impossible. Two unexplained car accidents, one killing Bryan's ex-wife, the second attempting to run Mackenzie off the road. What else?"

Jean came back right then. "One tough time gettin' her business set up, that's what else."

"What? What are you talking about?"

"You know, that letter she got and the newspaper ad, and that trash they dumped on the porch."

"Yeah, wait... let me get that. Okay, we know about those. But, Mackenzie, overall, haven't things been going okay? People want you here! Don't they?" Brooklynne looked confused.

"I'd have to qualify that," I mumbled through my sandwich. I cleared my mouth and explained the other part of my afternoon - Dianne Franklyn's revelations about her brother Mike.

Lloyd gave a low whistle when I finished, Brooke stared at the table, and Bryan nodded. Jason looked on.

"I helped put Mike away last time," said Bryan. "Dianne's not too fond of me, either."

"Did you know that went on when we were kids?" I asked him. "I didn't have any idea!"

"There were rumors, but nobody was really sure. You didn't exactly spread it around, even if you were a guy. I heard our folks talking one night - "

"I knew," said Brooke. She doodled on the edge of her pad, a very black, very jagged doodle that looked like a bomb exploding.

"Bryan," she said softly. "Remember that summer after fourth grade? That exchange kind of thing Mom did with a friend of hers in Saratoga? I went and stayed with them a week, and their daughter came and stayed with us the week after?"

"No, not really."

"You remember. You were mad at me afterward because I wasn't able to do stuff with you, even though it wasn't my fault. You put a 'NO GIRLS ALLOWED' sign on our clubhouse."

"Oh, yeah. That." He laughed.

"Well, when I met Mom's friend, her daughter, Erica, asked me if I knew Mike Franklyn. I told her no, but his sister was in my class. Erica was a year older than us, going into sixth grade. Mike was seventeen. Erica knew Mike. She was the girl he got sent away over. She told me what happened, and I told Mom. I didn't know what else to do. I barely understood what it was all about. Bryan, he did all those things they accused him of, every one of them. Erica stayed with us during the trial, then her mom moved her away. That's why you heard our folks talking, Bryan, because they were so closely involved."

Now we all stared at Brooke. Lloyd took her hand.

"Why didn't you ever tell me about it?" Bryan exclaimed. "We talked about everything!"

"Mom made me promise not to talk about it while it was going on or while Erica was with us. The whole thing scared me, and you were still mad at me, so I kept quiet. Eventually I think I forgot about it."

"What about when Mike came back?" I asked. "I told you I had a crush on him. You never said anything to me about him."

"I don't know why I didn't say anything, Mackie. Unless I didn't realize the danger. By then, with the crowd I was hanging around with, who knows? Maybe I thought it was exciting."

If I hadn't known so clearly what Brooklynne had gone through, I might not have understood. I would have been angry. But how angry do you get with a best friend over something that's deep in the past and no longer important?

"Well, okay," I went on briskly. "So Dianne Franklyn doesn't want me around stirring up bad memories. And she's got a following. But would they go so far as to put out a contract on me? That would be expensive! That is what we're talking about, right?"

There was a general sound of agreement.

"Jean, you've been handling this -   this negative campaign business. I know you know who's involved. Would they get that serious? Jean? Yoo-hoo, Jean!"

Jason waved his hand in front of her eyes.

"What? Oh, no. No, they wouldn't get that serious. At least, I don't think so." She frowned.

"Who are they, Jean?"

"It's okay, Bryan. Jean's doing fine with it. I don't really think it's the problem."

Lloyd spoke up. "Okay. We know you think it's someone connected with your father's case, but we still don't know how. Trying to keep the investigation open by insisting your father didn't do it is a normal thing for you to do. Hardly threatening. Police don't believe you anyway. They still think your father is guilty."

"They think he's guilty of pushing hard drugs, too, but they're wrong!" put in Brooke.

"Well, twin, they're probably right."

"No, they're not. Mackie and I proved it, didn't we, Mackie?"

"Uh, well, yeah, we did. At least I think we did."

Brooke and I explained to the others about going through the records and finding no evidence of hard drugs among Pop's teen charges.

Bryan still looked skeptical, but Lloyd nodded thoughtfully. "Write that down, Brooke. And congratulations, honey," he told her warmly.

"This doesn't do much to explain a connection between your stand on your father's innocence and the attempts on your life. If there is another murderer out there, he was in trouble day the bodies were discovered. No one took after the Hicks or the State Troopers. Why pick on you?" He leaned across the table.

Jason stared thoughtfully at the tablecloth.

Lloyd pressed on, "What is there that you know, Mackie, that makes you a danger to this guy? Where's the threat?"

"Lloyd, she doesn't know anything. She can't," said Bryan.

I could feel the blood rush to my face. Jason had transferred his thoughtful gaze to me. Fat lot of help *he* was.

"Bryan, she's got to know something." Lloyd leaned forward. Maybe it's something she doesn't know she knows. Maybe she was here when the murders were done and doesn't remember, or even doesn't realize it. Maybe she knows who one of those bodies is - "

"Impossible!" Bryan was so sure of himself, he didn't even turn to look at me.

Lloyd shrugged. "Mackenzie?"

I looked at Jason. This was why I'd wanted him here. I looked at Brooklynne, whose expression read that she knew that with me anything was possible. She was my ally. She thought we agreed Pop hadn't murdered anyone. I looked at Bryan, waiting for me to deny any knowledge that might be endangering me. I looked at Lloyd, still not looking at me, whose lawyerly instincts had told him I was holding back something important. Sometimes I hate lawyers.

I put my hands on the table and stood up.

"All right. I'll tell you what I know. You probably won't like it."

Rachel came running down the stairs screaming.

CHAPTER 22

Mom laughs at me.

"Okay. Go on. Stand in the corner. Five minutes." Then she chuckles again.

I told on myself for drawing on the woodwork. I had to tell, didn't I? I was bad.

B ryan was at the foot of the stairs by the time she hit the next to last one. He grabbed her by the arms as she flew down and swung her up to his chest. Jean and Brooke hustled over there in a dead heat.

"Shhh, shhh. Rachel, what is it? What is it?" Bryan smoothed the back of her hair.

"Daddy, Daddy! It was awful. There -   there was - " She hiccuped. "There was a great big spider on the floor by the bookshelf. Daddy, it was big and hairy and had all these legs! It was brown with stripes and - Oooh! I hate spiders! Daddy, do I have to go back up there? Can't I stay down here with you? Please!" She hiccuped again.

"Rachel, honey. It's okay." He smiled at us over her head. She'd burrowed back into his shoulder. "She's got a real phobia about spiders. Especially big ones."

"I've got an idea," said Jean. "You come on with me, Rachel. We'll go up and take some of those books, and I'll settle you on the bed in the guestroom. There's a radio in there, and a great big lamp that's guaranteed to keep all the spiders away. You can set yourself up on the bed and be snug as a b - snug as snug can be. All right? You okay now? Come on."

Bryan murmured to her, and she hiccuped again, untwined herself from his body, and returned upstairs with Jean, dragging her feet on each step as if she couldn't quite convince herself to go. Bryan and Brooke returned to the table. Bryan stood his chair back up and shook his head as he sat down.

"Sorry about that. She really can't help herself. Where were we?"

"Mackenzie was about to tell us something we wouldn't like. Right, Mackenzie?" Jason leaned back in his chair, twiddling his coffee spoon.

I glared at him. I couldn't speak yet. Rachel's vulnerability. Bryan's protectiveness. Our great assurances to her that she'd be safe -   from spiders or anything else. What kind of a hypocrite was I?

I cleared my throat.

"There is something I know, Lloyd. A couple of things, actually. The identity of one of the victims. And what killed the other one." I looked at the ceiling as I added the next part. "Actually, I have the murder weapon upstairs."

Brooklynne gasped. Jean, returning from settling Rachel, headed for the coffeepot and began refilling cups. Lloyd nodded and made notes. Bryan started as if he were about to speak, but a movement from Jason caught his eye, and now his glance darted from me to Jason and back.

"When I first read the autopsy report and Betty let me examine the piece of rock she pulled from the skull, I was worried. I recognized that kind of rock, and I was almost sure I knew where it had come from. As I told Betty, it's not native to this area, yet there it was, inside the skull. It could only have gotten there by an outside force." My cheekbone was hurting. I touched it with my fingertips.

"You know, it's ironic. Outside of an archeologist or maybe a paleontologist, I'm probably the only person who would have known that rock of that type was often used by prehistoric man to make rough tools such as hand axes."

I took a deep breath.

"Lloyd, you're my lawyer, right?"

He held out a hand, palm up. I reached into my pocket, pulled out a dollar and slapped it into his hand.

"Now I'm your lawyer."

"How much can I tell everyone before it gets sticky?"

"Hmph. It's already sticky, Mackie. You're sharing information you should have shared with the police. I've got lawyer-client privilege, but if they ask any of the others, they could be made to answer -   although it could be ruled hearsay. Bryan's a cop. He has a duty to turn over any information pertinent to an investigation."

All eyes turned to Bryan who was still gazing speculatively at me.

"You're right, of course, but we're in an odd situation here. The case is being closed. Has been closed, really. I have no jurisdiction, but I'm - involved. If there's something that indicates a present danger to someone - in this room or otherwise - then I have to act on it myself or pass it on to someone who can." He paused. "That's a judgment call. One I can't make until I know everything. *Everything*, got it? No holding back." The words came sternly, and his eye was steady.

My resolve wasn't. "Bryan, what if - "

"Mackenzie, you can't withhold anything. Apart from the fact that you could be charged with hindering an investigation, it's not fair to expect me to make a decision without all the facts, is it?"

"Bryan the cop or Bryan the friend?"

"One and the same, Mackie. It's what I am."

I bit my lip. *Fair enough.* "Okay. Well - I told you about hand axes being made of that kind of stone. I knew of such a hand ax. It was passed on to me some years ago. When I got home, I took a good look at it. The blade was made from the same stone as the chip in the evidence bag."

"You mean, the same kind?" asked Brooke.

"No, the same stone."

"How could you tell if it was carved from the same rock?"

I sighed. "It's not that it was carved from the same rock. The chip is described in detail in the report. Have you seen it, Bryan?"

"The report and the evidence."

"All right. The hand ax I have is missing a chip. Measurements on the ax correspond to those of the one in the evidence bag. And," I winced, "I have documentation that the blade of the ax in my possession was chipped some time in 1988."

Even Jason was startled at that news.

"Who gave you the ax, Mackenzie?" Bryan's voice was low.

"It was my father's. It came to me with some of his things."

Lloyd stared at his notes, silently underlining the last three lines. Brooke clicked her tongue against her teeth. Jean made another round, this time with tea. She patted my shoulder as she passed by. It would have been reassuring if my muscles hadn't started to stiffen up.

"Basically, you are telling us we have a murder weapon clearly traceable to your father." Bryan spoke aloud as he thought. "Well, that would strengthen the case the State has made. It isn't absolute proof, but it doesn't lead anywhere new, either. Therefore, it doesn't put you in any danger."

Jason halted Bryan. "Excuse me. You mean, a stronger case against her father actually lessens the danger for Mackenzie. What if you had indication that her father never let the ax out of his hands, that he was the only one who ever used it?"

"That would increase the case against him. Sure," Bryan agreed.

I was furious. Jason was supposed to be on my side, making things easier! Bryan had another question.

"Mackenzie, what about the other thing you said? The identity of one of the victims? Which one?"

"The first, the one found under the cedar tree." I circled the table once, sipping tea. I set my cup down and rubbed my arms. "You're right, of course. The ax is more damning to my father. That's why I was so unwilling to share it. The case against him keeps building. But see, this is what shatters it. The first body is Jake Terry."

"Who?" went the general cry.

"Jake Terry, my father's best friend, and incidentally, the only other person Pop might have let handle that ax."

"Oh! Black hair, funny-smelling clothes, sure!" Brooklynne was the first to recall him.

"Are you sure about this?" asked Lloyd.

"As sure as I can be without more sophisticated tests. We'd have a hard time doing some of them. Jake didn't leave any kin for DNA convenience."

"So how do you know this is him?" Lloyd pushed.

I ticked items off on my fingers. "The age is right. The wear and tear on the bones is consistent with his lifestyle. The teeth are in horrible shape. There is a bullet-crease above the eye exactly where a stray bullet - all right, of my father's - accidentally hit him one year."

"Thought you said your father didn't miss," murmured Jason.

"Technically he didn't; he thought Jake was a deer, and incidentally, you're not helping!" I snapped.

"That's still not conclusive, Mackie. It might be coincidence."

"Bryan," I groaned. "Do you remember Jake?"

"Yeah, some. I've never seen a missing person's report on him. Even with reviewing the files the way we did."

"No family to do it. Pop would've been the one to report it."

"And he didn't. Why?" His eyes, though sympathetic, were penetrating.

Lloyd explained, "The first thing most people are going to say, Mackie, is that your father didn't report him missing because he knew what had happened to him."

"I agree," I said quickly.

"Well, then...."

"I think my father knew Jake was dead. I think my father buried him."

The room seemed to grow darker as everyone digested that. Bryan leaned in and moved his glass toward Jean so she could refill it with lemonade. "Explain."

"Jake was buried at the base of a cedar tree. His grave was sided by daylilies, and there was actually a large stone at the head of the grave. Now that may not seem like much, but it says that whoever buried the body had regard for him, and the opportunity to do something about it."

"Okay, so your father buried him, if this is Jake."

"That's the other thing. The way I know it's Jake is also the way I know Pop buried him. Betty let me see all the physical evidence. That included the guy's shoes. Inside one of them I found a ring that was my father's. It was a custom-made one-of-a-kind ring given to my father. It couldn't have got inside there without Pop putting it there. And Pop wouldn't have given it to anybody else - except maybe me. By the same token, he wouldn't have killed Jake. He'd have sooner killed himself."

Lloyd glanced over at Bryan. "Maybe your father killed Jake in a fit of anger, or by accident, and gave him the ring and buried him out of remorse. Or fear."

Brooke spoke up, looking worried. "Maybe Jake even stole the ring, Mackie. Or - or maybe he took it for safekeeping. Somebody else killed him, and your father just buried him!"

I spread my hands out. "Look, I admit these are all possibilities, but they're not what happened. I can't explain it, but I know!"

Lloyd shifted uneasily in his chair and jotted something down. Bryan was studying me intently. Then he grunted and stood up. He came over to me, put his hands on my upper arms and squeezed me very, very gently.

"All right, Mackie. I see what you're saying. Given what I know about your family, it fits. What about the hand ax? It was used on the other guy's head. Who else but your father would have handled it?"

"Well, really, almost anyone *could* have - " I began, squirming gently in Bryan's grasp. Secretly I was fighting the urge to throw myself into his arms. "The way Pop kept himself those days, somebody could have taken it for a while, but actually, probably no one except Pop himself - or, like I said, maybe Jake."

"So, okay, he didn't kill Jake," Lloyd directed firmly, "but he might - might have killed the other guy."

I nodded. Bryan slid his arm around me.

"I've been thinking about this," said Jason. "Let's throw another scenario into the lot. What if Jake killed the other man, then afterwards someone shot him - on purpose or by accident, who knows? But Jake, since he hung around the farm so much, would've had the opportunity to bury the other fellow under the ramp. We don't know how close together these killings were. Maybe your father simply came along and buried Jake out of feeling for him."

"Jason's got a point. Willie Russell wouldn't't've wanted to - or had the money to - spend on a cemetery plot. And you know Jake wouldn't have had any insurance," Brooklynne added.

"Thought about his a lot, have you, Fields?" Bryan asked.

Jason glanced at me.

Bryan dropped his arm from around me and walked away, shoving his hands into his pockets.

"GI insurance!" I cried.

"What?" Bryan turned.

"Jake Terry was a veteran. That means he'd have GI insurance to bury him with. Or he could've been put in the Soldiers' Cemetery. That's what it's for."

Lloyd nodded. "Wouldn't your father have known about that?"

"Yes, I suppose so. Plus, he was in the process of selling the farm to Vince Lamberson. He wouldn't have left Jake on what was going to be Lamberson's land."

"But he did just that," Jason reminded me.

I shook my head (a mistake when you've been jouncing around and banging it against the steering wheel a few hours before). "No, you're right. I'm getting confused. He did bury Jake, so okay, he didn't want to mess with the authorities. He buried Jake quickly - and he didn't know the land was definitely going to Lamberson yet."

"Of course," chimed in Brooke. "He couldn't leave a raw grave there for a new owner to see. Lamberson would've investigated any newly-turned earth on his new purchase."

Bryan and I stared at each other.

"Did Lamberson say anything about that when Matheson told him about the bodies?" I asked him.

"No. He just denied knowing anything about the bodies. Said he'd bought the property off of your family, moved in and set up shop. He couldn't have done that without spotting the new grave, no matter who dug it!"

"The sale couldn't have been much later!" I said.

"Seems to me he would have noticed something anyway, the way you said he had trucks going in and out of there so often," Brooke said.

"I think we need to speak with him again," said Bryan

Jean picked up plates and cups to take to the sink. Lloyd started shuffling papers. "Bryan, if you can do that, I can check out Jake's GI insurance. If that policy was ever used, it will tell us what happened to Jake. If it wasn't, well, that's cause for speculation. Either he's still alive someplace, or...."

"Or Mackenzie's right," finished Brooke.

"Of course Doc Wilder's right," said Jean stoutly.

"I'll get on to Lamberson," Bryan told Lloyd quietly.

"Can you handle it?" Jason drawled.

Bryan gazed past me at him. "I can. I will. I intend to solve this. Mackenzie needs to get out from under this. There're other things she needs to do with her life."

"Provided she's got one."

"What do you mean?"

"We all seem to have lost track of the fact that she's been the target of a couple of attacks here. One of which, technically, was successful." The room went silent under the weight of Jason's statement. "All we've established here is that she does indeed have knowledge the real murderer could consider dangerous."

"Yeah, and we've come up with a couple leads. Solving the murder will make her safe," snapped Bryan.

"What about in the meantime? Are you going to do your job and protect her or what?"

Uh oh. I could see Bryan's jaw clench. His face was suffused with color.

"Look. I'll be careful. And maybe Bryan can convince Matheson now to give me police protection. "

"Never mind that." Bryan spoke in clipped tones. "Brooke, can you and Lloyd take Rachel for a few days?"

"Sure."

"I think we can be sure that Mackenzie is the target. That means Rachel is safe, so if she can stay with you, I can stay here."

"Bryan, Rachel needs you - not just for protection, but to be there for her. She's going to be worried." *You're objecting to him staying?* It was as if my little voice was shaking its head.

"Mackenzie, it's all right. Rachel stays with Brooke and Lloyd a lot. This will feel normal to her. Normal is what she needs, remember? Jean, make me up a bed upstairs, please. Then bring Rachel down. Lloyd, you've got notes on all this? Keep 'em safe, and check out that insurance thing. I'm presuming we all have the same goal here? No discussing what we've talked about. I'll report to Matheson when I'm ready. Fields? You got that? Keep your thoughts to yourself."

"I'm good at it, or didn't you figure that out yet?"

I thought Bryan was going to slug him.

Suddenly, everyone was up, the table fully cleared, jackets being picked up or put on. Rachel came downstairs, rubbing her eyes. She nodded when Bryan told her she'd be spending a few days with her aunt and uncle. Then she stopped and looked at us anxiously.

"Mackie? Daddy? Are you okay? What's going on?"

"Shhh. It's okay, Rachel. There's just a little problem Mackenzie and I are working on. I want to make sure you're taken care of while we clear this up. It's work, but - no danger." He hugged her tight.

"You sure?"

"I'm sure Aunt Brooke is going to love taking care of you for a few days while we straighten things out."

"Uh- huh. Okay. B'sides, I left my Gameboy there last week. It needs batteries. 'Night, Mackie."

"We'll get batteries in the morning, Raitch. Come on." Lloyd picked her up and carried her against his shoulder where she looked like she was going back to sleep.

"Whew, like you said, she's perceptive," I whispered to him.

"Yes - look, I don't know how much you've been relying on Fields, but from here on out, I want you to rely on me. Okay?"

"Okay, but...."

He tipped my chin up so I'd look him in the eye. "No 'buts'."

The noises of good- bye crowded in. They all left, Rachel taking her new circumstances good-naturedly. Jason less so. Brooklynne simply grinned at me behind Lloyd's back.

Jason kissed the top of my head gently. "Be careful, Mackenzie," he murmured. "Take care of her, Jamison! I hold you responsible!"

"You don't need to worry, Fields!" Bryan said tightly.

Jean came up, two clean platters in her arms. "You're in a helluva spot, Doc."

"Jean, I hope this doesn't scare you, working for me under these circumstances."

"Nah. I figure nobody will think I'm a threat. 'Course, if they come after you and run across me with a frying pan in my hand - or a hammer! Cut that out. Don't hug me, now! Maybe she'll be better company for you, Lieutenant Jamison. She was pretty boring Saturday night, I'll tell you! Take care of her."

We closed the door on everyone. The house seemed to lower sheltering wings about us, wrapping us in its own protective security. Which was good, because my body was rapidly letting down. My head throbbed, and my cheek and neck and shoulders had decided they'd had enough of my ignoring them. All of me cried out with pain.

Slowly we climbed the stairs, Bryan supporting me casually, as if it were no big deal. I found some Tylenol 3 and took as much as I dared. Then he escorted me to my bedroom door. I stopped just inside.

"Why did she do that, I wonder?"

"Who? Do what?"

"Jean. She put extra blankets and stuff in my room."

"She may have felt I wanted to keep a closer watch over you." He pushed back my hair from my face, his hands as gentle as if I were Rachel.

"Oh. Well. That's not really necessary, is it?"

"Maybe not. But it's what I want to do." There was just a hint of question in his eye.

I opened the door wider.

"Do you want me to?" he asked, following me a couple steps into the room.

"I want you," I answered slowly, picking up the extra pillow and stuffing it alongside mine on the bed. Despite the pain, despite the exhaustion and the underlying worry, it was true. I wanted to be held, and I wanted to know I was loved. I straightened up to find myself already in his arms.

It flitted through my head that what we were doing would not be understood by everybody. In the midst of fear and pain and death we cling to life and love with passion.

Later Bryan looked at me with a gleam in his eye. "Does this mean I don't need to be jealous of Jason Fields?"

I pulled him back to me, saying, "You don't have to be jealous of anyone, ever."

"This has been building a long time, Mackenzie," he murmured.

"Mmhmm."

He rolled to his side and gazed at me, his eyes searching out mine, his arm draped over me, caressing, massaging the sore spots. "No, I mean it. It's like we started on a journey way back when we were kids. Then we both got off on detours, and now we're together again, where we're supposed to be."

I stroked his chin. "I thought that was my imagination."

"No. I felt it from the moment Brooke told me she was trying to get you to come back. I could feel then that changes were coming. Somehow, I was getting back on track."

"This was meant to be, then?"

"Don't you think so?"

"I think it's a rough way to bring us together. Scary."

He tightened his arm around me. "I'm here," he whispered.

I nodded. I was growing sleepy, but Bryan's talk reminded me of a question I wanted answered.

"Bryan, did my father ever warn you to stay away from me in high school?"

"Wha- ? How'd you find that out?" He raised his head.

"Doug Pulaskey was in the office the other day."

"Conversation got around to that?"

"You know Doug. But, what he said, it's true?" I roused myself enough to send him a stern look.

"Yes. Your father pretty well said if any of us laid a finger on you he'd shoot us."

"Oh, great. Do you remember what my non-social life was like back then? Why didn't anybody tell me?"

"We were scared to. I'm sorry you were hurt like that, but with Rachel? I can understand why your father did it. Daughters are precious things."

"We're people, not things!" I argued absently, still considering the bigger question. "Are you sorry you never took a chance on me anyway?"

"Oh, no."

"No? Why? Wasn't I worth getting shot over?"

"Actually, I think you were, but if I'd gotten shot then, we might not have right now."

"Mmm," I said, tracing the line of his bicep to his shoulder. "If we aren't careful, we may not have a future."

We drew each other closer, and kissed, and slept deeply until morning.

CHAPTER 23

It took Mom years to plant that hill in irises. Every year she added new ones in exotic colors that she purchased from mail-order houses, plus others that she cadged and traded from friends. Each fall I held my breath as Pop rolled the mower over them, sending the green-hued swordblades flying, scattering over the hillside like so many war casualties. I figured she'd be mad at him for mowing them down. After all they were her favorites. I was eleven before I realized it was an agreed-upon technique for helping the irises grow strong and bloom better. One of those life-secrets parents neglect to let their children in on.

It was never Pop she got angry with over the irises. It was Vince Lamberson when he dredged them up with his backhoe and had the dirt carted across the road to fill in the embankment. Which of course explains the glorious profusion of iris that blanket that hill right now.

T he breeze at the top of the stairs was blowing off the river, carrying smells only a river rat can love: oil, fish, mussels, green algae. Silver-and-blue glinted through the trees at me. The river was happy, and I was loved. I couldn't ask for much more.

Bryan had left for work intent on interrogating Lamberson at the earliest opportunity. I was headed to the office.

I spent the morning passing along information. I told Andrea that I'd be seeing Matheson again after all. She reminded me to check into his marital status for her. I messengered the medical records of the entire Kings Hill baseball team to Dr. Jenkins of Fieldcrest. (There was a defeat of major proportions!) And I informed a young married lady that she indeed was going to have to convince her husband to give up smoking because their first baby was on its way.

After she left, I took a break. I stretched my arms overhead only to discover my bones had been rattled more than I'd realized yesterday. Of course, last night had been a vast improvement over the afternoon.

It seemed strange in some ways. I'd been alone a long time. I'd hardly been back long enough to get reacquainted with Bryan. The impact of events was compressing time, stripping away the formalities and leaving room for only essentials.

"Medical thoughts, Mackenzie?"

I looked up. Bryan stood in the doorway. He chuckled and bent over to kiss me as he reached my desk.

"I've come for lunch, and to let you in on Lamberson's interview."

"Lunch is at the house," I said, standing up.

"So are some other things," he commented.

"Including Jean," I reminded him, walking with him to the door.

Andrea waved, smiling at us. We crossed the road and climbed the stairs, the brook singing, though not so fully now. As we entered the kitchen we heard Jean at the front door and looked up to see Brooke walking toward us. She tossed her blond hair and said, "I thought you were here, Bryan."

"Yeah. Me, too."

They grinned and hugged. I gaped at them.

"How do you do that?"

"Twin stuff," they said simultaneously.

"That's eerie. Does it happen often?"

"Not so much as it used to," answered Bryan. "I kind of miss it. Can you stay, sis?"

"Yes, stay and have lunch. Bryan is going to report on Lamberson."

Soon the three of us were again seated about the table discussing Pop's case. Bryan laid two mini-cassettes alongside his plate, followed by a tape player.

"What's that?" I asked.

"We recorded the questioning with Lamberson. Matheson let me take this one from the previous session for comparison. Listen."

I hadn't expected this. Having to hear Lamberson's voice again. The tape squealed a little at first, then it settled down.

"...don't understand why I'm here, officer."

"Lieutenant."

"Lieutenant, then. I didn't come up here to spend my time at the police station. I'm on vacation!"

"Mr. Lamberson, I'm sorry to take up your time, but we're trying to clear up this case."

"Don't see how I can help."

"I wanted to see if you could recall any disturbed areas on the Russell property."

"Disturbed areas?"

"Places where the ground was dug up, or turned over. Something like that."

"How the hell would I know?"

"I thought maybe you might have noticed something when you took over the place."

"Oh. Let me see. We bought the Russell place in 1988. I was expanding a lot back then. No, Lieutenant, I'm not remembering anything. Like I told you before, I don't see how I can help you here."

"Mr. Lamberson, maybe I can help you remember. You bought the Russell farm. Surely you must have walked around the property when you took possession...."

"My manager was in charge of that. He helped my wife move in because I was in Denver. You'd have to ask Carl -   and I don't know where he is. Retired four or five years ago."

"You don't recall this - Carl - saying anything about some dug up areas?"

"No. All he ever mentioned was the place by the barn where Willie had planted some bulbs and a tree. But we'd covered that in the contract."

I jumped at his words, but Bryan kept me quiet with a raised finger. He'd caught it.

"...bulbs, Mr. Lamberson?"

"Oh, daylilies, I think it was. Some flower, cedar tree. It was in the contract."

"What was in the contract, sir?"

"Oh, hell. Leavin' that ground undisturbed. Russell wanted it to be some kind of memorial or something. Sounded stupid to me, but ol' Willie, he was startin' to lose it back then. No skin off my nose. I didn't have any plans for that strip. If I ever changed my mind, well, hey - it was my land."

"You never dug that spot, did you?"

"Nope, guess not. Or I might've gone through this a lot sooner, huh?"

Bryan switched the tape off.

I dropped my head on my hands. Lamberson's voice had sounded as thick and scornful as ever when he referred to my father.

"So, the grave was there. Lamberson knew about it," I said at last.

"He knew there was a place that had been dug up, but only because this Carl or whoever told him."

"And because the contract covered it," Brooke reminded me.

"Wasn't that an odd clause to put in?" Bryan asked.

"Not if Pop was trying to protect Jake's grave." I shook my head. "What's odd about it is Vince Lamberson honoring it."

Bryan slipped the other tape into the player. "Listen to this part from the first interview."

Matheson's voice was smooth and friendly. "Strange, don't you think, Mr. Lamberson, that it was so long before anyone stumbled on these bodies. I'm surprised you never dug them up."

"Never had any reason to dig back there. Most of our work was on the other side of the road in the gravel bank. Besides, Wylvern had so much crap out there, it was a pain in the ass to move it out of the way."

"Crap?"

"Junk, old cars, washing machines, you name it. Even a 1919 tractor. Jeez, what a mess!"

"So you don't know anything about these bodies?"

"No, how could I?"

Bryan stopped the tape and looked at us expectantly.

"He didn't mention the daylilies, or the contract," I said slowly.

Bryan agreed. "I picked up on that. Of course, he may not have remembered it at that point. Another thing. He says the contract no longer exists, that it was discarded when he turned the company over to his sons a few years ago. So there is no way of proving - or disproving - what he said."

"I don't like it, Bryan. I don't like it. I'd love nothing better than to hang this on Vince Lamberson, but I can't see any reason he'd have for killing Jake. Who was the guy Pop killed? If he did, I mean."

Bryan snapped his fingers and changed tapes again. "Mackie, as far as you know, did Vince Lamberson know who Jake Terry was?"

"Sure, he had to. Jake was around Pop's all the time."

"Listen to this, from this morning."

He fumbled with the little machine.

"How well did you know Jake Terry, Mr. Lamberson?"

"Who?"

"Jake Terry, sir. We believe that may be the identity of one of the bodies."

"Never heard of him."

"Wha - ? Excuse me, I mean, are you sure, sir?"

"Yes, I'm sure. I know who I know, and I never heard of any Jake Terry!"

By now my jaw was at table level. The exchange continued to play out.

"Mr. Lamberson, Mr. Terry lived at the Russell place and was with Mr. Russell almost constantly. You negotiated a deal for the farm and never met him?"

"I told you I never - wait, Jake Terry? Old guy, geezer in rumpled clothes? I never knew his name. We weren't exactly what you'd call formally introduced. Don't think he ever spoke more'n a dozen words around me. So, yeah, I guess you could say I knew him, although I didn't know him, if you know what I mean, Sergeant - sorry, Lieutenant. Are we almost through?"

"Bryan!" I yelled as he stopped the tape again. "He's lying! I know he knew Jake. You couldn't know my father and not know Jake. And look. I know I remember standing in the driveway with Mom and Pop and Jake and that s.o.b.!"

Bryan nodded even as he told me to calm down.

"I don't want to calm down. He's lying! Jake told us he'd seen Lamberson get Pop drunk. How could that happen and Lamberson not know?"

Bryan answered mildly, "It could happen. What's important, is that Lamberson *denies* ever knowing him."

"Bryan!" I started to wail. "Bryan! That's a point-blank lie we've got him in! If he's lying about that, what else is he lying about? And why? After all, if he were completely innocent, what would it matter if he knew Jake Terry?"

"There could be explanations for all of this, Mackenzie," Bryan warned.

"Do you really think so?" Brooklynne asked, seeing me ready to spout off.

"I don't know," he said, shaking his head.

"Well, I do. Lamberson is no more trustworthy than Dr. Frankenstein at a mortuary convention! He's hiding something!"

They burst out laughing. "Where'd you get that line?" Brooklynne asked.

"Oh, never mind. I'm sure he's not telling everything, Bryan!"

"Look, I'm going back this afternoon and work on it. If there's anything more I can find, I'll find it."

"All right," I acquiesced. "But I bet I'm right." *And I won't give up until I show you, either!*

At three o'clock, I drove out to the farm.

I went in the house, the replacement subfloor squeaking beneath my feet, its new wood smell of pine and resin permeating the atmosphere. Boxes stood in the living room -   the kitchen cabinets Jean and I had ordered. Lying across the top of them was a wooden mantel salvaged from an old row house in Albany. One of our carpenters, Bret Guthrie, had found it and brought it out for us to see. He'd only brushed it clean. Remnants of bird and rat guano still dirtied the carved images. Dogwood blossoms graced each end, tying down a garland eternally captured in the mantel's magnificent teakwood. The wood had dried, and a large gouge channeled one end, but some TLC would bring the whole thing back. As if meant, it was the perfect size for our irregular location. I jotted down a note and stuck it under one end of the mantel, thanking Bret for bringing it out and inquiring after his asking price. As an afterthought, I asked him if he thought we could find some matching wood to use as window moldings - or salvage some existing ones.

Next stop: upstairs. I wanted to search for papers we may have missed. I don't know what I was thinking. Jean had already cleaned things out. I burrowed back into the storage closet off my parents' room. The closed-in smell brought back Christmas memories of wrapping paper and hidden boxes and ornaments nested in boxes left over from Christmas presents. All in my imagination, of course, because the flooring in here was the ridiculous shiplap Lamberson had put in, and the walls sturdier than what my father had built. Aside from its location, the room had nothing in common with my parents' closet. I sighed and rose to my feet, dusting off my slacks. One more empty room. What did I expect?

I continued to search, however, just so I could say I had. The bedroom was totally empty. Someone had replaced the swinging casement windows with sliding aluminum atrocities. I envisioned dormer windows, window seats with built-in drawers below, calico wallpaper, and bare wide-board floors dotted with rag rugs. More notes to Bret were in order. Could he find genuine wide boards to salvage? Would adding the dormers be structurally sound?

I wondered at myself, able to come up with this when I ought to be focusing on solving Pop's case. But then, I'd always found re-doing old houses to be relaxing.

I checked the other closet. There was a shelf over the clothesrod, stretching from one end of the closet to the other. Shoved to one end of the shelf, where I hadn't seen it before, was a shoebox. I had to jump a couple times, batting at one end to jiggle it forward. I took it over to a corner, and opened it.

Inside, three-by-five cards were divided up into a sort of file. Cards with large Roman numerals on them created twelve sections. Pencilled beneath each numeral, as if for clarification, was the name of a month, 'January' written below 'I', and so on. Within each section, further divisions were made, breaking them down into years: 2004, 2005, 2006, 2007, 2008 (this one went only through March). You could read through what happened in the same months each year, like anniversaries.

I took out the section for January 2004. There were about thirteen cards in it. A sturdy script written in blue pen covered the first one. "9th - We've just moved into our house on the hill. David says it's a dream come true. I hope he's right. The barn is so old, I don't know how it'll hold any horses. What a mess inside! David talks of a riding arena. Such big plans! It's awful cold here. I miss Center Hill pretty bad, too. I hope David knows what he's up to - what we're up to, I guess."

The next card I read said this: "15th -   I can't believe there is so much unpacking to do! David has been to the bank, and he's discouraged. He said the banker's as cold as the weather up here, not like home. They told him he'd have to wait before he could get a loan for the horse arena. Lamberson let it slip we're spread pretty thin, and that he let us skip our first payment. Bet he didn't say anything about raising our interest rate a point because of it. I don't like him much. David's mad. Says we'll refinance with another company as soon as we can. Good!"

This was fascinating! I looked again at the box cover, but there was nothing written on it. Rummaging around in the front, however, I found an extra card that read: "House on the Hill, Wexford Road, Kings Hill, New York - My house diary - Marlene Hicks 2004 - "

House diary? I flipped through some more, checking out May 2007. I read:

"21st -   I begged and begged. Finally David carpeted the kitchen. That old tile had so many cracks in it, it looked like bad marble! Re-financing looks good. Thank goodness. I hate Vince Lamberson!"

"31st -   Went to the Memorial Day Parade. Stood by the Elementary School. Danny and Mirande look so fine in their band uniforms! But what was really wonderful was the look on Lamberson's face when David corralled him and made him accept the bank's check and sign the papers. In front of witnesses! We're out from under the thumb of that money-grubbing snake!"

What had happened during those years? Apparently Lamberson had been holding the note on the property himself. What could he have done to make them so angry? Surely there were limits to what a mortgage-holder could do! Wait a minute, I told myself, this was Vince Lamberson we were talking about here. Normal rules did not apply.

I sat back, my mind spinning furiously. Perhaps there was more evidence in here. Lamberson had done something that a) made Marlene Hicks hate him and b) made them determined to get out from under his thumb. What could he have done legally to make them that angry? Okay, what could he have done *illegally* to make them that angry?

This was going to take time. The sun was setting, and I didn't have too many lights hooked up out here. I wanted to check out two more things, and then I'd take the box home with me. I rustled through February and March of this year. February:

"23rd -   I can't believe it! All the money we've poured into this place and now this. A dead body! The police have been all over the farm. Mirande is having nightmares! Pro'bly Lamberson did it -   bumped off some poor guy who got in his way! With his methods, it wouldn't surprise me."

A week later, in March:

"2nd - This is too much! Another body! We're getting out. I can't take this anymore. We're going home, to Center Hill. This house is bad for us. I don't even want this diary anymore!"

That was the last entry, just two months ago. I felt bad for the Hicks. I was glad I had paid them a good price. I wanted to read this whole thing. Marlene had hinted at wrongdoings by Vince Lamberson. What if she had proof? What if it was right here? What if this diary showed that he was the kind of man to bump off those who got in his way?

I went back to January 2004. I'd go chronologically. Maybe I could get through 2004 before I went home. I struggled to my feet and took the box down to the kitchen where the bare overhead light was harsh but powerful.

I settled down to read. A half hour later I sat back and stretched. Their first year had been tight, what with Vince raising the interest rate and all. He'd made it hard for them to get financing for other projects. Their farm had survived, however, and they'd each made small improvements (well, so they considered them -   I couldn't get over the kitchen carpet myself). Marlene worked as hard as David did. The kids seemed involved as well. Still, I hadn't found what I was hoping for against Vince.

It was completely dark out now. I'd better leave. I checked the front door. Habit, since I almost never unlocked it. Then I checked a few windows, and went to secure the door to the basement. My hand was on the latch, when I heard something upstairs. Slow, measured steps, as of workboots, across the floor overhead. My mouth went dry. An intruder's bad enough. Why did those footsteps have to sound like Pop's? I stepped towards the table with my purse and keys on it. If he was upstairs, I should get to my car and get out of there. I froze mid-stride.

The front door handle rattled. There was a tap on the glass windowpane.

I swiveled my head toward the back door. I still stood a chance that way. The door handle was turning even as I looked. I was trapped -   and outnumbered! I'd have to hide in the basement. I pulled open the door and started downward. In my mind I saw the wood lathe and plaster and cleaning products of my nightmare. My hands were cold. Sweat trickled off my shoulders down both front and back. I heard more footsteps, and someone yelled. I heard my father's voice. "I'll get you!"

I plunged down the stairs, terrified. Breeze cooled the sweat on my skin. The outer door was open! It was dark now, as in my dream. As in my dream, I flung myself down the hill and through the fields.

This was wrong. This was forest, now, not fields. I was grown up, not a child. There was real danger behind me, for no one with a legitimate reason approaches a house this way. The white terror ebbed, but I still had to get away to safety. Wracking my brain, I remembered a path. The moon was up sufficiently to help me see between trees, and soon I found the pale swath I was looking for. I followed the rise until I was at the crest of the hill. Then I turned ninety degrees right and went downhill and back up again to find the road. When I saw it, I paused, hanging back among the pines a bit. I didn't relish walking in the dark along the road. It was too exposed.

Who were they? Burglars? Someone just up to no good? Someone paid by my invisible enemy?

I started trembling again.

A car was coming. I drew back behind the skirts of a full white pine. It came slowly, rolling along as if on momentum alone. Voices accompanied the crunch and rattle of the gravel.

"I tell you, I saw her come this way. She was over there. Next minute she was gone. Right about here!"

My blood was cold in my veins. I stepped behind another row of trees. The car passed. I nearly fainted - it was a pickup truck. In the back were two figures, standing upright, husky and tall, peering out into the trees.

"Dr. Wilder! Dr. Wilder! Hey, c'mon. It's Kyle Anthony, Doc! Please answer!"

There was mumbling between the two. Was that Kyle? I tried to remember his voice.

"Dr. Wilder! Please! We're sorry! We didn't mean to, honest. We didn't mean to scare you like that! Doc?"

It was Kyle! I drew a deep breath. Whatever mischief they'd been up to, I was not in mortal danger from these youngsters.

"Kyle! Over here!" I called out and stepped onto the road.

The brake lights brightened. As I watched, the back-up lights came on, the truck rolled back slowly, two figures hunched over the tailgate like combat lookouts.

"Hold it, stop!" Kyle jumped out the back and skidded in front of me.

"Are you okay, Doc? I mean, you didn't hurt yourself runnin' through there, did you? We weren't trying to scare you like that... I mean - oh, hell!" He looked miserable, and pretty scared himself. The second boy, Tony, climbed out of the truck, too.

"It was you upstairs - and at the back door - and yelling things?" I asked them each in turn. They shuffled and nodded.

I sighed and started pulling weeds out of my hair. "Let's go back to the house and sort this out. I'll ride in the cab." I glared at the driver when I climbed in.

The kitchen light shone bright on the papers and keys on the table. I stood beside it, watching them file in to face me: three very embarrassed, fidgety ballplayers. One shifted back and forth from foot to foot. Kyle stood with his head down and his hands jammed in his jean pockets. The third, James I thought was his name, kept running his hands over his hair. I let them wait.

The cellar door swung gently. I closed it. My reflection in the side window showed my hair in disarray. I smoothed it into shape, and brushed dirt off my clothes. A hole was torn in my Liz Claiborne slacks, and a grass stain ran up to my left knee. Great.

"Sit down," I ordered.

Chairs scraped. I remained standing, folding my arms. "What has been going on around here?"

"Well, - "

"You tell her, man."

Kyle spoke. "Doc, I'm sorry! We didn't mean to - It wasn't our idea to - I mean, everyone was saying how you didn't belong - We just thought we'd - oh, hell, Jean tried to tell us!"

He slumped down in the chair.

I waited, pulling my arms tight against myself. The other two boys darted looks at each other over Kyle's lowered head. One of them yawned.

"C'mon, you guys. You could do some talkin', too, you know." Kyle looked at Tony.

"Yeah, well. Jean - Mrs. Hesford - she tried to warn us the other day. But - " Tony shrugged.

"Jean." I frowned. "You were the guys cleaning up my driveway - Wait, you're the ones who messed up my driveway, weren't you? No wonder Jean said not to tip you! What is going on here?"

One more look at their sorry faces as they tried to squirm out from under did it. I snapped, "Answer me!"

Three heads shot up.

"We were just trying to get you to leave," James said plaintively.

"We figured if we bugged you enough, you'd decide it wasn't worth stayin' around." Tony was starting to look like he thought it had been a mistake.

"Mom told me how you might be scared about being alone out here. About how your old man used to chase you downstairs. She said if we came out here some night, maybe you'd be here and we could scare you by actin' like him." Kyle's whole face seemed to grow longer as he told me, and his eyes poured out misery.

But my 'old man' never did chase me downstairs. That had just been that old nightmare of mine. A recurring nightmare, that started when I was ten years old. That I had shared with my 'best friend' Dianne Franklyn. Carmen's cousin.

My jaw twisted. "Your mother."

Kyle nodded.

James spoke with firmer conviction. "We shouldn't have done it. No matter what she said. She was wrong. Dr. Wilder, you're okay. I'm going to ask my parents if we can't come back to your office. It's dumb to go to Fieldcrest."

Tony nodded agreement. Kyle was still staring at my table. James nudged him.

"Yeah." He looked up at me. "She was wrong, Doc. So were we. I'm sorry."

My arms disentangled themselves. There's only so long you can be angry at a trio of truly contrite young men who want no more than to be let alone to play baseball and chase girls. And these three had been grievously misled by their elders.

Which gave me more to think about. This whole campaign to get me out of here was nothing more than an effort organized by the people I used to know. A *few* of the people I'd known. Not people like Bob and Sandy Cooper, but people who despised me. How far would they have gone? How far did they go?

"All right, boys. You told me the truth. So far. Now tell me some more."

They looked at each other, questions in their eyes.

"I don't know if we can," said James.

"Just tell me everything you guys are responsible for."

They sighed.

"Tonight, obviously," I coached.

"Yeah, and the trash," muttered Bob.

"Some letters. And that ad in the paper," added Tony.

"Anything else?"

"That's pretty much it. Except for persuading the team to go over to Fieldcrest. Coach would've just as soon stayed with you. He said you were a good doctor, but Mom pushed it. She's his older sister," Kyle explained.

I licked my lips. "This is important. I want an honest answer. You heard about my almost being run off the road yesterday. Do you know anything about it? Was it one of you? One of the team?"

They all shook their heads. Kyle's eyes grew wide.

"No! We never wanted to hurt anybody. We just thought we'd get you to leave!"

"Okay," I said slowly. "I believe you. Kyle, do you think your mother or her cousin Dianne might have done it?"

The question brought a shocked, honest silence. Then Kyle shook his head at me like a mechanical doll.

"No, never. I heard about the car you said drove you off the road. I know that sounds like Dianne's Jeep, but I worked on it for her early this morning. It was dirty and needed a tune-up, but it sure wasn't smashed up like the one that was after you must've been. And my Mom doesn't like driving' those things."

"Okay. I believe you. Now - what about tonight? Did you get into anything else?"

They shook their heads.

"You didn't go up to the barn or anything? Mess with my boat?"

"No, ma'am - I mean, no. Why would we?"

"Yeah, it's just an old boat."

I sighed inside. "Okay, now - "

Tony pulled his head up from where he'd been contemplating the color of his jeans. "Old boat? You mean like antique? What kind is it?"

I recognized that look and tone. "It's a 1941 barrel back Chris Craft. My former husband and I restored it."

Kyle groaned. "I don't get what's so cool about antique boats. Tony won't shut up about them."

"Hey, my parents take me to that Antique Boat Show every year in Clayton. Can I help it if I think the boats are cool? You've never even been in one, so how would you know?"

"You're almost as obsessed with the things as your parents."

"Looks like Dr. Wilder thinks they're pretty cool!"

"Guys, wait. This is getting out of hand. Tony, I'd love to talk with you and your parents about old boats, but you guys need to get back home."

Their faces fell. It was clear their troubles weren't quite over yet.

I studied them carefully. No matter how much they'd been deceived and misguided, they hadn't been corrupted entirely. This had been a small- scale operation, aimed only at shooing me off, not shooting me down. The junior team, at least, was sorry. Maybe their remorse could be contagious.

"I want you to go back to your parents, and let them know we've talked. Tell them how you feel. Maybe it'll knock some sense into them. Since I don't know what they've told you exactly, I'll tell you this. For the record: I don't know who killed the men whose bodies were found here. I do know the reputation my father had. I am his daughter, but I am not him. I believe differently than he did; I act differently than he did; I am not him. I am, I think, responsible, law-abiding, and a damn good doctor. The one thing I do have in common with my father is that I am stubborn. I will not be chased off. I can be good for Kings Hill, and I plan on sticking around to prove it. Now, go home."

The door closed behind them, and I sat down at the table, rubbing my eyes. They focused blearily on the box of papers on the table. A helluva day. I stared for a moment more, then I gathered up my stuff and took my own advice. I went home.

CHAPTER 24

All my life, every time I ride into Albany, the thought runs through my head that this is one old, old city. Cobblestones on the streets make me think of what it must have been like in colonial days. Dioramas in the State Museum, with their exhibits of old pottery, weaving, and arrowheads remind me of the Indian past that surrounds us.

Sometimes, walking in the woods, I stare at the ground, hoping to find one of these arrowheads on my own. Always looking for links, links to bind me closer to the land. I'd be thrilled to discover I have Indian blood in me.

But there's never been an arrowhead or any Indian blood. I have no concrete sign of the bond that exists between me and this land. The bond that even my father's weakness and Lamberson's treachery can not break. The bond that years of separation did not undo. The bond that has drawn me back and put me in my current predicament.

B ryan was spending the night at Brooke's. Rachel hadn't handled being without her dad quite as well as we'd hoped, so he was going to alternate between the two houses for a while. He'd called a private security firm, and I found their man under the portico when I got home. I nodded to him, touching off the pain in my head again. I didn't know whether it hurt more from the physical exertion I'd been through, or from all the new information I'd garnered. Hurt it did, so I treated it and went to bed.

It hurt a little less by morning, and was almost clear by the time I was facing Andrea's latest hairstyle - a complicated French braid with a poofy bang - across an empty waiting room. She looked a little forlorn over all our nonexistent patients, so I paused to tell her what the kids had told me last night.

"Business should pick up soon," I reassured her.

The telephone rang.

"Just a moment, Kyle. I'll see if she'll speak with you." Andrea's tone was severe.

I took it in my office, Andrea following and hovering under pretense of checking files.

"Yes, Kyle?"

"Doc, I wanted you to know. James and Tony and I talked to Coach and to our parents. James and Tony's parents are cool about it. Mom's not. She's mad we got caught."

"I'm not surprised, Kyle. But you know you did what was right."

"Yeah. Coach wanted me to ask you to come out to today's game. It's a home game. Three o'clock. I think he wants to talk to you, too."

"Thanks, Kyle. I'll try to make it."

"Mom'll be there. Maybe you can talk with her."

"We'll see. I don't hold out a lot of hope."

"Yeah, I know." He paused. "See ya'."

"Good- bye, Kyle."

"You'll see what?" Andrea fussed over my desk.

"I've been invited to a ball game this afternoon, Andrea. The boys talked to their parents. Ms. Anthony is the only holdout so far." I reached for Brooke's number. "Maybe Bryan and Rachel would like to go with me."

I heard Andrea chuckle as she left the room.

"Hello, Brooke? It's Mackie. Let me speak with Bryan, okay? .... What are you doing around three this afternoon? You and Rachel?"

"I have to be at the station - reports, and so on. Rachel's free after school, though. Why?"

"I'm going to the ball game over at the school. I wondered if you two wanted to come with me?"

"Going to brave the lions' den?"

"That's right! You don't know what happened!"

"What? What happened?"

I related the events of last night.

"Anthony and Franklyn!"

"Yeah. Again! Kyle called with another apology and said he and his Coach wanted me to come to the game. It wouldn't hurt me to show up at something like that."

There was a thoughtful pause. "You could talk with people."

"Exactly. Bryan," I dropped my voice. "Do you think it could actually be Lamberson?"

"Careful what you say. Maybe."

"Damn him!"

"I'm still checking some things out. So is Brooke. It's okay if Rachel goes with you this afternoon. As long as you are both careful."

"I wouldn't endanger Rachel. Of course I'll be careful!"

"I want you to be careful for your sake, too, you know."

"I know," I said softly. "Tell Brooke I'll pick Rachel up about two-thirty."

"She'll be at school then, but they'll let you take her out a little early. I've cleared it with them that you can take her anytime." His voice was a trifle embarrassed.

"Well, thank you."

"They probably think it's because you're her doctor, but..."

"Thanks. Bryan, I - "

"What?"

I couldn't say it yet. "I'll see you this evening."

"Fine. I'll tell Brooke. Mackenzie?"

"What?"

"I love you." The phone clicked softly.

I looked over the crowded bleachers and past the concession stand at the playing fields of Kings Hill High School with its short-shorn grounds, wild woods stretching between it and the neighboring middle school. There was the crack of a bat as Kings Hill's tradition of batting a ball into the woods from the pitcher's mound signaled the beginning of the game. Two young boys sprinted into the woods to retrieve the ball. Rachel and I hurried to find seats behind the team. Coach Franklyn nodded to me as we clambered up the bleachers. Kyle waved.

"Mackenzie! Up here! Come join us!"

Sandy and Bob and their spouses and assorted children roosted on seats three rows up. Bob nodded towards the field. "My daughter's cheerleading. Good to see you!"

"Come on up, Mackenzie!" urged Sandy. "Who's that with you? - What, Amanda - oh, is that Rachel Jamison?"

"Yeah. She decided to keep me company. I wanted to get a better look at the team."

Bob narrowed his eyes. "Carmen giving you any more trouble?"

I glanced quickly downward. "No-o, I don't think I'd say that. Come on, Rachel." We settled on a seat halfway between the Coopers and the team.

Rachel waved to Amanda. "What did you get on the spelling test today? I got a ninety-five. - Yeah, me too!" Then she studied the field for a moment before turning to me. "That's Ted Stuart, Mackie. He's Standish's best hitter. He pitches, too. He's a senior. Some scouts have been eyeing him for the pros, but he's probably going to take a scholarship to Ohio State first." Rachel pointed to the young man warming up near first base. "Daddy brings me to the games a lot. These two guys over here are awful. Ted's their best player. Daddy sometimes says he's their only player! Kings Hill'l clobber 'em."

I laughed at her expert assessment. The game got going. Soon we were cheering and booing with everyone else, ducking when pop-up fouls came our way. Bob's daughter's cheerleading was acrobatic and enthusiastic. I gave him a thumbs-up and noted the picture of my high school buddy as a proud Dad.

About the third inning I offered to get us sodas. I ordered our drinks from the mom minding the stand. As she pushed the cups of crushed ice and brown liquid toward me, I asked her, "How good is the Standish team, anyway? This is my first game."

"This team? They're terrible! Well, Stuart's actually pretty good, but everybody else is so bad, it doesn't make a difference."

A familiar-looking redhead stomped purposefully toward the stand loaded with two baskets of baked goods. We nodded to each other.

I paid for the drinks. "Is it a big rivalry?"

"Nah. Our boys are like their big brothers. This game is more like a scrimmage than a real game. The coaches are best buddies." She waved the bills around, finding change and emphasizing her words simultaneously.

The redhead hefted the baskets onto the table. "Here they are, Eileen. Fifteen dollars."

"Hi, Dorsey. Another one of your jobs?" We grinned at one another. I liked her.

I walked back to the stands. Jean's friend Arthur arrived, a grunt serving as a greeting as he passed me.

"Thanks, Mackie. Look! They only scored two runs. We're still ahead." Rachel took her drink from me and sipped.

"Hey, that's great - "

"Mackenzie? Mackenzie Russell? Is that you?"

A vigorous old woman raised a bony arm to shield her eyes. Her hair was white with touches of yellow at the edges, like old newspapers. She wore a sun hat atop the curling mop and sunglasses, peach slacks, a white tailored blouse, and a beige cardigan tied around her shoulders. Her voice was as distinctive as ever; crows cawing in the sun never sounded worse.

"Miss Davenport! How nice to see you!" I leaned down two rows to take her hand. Tennis had left her arms powerful.

"How have you been, my dear. And your mother? It has been years, hasn't it? Merton tells me you're our new doctor. That's marvelous! Your mother must be so proud."

I found myself nodding my head in several directions at once. "My mother died some years ago, but yes, I'm the new doctor for Kings Hill. It's been twenty years since I've been here. I don't believe I know Merton...."

"That's right, you wouldn't. Merton and I were married eleven years ago!" She leaned towards me. "Actually, we weren't married at all! We moved in together to save expenses!" Her eyes twinkled roguishly. "I'm sorry about your mother, dear. I remember her in her blue hat."

I grinned at her. "Let me tell you about that hat. Mom hated that hat. She thought it was the ugliest thing on earth, but her sister gave it to her, and it wouldn't wear out no matter how badly Mom treated it. The first Sunday of every month, Mom and Aunt Mildred met for lunch after church. So Mom always wore the hat for those luncheons, just to please Aunt Mildred. Finally, one time, Aunt Mildred evidently forgot she'd been the one to give Mom the hat. She was moaning and groaning about how she needed a new hat to wear, and Mom, thinking this was her chance, offered the blue one to Aunt Mildred. Aunt Mildred said 'That old thing? It's terrible! I don't know what possesses you to wear such an awful hat month after month! I'd throw it out!' Mom was so astonished, she didn't say anything, but when she got home, that's exactly what she did. And Aunt Mildred never noticed."

We laughed. "You need to come by the church. We have a very nice young pastor. I don't believe he's married, is he, Merton? You'll see some of your old friends there. Helen Oglethorpe is still with us, eighty but healthy as an ox. Charlie Osterhout, too, silly old fool. And - oh, did you know Anne Marie Harris?"

"No, I don't think - wait a minute - very fine hair, sort of blonde, maybe a little heavy, with really blue eyes?"

"And very flighty," she added firmly. "She's been our organist and church secretary for twelve years. She's a redhead now, by the way. Anne Marie's a wonderful organ-player, but her secretarial skills! Last week all the bulletins had different covers! I asked Pastor Reynolds about it, and he told me Ms. Harris had saved up leftovers and used them. Trying to save paper. Hmph!"

"Well, I suppose that's an admirable goal."

"Covers from Easter and Christmas?" She looked shocked. "That girl just doesn't think things through!"

I chuckled, and Miss Davenport smiled at me.

"I'll be by to see you, Mackenzie. Check-up time, you know. Oh, look, there's Anne Marie now - with Pastor Reynolds, no less. That girl just does not think!"

I slid back to Rachel, reflecting that here at least was one person who didn't question my wisdom in moving here. Not only that, she didn't even mention my father! Things were looking up. Well, sort of. I saw Carmen Anthony approach the team's bench.

Her eyes met mine, and with a resigned squaring of her shoulders, she climbed up beside me.

"All right, the boys told me. What are you going to do?" Her jaw set in a tense line.

"Do? About what?"

"About the stuff that was done."

"You mean, what am I going to do about the stuff you and your cousin organized the kids to do? Actually, nothing. I don't see any reason to get the kids' into trouble over something other people are responsible for. Look." I waited for her to actually look me in the eye.

"You've apparently spent a lot of time listening to Dianne carry on about me and our relationship when we were kids. I can't fight that you sympathize with her. After all, you're her cousin. But that was a long time ago - longer even, than those two stupid bodies have lain buried out on that piece of property. Now I don't know who was responsible for those bodies, but Dianne and I - and only Dianne and I are responsible for what happened in junior high. We were kids, and we had the kind of misunderstandings kids that age do. It's over now, and I wish everyone would realize that. I think we all need to give our adult selves a chance. I don't know if Dianne will go for it, but what about you, Carmen?"

She met my challenge with a stony stare. Then she looked at the outfield where Kyle was playing today. Her throat constricted. "Kids make mistakes," she said softly.

"So don't we all."

She looked at me, then slid off the bleacher and moved to rejoin the team.

The game was progressing. Rachel barely spoke to me, she was so absorbed. It was just as well, since every time I turned around, someone else was hailing me.

Maude and I got into a discussion of old boats. She'd heard about my interests and told me that she knew - although he didn't know she knew - that Charlie Osterhout had an old launch in the back of his garage. It had been old when he'd put it up for storage in 1959, and Maude knew for a fact it had been brand new when Charlie's Dad bought it, although she couldn't recall when that was. Merton, she told me (because she wouldn't let Merton get a word in himself), had heard about my talk with Gary about the Boat Club. He shook his head over the prejudices, finally speaking up.

"If you check around the village, I think you'll find enough interest for a classic boat club. There's enough of us old farts around who remember those boats."

"Merton!"

"Why? What'd I say?" I caught the twinkle in his eye as he teased Maude with his talk.

I ran into Anne Marie Harris on a return trip to the concessions. She eyed my drink container critically.

"I thought I told the Concession Committee to start getting cans! Honestly, you'd think they didn't care about the planet at all! Hi, I'm Anne Marie Harris. You're Doctor Wilder, right?"

I nodded. "If it's any consolation, I think this came from a box labeled 'biodegradeable Styrofoam'."

"Well, that's better than nothing, I guess. How about you, Doctor Wilder, do you recycle? Does your healing practice extend to the earth as well?"

I opened my mouth to answer, looking her over sharply as I did. She wore a khaki linen shirt and shorts and woven leather sandals. Her wispy hair was pulled to one side with a clip that had spent a prior life as a series of pop-tops and bottle caps. Indian dreamcatcher earrings dangled from her ears, and the cross she wore was made of twigs lashed together with wire-thin grapevine. It shared space on a strip of rawhide with a two-inch long crystal.

Which prompted me to think of the dilemma I often pondered. Does someone who cares about resources wear animal hide (the more natural choice) or plastic (to preserve animals and keep plastics out of the landfill)? What is the ecologically consistent answer?

"Um - sorry - yes, I do recycle. I think it's very important. That's an interesting way of thinking of it: healing the Earth."

"That's what it's all about. People don't stop to think about all the things we can do to make life better. The responsibility we have to do that. Take re-using paper. Use both sides and it lasts twice as long. Then recycle it. Everybody saves. You don't buy as much paper, and the landfills don't fill up so fast. Paper's my big thing, I guess because I'm a secretary. I'm always looking for ways to make it last longer."

Finally she paused for breath. A thought glimmered.

"Anne Marie, was that the real reason for using Easter and Christmas bulletins last week? I mean, saving the planet, not just money."

She sighed. "Who complained?"

I indicated Miss Davenport.

"Figures. She's always at me over something. She doesn't understand. Probably Alzheimer's."

I raised the cup to my lips to hide a smile.

"Well, I have to talk to Eileen about those cups. See you, Doctor Wilder."

I watched as she clomped away on her sandals. With all the people I'd spoken with, nothing had any bearing on the farm or what had happened there, or any of us who had owned it.

I was thinking about that as I went back to the stands, pausing beside them. I was handing up a drink to Rachel when a gravelly voice broke out behind me.

"I hear your old man left you with a real problem on your hands, Ms. Russell. Don't surprise me."

I froze, my arm upraised like the Statue of Liberty's. Rachel looked at me anxiously. I lowered my arm with care and turned 'round. Close-cropped grizzled hair circled a nearly bald pate. His head was bent low over a match and cigarette. He drew himself back up to his six feet and blinked his piggy little eyes at me from behind his glasses.

Then he added, "Nope, your pop never was much good for anything except trouble."

"My father had nothing to do with those bodies, Mr. Lamberson."

He wore a cream polo shirt and khaki slacks. His shoes were sneakers, top-of-the-line discount store. He looked like someone aspiring to middle-class prosperity but not quite making it. Money for two decades, but the early years of blue-collar labor still showed.

"I'll thank you to keep your cop boyfriend out of my hair. I don't appreciate having my vacation ruined bein' dragged into some police station to talk about something I had nothin' to do with!"

"You know, it's funny you should say it that way. After all, you owned the property most of those twenty years."

"That doesn't mean a thing!" he said sharply.

Arthur, who was seated on the other side of Rachel, peered over the bleachers at us. "Lamberson, that you?"

"Yeah, who's that?" Lamberson squinted up at him.

"Arthur Swandeck."

"Art Swandeck, how the hell are you?"

Arthur looked at Lamberson's outstretched hand like it had spit on it. "He botherin' you, Doc?"

Vince's eyes grew blacker. "No, I'm not. Mind your own business!"

"Is he, Doc?"

"It's all right, Arthur," I reassured, marveling at the number of words he'd spoken.

"Okay." He looked back toward the game, but I noticed he kept an ear cocked towards our conversation.

Lamberson was studying Rachel and Arthur. "She yours?"

"No," I said firmly and redirected the conversation. "What was it with you and that property, Lamberson? First you pressure my parents into selling it to you, then, even when the Hicks bought it, you still kept your fingers on it. You didn't like it when they got a new mortgage, did you? Why? How did you talk my father into selling to you, anyway?" I took a step towards him, and he fell back, his face reddening. The words poured out of me of their own accord. "Just how did you - ?"

The bleachers shuddered under the collective weight of spectators rising to their feet. A woman screamed. I turned toward the thudding sound of running feet as players converged on first base. A player was on the ground, clutching his throat. Kyle was waving frantically at me.

Carmen was at me, grabbing my arm.

I looked from Lamberson to Rachel wildly. "Rachel -   stay with Arthur. Don't move!" I slung my shoulder bag higher and raced out to first base.

The boys made a thick circle around him. An arm snaked out and tugged me in as Carmen pushed aside crowding bodies. It was Tony who lay on the ground. He still held his hand to his throat, and his face was reddening, his eyes wide, frightened, threatening to bulge. A few inches away lay the ball.

Kyle looked gray. "It hit him right in the throat, Doc! Straight out from the bat!"

I nodded, opened my purse, and fished around in the side pocket. Men may joke about large shoulder purses, but they make the best friend a female doctor ever had. I was never without tools. I whipped out a sterile-wrapped scalpel, and a packet of tubing, and cloth tape. I thrust the tube packet at Carmen. "Open it and hold it ready. Somebody get his shoulders!"

His coach held him down.

Locating the telltale notch, I cut a slit, inserting the tube almost as I removed the knife. His color eased even as I taped the tube in place. Gingerly I felt the surrounding tissue.

"Someone call an ambulance?"

"Yeah," panted a heavy-set man with freckles mapping out large areas of his arms. "They're coming. I'm the principal. Is he okay?"

"He will be." I finished checking Tony's heart and other signs. Then I addressed the scared eyes that made him look so much more a child than he had the other night. "This is temporary, Tony, so you can breathe. Your trachea -   your windpipe -   took the hit. The tissue swelled so rapidly it cut off your breathing, but I'm almost sure there's nothing broken or crushed. We'll make sure in the hospital. You'll be okay. Don't worry."

I looked at the players. "Anyone know if his parents are here?"

"We're right here, Doctor Wilder."

I looked up at a couple demonstrating remarkable restraint. They'd said nothing, made no distracting scenes, though they'd obviously seen the whole operation. Quietly, Tony's mother came forward and knelt next to him, tenderly wiping his hair out of his eyes, and grasping his hand with a serenity that seemed to pass right to her son. It was clear her presence would keep him still until the ambulance people maneuvered into position. From the corner of my eye I saw the orange and white rescue unit pulling up the gravel drive. I rose and spoke to Tony's father.

"Thank you for not coming up to him too soon. He will be all right. Do you want me to treat him?" I had to ask, and I had to ask right then, before I did anything further than emergency care.

"I'm an orthopedic surgeon, Dr. Wilder. My wife was an Army nurse in the Gulf. We know when to let a professional do her work. I'd be pleased if you would continue to be my son's physician. There's no reason for us to go elsewhere." He looked across at Carmen. "If there ever was."

The paramedics came up then, and started their jobs. With the help of Tony's father (Dr. Fortescue, I discovered), I established myself with them and agreed to meet them at the Medical Center.

Rachel! I scanned the bleachers. Good, she was still sitting with Arthur.

"Dr. Wilder!"

It was Maude Davenport's friend, Merton, calling me from one side. "We'll take Rachel to her aunt's house if you need to go on," he nodded his balding head towards the ambulance. At my startled expression, he added, "Mr. Swandeck says he has a job to go on, and we've known the Jamisons a good long time. Lloyd Kerns is Maude's attorney."

"Thank you, so much! And - make sure you don't let her go with anyone else, okay?"

He nodded slowly, his eyes squinting as if he were puzzled I'd mentioned it. I hadn't seen Lamberson as I was looking for Rachel, but I didn't want him anywhere near Bryan's daughter. I was taking no chances. With her welfare safely disposed of, I had a patient to attend to, so I strode off to my car and lit out for the hospital.

CHAPTER 25

I've finally done it. I've returned home, and claimed Kings Hill for my own.

It 's different than when I was younger. Being born into a place doesn't make you a part of it. It took my rejecting it and leaving to teach me what there is to like about Kings Hill. Now I am staking a claim on it, just as my father once did.

Has it really been just a few weeks? With so much that's happened, so much I've discovered... the memories are running together, all intertwining, past meeting present, and turning back on itself again.

Am I me? Or am I just my father's daughter?

D oc, I got that estimate on the dormers!" My enterprising carpenter- friend called out the news to me.

"Thanks, Bret."

"Dormers? You're putting on dormers?"

"I'm thinking about it, Jean."

She shook her head at me. "Don't do anything halfway, do you?"

A familiar red Land Rover rolled into the driveway and laced its way through the myriad of loaders, dumpsters, 4-wheel drives and pick-ups.

"Looks like Mr. Fields is here," said Jean.

I laid down the list I'd been checking against the blueprints and dashed outside, jumping off the front porch and letting Jason scoop me up into one of his bear hugs.

"Hi. Just wanted to see how your work was coming along. And check on security." His eyes sparkled as he took in the activity, men on the roof, electricians stringing wire, wood scraps shooting out an open window into a dumpster, hammers pounding somewhere on the back side of the house, a saw whining as new framing was cut. "Where's Bryan anyway?"

"He's working. Now don't worry. I'm here with Jean and the entire crew. No one is going to try anything with all this going on."

"At least you're working over here. There's been a hold-up on permits and materials at my site. My crews have been sitting on their hands for three days. Let me know if you need any help."

"Come on, let me show you the inside." I tugged at his arm. He walked through alongside me, smiling approval and praising Bret's finds. As we watched demolition on the second floor, I told him about the last couple of days.

He grunted when he learned about what Carmen had put the boys up to. Then I told him about how yesterday's events at the ball game had seemed to eradicate for good any problems from that quarter. We wandered back outside so he could see the barn.

"Good," he said. "You've eliminated one problem. I take it you hadn't expected to run into Lamberson at the game. Why was he there?"

I shrugged. "Probably to see old friends. He has family here, too."

"From what you told me, I'd've thought he didn't have many friends. Does he have a grandson on the ball team or something?"

"I don't think so. I'm sure I'd have heard about it by now with all that's going on."

"I repeat, why was he there?" Those penetrating emerald eyes probed mine.

"You think he was following me?" My rising tones drew looks from the workmen.

"Maybe not exactly following you, but how about checking up on you? After all, he's ticked off about Bryan questioning him. Maybe he got wind of the fact you were going to be at the game. I don't like the sound of what he said to you."

We were standing in front of the barn now. Jason's head tilted back as he inspected the roof line for sags and took in the old creosote-colored boards, the gaping opening, the timber-lined concrete ramp leading inside.

"You know," I gave a weak laugh, "this is starting to sound like one of your mysteries."

He turned his gaze to watch a circling hawk. His eyes slid down to look at me sideways. "What did Bryan say about all this?"

"He was as relieved as you were about nailing down the identity of my 'stalkers'. He was happy the Fortescues and the others changed their minds about me. He didn't say what he thought about Lamberson being there - other than to say he was glad I kept Rachel away from him."

It was obvious I hadn't made Bryan wait two whole days before bringing him up to date. I walked ahead into the cool interior of the barn with its sense of immense space. Despite everything, this was the same spooky old barn that had haunted my childhood. There were the same old chicken coops my parents had built, even some of the same old junk in the hayloft where Pop had struggled up the creaky open stairs to chuck things - "in case he needed them." I swore I spotted the very car seat (not infant seat, but the bench seat from the back of Pop's old Chevy) in which Wrinkles had her last litter of kittens.

"I'll have to clean this out," I said unnecessarily. Jason put his arm around me loosely.

"At least enough to make better room for your boat. How on earth did you get it in here?"

"It wasn't that hard," I protested.

"I know a guy who could probably haul away most of this junk."

"Not until I go through it. There might be treasures here, at least, someplace," I muttered, peering around me.

Jason bent down, examining the *PsyKe*. He eyed the curve of the deck, and wiped some dust off the chrome trim, ran a hand along the finish. "Have you shown this much?"

"Just once. I want to get her up to the show in Clayton - the Thousand Islands - some year. I got her in the water last week. Found a ramp behind my office. It's in pretty bad shape. Had to fight the weeds to get the boat out into the river."

"So you've got access? Want me to send a crew down? They can rebuild the ramp and even put up a boathouse, if you want. And I know a guy who sells portable boat repair racks for when you're working on them."

"Jason, is there anyone you don't know? For someone who just got here, you seem to know an awful lot of people."

He blushed. "Tell me about this boat, Mackenzie."

I sat down on an old bench a couple feet away from the boat. "The *PsyKe* is the first boat Brian and I bought. I think I told you about that. We found her in a tiny marina down near Wilmington, North Carolina. The owner had left it with the marina in trade - I don't know what he got for it. The guy at the marina didn't know either, because the boat had been in the back when he took over the place ten years earlier. There were a couple of papers that went with it, and a picture the guy had hanging on the wall."

I stood on the bench and leaned over the side of the boat, reaching into a glove-type compartment. "See here? These are sale papers from New Jersey. 1946. And it sold again in 1963. But that leaves these gaps before and after. We *think* it was built in Algonac, Michigan -   that would have been the right time for that plant. But we don't know who bought it first, and we don't know anything about the thirty years before we got it. There's no telling what this boat has seen."

Jason examined the boat from stem to stern, his gaze traveling her length steadily. He reached in and fondled the steering wheel, tapped a gauge, patted the leather.

"They do capture the imagination, don't they? I can feel the pulse in the wood, water slapping the sides of the hull, the smell of the fuel, the breeze going by, the fish hauled in on a summer's day, and the cocktails spilled on the seat after an evening on some lake."

"You want to know what grabs me? The stories about the racing boats. Do you know who Gar Wood was?"

"Isn't that the name of a kind of boat?"

"Gar Wood was a man who invented the hydraulic lift used on dump trucks. He also designed and raced wooden boats. In 1928, he was entered for the Harmsworth Trophy in England. Seventeen days before the race, he and his mechanic crashed the Miss America VI. It was powered by 2200-horsepower twin Packard aircraft engines. The mechanic broke his jaw and some ribs. Get this, they still raced in the Harmsworth -   what a name, right? -   in a new boat, with the *same engines* installed. And they won the trophy!"

"Sounds like my kind of people," Jason said.

"I suppose, in a way they were. They were crazy! I've seen books refer to them as fearless, but I've heard it called reckless, too. And anybody who races a wooden boat with aircraft engines is just asking for trouble!"

"Reckless, huh? Maybe about as reckless as someone who keeps trying to find a murderer?"

"I - it's not the same thing! I'm not deliberately putting myself at risk - I mean, we don't know that - Oh, it's just not the same thing. At all." I got up and moved back to the main corridor we'd cleared between the stuff packed into the barn.

"Anyway, to return to the conversation, I do have to clean this place up. I could store a dozen boats in here if I wanted."

"Well, while you're planning where to stack the watercraft, maybe you'll find something. I mean, the bodies were found here, there may be more clues."

I stared at him. "You know you're brilliant?"

"Of course I am, it's my stock in trade."

We wandered about the perimeter of the interior, poking into things. I realized this would be a tall order, but the very scope of the job lent plausibility to Jason's theory that we might find something here.

"Mackenzie! Mackenzie! You in here?" Rachel stood in the doorway to the barn, her hands clamped around her eyes like binoculars as she peered in. She scampered towards me as I moved to the entrance.

Brooke followed behind her. "Jean told me I'd find you here. Mackie, we need to talk. Can we go back to the house?"

Walking back I mentioned Jason's suggestion that I might find more clues in the barn. Brooke held up her hand to me, a funny look passing over her face.

"Doctor Wilder!" The shout came from atop a teepee arrangement supporting an electrical meter. "We're turning off the power until we can re-wire the kitchen!"

The man scrambled down from his perch and walked over, moving like a cowboy too long in the saddle. He jerked a thumb over his shoulder. "I have to go. A job I was on last week is in trouble. I'm leaving the meter unhooked 'til tomorrow. Everyone's ready to break for the day anyway. Okay with you?"

"Well...."

"What's on that line?" Jason asked briskly.

"Phone and electric." The worker grimaced. "I don't like running them together like that, but the way this place is hooked up, I more or less had to. Is that gonna be a problem, Doc?"

"Want me to send some of my people over, Mackenzie? It might speed things up a bit."

Brooke was flashing me signals. Whatever she wanted to talk about, apparently it was something she didn't want workmen to hear. Now I was curious.

"Never mind, Jason. You guys go on ahead for today. Jason, Brooke, let's grab something out of the cooler, then go sit on the front porch."

We settled on the cement porch, surrounded by stacks of lumber putting a tang on the air that mingled with the scent of bursting lilacs. Rachel slurped some Coke®, then set it beside mine while she turned cartwheels on the grass. The lilac guarded her shadow much as it had mine when I tumbled about twenty-plus years ago.

"Okay, Brooke, what is it?" I asked.

She glanced around, taking in Jean and Jason and Rachel and myself. "It is just us now, isn't it? No one else left?"

"Yes. Sure. What is it?"

"I pulled out the papers on the farm. You know how Lloyd makes me keep copies of everything I do?"

I nodded.

"Well, being as how it was you, I was twice as careful. I kept copies of notes, phone calls, everything. I especially kept copies of things going on file. Like the papers I filed with the title office. Besides your normal copies, I have copies of the contracts on this house going back for the last five owners."

I cocked my head at her. "Five? That would be me, the Hicks, Lamberson, my folks, and the -   the -   oh, who'd they buy it from? It doesn't matter -   you've got the Lamberson contract? What does it say?"

Jason watched us quizzically.

"Actually it's all really interesting. I followed it back through the Hicks' refinancing contract, through their contract with Lamberson, then his with your parents. Remember, he said he didn't have his copy of the contract. No reason he should, really, but many people would."

Jean nodded. "I have copies of every paper I've signed since I was eighteen years old. I even have my first driver's license."

"See? Yet Lamberson says he doesn't have a copy of the contract he made to purchase a piece of land that was used for both his residence and his business. Remember, this land made his business. Now the Hicks' refinancing agreement made no reference to any special parcels of land or treating any bit of the property differently than any other. It's a very brief and simple contract, almost Spartan. Lloyd spent a lot of time admiring it."

I smiled.

Brooke went on. "In the original purchase agreement the Hicks had with Lamberson, where he held the mortgage -   "

Jason interrupted. "Wait a minute -   he held the mortgage himself? That's odd, surely."

"He held the mortgage all right," I put in. "I read in Marlene's diary that he let them be late with their first payment, but then he raised their interest rate! And apparently bad-mouthed the Hicks to the bankers in town. Marlene hated him."

Brooke was nodding agreement with Marlene's sentiment. "With good reason. Lamberson's interest was already two points above average. When he raised it, it must have been four points higher than anyone else's."

I stared at her. "You're kidding! We held his mortgage on the place when he bought it, but it was at a lower rate. So all that money wouldn't be wasted going to a bank, he said. That son of a - "

"Wait, it gets better. That clause about the stretch of land behind the barn? It's in Lamberson's contract with the Hicks!"

"Why? Pop put that in to protect Jake's grave. Why would Lamberson keep it in?"

"That's what I wondered. I thought maybe he'd just left it there to save time. In reading the contract, however, substantial changes were made in the rest of it."

"Excuse me, but what are we talking about?" Jason wanted to know.

"When Bryan asked him about what condition he'd found the farm in when he took over - that is, if there'd been any freshly turned earth or anything - Lamberson told him no, except for the piece of land Pop had planted in daylilies and a cedar tree and asked him not to touch. Pop had it put in the contract that the ground was to be left alone. Lamberson laughed about that and told Bryan he'd agreed to it because he'd known he could always change his mind and Pop wouldn't be able to do anything about it. What?"

Jason was shaking his head in surprise and sympathy, but Brooke's head was moving back and forth in emphatic disagreement with something I'd said.

"It wasn't your father who put that clause in. It was Lamberson."

"But - then he - so - No. That can't be right."

"It is, though."

"How can you tell?"

"I said I had copies of everything, remember? Including Lamberson's original contract offer, and the subsequent changes it went through. The original offer has a specific clause in it stating that that piece of land would not be dug up or developed."

"That's the clause Pop put in."

Brooke contradicted. "No, Lamberson put it in. The realtor who handled this was the guy I took my courses from. He had this little trick he taught us. You know how you have to initial every change you make in a contract?"

I nodded.

"Well, Mike Schwartz always had the person who put in the change initial it first. The other party put his initials right under it. That way, he said, he could always tell without checking who had asked for what in a deal. It was just a little shortcut he used, but he always used it. So do I. In the contract, it's Lamberson's initials on top by that clause. Your father's are below them. *He* agreed to a clause that *Lamberson* put in."

"It's phrased as if Pop wanted it. It mentions the daylilies and the tree he planted. Keeping it as a memorial. Why would Vince Lamberson put it in there? Unless - oh my God - he wanted it to look like Pop wanted that clause in there!"

"The way you say it's worded, I'd say you're right," Jason put in. "Question is, why is it there at all?"

"The logical reason - and the reason I like - is he knew the bodies were there, and he didn't want them dug up."

"But why bother putting the clause in the contract? Why not just let things lie? Oh, sorry." Jason apologized for the pun when Jean shoved his shoulder.

"I know. The clause draws attention to the land. You'd think he'd want to keep it as quiet as possible. It doesn't make sense."

"It's something to think about. It's another lie he told, for one thing. Your father didn't ask that the land be left alone - so maybe he isn't the one who buried Jake there," said Brooklynne. "Although Lloyd did check up on Jake's GI insurance. It was never used."

"Oh, it was Pop who buried him all right. The ring proved it to me long before anything else did. It makes this clause thing that much more peculiar."

"I wanted to tell you about it as soon as possible. I'm telling Bryan everything as soon as I see him. Meet me at his house tonight, why don't you? Jason, you come too."

"Sounds all right to me. I may do some checking up before I get there." He stood up to leave, Brooke right behind him.

"Mackenzie, can I stay with you? I won't be any trouble." Rachel was hanging on my arm. She passed me a sly look through her strawberry blond hair. "Besides, you're going to my dad's anyway, right?"

Brooklynne laughed. "Mackie, you want her?"

"Sure. I'm going to settle a few things here, then I'll be over."

"Yay!" Rachel jumped up and down.

"You don't have any electric," warned Jean.

"I know. I won't be very long. I just want to close up and take a quick look through the barn."

In no time, the others were gone, and I'd put away my papers, checked the demolition upstairs (sweeping some of it aside for tomorrow's crew), marked off Bret's lists (he really was my favorite carpenter), and tidied up some stray cans and litter. Together Rachel and I walked down to the barn.

The timbers looked warm in the late afternoon light. Pigeons circled the roof-peak, perching momentarily to bustle about and coo, then plummeting down in free-fall before flapping up and away again. One flew in the window set high in the gable and disappeared into the blackness behind it. The cavernous opening drank in light from the westering sun.

"Can I mess around in there, Mackie?"

"Yes, watch your footing, though. Stay away from the haymow. If you're not sure about something, don't do it," I called after her.

"I know," she hollered, then vanished under a timber railing and up onto the old chicken coop. As I prowled throughout the barn, I heard her clambering and tunneling her way about.

I realized that if I were going to find anything, it would probably be in the back. That was where things seemed the least touched, as if both Lamberson and Hicks had simply shoved things back to make way for their own. I pushed past where Pop's old table saw had stood where he'd cut lumber for shelves and stools and that funny ride-on airplane he'd built me. Of course, he'd also cut frames for the crates for his marijuana plants, as well as simple plank huts to shelter his stills on that same saw. Let's not forget who he really was.

Back in this corner was the door to another room. It had to be one of the grungiest, oldest parts of the barn. There were things back here that predated even our tenure on the farm. Ancient tools coated with the grease and sawdust that seems to protect tools as much as it ruins clothes. Car parts, grain feed bills -   good Lord, here was one from 1947! A notepad with its disintegrating leather jacket. Notes -   parts lists mostly - printed in that peculiar mix of large and small caps my father used. I read in wonder, smelling in my mind the sunny, outdoor smell my father's brown skin always had. I thought that time was wiped out of existence, the time when I admired my father.

I squatted down and peered under the workbench. Tucked in back, against the wall where it couldn't have been moved for years, was an old wooden box. I pulled it out and opened it. The inside was lined with felt. A black-barreled, wood-handled gun lay to one side, secured by clean rumpled cloths. The gun looked remarkably like Pop's .357 Magnum. Beneath it lay a piece of paper.

I didn't recognize the handwriting. The word was puzzling: 'insurance.'

I sat back. This was a momentous discovery, right? It had to be. A clue - but to what? My father's gun (I felt sure) and - insurance?

I left the gun alone. Fingerprints, I thought. The bullet that had killed Jake Terry had been from a .357. The thought revolted me. Pop? Kill Jake? Not likely. Oh, I knew he could kill. I'd faced up to that. But Jake was his best friend! Pop shooting Jake didn't make sense. Jake's death had been no accident. That bullet had been carefully aimed, and not from far away. And possibly fired from this gun, but not by Pop.

Somehow someone had gotten hold of Pop's gun and shot Jake with it. I saw in my mind a stranger's hand stealthily pulling Pop's gun off the cabinet where he'd kept it. It had either been handy, or the person deliberately stole it to implicate Pop. That would be the main reason to use another person's gun. Then that same hand, from not far away, fired the gun and shot Jake dead. My mind's eye saw another hand raising a primitive hand ax and bashing in the stranger's skull.

I gasped.

If Pop had caught the person who shot Jake, the first thing he'd have done was grab the nearest weapon and take out after him. It made sense! Stranger kills Jake; Pop kills stranger. Pop buries both to cover up murders.

Who was the stranger?

What was it with this box? 'Insurance.' It read like a label. Could this gun really be the one that killed Jake? Would it have incriminated Pop - was that why the stranger took it? Only if Pop's fingerprints were on it, but Pop would have wiped them off, wouldn't he? And who was I talking about? If I was right, Jake and his killer were dead. So what did it mean?

I tried to remember what it had been like. Pop trying to get us to sell the farm to Lamberson. Lamberson pulling strings, getting Pop drunk, having him call us. Trying to get Pop to forge our signatures on the sale papers. Jake talked with Mom more than once about how he didn't trust Vince Lamberson, didn't like his tactics.

"I been talking to Wylvern. Tryin' to get him to see sense. He shouldn't sell that land. It's all he's got. I know Lamberson won't give you a fair price. He's the meanest, cheatin'est man I ever knew. Don't worry, missus, I won't let him get to Willie."

That's the last thing I ever remember hearing Jake Terry say. So... it had to be. Somehow it had to be... that Vince Lamberson was involved.

I heard a noise behind me. Rachel, probably climbing back down from the hayloft.

A hand lay heavily on my shoulder. Another reached forward and shut the box. Before I could protest, I was pulled to my feet, my hands jerked behind me and rope looped around them.

"My son told me you'd bought the place back. Right after they found the bodies, too. Damned inconvenient. And you decidin' you gotta solve things! As if that damn policeman boyfriend of yours wasn't enough!"

More rope was wound around my waist and up under my shoulders. Shock had kept me silent so far. Now my mind set off a warning klaxon. Where was Rachel?

The ropes were being gathered together behind me near my hands. More rope snaked through them.

"I'm not sure what I'm gonna do with you. I've got to be somewhere, so this'll do for now."

The man whirled me about to face him. Age did not seem to have slowed him down any. He was amazingly strong for someone of sixty-odd years.

"It *was* you! But who - "

"Shut up! That fool Jake. Always interfering. Almost had your father convinced not to sell! I needed this land! I wasn't going to let two worthless old bums keep me from what I wanted!"

"So you murdered him - just to get some land!"

"I said shut up! It doesn't make any difference what I did - or your old man. He wasn't worth much anyway!"

"You son-of-a-bitch! This place meant everything to him. He couldn't live without it! You might as well have killed him, too. As far as I'm concerned, you did!" I spat the words at him.

He shrugged. "Don't matter." He grinned, a big, jovial, hate-able grin. "Look at it this way, it's something you two'll have in common."

He jerked me about. He'd tied a long rope onto the ones binding me, like a lead. "Come on. I've got to get out of here."

He tucked the box under one arm and held the rope in the other fist. He dragged me forward with him, not even bothering to look back at me. He just kept moving forward with me stumbling over the rough boards.

We edged through the corridor that ran along the barn's center. My elbow caught briefly on a rake handle, toppling it. He responded with a grunt and a harder tug on the rope.

There was no sign of Rachel at all.

We paused next to my boat. Still holding my tether, Lamberson hoisted the box over the side, dumping it with a clatter onto the front seat. He sneered at me as if he appreciated the irony of putting it there, then shoved me in the direction of the lower haymow, the one that had never been cleaned. Someplace in there was hay that had been grown before I was born - or at least its dust. He pushed me under the beam that ran alongside the old chicken coop. The same beam Rachel had ducked under maybe twenty minutes before.

Where was she?

He bent beneath it, hand gripping the lead firmly, pulling me along. The chicken coop came almost to the edge of the haymow. We stood on the narrow walkway. Maybe fifteen feet below lay the hay: dirty, moldy, rat-infested.

Lamberson was busy tying his end of the rope to the beam.

"Siddown," he muttered.

"What? I can't."

"I said, sit down!" He pushed me down with one hand. I fell to my side, squirming to roll back from the edge. I sort of wiggled my legs around, but I couldn't really sit up.

"Over you go!"

I gasped as he shoved me over the edge.

I stopped after only three feet. My face banged into the old plank wall. My body planed out at about thirty degrees, my hands jerked behind me, the ropes about my chest and waist cutting into me. Dust and mold wafted toward me.

Hand over hand he lowered me further into the pit-like mow. He stopped me somewhere above the hay. I couldn't see around me, and I couldn't turn my head to look up. I swung about, dangling in space, bumping against rough boards. I could feel the scrapes and bruises forming.

"There!" he said smugly. "I'll be back when I've decided what to do with you."

"Lamberson!"

"I don't think I have to worry about you hollering. I'll be back later."

I listened as his footsteps echoed off the dark walls. Gravel crunched, and I heard an engine start up and roar away, disgusted I hadn't heard it earlier.

My feet thumped the boards, the hollow sound underscoring my helplessness. At least it wasn't my face again. The scrapes were starting to sting. I tried to think, but my thoughts raced too fast to catch. Fear chased them round and round. I tried to stop my swinging, but I couldn't really do anything effective. Everything had begun to hurt dreadfully.

"Mackie?" A very small voice floated down to me. "Mackie?"

"Rachel! Where are you?"

"Up here. On top of the chicken coop. Is he gone?"

"Yes, honey."

"Mackie, are you hurt bad?" She sounded more concerned than scared.

"No, honey, but I can't do anything. He's tied me up and hung me over the side into the haymow."

"Just a minute."

I heard a scramble. Her voice came again, closer.

"I'm down on the ledge. He's got the rope tied really tight. I can't untie it."

"That's okay. I don't think we should do that anyway."

What could we do? How soon would he be back? I couldn't keep Rachel here. Way too dangerous.

"Rachel, go back to the house and - " I stopped. The phones - the electricity - both off!

"It's okay. I've got an idea."

I felt a tug and a pull, then a strain on the rope. Everything tightened.

"Rachel, don't! You can't pull me up, honey."

"That's okay - I'm - not - trying - to." She grunted.

She was shinnying down the rope, trying to come slowly so as not to land on top of me.

Bless her! I had a flashback of the pretend games her father and I had played in kindergarten: Bryan rescuing his damsel in distress. Like his daughter was now.

"Careful, Rachel."

"Mackie, I can't see. Look out, here I come!"

She'd reached my back. I could feel her being careful as she slid along my back and down to the hay.

"Oh, no! Mackie, I can't reach you to untie you!"

She sounded so disappointed.

"Rachel, feel around. Are there any bales of hay still bundled together?" I had a sort of idea.

"I don't think so - wait a minute. Here's one. And here's an old crate or something. Here's some more hay."

"Okay, great! Take the crate and those bales of hay and stack them under my feet. Can you?"

"Sure. I'm strong." I heard her grunting, but there were no complaints. Now that she knew what to do, her nine-year-old confidence had kicked in. It seemed to take forever, but I was able to feel hay beneath my feet.

I got a grip and struggled into an almost upright position. The sudden relief to my arms made them tingle. I felt a small body beside mine.

"Let me try to undo that, Mackie. Daddy taught me a lot about ropes."

He would have. Bless him, too, I thought.

She struggled, her fingers maybe too small for this job. It was taking twenty - thirty minutes. We both were getting anxious, I for her safety, she for mine. Maybe she wouldn't be able to do this. She had to. What else could we do?

Suddenly the rope slackened. She'd gotten the first one off. The second came faster, and the third one right after that.

In relief we dropped down onto the hay in a heap.

"Mackenzie, why did that man want to hurt you?" She started to shake.

I squeezed her tight. "Rachel, he is a very bad man, and he knows I've found him out. Honey, he's very dangerous, but we're going to get out of here and get you back to your Dad so you won't have to worry. Okay?"

"Mackenzie? Did he kill my mother?"

Oh, God! "Rachel - I - don't know. But he is dangerous, and we need to get out of here fast. Hang in there."

She nodded, but I could feel the tension in her body. Small wonder. I had no idea how soon Lamberson would be back. Plus I thought I heard scuffles and squeaks in the shadows' depths. We had to get out now.

"Sit on the crate there. I'm going to check something out."

I made my way to the back of the haymow, feeling along the wall. There it was! Now where exactly did it come out?

"Rachel, can you meet me? Follow my voice."

I kept talking to her, moving slowly across the straw. I didn't want to think about what was crawling around in it - and I didn't want either of us to stumble in it! She met me part way, and I led her to the wall.

"Okay, brave girl. Here it is. This is a ladder that goes up the wall to a window. It's probably not latched, and I know it's big enough for us to climb through. But it's pretty far above the ground, right by the milkhouse outside. I'll go up first. You come up right behind me. When I go out the top, you wait until I say to come out. I'll probably have to catch you. Okay? Can you do it?

"Sure, Mackie."

She sounded tired now, but trusting. I hoped I wouldn't be letting her down.

"Watch the cobwebs," I warned, and started up, wincing as movement tore at abused muscles.

It worked. The window wasn't latched, and instead of being stiff, it swung out so loosely I thought it would fall off. There was a ledge outside the window. I climbed out and lowered myself down. The stretch was agony on my arms. I dropped to the ground. It couldn't have been more than eight feet.

"Rachel?"

She popped her head out of the window, a white blur in the failing light. I heard the grin in her voice.

"Yeah, Mackie?"

I raised my arms. Rachel had already climbed out on the ledge, and was letting herself down in the same way I had. I stepped forward and hugged her legs. Then I pulled her off the wall and held her close.

CHAPTER 26

Has everything become a nightmare?

Is any of this real?

Will it ever stop?

I catch myself. That isn't really what I mean. I want this *trouble* to stop. I want to stop Vince Lamberson.

I want my future to go on, a future that includes Bryan and Rachel and Kings Hill and this farm. I want that to go on forever.

O kay, okay. It's okay." I wiped our grimy faces. "We have to get out of here. Come on -   no, wait a minute. Come up here."

We circled the milkhouse, and I started up the barn's ramp.

A small whimper from Rachel as she hung back.

"It's okay. I'm getting something from the boat. Stay right there."

"Okay." But her answer was small, and fading.

I strode up to the boat and stood on the trailer fender. I could barely reach it, but concern for Bryan's daughter fueled me. I lifted the box out, jumped down and was back at her side.

"Let's go."

I grabbed her hand, and we ran to the Subaru. My purse was on the seat. I flung the box onto the back seat while Rachel scrambled into the front. I fumbled through my bag and snatched out my keys. Trembling as I fastened the seatbelt, hands shaking as I jammed the key into the ignition. I wouldn't begin to feel safe until I pulled out onto the state highway.

It wouldn't start. It cranked and whirred and made all the right noises, but it wouldn't start.

"Damn!" I hit the steering wheel with hands that couldn't feel.

"Mackie? Why won't it start? Mackie, you said we have to get out of here!" Her voice was ragged. She shook my shoulder.

"Rachel, I can't get it started. Look, he shouldn't be coming back this soon. If we wait a few minutes, maybe it'll start. It does this sometimes." I tried to count, to make myself wait for the car to adjust itself.

"Mackie! Mackie!"

"Rachel, it's going to be okay, honey - "

"No, Mackie, I see lights coming up the road! Look!"

I didn't even bother. I grabbed her wrist. "Come on!" I yelled, and pulled her past the steering wheel and out of the car. All the greens were gray, and the sky was the blue of ink. Lights were coursing up between the trees. Without thinking twice I dove inside the grove of white lilacs, dragging Rachel in with me and wrapping my arms around her. The lights slid from being reflecting beams into balls of yellow-white light. There was the unmistakable rattle of a loaded pick-up truck.

Would Lamberson drive a pick-up?

Rachel squirmed in my arms. "Mackie!"

"Shhh! We don't know who it is."

"Mackie, yes I do! It's Dorsey Wegman! She can help us!"

I let her go. She darted out and stood at the road's edge, waving frantically. With a prayer I came up behind her, hobbling over the ground, my adrenaline deserting me. I stood in the road itself and flagged Dorsey down. She rolled to a stop and stuck her head out the window.

"Doctor Wilder! What on earth! What are you doing out here in the pitch dark?"

I glanced at Rachel and shook my head ruefully as I talked to Dorsey.

"We got ourselves kind of caught up in the barn. They've turned off the electric temporarily. And now my car won't start. Do you suppose you could give us a lift? To Bryan Jamison's house. I have to get Rachel back."

"Sure, I can run you over there. Tupperware party can wait." She reached over and opened the passenger door. Rachel scrambled in first. I grabbed the doorframe to raise myself in, grateful for cold solid steel and sturdy purple pick-up trucks.

"Uh, Dorsey? Swing by my car, will you?"

"Sure, Doc."

She pulled alongside it and I popped back out. Opening the back driver's side door, I grabbed my medical bag and the box and threw them in the back of her truck. My hand slipped on something wet on the truck's door handle. I couldn't grip with my fingers. My hands were stiffening, and the adrenaline rush was dying. Tears started to shudder their way through my body as I listened to Dorsey.

"Truth is," Dorsey kept on as she spun through the driveway and on down the hill, "Truth is, I really don't like Tupperware. I'm thinking of dropping the parties. What do you think, Doc?" She looked over at me. "Good Lord, Doc, what happened to you? You're a mess!"

"Bet I am. We had a sort of accident in the barn. We're all right, though."

"I just want to get home," said Rachel in a small voice.

Dorsey looked from me to Rachel. "Home it is, pumpkin!" Then she spoke no more, but headed straight for Bryan's.

The house was lit up when we pulled in the driveway. Dorsey laid on the horn. Brooklynne and Bryan and Jason spilled out of the door.

"Daddy!"

I let Rachel out first, then climbed out, stiffness settling in. Dorsey got out to hand me the box and bag from the truck. She stopped when she saw me in the light.

"You sure you don't need to go to the hospital, Doc?"

"I'm sure. And thanks. You're a Godsend."

"He does put me in the darndest places." She grinned at me, and dropped the items on the porch and took off for Tupperware parts unknown.

Bryan scooped Rachel into his arms, smoothing her hair, hushing her gently. His eyes widened when he saw the condition of my face and clothes. He rushed us into the house, Brooklynne holding the door, Jason at my elbow. Gently Bryan set Rachel down and looked her over. She was not so bruised as I, but her hands were bloodied. Before Bryan could speak, I took them in mine.

"Rachel? What - ?" Then I saw my hands. They were red, swollen, the wrists scraped raw and bleeding.

Brooklynne made a choking sound and disappeared. I heard the sound of running water. Meanwhile, Rachel looked up into my face. "I didn't get hurt bad, Mackie. I just broke some nails untying you. That's your blood."

Bryan stared. Brooke came out and ruffled Rachel's hair.

"Come on, I've run some water to clean you up. Let your Dad talk with Mackenzie." She looked back at me. "She is all right, isn't she?"

I nodded. "A warm soak should do her good."

"You're next."

She started to lead her out of the room, but Rachel ducked back to me, wrapping her arms about me in a fierce hug.

"Everything's okay now, right, Mackenzie?"

I rubbed my cheek against her hair. "You bet. Thanks to you."

She squeezed me again. "You sure? I -   I don't want that man to hurt you - or kill you like Mommy."

Bryan started.

"Everything's going to be okay, Rachel. Your daddy and I will see to it."

She went at last to a curiouser-than-ever Brooke.

My spine melted. Strength seeped from my knees. Jason started to help me to the table, but Bryan stepped between us. He drew me over to the sink and began to wash my hands and face for me. I leaned against the countertop, certain I'd drop. His tenderness as he soaped and sponged and wiped was at odds with the tight jaw and terse command.

"Tell me what she meant."

My tongue had grown thick in my mouth. It felt as if it too had been tied up and unused for a while.

"She - I don't know - somehow she made the connection. She's smart, Bryan. She knows this is all related."

His lips tightened. He wrapped my hands in a towel and led me to the table. He sat close by my right, one arm along the back of my chair.

Jason brought over mugs of hot tea he'd made. Tonight he looked more than ever like Albert Einstein after a perm.

"I didn't know - hadn't realized - " lifting my hands, "I knew they hurt, but I didn't know what bad shape they were in. I couldn't feel anything. I just wanted to get here."

Bryan's fingers toyed lightly with the wrappings. In a soft, controlled voice he asked, "What happened out there, Mackenzie?"

I still fumbled. Why, when all I wanted was to get it out, did the words stick and scratch?

"He was there. After Jason left. It was him. He did it. He killed Jake. And he did this to me."

"And Rachel?" His voice trembled.

I put my towel-wrapped hands on his arm. "No, not Rachel. He didn't know she was there. Bryan, she saved me. She rescued me! He never touched her, never even knew she was there."

His voice was hard. "Tell me."

"Vince Lamberson."

He smacked his fist against the table. "Damn him!" His eyes went to mine. "Are you sure you're all right?"

"I'm okay. Now. He - he found me in the barn. Somehow he sneaked up on me. He tied my hands and wrapped some more rope around me kind of like a harness and he - he dropped me over the side of the haymow and left me hanging there. He had to leave, he said. But - but he said he was coming back and then Rachel got me loose - Bryan, she was great - but, he's going back out there, Bryan!" I was starting to come unglued.

His left arm slipped around me. I felt him motion with his right hand to Jason. Jason handed him the portable phone. Even as he patted my back and crooned comfort in my ear, Bryan was dialing the State Police.

He stood up and started pacing. Jason held my mug for me while I sipped some tea.

"This is Bryan Jamison. Get me Trooper Matheson - I said, get me Matheson right now."

The pain in my hands and fingers was subsiding. The swelling had halted and seemed manageable. With difficulty I held the mug myself as I finished off the tea. Jason refilled it. Bryan continued to bark into the telephone.

"I don't care if he's busy or off duty or talking to the damned Governor! This is Lt. Bryan Jamison of Albany Homicide. This is urgent and I want - *damn*!"

He came over and knelt down beside me, cupping my chin in his free hand.

"He isn't going to get away, Mackenzie. I promise."

My heart lurched at the darkness in his eyes and the steel edge in his voice. I stretched forward and kissed him.

Suddenly Matheson must have come on the line, for Bryan pulled back.

"It's about time! This is Jamison! Pick up Lamberson. Because he assaulted Mackenzie, that's why! And endangered my daughter! I'll tell you what happened after you put your men out! - Okay. Mackenzie's here with me. So's Rachel. They're all right, but Mackenzie's got a banged- up face, rope burns, swollen hands, and, it looks like - "

He tugged at my blouse, raising it to show my skin - red, bruised, streaked with raw marks where the rope had cut into me. Gently he dropped it. I couldn't tuck it back in.

He gulped. "It looks like she's got other injuries: scrapes and contusions. I don't think he hit her."

I shook my head at him.

"No, he didn't. Did he threaten you? I mean, to do more than he already had?"

"Yes. He said he was coming back as soon as he - figured out what to do with me. I'm sorry." I started to shake all over, gasps ripping out of me. My body responding to the fear I hadn't let myself feel.

Jason took the phone from Bryan's hand. "She needs you," he said, pushing Bryan towards me. "Trooper Matheson, this is Jason Fields. I can tell you what's going on. I know I don't have official standing. That doesn't matter; Mackenzie was attacked. Lamberson's coming back for her. Rachel wasn't harmed - seems she kept herself out of sight until Lamberson took off." He paused. "Yeah, well, it fits. Let me tell you what one of my people discovered in Florida. Lamberson hasn't exactly been in peaceful retirement down there."

He turned away, muffling his voice. I leaned against Bryan. I jumped when I heard Jason say the word 'kill'. That set off hiccups. My body definitely did not like hearing about its possible extinction.

I'd never really faced death before. Not since Brian died had I thought about it, and then, bluntly, it was my loss of him I dealt with, not the prospect of my own death. Struggling in the rope, dangling over the haymow, scheming to get Rachel and myself out of there, I was too involved to reflect on possibilities. Adrenaline-fueled I'd concentrated on fighting the battle without focusing on the consequences. Now I contemplated all I could lose.

You're okay. You made it out all right. This time. I stomped on my little voice and put my arms around Bryan.

"... that's what I thought, too. We're at Jamison's. Mackenzie needs attention, but we can manage. All right. All right." He laid the phone on the table and sat down across from us.

"Matheson will be here soon. He needs statements, and so on."

Bryan glared at him. "Yeah, I know, Fields."

Jason shrugged mildly. "I thought you'd like to know."

"Thanks, Jason. Really. Bryan, can you get my medical bag from the porch? I'll need more towels. Jason, could I have more tea?" I found the prospect of Matheson coming enervating. Bryan would be ready for action, and I wanted to show that I was, too. To my surprise, I felt I was.

"Ordering everyone around again? You're okay, then." Brooke stood in the doorway with a terry cloth robe over her arm. "I suppose this is out of the question, huh?"

"Well, for now, yeah." I grinned at her. "I seem to be getting my strength back. Thanks, Bryan."

He put the bag on the table and began rummaging around in it on my orders. Between us we pulled out what I needed, then Brooke and I went to work wrapping my wrists and washing the wounds on my sides and abdomen. The treatment took about twenty minutes.

"Rachel's sound asleep. That adventure took a lot out of her. I hope she'll get through the night okay."

"If she wakes up or has nightmares, just comfort her and give her some warm milk. I don't want to give her a sedative if it's not absolutely necessary. She was scared - mostly for me - but we got away. She didn't hear everything he said, and she didn't see what was in the box. The box! Bryan! Was there a box on the porch just now?"

"Yeah. Why? Is it important?"

I waved at the door. "Yes! God, I can't believe I forgot about it. Get it in here now. Ow! Damn! Brooke, there's some pills in here. They won't affect my thinking, but they should knock out this pain."

Jason smiled at my efforts. "I'd better tell you what my people found out about Lamberson."

"Your people? What, your spies?" I joked.

"You could call them that. They're people who check things out for me."

"All right. What did they find?"

"For a gentleman retired from what is essentially a small-time gravel and construction operation up here, he's managed quite an income. Last year he filed income well into seven figures. Very upfront paperwork he had, but there was rather a lot of it. A bit confusing as to exactly where his money came from - although all of it was obviously reported."

"Meaning what?"

"Meaning Vince Lamberson probably has connections - ones that could easily put him in touch with people such as your average work-a-day hit man." Jason's eyebrows disappeared beneath his curls.

"Hit men! Like the car that hit Deb!" Brooke lowered her voice.

"Not only that," put in Bryan, returning with the box. "Remember the old fractures in that one autopsy report? Not Jake, the other guy."

I shuddered. "You mean, he would have been a hit man, too? Betty said something like that. But I thought broken legs was what usually happened to their victims!"

Bryan explained, "It can be an occupational hazard for anyone working for the mob. If I remember what Betty said, it had apparently happened only once, so he must have learned his lesson. Point is, Vince's connections may go way back. That guy may be the actual shooter who killed Jake."

"But Vince said...! Well, I suppose he could have hired it out. After all, he did now, he may have done it then, too. But wait 'til I tell you what I found. Where does this fit in?" I pulled the box toward me and opened it. "Don't touch it!"

Bryan gave me a look. I smiled weakly. "Sorry."

They looked over my shoulder at the gun, murmuring. Bryan touched it gingerly with a pen.

"Is it the right kind?" Jason asked.

Bryan grunted. "Yeah. Jake was killed with a .357. Was this your father's, Mackie?"

"I'm pretty sure. See the note? What do you think?"

" 'insurance'. Hmph. What is that supposed to mean? Lamberson's insurance, maybe?"

"Bryan, remember those logs my father kept of his collections? Pop had marked though the listing of this gun with a line - but a faint line, with a question mark beside it. What if it was suddenly missing? What if he couldn't locate it? That's how he might have marked it. And - just before Vince nabbed me, I had this idea come to me...."

"Mackie - "

"No, listen, let me finish. Supposing someone stole Pop's gun, maybe with the intent to frame him for something. They'd be sure to keep his prints on it, right? And that would be their insurance against getting caught - or against Pop talking. So, this guy takes Pop's gun and shoots Jake, *on Vince's orders*. Only Pop catches him at it and - mad as hell like he would be - bashes him on the head with his ax. Then he gets scared and buries them both. And sells the land to Vince Lamberson in a rush to get out."

Jason stared at me. "It makes some sense. If that's what your father was like."

"You didn't know Pop. His temper was quicker and hotter than Texas hot sauce. And Jake was his only friend left."

"That still doesn't explain this note - or why the box was in the barn," Bryan said.

"The other guy could've written the note and stashed it all there planning on coming back for it afterwards. - No, wait, he'd be dead - "

"I thought you said Vince was taking credit for Jake's - "

"He was. He did. Okay, he stashed it. Bryan, that's it! I'm sure. That's how he maneuvered Pop into selling! And tonight, when he was talking, he was *proud* I blamed him for Pop drinking himself to death. He boasted that he'd send me to join him!"

Bryan's jaw clenched, and his eyes grew hard as he stared at the box. He glanced at his watch. "How long ago did we talk to Matheson?"

"Not all that long ago. But I expected him to be here by now, didn't you?" Jason reached out and nonchalantly shut the box.

Bryan tapped his pen on his hand. "If you were Vince Lamberson, and went back to finish a job and found your victim gone, what would you do?"

"I'd either get out of town, or, if I were losing my senses, I'd try to find my victim and finish her off anyway."

"Where would you look for her?"

"At her boyfriend's."

The two men stared at each other, my head swiveling back and forth between them.

"On the other hand," continued Bryan, "If you have someplace to be, and you think your victim is relatively secure...."

"...you might not know. You might not even be back yet."

"Oh, no," said Brooklynne.

Both men reached for their jackets. I stood up, and they froze in their tracks.

"I am not staying here!" I said.

"Now, Mackenzie, you've been through enough - " Jason began.

Bryan gazed steadily at me, a flood of memories flowing through his eyes. The predominant one was 'STUBBORN'. "If you're ready, come on."

I grinned.

"But first, take off your clothes."

"What?!"

"I've got an idea. Brooke -   get me Resuscitation Annie. The one with the radio hook-up. C'mon, Mackie."

"Bryan! I need something else to put on, for heaven's sake!"

"Oh. Yeah. Help yourself to some of my jeans and shirts. Second drawer of my dresser. I've got a new battery pack here someplace," he muttered, rummaging through a drawer.

"Yeah, right, like your jeans are going to fit me." I went off in search of, wondering what on earth he was up to.

There would never be a pair of Bryan's jeans that would fit me unless I spent about six months on a torture rack, but I found a pair of long cut-offs that fit me about like capris. A long-sleeved blue and white soccer shirt tucked in okay. I wandered back out, my clothes in hand, in time to see Bryan performing what looked like brain surgery on a very short brunette dressed in a tracksuit. Jason looked on intently, holding a minute antennaed radio at the ready. Bryan flipped a patch of skull into place and nodded.

"Testing - testing - one, two, three, four. Mary had a little lamb."

"Bryan? What is all this?" I handed him my clothes, catching the twinkle in his eye as he saw what I was wearing.

"Help me get these on her and I'll explain. We've got to hurry. This is Resuscitation Annie. We use her in rescue training."

Rapidly we stuffed her unwilling limbs into my jeans and Jaclyn Smith shirt. (Okay, so sometimes I shop at K-mart. Want to make something of it?)

Bryan went on. "To make training as realistic as possible, we use this model with the radio receiver in the head. It puts spontaneity into the exercise. With these clothes on her, we can make Annie look like Mackie."

"Gee, thanks."

"I see the likeness," offered Jason. "Especially around the ankles."

"Uh- huh! Okay, she's dressed like me and she's got a radio mouth. What good does this do?"

"No, no sign of Matheson yet, Bryan," said Brooke as if answering a question.

I caught Jason staring. "It's a twin thing," I told him. "Bryan, what - ?"

"Come on. Brooke, when Matheson gets here, explain everything to him, okay? Jason, Mackenzie, come on." He jammed the radio in a pocket and slung Annie over one arm and headed out the door.

Jason strode out behind him, holding the door for me. I tried one more time. "Bryan, what are we doing?"

By the time Jason had followed Bryan to his car, he'd thrown Annie in the back and was stretched out across the front, reaching under the seat. He pulled out a gun and checked to see if the clip was full.

It hit me then, a thump in the chest. Whatever we were about to do was dangerous and serious and probably permanent. I hesitated, until I remembered how permanently Vince Lamberson had wanted to hurt me. I had an idea how angry Bryan was with the man who had assaulted me, endangered his daughter, and murdered his child's mother.

He pulled out a small device and held it up, contemplating it. Jason reached out a hand.

"What's this?"

"Taser. It won't really be useful for this. Too many wires. Stun gun might work, though." He grunted as he fished another device from under the seat. "Think you could use this? I've pre-set it."

"What do I do?"

"Get close enough to Lamberson and hold it like this. Press here."

A zap and blue light and a faint smell of ozone.

"Ahh," said Jason. "Nice gadget. Are you sure it will do the trick?"

"At that setting, stunning him is the least it will do," Bryan said grimly.

We climbed into the car silently. Bryan started up and backed out the drive. He picked up the radio and handed it to me.

"Take a look at how this works. Try it out."

It was small, smooth, and easy to use. Sophisticated. I pressed 'on' and held down the red talk button.

"Hello. Hello? Test - one, two, three, four."

"Okay, now. Turn the volume way up, then try it with a whisper."

I turned it up to 'max'. "Test - one, two, three, four. Is that better?" I croaked into the mike. The sound emanated from the back seat where Annie accompanied Jason. It had an eerie quality, seeming to come from her lips. Jason stared.

"That is uncanny. I could barely hear you, but I could hear Annie. It was as if you were saying something to Bryan and Annie was talking to me. Fascinating!"

Bryan grunted. "Her electronics are top quality. Okay, here's what we're going to do." The car slowed as he explained in detail what we were going to attempt.

"We're assuming Lamberson is still out. He's left you hanging - literally - and he's figuring on finding you there when he gets back. If you've been there this whole time, you're tired, maybe not even conscious. Your arms at least have gone numb, maybe your legs, too. You've probably been screaming for help, even though you know there's none coming. You might be hoarse." He looked meaningfully at me. "You're discouraged, scared. After all, you're Wylvern Russell's daughter. How much of a problem can you be?"

"Okay. I get it. We're putting Annie in my place. And, the part about being hoarse, you want me to whisper into the radio. What do I say?"

"Try to get him to talk. Isn't that it, Bryan?"

"See if you can get him to tell you exactly what happened. Push him to spill as much as you can. Like how he had Deb killed, how it was really meant for you and so on."

"After he's told me everything, what's to stop him trying to finish me off and finding out he's dealing with Annie? That's not going to make him happy."

Jason leaned forward. "We'll stop him, Mackenzie. That's what we're for. We wouldn't - Bryan wouldn't let you risk anything more."

Bryan turned onto Wexford Road. We drove openly, high beams on, and with the AM radio blaring out the windows. I sat rigid in the front seat, barely turning my head to look at the barn as we drove by. The bandages on my wrists were soaked through with sweat.

We rode past the house. I saw my car sitting there. Under the circumstances a good thing it hadn't started. It looked like I'd never left. Bryan turned everything off but the engine, backed the car up and pulled in by the barn, coasting at my directions down the tracks that wound behind the barn, screening his car behind tall weeds and the mounds of earth the diggers had moved.

"No sign of anyone here, but I don't want to take chances. Be as quiet as you can."

The four of us (counting Annie) moved out, climbing the hill as silently as possible in the blue dark created by the partial moon. At the entrance to the barn, Bryan used his flashlight. The rope, now slack without its burden, wrapped the beam a few times before knotting and snaking onto the floor. I led the way under the beam to the lip of the ledge where Lamberson had dropped me over. My knees shook as I knelt to pull the rope up. Bryan said nothing but worked briskly. Jason watched the door and scouted around the chicken coop behind us.

"How did Lamberson tie you?"

"It - it went, I think," I drew a deep breath, steadying myself. I was a doctor, not a heroine. I tried again. "It was like this." I bound Annie's hands, then laced her up the way Lamberson had done me. "Then he tied this one through here. Like this, I guess."

"Good. Now, help me lower her down. How far?"

"Umm, my feet were about four feet off the ground. That's why it was so hard. Yeah, that should be about right. God, it does look real. In this light, you can't tell. Bryan, what if he shines a flashlight right on her?"

"He probably won't. He won't be expecting anything unusual, and he'll probably figure that the dark would terrify you more. We should be all right. Jason?"

"Right here."

"Think you can find a good hiding place?"

"I've got one picked out already. In here. I can prop the door so I can see out. Hearing's no problem."

"Watch your step in there," I warned. "Even petrified chicken crap is slippery." He groped his way into the chicken coop.

Bryan was setting up another rope - one he'd carried in around his waist. It was a climber's rope, complete with knotted intervals and a looped end. He passed an end around the beam and over to Jason who'd returned to the ledge.

"I hate to ask you this, Mackie. Will you let us lower you back down there?"

I swallowed. I stared down at that filthy, scary hole. Then I thought of Jake. And Pop. And no one to provide justice. I turned and picked up the rope, stepping into the loop like a stirrup. Nodding to the two men, I sat down on the edge once again, this time going over it of my own free will.

They lowered me slowly 'til I touched down in the hay, stumbling some over the uneven layers. I slipped the rope off my foot and gave it a tug. Bryan climbed down next, his gun in his belt. Beside me, he tugged the rope a second time, and with a chill passing over me, I watched it bob back up into Jason's hands. He leaned over and saluted us briefly, then disappeared from view as he went to his hiding place.

I stood there fingering the radio, while Bryan scouted out some cover for us.

"Our only choice is this corner over here, right under the ledge. I'll be able to cover him when he goes to pull 'you' up."

"How will we know what he's doing? We can't see anything from here."

"I can see some. That's why I wanted Jason up there. I'll protect you here. It may be better if you can't see him. You wouldn't be able to see him if you were still on the rope. This way you can't slip up."

"How do you do that?"

"Do what?"

"Go all professional like that. I know you care. How do you keep it under control?"

He looked over at me, then tucked his gun back into his belt, and wrapped his arms around me and kissed me as he never had before. Locked in the framework of his arms I felt safe. Excited. An excitement caught from him, from the fever of his work. A glimpse into his world affording me a comprehension I must hold onto for the future, I told myself.

He looked me over and gave a self- satisfied grin and told me, "Hide that light in your eyes. We have a trap to set." We moved back into the corner, and settled in to wait.

CHAPTER 27

There is a special quality to the sun, in autumn, when you're thirteen. The light is orange, but not too bright, the air still and dry and clear. A day for walking down a country road and collecting bittersweet.

Pine cones will be next, I think, as I picture snowfalls to my knees and forests made of sticks and stones like names that stick like the falling snow itself.

Deeper meaning in the memory than ever was in the live event. Only in memory am I aware that by spring I will not be here to walk this road.

W aiting is terrible. Time rubberbands -   stretching out, snapping to, stinging your emotions in the recoil.

Bryan had literally backed us into a corner. The concrete walls rubbed my shoulders. I kept thinking I felt spiders crawling on spindly legs all through my hair. My feet sank in the mossy bed of hay. He stood to my left, peering up into the lighter patch of dark above us, his gun ready. Annie hung against the planked wall some six feet away, her face not much higher than ours. I fingered the radio for comfort. The sight of Bryan ready to kill someone -   not in one of our make-believe children's games but for real - was troubling me.

Bryan had been the only guy I knew who baby-sat young children. I'd seen him bandage little girls' knees with infinite tenderness and play pat-a-cake with grinning infants. Now he held a police weapon in his hand, prepared to kill.

Was it right?

I felt a self-righteous burning to wipe out this vermin myself, to bring justice to Jake's memory. I wasn't holding a gun.

"Bryan!"

He turned, lowering the gun.

"How long have we been here? My feet are getting stiff."

He grinned. "About fifteen minutes. It just seems longer." He started to turn away.

"Bryan!"

"What?"

"Thank you," I said softly.

He kissed me again, hard, then turned back to his lookout position. I swear his eyes were twinkling.

I jumped once when Jason's head popped over the side as he checked to make sure we were okay. My fingers explored the surface of the little radio until I had it memorized. I gazed at Resuscitation Annie, thinking that if I'd really been hanging there myself all this time, I'd be half-dead.

My hands would be totally numb; the circulation cut off; serious tissue damage might have begun. My skin would be chafed and the muscles under my ribs bruised. My shoulders, unable to withstand the stress, would be displaced. Back and neck muscles would have passed through pain into tingling numbness as they lost the battle to maintain any position on their own. My head would hurt, and my throat would be sore. It felt dry now, just thinking about it.

I can't tell which happened first: Bryan's shoulders tensing or my ears picking up the hollow clop of heavy shoes meeting the barn floor. The skin on my arms prickled.

There was a metallic scraping sound, then a scuffle. Lamberson had come under the beam to stand at the edge of the haymow. He grunted as he tested the ropes.

Bryan pushed me further into the corner, then nodded upwards. I was to say something.

My hands shook. I raised the radio to stiff lips. Bryan's thumb circled about the gun handle.

"Who - who's there?" I croaked. "Help me!"

I knew I'd spoken the words, but even to me, they seemed to come from the body suspended from the rope. He bought it.

"I told you before, callin' for help wouldn't do you any good!"

"Lamberson! You son-of-a-bitch! Let me go!"

"I don't think so. You've given me too much trouble."

"Lamberson! You - you can't be serious."

"The hell I'm not! I'm not letting you take everything away from me. Not now! Not after all I've been through!"

"Been through? You?" I held my breath.

"Yeah."

"Like what?"

"Like trying to get that mother of yours to sell. Like keeping the police far enough away from that farm so they wouldn't figure out what was really going on. Like spending my good hard-earned money keeping myself out of the courtroom."

I cut off a gasp. He'd sat down. I could hear his shoes thumping against the boards above our heads. Then I heard the scratchy clicks as he flicked a lighter twice before the flame held. I smelled the cigarette as he lit up.

"Is that a cigarette?"

"Why, you want one?"

"Put it out! You want to set off this hay?" I made my voice frantic.

"Don't worry, nothing like that is going to happen. I know what I'm doing."

I thought I detected a slight movement, and I felt him laughing. I grabbed at Bryan's hand. He frowned at me and motioned me to start talking again.

"Be careful! When are you going to let me down?" I let myself whine.

"In my own time. Don't you want to know what's going on? Hang on and I'll tell you." There was a sort of a wheeze (more laughter), then he continued. "About twenty years ago there was this piece of land. It had more than enough gravel on it to keep my trucks busy for a good long time. Not just gravel, either. Sand, fine black sand. For a while I had a deal with the owner, and I worked the gravel bank. I moved another one of my hauling businesses in. Of course, that was without his knowledge, but I didn't really think he'd mind. After all, he was on the wrong side of the law himself over a few things. Worked out fine for a while. The cops had their suspicions, but I wasn't their focus. Wylvern was. That was all right by me."

"Go on," I croaked.

"There I was, surrounded by all that gravel, all that opportunity. No one knew about my sidelines. Where there wasn't gravel or sand or drugs, there were Christmas trees, ready to sell. There was a house to live in and a barn big enough to store my boat. The perfect set-up, just waiting for me. I wanted it. But the owners wouldn't sell. Sound familiar?"

I snorted into the radio, wishing there were some way I could toss 'my' head for emphasis.

"One of the owners was an old drunk. The others were his wife and teen-age daughter. Got them figured out, right?

"I tried everything I could to get these people to sell to me. After all, I'm a fair guy. I offered a good price. They couldn't get it together. One day old Wylvern, he'd be ready to sell. Next day, when he sobered up, he wouldn't. But it seemed we couldn't ever talk his wife and kid into selling. So I tried out a few ideas...." He paused to draw on his cigarette.

"I know this part of the story, Lamberson. I was there!"

"Yeah, well, did you know about when I almost had your old daddy ready to forge his little girl's name to the papers?"

"Yes, I did. Jake told us!"

"That's what I figured. That's when I decided Jake had to go. He was gettin' in the way too much, always pullin' your old man away just when he was drunk enough to sign."

Lamberson stood up. He tugged on the rope, causing 'me' to swing and bobble against the side. Bryan signaled me worriedly.

"Hey!" I cried out. "Stop!"

Lamberson ignored me. "That's when old Wylvern decided to get in the middle of things. But, it all came out the way I wanted."

He stepped away for a moment. We heard the sound of a metallic screw top, then the velvety slop of something pouring, like a canteen. The top screwed on again. He came back.

"Yeah, Wylvern got involved in Jake's death. That was his mistake. But it worked out just fine. Gave me an advantage over him."

"Your 'insurance'. Right?"

"You've been thinkin' while I was gone. I hired young John-o to take out Jake. Set him up with Wylvern's gun. Easy to do. Your old man didn't know where his ass was, let alone any of his guns. I'm watching from up on the hill. John-o goes and plugs old Jake, shuts him up fine. Your old man sees him. I don't know where the hell he came from, but he had that old hatchet with him, and he let John-o have it in the back of the head. I high-tail it down there, and there's Wylvern standing over John-o. I come up, and Wyl pulls the gun out of John-o's hand and gives it to me. He trusts me, see? So he says, 'Hold this on him while I get some rope. Then we'll call the cops. He killed Jake!' He hands me the ax too, and then goes for the rope."

I felt sick. Jake's loyalty to our family had killed him. And Pop had killed a man.

"Then," said Vince with a snigger. "Then it started to get funny. John-o was comin' around. Now I'd already - "

"What!" I screeched, barely keeping it down enough not to be heard directly.

" - already planned to get rid of John-o," Lamberson continued calmly. "This just made things better. Before he could sit up, I whacked him again, harder, finishing him off. When Wylvern got there, I just let him think he'd done it.

"Well, he went off the deep end, stuttering and carrying on about how this guy had deserved it and how great a friend Jake was. I suggested to him he'd better just bury them then and there. Jake'd like it, I told him, and it was no better than what this other guy deserved. Besides, I said, the police might not believe your story. Well, that did it. He buried 'em. I gave him back his ax, but I kept the gun. I don't know if he even knew it was his."

I was stunned. Pop hadn't killed anybody! But Vince, had - and admitted it.

I craned my neck trying to see Vince. He'd stepped away again. I thought I could hear the sound of something pouring again. A slight acrid smell drifted down. Vince returned and sat down. He lit another cigarette. Then he sat playing with the lighter, flicking it every now and again.

I looked down at the straw beneath my feet. How dry was it? I glanced uneasily at Bryan. He touched my arm to tell me to continue.

"The gun in the box. That's your note, your handwriting."

"Yeah, that's it. Few weeks later, I told Wylvern that as I saw it, if you went by fingerprints, it'd look like he killed old Jake. I told him it might be my civic duty to turn that gun over to the police. Well, he sputtered some - made a disgusting spectacle of himself - but I made him see if he just sold me the land, getting you and your mother to sign too, well, it would work out for all of us."

"You son-of-a-bitch, you blackmailed him!" I wished I could make Annie kick. It was what I would've done.

"That's not a nice mouth you have, young woman. But then, you're Wylvern's daughter. Trouble, just like he was. I'm going to have to take care of you, like I did him."

"What do you mean?"

"Got to know everything, don't you? Okay, sure. About ten months later, Wylvern came to me. He'd got wind that John-o was a 'for hire' killer, and that I'd been the one who hired him. He'd been drinking. He said a lot of crap about me killing Jake and blackmailing him into selling the farm. He was going to the police." He laughed. "His story wouldn't have held up! But I couldn't risk it. We fought, and I knocked him out. I took him back to his crummy little apartment, and started dumping more whiskey down him until he stopped breathing. Jesus, that was messy!"

The blood drained from every inch of me. He'd killed my father! We'd thought he'd drunk himself to death! Lamberson had killed him!

Bryan's free hand shot out and gripped my wrist. I realized I'd dropped the radio, my hands clenched into claws. I wanted to rip Lamberson apart, and I'd been about to blow everything.

I dove down and grabbed the radio. "You - you bastard!" I growled. "You murdering bastard! God damn you to Hell!"

Bryan stared at me.

"Goddamn you!" Lamberson snarled back. "Everything was fine 'til you went and bought this place. Decidin' you had to clear your daddy's name!" He sneered. "What for? Your father was a loser! And you know? You're real slow at picking up hints. If you'd just got lost, you wouldn't be where you are now. And that fancy model wouldn't be dead! Jeez, you can't get good help these days! I'm gonna have to take care of you myself!"

He stood up again, and reached for something under the beam. I could hear the metal lid unscrewing again, and something pouring. This time I could smell something, too.

"What is that?" The fear in my voice was real. I knew what it was. *Gasoline.*

He splashed it over the sides, dousing the wood and concrete. Some of it hit Bryan as it fell. He grimaced and shook it off.

"Bryan! Can't we stop now?" I whispered. "Don't we have enough?"

He nodded. "I'm waiting on Jason. I can't get a clear shot from here."

"Bryan, you've got to. He'll set - he's going to - " I stared at Annie. "My God, Bryan, he means to roast me alive! Oh, God!" My knees gave out, and I dropped the radio. I started to wail.

Bryan leaned down to help me up. "Shh! Mackie, shh!"

"Well, if it ain't the cop. How'd you get over there, Doc?"

We froze. A flashlight shone on us from above. I couldn't stop sobbing. Bryan started to turn, slowly, but Lamberson stopped even that.

"Don't move - "

Bryan whipped around anyway, his gun ready. But he didn't shoot.

Lamberson was holding his lighter, already flaming, inches away from the gas-soaked wood.

"Hold still, you two. This isn't exactly according to plan, but it'll work. A real pity, I think I spilled some of this gasoline on those nice clothes of yours, Lieutenant. A real shame. It'd be awful if they caught fire while you were down there. No place to roll in to put it out - the hay would just catch fire." He moved the lighter downward, towards Bryan.

"Hie-yahh!" came the scream, and a blur flew from the chicken coop, Jason, bowling Lamberson over, rolling both of them into the haymow with us.

Flame jumped from the lighter as it fell, and caught on the gas running down the wall, and leapt from there to Bryan's shoulder.

"Bryan!" My scream was muffled by a gulping sound as air was sucked up by flames chasing along the streaming gas. I glanced at the wall behind me. Flames raced for the straw like a downhill roller coaster. The matted straw seemed to dampen their enthusiasm, but only briefly. Flickering triangles of yellow poked out through openings between the strands of hay. I watched, paralyzed, part of my mind screaming that Bryan needed help. He'd dropped the gun and was slapping at his shirt. The flames needed to be smothered. There was nothing here we could use.

As Jason struggled to regain his balance and Lamberson crawled away on hands and knees, I grabbed at the ends of the soccer shirt I'd borrowed from Bryan. I jumped up, whipped my hands over my head, stripped down to my bra, and lunged at the flames, wrapping the shirt shawl-like over Bryan's shoulder. He ripped open the front of his shirt and slid out of it. Already his skin was blistering. He shook me off and jumped for Lamberson.

Lamberson was a big man. Bryan was tall, but not as bulky, and nearly thirty years younger.

Someone like Lamberson wouldn't go about unprotected. As Bryan reached him, Lamberson rose to his feet like a great brown bear, right down to a gleam of silver claw at the end of his arm. A knife!

I wanted to scream again, but all I managed was an indrawn breath. Smoke was starting to accumulate.

Bryan sprang at Lamberson, grabbing hold of the arm that held the knife. Lamberson punched his stomach, but it was close in and not effective. Bryan swung away from the blow and got behind Lamberson. He tried dragging the knife arm around with him, but Lamberson seemed made of iron. The arm did not budge. Then Bryan drove a leg behind Lamberson's knees, making him bend. He flung one arm around Lamberson's neck, forcing his head back. They stumbled on the hay, but Bryan recovered first, and immediately kneed Lamberson in the back. The knife arm swung down like a slot machine's. Bryan caught it and snapped it back. The knife dropped. He watched its path, making sure Lamberson could not retrieve it. Suddenly Lamberson threw his other arm back, grabbed Bryan's head and flung him over his head onto the straw. Lamberson lunged and picked up the knife.

Bryan rose, more wary now. I spotted flames behind him popping up out of the straw. The fire was traveling along the underlying layer! Something there, maybe a by-product of the straw's decomposition, was fueling it more quickly than the top layer. The wood of the walls had caught now, too. I whirled to look behind me. Flames had climbed the ledge and jumped to the chicken coop. Jason - whose help I expected - was cut off from Lamberson and Bryan by a line of flame. As I soon would be.

"Jason! This way!" I started to try and cover myself, but this was no time for modesty. We might yet need this shirt for protection from flames again. Jason was peeling off his own as he leapt over the fire. Smoke was billowing about us now.

Bryan's skin glistened. There was an ugly patch of red where the skin had burned. Some of the blisters had scraped raw in the struggle. No time to attend to that. The twin enemies of Lamberson's knife and his fire commanded our attention.

Lamberson held the knife like a street fighter, low and sweeping, thrusting every time Bryan moved in close. He couldn't leap out of the way easily, footing was too unsure on the uneven hay.

Jason gripped my arm and pulled me toward the outer wall. Panicked, I whipped around.

"Where's the stun gun? Use it!"

"I don't have it. I think it fell out when I came over the side. Mackenzie, come on, now. We've got to get to that ladder!"

He was right. The only way out was the ladder Rachel and I had used earlier. I didn't know how much longer we'd have that.

"Bryan! Come on! Please!"

It went unheeded. The two men were together again, grappling for the knife. A gash flowed red on the burned shoulder. Lamberson had struck home!

A blur of Bryan's arm and a flash flew from the two men. He'd gotten the knife away. Lamberson breathed heavily. Bryan, hampered as he must have been by pain, seemed to be gaining strength from his victory over the knife. He punched Lamberson twice in the stomach, then threw a final blow to his jaw. As he went down, Bryan reached over towards the wall and fumbled in the straw. He'd found his gun. He held it on Lamberson and ordered him on his feet.

Jason urged me toward the ladder. Smoke and heat and roar swirled around us.

"Bryan, we're over here! The ladder!" he called out.

Bryan nodded and jerked Lamberson to his feet. He pushed him forward, and together they stumbled toward us.

Jason pushed me in front of him. No time to feel relief yet. Nothing else must go wrong. I gripped the ladder and scrambled up. Once again the ledge spelled safety. This wall was all stone foundation and not yet affected by the heat of the fire. I climbed through the window and scooted aside. Jason followed me. He moved to the opposite side of the opening and braced himself in case Bryan needed help. Lamberson was a big man.

No one appeared. I leaned my head in. Bryan and Lamberson were still at the foot of the ladder. Bryan held the gun. Lamberson's arms were on the ladder, but his head was turned over his shoulder. One foot on the bottom rung, he wasn't moving.

"Bryan! What's going on?" I called anxiously.

"Lamberson won't go up."

"Hey, you've winded me, boy. I can't fit out that opening anyway. I'm not goin'."

"Come on, Lamberson. Thanks to your little games, this place is going up. Now get up that ladder. We'll get you through."

Jason's head bobbed next to mine. "What's taking them so long?"

"Lamberson claims he can't make it up here or through the window," I said uneasily. "Jason, this barn is burning faster and faster. We have to get them out of there!"

"Hey, Lamberson! Here, take my hand. I'll boost you up." Jason reached down his arm. "Wait, I'll come part way in."

He shifted around and inserted his feet and backed down the ladder part way. I watched as he turned and reached down with his right hand, steadying himself by wrapping his left arm around a rung.

Lamberson was watching even more closely than I was. Before Jason's left arm was secure, Lamberson had gripped his right hand - and yanked him to the left, pulling him off the ladder and back into the haymow. Without pause he lashed out with a foot and kicked Bryan deep in the thigh. Bryan fell back, and Lamberson shot up the ladder.

My head exploded. This was the monster that'd tried to tear apart my world all my life. Stealing my land, undermining my father, killing him, killing Jake, chasing me down, trying to kill me and now Bryan!

My rage was the echo of my father's, my inheritance from him. In righteousness I acted; as Lamberson leaned out the opening to bring his knees to the ledge, I kicked his arm out from under him and followed through with my foot in his side to send him part way down the wall. A final tug at his belt sent him the rest of the way.

CHAPTER 28

I am my father's daughter.

B ryan appeared at the opening. "Mackenzie?"
       Firelight glinted off his hair as he stared at me. I heard
Jason's voice right behind him. My fingernails clawed the ledge.

"Oh, God, Bryan! Hurry!"

I pushed off, scraping my back on the wall as I dropped down. Bryan
followed, then Jason. Bryan kept looking from me to Lamberson and
back again. He didn't say anything.

Lamberson had landed on his head. His body had slumped over
him in a sort of backward somersault, and toppled to one side. I felt the
carotid - the pulse was strong - pounding slightly - but he'd just been
fighting. I wanted to move him, but I didn't dare. I couldn't tell if there
was a neck injury or not. There could have been.

"We've got to move him, Mackie."

"Bryan, we can't - "

"We have to. Look!"

The outer wall of the barn was glowing about five feet above the
foundation. Bright slivers of light licked along the edges of the boards.

Flickering at the edge of my brain was the recognition I was losing
something important.

"I - all right. But we need a board or something. We've got to
immobilize his neck." This was my fault!

His leg shifted. He groaned and rolled over on to his back,
straightening out his legs, and raising his hands to his head.

"That's all I need," said Jason. "His neck's not broken!"

Bryan thrust the gun at me and grabbed Lamberson under the arms
and lifted. Jason took his legs. We crabwalked our way around the milk
house to the front lawn. Bryan took the gun from me and gave it to Jason.
I didn't trust me with it either. Then he raced down the hill to his car.
Gunning the motor he charged around the sparking and flaming barn
and swung the car onto the lawn, headlights aimed straight at us. He

opened the door, and I could see him radioing for assistance. In seconds I heard sirens approaching from both ends of Wexford Road.

"Good of Matheson to show," commented Jason.

"Yeah," I answered. I looked at Lamberson. There was a glitter at the fringes of his eyes. He was conscious. I was aware of malevolence more potent than any I'd ever encountered.

I stood up and moved away. I still had the shirt with me. I tugged it back on. Singed, scratchy, it had a couple holes, but it was better than nothing.

Cars and trucks were pulling in now. Fire trucks, rescue vehicles, State Trooper's cars. Paramedics rushed over to Lamberson. Matheson loped behind them.

"Keep a guard on this one," he ordered.

The paramedics were examining Lamberson. I stepped over to them, clearing my throat. "I'm a doctor. He's had a fall, check for concussion - although he was coming around a minute ago. His pulse was okay. Get some heart meds handy. He - " I swallowed.

The lead medic looked up at me, clipboard and record in hand, even as the other placed electrodes and plugged in wires. "What happened to him?"

"I - he - " My hand went to my throat. I was cold suddenly.

"Doctor Wilder told you. He fell. About eight feet, onto rocky ground." Bryan's arms came round me. "Come over here, Mackenzie."

Matheson stepped up. "I need statements from you two."

Bryan nodded, but he drew me along anyway. We sat in the back of his car, the barn aflame behind us. We kept turning to watch. Still, I felt detached. There went the upper stories -   all those old things I'd been going to go through. That was before I'd found the gun. I didn't have to anymore. We'd learned the truth. But now I wanted to go through them. I wanted to see if there was anything else left from my childhood. Anything left from the days when my father had still been my hero.

I looked at Bryan. He was answering Matheson's questions patiently, exhausted though he was. Straw still clung to his back. I picked some away. He reached over to cradle my knee with his hand. His face was greasy with sweat, and his shoulder looked painful. He'd better see the paramedics about that, I thought. He was my second hero. A much better one than my father.

Yes, but Pop hadn't been a murderer after all. He hadn't actually killed anyone. Neither had I.

"Doctor Wilder? Jamison's statement is pretty complete. Why don't I take yours tomorrow?" Matheson added gently, "It'll be routine."

I managed a stiff sort of nod. Firemen were shouting less now. They'd managed to get the pumpers going, one to a tanker that had arrived, one to a hose they'd run to the creek. They poured water on the barn, but only to contain it. No one felt compelled to try and save it. There were creakings and crashes. Beams going, I thought distractedly. I hoped the pigeons got out.

A shout went up over by the rescue vehicle. Matheson went to check it out. Jason tagged along.

Bryan tilted my face to his. "Talk to me."

I shook my head.

"I can't. Bryan - I - Bryan, I almost killed him!"

"Mackie, he didn't even break his crummy neck!"

"Bryan, I shoved him off that ledge. I'm not supposed to do that kind of thing! I'm a doctor. You're the one who's supposed to go around killing criminals!"

"Not exactly."

"You know what I mean. You were ready to do it tonight!"

"Yes, because he couldn't be stopped any other way. I was prepared to do what I had to."

"You see?" I cried, my hands shaking. "When you had Lamberson at the base of the ladder, you didn't shoot him because he'd fought you or hurt you. You captured him!"

"You don't know what I was going to do when I got to the top of the ladder."

"You waited, though. I didn't."

"You wanted to stop him from getting away. There's nothing - "

"That wasn't it. It was everything he'd done. The anger, the rage. I felt such terrible rage, Bryan. It's like everything he said was just one more way he could hurt me. It made me so mad! I wanted revenge! I wanted him dead!"

"He's still alive."

"Don't you see? His being alive is luck! I tried to kill him!"

He held me.

I gulped a few times. "I didn't know I could get that angry. Just like my father when he tried to kill John-o. I'm just like him! It scares me!"

"Of course, it scares you to think of it that way. But you did what you had to do, Mackie. Lamberson - and John-o - weren't ordinary men. They stopped being ordinary men when they profited from their first killing. You followed an instinct when you pushed Lamberson. Not necessarily a noble one, but a natural one. It really was self-defense, you know."

"Bryan, no amount of rationalizing is going to make it go away. I tried to kill Vince Lamberson!"

He looked me in the eye. "Yes, you did. You tried to kill a killer. Mackenzie, you'll get past this. I'll help you. I love you."

I laid my cheek against his.

The fire was slowing now, lack of momentum, lack of fuel, I thought. I saw Matheson and Jason approach the car. I pulled back, and Bryan turned to face them. A sudden 'whumpf' announced one final explosion.

Firemen jumped, and the chief shouted, pointing to the left side of the barn, opposite the haymow, where I'd parked -

"My boat, oh Brian, our boat!" I started to shake and sob. It was gone. Everything, the last tangible connection....

Bryan held me tightly. I knew he knew it wasn't his name I'd called. He stroked my back, murmured in my hair anyway. Total compassion.

I pulled back for a moment and looked as deep into his eyes as could be done.

His wonderful, blue, blue eyes.

Brian's had been brown.

Brian had been shorter, stockier of build.

Brian and I had already shared a lifetime.

The blaze was destroying the *PsyKe*, the barn one massive funeral pyre to my entire life before now.

Bryan's eyes held love for me. I could see that. Love not much different than Brian's. Could I *be* that lucky? I wasn't sure.

Matheson spoke to us, Jason hovering behind him.

"Lamberson's dead."

"Oh God." I clutched Bryan's shoulder.

He tightened his arm around me again, steadying me. "How?"

"They had some trouble over there. Seems whatever was wrong with him, he was in a lot of pain. He kept screaming for some painkiller. The medic told him he'd have to wait until they finished transmitting the readings." He glanced at me.

"Yeah. Medication can affect the vital signs. They can be suppressed or elevated. Anyway, we don't give pain medication until they've been recorded - in this case, transmitted to the base hospital." I sniffled.

"Right. Well, that wasn't good enough for Lamberson. He must be familiar with these rescue set-ups. Or at least he thought he was. He grabbed what he expected to be a syringe of pain medication prepared for him and injected it himself."

"What was in it?" asked Bryan.

"Potassium concentrate."

"For his heart," I said automatically. "But...."

"Apparently they'd gotten the syringe ready with a dose. One of the beams in the fire cut loose and everybody shouted, just like now. The medics turned around. Lamberson grabbed the syringe and injected himself."

"Oh, God! That stuff's supposed to be given with an IV solution! Of course he's dead!" I spoke my next words slowly. "He never could wait for anything."

Exactly. Lamberson never could wait for anything. He was greedy. He was evil, and his own deeds were finally his undoing.

He'd been the root cause of it all. Not me. Not my father. Lamberson, with his arrogant greed that put his own desires above everything else.

"You're losing a barn, Doc Wilder," observed Matheson. "But you'll be getting your place back once we've got our reports all written up."

"Sorry about the boat and all, but you've got another coming in, right? And if you want to rebuild, Mackenzie, I know an architect who specializes in old barns," Jason offered cheerily.

"You know just about everyone, don't you?" I laughed a little wildly. "We'll see. I don't know what I'm going to do. I might build a riding arena like the Hicks were going to do. Maybe let underprivileged kids camp out here."

"If you need some support, I know of a foundation that could... right. Well, just call me." Jason's voice trailed off.

Bryan's arms encircled me once more.

Some homecoming. Red flames devouring the barn timbers. And probably the last planks of the *PsyKe*. Jason consulting with the Fire Chief. Matheson writing his report. The rescue vehicle slowly bumbling over the lawn and onto the road. Like a wild party with a bad ending.

The big white farmhouse, dark without its electricity, had once overseen my first homecoming. Now its empty eyes looked out on this turbulent scene. I turned my head back to the other end of the driveway. No barn. The whole view, the whole setting was altered. It wasn't the same anymore.

Never was, said that little voice I carried with me. *It isn't the way you remembered it now, and it never really was.*

But my house, the trees....

They're still here, still yours, just not the same.

The voice was silent for a minute.

Did you really want it to be the way it was when you were a child?

I closed my eyes. I felt the land stretching out around me, as far as ninety-some acres could stretch. I felt the Christmas trees, the woods, the creeks, even the gas pipeline coming down the hill from Murrays. I wanted it to be a part of me. I wanted it to be home.

Home. Home is supposed to mean safe haven. But, as my little voice had just reminded me, things aren't always what they seem. Maybe this hadn't been a safe haven for me. That didn't mean it couldn't be, someday.

I opened my eyes again. All right, it wasn't the same. But it was mine. I could make it what I wanted it to be. That was more than some people ever got. And maybe, with Bryan....

Yep, agreed my little voice. *You could even count yourself lucky.*

The last flaming timber cracked and toppled into the darkness.

Lucky.

Where the Bodies Lie Buried

acknowledgements

It may take a village to raise a child, but it sometimes takes almost that many to care for and cosset a writer. Thank you to my family for lending me support - literal and psychological - as I work, making sure I eat, sleep, and get to my other jobs on time.

Thank you to Kelsey Shaver for her support and editing skills, and to the members of WORN *(Write On, Right Now)* led by Robin Deffendall whose support, critiques, and suggestions keep me on my toes.

A special thanks to my husband, Dave, for introducing me to the Thousand Islands and the magical beauty of antique boats.

And thank you to the many boat owners who've gladly shared their stories and their boats with us over the years, most recently Jeff Gelm of North Carolina.

about the author

R.J. MINNICK has spent a lifetime working at various jobs (she even sold Fuller Brush!) and another lifetime raising six terrific offspring with her husband.

During both those lifetimes she kept writing - poetry, reviews, short stories, nonfiction, mysteries, mainstream novels, and Christmas epics. She has credentials in national and local magazines and community news publications.

Where the Bodies Lie Buried is her first mystery, and the first in her Mackenzie Wilder/Classic Boat mystery series.

R.J. Minnick lives in Fayetteville, North Carolina with her husband, two dogs, five cats and - from time to time - a child or two.

Where the Bodies Lie Buried

FICTION

Printed in the U.S.
Wingspan Books